In Your Arms Again

Other **AVON ROMANCES**

IN MY HEART *by Melody Thomas*
LEGENDARY WARRIOR *by Donna Fletcher*
ONCE A GENTLEMAN *by Candice Hern*
THE PRINCESS MASQUERADE *by Lois Greiman*
THE PRINCESS AND THE WOLF *by Karen Kay*
THE SWEETEST SIN *by Mary Reed McCall*
THREE NIGHTS . . . *by Debra Mullins*

Coming Soon

KISSING THE BRIDE *by Sara Bennett*
ONE WICKED NIGHT *by Sari Robins*

And Don't Miss These
ROMANTIC TREASURES
from Avon Books

A DARK CHAMPION *by Kinley MacGregor*
AN INVITATION TO SEDUCTION *by Lorraine Heath*
IT TAKES A HERO *by Elizabeth Boyle*

AVON BOOKS
An Imprint of HarperCollins*Publishers*
10 East 53rd Street
New York, New York 10022-5299

Copyright © 2004 by Kathryn Smith
ISBN: 0-7394-4419-0

Printed in the U.S.A.

KATHRYN SMITH

In Your Arms Again

AVON BOOKS
An Imprint of HarperCollinsPublishers

This book goes out with love and appreciation to
two of the best friends a girl could ever hope to have—
Lisa Kleypas and Adele Ashworth,
my sisters of choice. I adore you both.

And, of course, to Steve, my always.

Smoochies
Kathryn

Chapter 1

⌒⌒◯◯⌒⌒

London
April 1818

She was a fraud. *He* was a fraud.

From his position near the upper balustrade, North Sheffield watched his prey as she twirled around the taupe and cream marble dance floor, smiling in the arms of a handsome young lord. Diamonds glittered in her hair, and her gown was the height of fashion.

She looked as home there as he knew he did, weaving in and out among the upper ranks of society. There was one big difference between her and him. She wanted to belong. North had given up caring about what society thought of him years ago—when the upper ranks of the *ton* let him know in no uncertain terms that while he might *look* as though he was one of them, the simple accident of his birth ensured that he was not.

Bastards weren't equals unless they were born under the guise of legitimacy, and neither North nor the girl laughing far below him could claim such distinction. At least North's father had claimed him. This girl's father stood not even ten feet away from her. If he had any idea of her identity, he did a good job of hiding it.

Poor girl. She would be forever ruined before the night was over. No one would come to her rescue, especially not her father. She would be tossed into the street, if not sent directly to Newgate. Once he unmasked her, her fate would be out of his hands. The knowledge left him feeling dirty.

Sighing, he pulled the silver watch from his pocket and checked the time. A glob of wax from the sconce on the wall by his head dropped onto the glass facing, obscuring the numbers in a splattering of milky white. He wiped it away with his thumb before it hardened.

It was five minutes before midnight. His associates would be waiting for him outside, and he did not want to keep them or the person with them waiting any longer than he had to. It was a consideration he normally didn't extend to those helping him solve a case, but this one was special.

And he felt all the dirtier for it.

Turning his back on the glittering ballroom, he crossed the soft claret red carpet to the stairs.

"There are three men waiting in a carriage out front," he told a footman when he had descended to the next floor. "Have them come in."

The footman looked as though he'd dearly love to tell North to do it himself, but North was still the fellow's better, bastard or not. With a stiff nod, the young man went off to do as he was bid, leaving North watching him with a narrow and somewhat anxious gaze.

He stood alone, in a small opulent vestibule decorated in shades of crimson, cream, and gold, waiting for his companions to join him. He hoped Francis had left the restraints behind as he instructed. He would give the girl—Lady Amelia, she called herself—as much dignity as he could. Whether she chose to accept the consequences of her charade with the same dignity was up to her.

Christ, but he'd be glad when this was all over. The entire situation left a foul taste in his mouth. He could just let the girl go, forget all about proving her a fraud. It wasn't as though she was hurting anyone—at least not anyone who couldn't afford it. She was simply trying to claim a life she believed herself to be entitled to. Of course she had raised suspicions. If she hadn't, no one ever would have thought to hire North to ferret out the truth. The "Caraboo" fiasco of last year had made Society paranoid, everyone new was suspect.

Which was why North could not just let Lady Amelia walk away. Even when he'd first discovered her secret, he knew he wouldn't be able to let her go. To do so would not only be a lie, but if the truth was ever discovered, it would destroy his credibility among the *ton* as a man of discretion and honor. He could not afford to have his name tarnished any further than his birth and occupation had already tainted it.

The bastard son of the late Viscount Creed and Nell Sheffield, a Scottish actress, North had lived much of his life on the fringes of society. In his mother's world he had been readily accepted and loved. After her death he'd gone to live with his father and brothers—much to Lady Creed's disapproval. It was in that world—his father's world—he had so desperately wanted to belong. But eventually he gave up trying.

Now, those same people who hadn't wanted him hired him to solve their dirty problems, protect their nasty secrets. He was suddenly very much in demand and wanted by the aristocracy. He kept their secrets as though they were his own, and reminded himself to never mistake their offers of friendship for anything other than fragile overtures with no more solidity than the flecks of wax still clinging to the edge of his watch.

Now if only Francis and the others would hurry up so he could get this job over with. He had yet to meet anyone who knew him, mostly because he'd spent the better part of his brief time there skulking in the shadows, but now he was out in the open, and if anyone saw him, the whispers would soon follow. People would begin to suspect that he was there for a reason—he was rarely in society without a case being involved. He didn't want to answer any questions, and he didn't want the girl to suffer any more than she had to.

"Ready?"

North looked up. It was Francis. Six feet tall and barrel-chested, somehow the investigator had managed to sneak up on him. That wasn't good. It only proved how much this particular case affected him.

"I will take the girl aside," he told the heavier man. "A footman will lead you through a separate entrance with our guest."

Francis ran a hand over the silvery thickness of his beard. "I have a bad feeling about this."

That made two of them. Every instinct North possessed told him this night was going to end badly, that he should leave now. But he couldn't. He had a job to do, as distasteful as it was.

"Let's just get it over with." He turned toward the ballroom doors, leaving Francis to do his part. He wanted this night over.

He pulled the double doors open, filling the previously quiet vestibule with the noise and heat of the ballroom—every sense recoiled. His eyes narrowed at the bright lights and glittering jewels. His ears cowered as the strings of a violin clashed with the high-pitched laughter of a society matron. Incoherent voices rose up around him, driving him back in their efforts to be heard. His nose shrank from the scents of too many bodies—unwashed, overperfumed, overheated.

Stale sweat, fresh sweat, stale smoke. Too much perfume, too much bay rum. Not enough soap.

Even worse was that slight lurch of his heart.

His entrance soon attracted attention, as he knew it would. One of the pitfalls of his newfound notoriety was of course the notoriety itself. The fact that he had attended this party would be in all the gossip columns tomorrow, along with a declaration that the rout had been a great success. He hoped they would not know the true reason for his appearance. Certainly, the truth would leak out eventually, but for now he was going to do everything he could to give "Lady" Amelia a fighting chance.

He didn't owe her anything—didn't owe anything to anyone, in fact. Nor did he harbor the illusion that so many other bastards seemed to, that the world owed him. He settled all scores and debts as quickly as he could and when someone was left in his debt, he collected when it was convenient or forgot about it until it was. No expectations. So much easier not to be disappointed that way. Surely Lady Amelia would agree.

Would Octavia?

Lady Amelia was no longer dancing. She was standing beside her beau, the man whose father had hired him to investigate her, her dark eyes smiling up at him with uncensored affection. And North was going to ruin everything.

Someone in her group said something, and her gaze left her lover's and met North's instead. There was the briefest flicker of panic before her eyes went perfectly blank. She knew, or at least she feared, that he was there for her.

He didn't bother prolonging her anxiety. Weaving smoothly through the crowd, nodding to those who managed to snare his attention, North moved toward the young woman whose charade he was soon going to put to an end. He smiled, willing her to play along, to keep up pretenses. Tentatively, she smiled back.

Standing in front of her, he sketched a bow. "Lady Amelia. What a pleasure it is to see you again."

Bright girl that she obviously was, Amelia ignored the fact that they had never met before.

"Mr. Sheffield." She knew enough about him to know that he preferred to be called by his mother's name alone.

"I have a friend with me who longs to make your better acquaintance. I wonder if you might humor her with an introduction?"

Clearly the girl would rather run naked through the streets of Whitechapel than accompany him, but she was also apparently intelligent enough to know not to make a scene. Too bad. It made him feel all the more for her. But he wasn't a big enough man to let her go and risk his own ruin, not when he had worked so hard. Not when it would reflect upon his family.

Amelia placed her hand on his arm. "Of course, Mr. Sheffield." She cast one last look at her beau, and the shriveled remains of North's heart bled at it. She loved this young man and he her. Did he know her terrible secret? Did he know that she wasn't what she claimed to be? For a moment North was reminded of another young woman—one who hadn't pretended to be a lady, but had ended up one anyway.

"Do not be long," the young man urged. Amelia shook her head and turned away. North saw the sheen of tears in her eyes.

He felt for her, because at one time he had been very much like her—an outsider looking in, knowing that if it weren't for some cruel twist of fate, he would belong to the world he was watching, rather than being an interloper. The only difference was that he hadn't been given the chance to sneak in. Perhaps he would have done exactly what she had done. He would have risked everything just to feel as though he belonged.

"Amelia!"

The girl on his arm froze at the sight of the woman standing not five feet away from them, and North had no choice but to stop as well. Unfortunately, they stopped right next to Lord Barnsley, Amelia's father. Until that moment, North had been certain that Barnsley had no knowledge of his daughter. However, all that changed as the viscount's horrified gaze traveled from an impoverished woman standing stricken yet stately in the middle of the dance floor, with looks of haughty disdain focused on her from every angle, to the young girl on North's arm.

Barnsley recognized his former mistress, and now he recognized his own blood.

How had this happened? How had Amelia's mother gotten inside? North had told Francis to take her in through another route. This reunion was to have been more private than this show.

There would be no quiet escape now. Not unless North did something fast.

"My lord," he said to Barnsley, "would you accompany us please?" Then he turned to Amelia's mother. "Madam?"

Curious stares weighted their steps, watched their every movement and expression. North favored them with the briefest of bored glances. He just wanted to go home.

Then he saw her. Out of the corner of his eye, he caught a glimpse of hair the color of dark gold and ripe strawberries. He had only ever met one person with hair that peculiar shade.

Octavia. No wonder she had been in his thoughts the whole night. His heart must have sensed her.

Heart hammering against his ribs, he dared himself to look, both hoping and fearing that he was correct. He was.

Standing in the crowd was the woman he had once considered his best friend, his only friend. So many plans they'd made, so many adventures they'd had.

Still so beautiful. The years had been good to her. No longer all limbs and sharp angles, she was tall and slender, an ivory goddess with sapphire eyes and ruby lips. Once she had been within his grasp, and now she was as removed from him as one person could be from another.

As removed as his heart from his chest.

She moved as though she thought to come to him. How many questions would that raise? He'd spent the last twelve years avoiding her so people wouldn't realize they'd known each other. It hadn't been hard, they were rarely in the same circles. He'd made a promise to leave her alone, to allow her to have the life she deserved. Being associated with him wouldn't do anything to benefit her, that was certain.

She'd taken but two steps when he shook his head. She froze, a small frown puckering her brow. How quickly her smile died, the light faded from her eyes. She'd been happy to see him until he'd rejected her. Happy.

Dear God but he was happy to see her too! So happy it hurt.

Forcing his gaze away, he focused on the doors before him and walked toward them. The crowd parted easily, faceless guests firing questions at him as he moved. He answered none. He doubted, if asked, that he could even remember his own name.

"Are you quite all right, my dear?"

Her hands were shaking, her mouth was dry, and she was pretty sure there was sweat beaded on her brow. Did she *look* all right?

Octavia Vaux-Daventry placed a reassuring palm on her companion's arm. "I am fine, Spinton, thank you." But she wasn't fine, not by a mile.

The last person she'd expected to see here at the Whortons' was Norrie Sheffield. Or did he go by Ryland now? She had no idea. For many years she followed his exploits, but lost him the more removed from society he became. Lately, he'd become a person of great prestige among the *ton*. They all seemed to want him at their parties. He rarely attended, unless he was on business. It must have been business that brought him there tonight—of all nights for her to see him again.

He was no longer that sweet, gentle boy she had known. He was a man, full-grown and strong. He had stubble on his jaw and lines around his eyes. Oh, those beautiful eyes. Like looking into a lake on a clear winter morning. His hair was still a little longer than fashionable and still as wonderfully dark and unruly as it had been all those years ago. Someone had broken his nose during the last dozen years. It should have detracted from his looks, but it didn't. He was still as bonny as ever.

Bonny. That was one of his mother's words. Dear, dear Nell. She'd been gone so many years now. Longer even than Octavia's own mother. Nell Sheffield had been a remarkable woman. She wouldn't have changed her life for anyone. She wouldn't marry a man she didn't love just because she'd made a promise to a dead man.

And to think that Octavia had made up her mind to accept Spinton's proposal that night. It seemed the right decision at the time, but now . . .

Now she was glad she hadn't voiced her decision, because she wasn't so certain of her answer. She was expected to become Lady Spinton. It had been expected of her for years. She would do it. She had made a promise, and she always kept her promises.

Almost always.

She had made promises to North as well, but he was still alive and her mother and grandfather were dead, and vows to the dead were not to be taken lightly, especially when she owed them both so much.

North hadn't wanted to see her. So badly she had wanted to run up to him and throw her arms about his neck. Her heart fairly soared at the sight of him, like an old automaton wound back to life after years of being idle. For one second, it felt as though the world was just and fair and right.

Now he was gone, and that joyous feeling had left with him because he hadn't wanted her to run to him. Hadn't wanted her to know him. Why? Was he ashamed of her? Did he think she had turned her back on him and the rest of her past? She had. But was that reason to snub her? To pretend that they had never been friends? That they had never been more than merely friends?

One glimpse was not enough to satisfy her. One snub was not enough to dissuade her. She wanted to see him again. She would not—could not—believe that he harbored a grudge against her, not after all they'd been through, and been to each other.

"My dear," she said, turning to Spinton once again—good, dear Spinton. "I wonder if you might be so kind as to take me home."

Spinton's face, all smooth and freshly shaven and with nary a crease about his dark eyes, thin mouth, or brow, was wrought with concern. "Home? But it is still early. I thought you said you were fine."

"I am fine. Merely tired. Please, would you mind?"

It was wrong of her to do it, but she added just a touch of pleading to her tone, a slight tilt to her head, and a softness to her gaze. Spinton was a good man, a nice man, and he was as easily led as a toddler by the hands. One merely had to show him where to put each foot, and he followed.

"Of course I will take you. Are you certain you do not need an apothecary?"

She patted his arm. "Just some rest. I fear the evening has caught up with me."

He nodded, guiding her toward the exit. "It is a dreadful crush, and far too warm for my liking."

Octavia glanced at him, her gaze raking him from the top of his sandy head to the impeccable knot of his cravat. There wasn't a hair out of place or the shine of sweat to be found. He looked perfect. It was she who no doubt looked as wilted as a flower out of water.

The skirts of her ivory silk gown clung to her legs as she walked; her feet were hot and sticky in her stockings and slippers. Even her neck felt moist, and now a footman was slipping her cape over her shoulders, adding to her discomfort.

Yes, she wanted to go home, where she could lie on her bed, between crisp cool sheets, and feel the gentle evening breeze as it drifted through the window on her heated skin.

And think about North. Yes, she wanted the peace and quiet to think about seeing her Norrie again.

He had never come to visit her at her grandfather's, and she didn't blame him for that. But he hadn't written either, nor had he sent a message with any of his brothers whenever she saw them in public. It was as though he had completely erased her from his life. Why? He had to have known she would miss him. He had to have missed her. Had it been because of her grandfather? She couldn't imagine Norrie being afraid of anyone, not even an earl. No, he had decided on his own not to contact her, to forget her.

How unfortunate that she hadn't forgotten him as well. Oh, she'd certainly put him aside from time to time for a day's duration, even weeks, but never completely. She wasn't the kind of person who forgot her best friend.

"I do not believe you are as well as you insist," Spinton remarked once they were inside his carriage. "Have you received another letter? Is that what has you so discomfitted?"

Was he still there? Octavia's gaze flitted to the man across from her. She had forgotten about poor Spinton.

He was hardly "poor," however. He was the new Earl Spinton, and he was her grandfather's heir. He and Octavia were actually cousins—although distantly.

"No," she replied absently, her mind not quite ready to relinquish thoughts of North to think of something else. "Not since Tuesday."

Spinton pursed his lips. "They are arriving with more frequency."

Were they? Octavia hadn't really given it much thought, but then Spinton believed the letters to be of a far more sinister nature than she did. He believed them to be the work of a deranged mind, while she thought them nothing more than the romantic ramblings of a secret admirer. Bad poetry, foolish odes to her hair, her eyes, even her feet—how could she possibly believe the author to be dangerous? He was annoying at best.

"I do not believe they are worth this worry," she remarked, stifling a yawn with a gloved hand. Oh dear, she'd gotten lip color on the fingers.

Spinton did not look as sure as she felt, which was hardly surprising. "I do wish you would allow me to hire someone to investigate them."

"Really, Spinton, they are of no consequence." She yawned again. "I beg your pardon. I do not know why I am so tired all of a sudden."

Her companion eyed her knowingly in the dim light as the carriage hit a rut in the road, jostling them both from side to side. "I do. It is because you are not sleeping. You spend all your time worrying about money and these demmed letters. Do not try to persuade me to the contrary; I will not believe it."

No, of course he wouldn't. Spinton was a kind and gentle man, but he was as stubborn and bullheaded as an old mule. The proof of that was in how long he had been waiting for her to marry him.

Yes, he was correct that she often fretted about money, but it wasn't because she hadn't any, it was because she had too much. Never in her life had she ever had access to such funds, but after her grandfather's death a year ago, she found herself a very wealthy woman, and she had no idea what to do with it. The idea of just sitting on it and letting it go to waste seemed idle to the extreme, but she had very little knowledge of the Exchange and worthwhile investments.

She did not, however, worry about those blasted letters. The only time they interfered with her sleep was when some fool messenger delivered one at an ungodly early hour. No, she'd been up late the night before thinking about her mother and wondering how her life could have turned out. If her grandfather hadn't come for her after her mother's death, if she hadn't discovered that she was the legitimate daughter of an English lord, she might very well have followed in her mother's footsteps and ended up not only on stage, but becoming some man's mistress.

That had been the fear that had driven her to North with that shocking request—one he had hesitated to fulfill, but granted in the end.

"I know I said I would respect your wishes and not push you, dearest, but I do wish you would put your mind to the matter of our marriage. It has been almost a month since I proposed the idea."

Octavia merely smiled in reply. What was there to say? That she had made up her mind, but that seeing North Sheffield again suddenly made her have second thoughts? He might want to know why she was suffering such doubt and then she would have to lie, because there was no way she could tell him the truth about how it felt to see North again.

It had felt like everything was right with the world for once. He was a moment of peace in the cacophony of her life.

No, she couldn't tell the man who wanted to marry her that

another man made her feel something he'd never been able to achieve. And she couldn't tell him that this same man had done things to her that she'd never allowed him the liberty to do. When she finally did marry Spinton, she hoped he wouldn't realize that his blushing bride wasn't a virgin.

And she did plan to keep her promise to her grandfather and marry Spinton, just not right away. And she also had no intention of ever telling him that she had made love with North Sheffield twelve years ago—not because she wanted to deceive him, but because her memories of North were her own, and she would not share them with anyone else.

Spinton sighed. He didn't seem to notice that she wasn't paying attention.

"I am sorry, my dear," he said. "I did not mean to upset you."

Her reply was immediate, "You did not." North had when he'd shaken his head at her. *Do not know me,* his look had seemed to say, and she still couldn't fathom why.

No letters, no contact, but flowers on her birthday. He sent them still, for she had gotten a bouquet just this past birthday when she turned thirty. The card with them simply wished her a happy day in a hand she didn't recognize. North didn't even sign the cards.

This year's offering had been a sad reminder that she was getting too old to remain single any longer. Only her money made it permissible for her to do so, but even wealth had its limitations. Spinton's patience would have to run out eventually.

"I wonder what business Sheffield had at Whortons' tonight," Spinton mused as he glanced out the window at the darkened street.

Octavia's heart tripped at the sound of his name. "Something to do with Lord Barnsley, so it would appear." Actually, from what she had gleaned from the situation, she believed the lower-class woman who arrived at the ball to be "Lady"

Amelia's mother, and Lord Barnsley to be the girl's father, but only because of the way they'd all looked at one another.

"Perhaps I might speak to Sheffield about your letters. Would you rest easier knowing he was looking into the situation?"

Octavia swallowed an obscenity she had learned long ago on the streets of Covent Garden. "Do not you think you might be overreacting a tad to these notes? Really, they are quite harmless."

"I think you are not reacting seriously enough," came the petulant reply.

If Spinton told North about the letters, any rest she had would be uneasy rather than the opposite. North would either dismiss Spinton's claims—which would be the intelligent choice, but hurtful, knowing he didn't want to help her—or he'd believe there was some kind of threat and come barging back into her life, ready to take charge and fix everything as he always had in the past. And there was nothing for him to fix. If anything, things were more likely to be broken.

She sighed. "I appreciate your concern, Spinton dear, really I do, but I think Mr. Sheffield has more important things to attend to than my mail."

The look the earl gave her was so full of affection and warmth that it made her feel unworthy to receive it. "Nothing is more important than your well-being."

God, why did he have to be so kind and thoughtful? And why couldn't she just be grateful for it? Why did she have to feel so blasted guilty all the time?

Because she knew very well that Spinton's feelings for her ran far, far deeper than hers for him, and she knew that he deserved better. Well, at least one of them would be happy in their marriage—at least until her disinterestedness made him bitter with regret.

The carriage rolled to a stop. Finally, she was home.

"I will walk you to the door," Spinton announced, his tone brooking no refusal. Octavia knew better than to even try. She could only hope he didn't try to kiss her on the mouth again. It was becoming a disturbing habit as of late.

A footman lowered the carriage steps. Spinton alighted first and turned to offer her his hand. Octavia took it, hoping the cosmetics stain on her glove didn't rub off onto his.

At the door to her house, he faced her, her hand still caught in his. "You know I care for you, do you not, Octavia?"

Oh dear, this wasn't going to be one of his "I am the strong man and you the weaker vessel" speeches, was it? "Of course I do."

He smiled, giving her hand a gentle squeeze. Then he lowered his head and kissed her—thankfully—on the cheek.

"I will not allow any harm to come to you," he vowed before taking his leave.

Octavia didn't watch him go. She opened the door and slipped into the darkness of her foyer, where her butler waited to take her coat. She muttered a brief good night to him before running upstairs to her room. Spinton's words rang in her ears, setting her stomach to flutter as though home to a thousand caged butterflies. His promise unsettled her, but not because it bespoke deep emotion and abiding affection.

No, she had heard a similar vow before—the night before North Sheffield allowed her grandfather to take her away.

"Yer purse, guv."

In the eerie predawn hours, North sighed into the strange quiet that was Covent Garden. A sound here and there, a thump, a crash, a burst of raised voices—and then nothing but silence. A silence heavy with the keenness of too many ears—waiting and listening.

The man behind him, for example, had obviously been waiting in the shadows for some time, watching and waiting for a well-dressed cove to pass by so that he might stick his blade in the poor bloke's back and rob him of what blunt he had.

"Go away," North growled.

The knife pressed a little harder. Dull, it was. North couldn't even feel the point of it through his jacket. That didn't make it any less dangerous, however. Just meant it would take longer to find its path between his ribs.

Ale-stale breath brushed his face. "I *said* give me yer purse."

North smiled. "I do not have one."

"Wot do you tyke me for?" the man demanded incredulously. "All you kind carry silver on ye."

North shrugged. "I do not."

The pressure on his back eased just a fraction as the man tried to decide whether North was lying. It was all the opening North needed. He whirled around, seizing the man by the wrist and pushing the knife away with his left hand and smashing him in the face with his right.

The man grunted, but didn't drop his weapon. Capitalizing on his opponent's disorientation, North shoved, propelling him backward until he had the bounder against a wall. There, in the watery light from a candle in the window above and the increasing pale gray of dawn, the man who attacked him got his first good look at North's face. He paled.

"Sheffield," he whispered, eyes wide.

North smiled again, but there was no humor in the expression. Still holding the man's wrist, he wrapped his free hand around his throat. "That's right. And from that unfortunate growth on your face I'm going to guess that you're Mole Face Charley, am I right?"

The man nodded.

A certain amount of pleasure filled North at the thief's admission. "You work for Harker."

Charley didn't speak, but the subtle widening of his eyes was enough. North's smile widened, twisted. "Will your boss be impressed that you tried to roll me tonight, or will he mess your pretty face up some more when he hears you did not finish me off?"

A blink was his only answer. Obviously Charley was wondering that very same thing.

"I want you to take Harker a message for me," North said, flexing his fingers around the dirty column of the thief's throat. "Tell him to enjoy his freedom while he can. It will come to an abrupt end very soon. You know what 'abrupt' means, do you not, Charley?"

The thief might have looked fearsome if not for the blood running from his nose. North released him, relieving him of his weapon with one deft motion. "Get."

And Charley did just that, slinking off into the shadows as rats were wont to do. North pocketed the blade and continued in the direction of home.

Once in the comfort of his own study, he washed Charley's blood from his knuckles and fell into the chair behind his desk with a weary sigh. Unlocking the bottom drawer, he retrieved a silver flask and a miniature. The flask contained old Scotch whisky, which he saved for nights when he needed an excuse for the numbness he sometimes felt. Tonight it was to numb his reaction to the face in the miniature.

She had been so young when this was painted. He knew because he hadn't been much older at the time and had sat for one himself. Did Octavia still have it? Did she take it out on occasion and stare at it as he did, wondering what might have been? Did she ever miss him as he missed her?

He took a deep swallow from the flask and stared at the painting, stroking the ivory oval frame with the pad of his thumb. The smooth, round cheeks were gone, replaced by high, elegant cheekbones. The little chin was more stubborn, the nose more pert. But the eyes were the same—bright and guileless, innocent yet seductive. If the rest of her face was obscured from view, he would still know her just from those eyes.

He didn't owe her anything, yet he felt the sting of rejecting her as acutely as if the situation had been reversed. Did she owe him? He wasn't certain. Probably not, but it would be nice if she would just let him go—release him from this strange hold she had over him. His reaction to seeing her earlier was a painful reminder of just how much she had once meant to him. Now—if the gossips were to be believed—she was going to marry someone else. An earl. North probably wouldn't be invited to the wedding.

Yes, she owed him. Hell yes. She owed him a good-bye.

But did he have the courage to collect?

Chapter 2

"I will do everything in my power to keep you safe."

Black Sally looked at him with wary disbelief in her dark, dull eyes. It was an expression North had seen countless times here in the Whitechapel district, but it never failed to tug at his heart. It was the look of someone who had already resigned herself to a particular fate. In Black Sally's case it was death, and she didn't believe he or anyone else could prevent it.

Well, North did believe it. He would have men stationed outside this dismal building, watching Sally's tiny dark apartment and all those who entered. He would have her followed wherever she went. His men were used to the hard facts of life; watching Black Sally and her customers would hold no shock for them.

"You can't protect me," Sally informed him in a voice rough and nasal. "You ain't low enough to have arms that reach as far as 'is, and you ain't got the blunt to buy the loyalty of the people 'oo are afraid of 'im."

Maybe not, but North's reach was long enough, his pockets deep enough, his connections just strong enough that he might be able to keep Sally alive.

Black Sally wasn't even twenty years old, and she looked well over forty. She was approximately the same age as Octavia had been when she'd come to him, scared that she might end up some rich man's mistress. But there would be no fairy-tale ending for Sally. Even if North managed to keep her alive for the present, she would still die young, one more "unfortunate" the good charity ladies would pay to bury and then forget.

"I will protect you," he vowed with all the conviction he could muster.

Sally shrugged her narrow shoulders. The gown that bared them was a bright and garish red, a shocking contrast to her faded looks and the dingy, peeling wallpaper that covered the walls of her room. The carpet was as threadbare and worn as the woman herself.

"Keep me alive long enuv to testify, mister. After that, it don't matter. Death's a right bit of peace for a woman the likes o'me."

A right bit of peace. How sad. And yet, how he envied her for not fearing death. He feared it, feared the unknown, the darkness. It wasn't the dying itself that made him uneasy—he'd seen enough death to know that the pain and horror eventually stopped. The body had ways of dealing with suffering, as did the mind. It was the afterward, facing eternity that gave him pause.

"You are not going to die, Sally. Not yet."

The prostitute smiled, revealing teeth that were as brown and broken as the rest of her. It made her look younger, more like the girl she should be than the old woman she was. "Yer a good man, guv. You should be married to a nice lady rather than worryin' about cunnies like me."

Not a person—not even to herself. Just a body part, and

one she gave a vulgar name to at that, as though fornication were her only use.

He forced a smile. "Why would I want a woman at home to nag me when I have you ladies to do it for me?"

Sally's smile faded. "A man like you deserves better. Stop fussing wiv our lives and live your own. Now get out. I 'ave work to do."

No, Sally's life couldn't mean much to her if she was going out onto the streets again, knowing that Harker had put a price on her head. It wasn't that she was trying to test North's ability to protect her or even that she was trying to make his job more difficult; it was the fact that she had to support herself. She had to eat, she had to pay rent, and she wouldn't accept money from him to do so.

"Be careful," he told her. But how careful could she be when most of her time was spent frigging with complete strangers?

Sally rose off the narrow cot where she'd been sitting. "Tell those boys o'yours that I'll be keeping tally of how much they owes me for watchin'."

North had to smile at that. "I will."

He left her then, alone in the tiny, stained room with the uncertainty of her life. Society considered women like Black Sally beneath their notice, no better than dirt under their shoes, yet who of the *ton* would sacrifice themselves to catch a murderer?

His shoulders brushed the walls of the narrow stairs, the boards creaking beneath his boots. His childhood had been golden compared to those of London's lower classes. His mother might have been an actress—one step up from a courtesan—but she was popular and they were able to live comfortably thanks to that and his father's assistance. His life would have been very different without his father in it.

And yet there was still some bitterness that he hadn't been

fortunate enough to be legitimate. It colored his entire life, his perception of the world around him. He hadn't belonged in his mother's world, or his father's. After his mother's death, he'd desperately wanted to be part of something, but no matter how hard he tried, the aristocratic world would not accept him as one of its own.

The only place he'd ever felt accepted for himself was with Octavia, and then even she'd left him, finding a place for herself in that socially glittering world that wouldn't open its doors to him. What a joke—what a blow—that had been.

So he'd made his own world, found his own path. And the irony was not lost on him that now that he wanted no part of the *ton,* they clamored to him. He was fashionable because he'd turned his back on them. He was content in his own world—happy even. All those years of longing, and now that he no longer cared, he was being welcomed with open arms. Now *that* was a joke in itself. North appreciated the humor in the situation. What he didn't appreciate was that tiny, tiny part of him that he thought long dead, getting hopeful every time he was invited to a party or a ball.

He stepped outside into the gray, damp day. The rain had stopped, but the scent of it clung still to the breeze, along with the scents of refuse, horse, and all the other smells of Whitechapel. He walked down the street a few blocks, to where the hired hack sat waiting, and told the driver to take him home. He had more work to do, fees to claim, and problems to solve.

Perhaps throwing himself into a new case would stop these nagging thoughts of Octavia Marsh—Vaux-Daventry, she was now. What an awful, pretentious name. She would always be just Vie to him. Constant, loyal Vie.

There was only a few years age difference between them. When he was very young, her constant following of him had been annoying and unwanted, but then something had

changed. She changed. Or maybe he had. He couldn't remember exactly when, but gradually she'd gone from a nuisance to a friend. They would play in the theater together
when no one else was around, using the stage to put on their
own productions. They painted each other's faces, selected
each other's wardrobe.

Then one day they'd been playing at Romeo and Juliet and
Octavia kissed him. She changed everything that day.
Friends they remained, yes. Inseparable, always. But something new blossomed between them that day, an awareness
that North hadn't been able to shake. A possessiveness that
most people—perhaps even Octavia herself—mistook for
brotherly affection took hold of him. But it was far from
brotherly, as he realized that night she came to him, asking
him to be her first lover.

She'd feared her future, and then a new one was handed to
her. Society let her in without question, and the one person
who made him feel as though he belonged was lost to him
forever.

Until last night when he'd picked her out of the crowd with
frightening ease.

She had grown into a beautiful woman, his Vie. Tall and
slender, with skin like peach-kissed alabaster, and features
that were both sharp yet sensual. Her hair was still that
strange combination of copper, blond and brown, so that it
changed depending on the lighting. Her smile could still illu-
minate an entire room.

She was a woman, that was for sure; the soft breasts
pushed upward by the gown she'd worn—the color of which
he couldn't remember—were proof enough of that. But one
look in her eyes was enough to determine that no matter what
she looked like, how she dressed, or who she was with, she
was still his Vie. Once his shadow, then his friend, and finally
his torment.

And to think that she had almost made the mistake of coming to him, of speaking to him. Hadn't her grandfather warned her about socializing with people of his ilk? Surely he must have advised her to not reveal her past connections with North and the theater? No one could know of her sordid beginnings, that her mother had allowed her to be raised in such circumstances. Hadn't that been what old Vaux-Daventry, Lord Spinton, told North that day he'd actually tried to claim Octavia for his own?

She deserves better, the old man had told him. *If you truly care for her, you will never come near her again.*

So North hadn't, despite Octavia's efforts to entice him. He still had all the letters she'd sent, letters that arrived like clockwork for the longest time and then eventually dwindled as he refused to reply and she learned to stop trying. Even though he sometimes kicked himself for letting her go, he knew the old man had been right. He couldn't have given Octavia the life she deserved—the life her birth entitled her to. His one act of rebellion against this was the flowers he had sent to her on her birthday.

A casual hello at a party would not raise eyebrows, but Octavia hadn't looked casual; she had looked ready to call him some foolish pet name and rush into his arms. Obviously her grandfather had been able to teach her to act like a lady, but he hadn't been able to change her completely.

For some reason, that realization was as saddening as it was joyful.

The carriage rolled to a halt. Had he arrived home already? The trip seemed so short, but then he'd had his mind on other things.

He lived in his mother's house—the one his father had bought for her back when Covent Garden had still maintained some degree of respectability. His mother had named him North because that was the corner of the piazza in which the house was situated. It was an elegant yet simple structure of smooth red brick, and but a short walk from the theaters and the Bow Street offices.

Once it had been home. Now it was simply his house.

North barely stepped through the door when his housekeeper, Mrs. Bunting, rushed to meet him.

Little hands clasped before a generous bosom and a happy smile greeted him. Bunty was as much a part of this house as he was—having been there for more years. "There's a gentleman waiting for you in your office, Mr. Sheffield."

North often conducted business out of his home, and his address was public knowledge—it was one of the reasons he slept with a loaded pistol nearby, and why he had a very large man by the name of Johnson acting as his butler. Johnson searched every stranger who came into North's home. It wasn't just for of his own safety that North had this done, but for the safety of his servants as well. He hadn't made a lot of enemies in his career, but he'd made enough. Harker, for example.

"Is Johnson with him?" he asked, combing his fingers through the unruly waves on his head. If he wore a hat, his hair wouldn't get so messy, but hats made his head itch, and he hated the feel of anything around his skull.

"Yes, sir."

North relaxed as he walked through the main hall to the room that served as his office. The danger of his job was very real, but he trusted Johnson and knew there was no point in living his life in fear. Fear kept a man smart, but too much of it got him killed.

Other than his bedroom and small dining room, his office was the only room in the house he used on a regular basis. He'd had it redecorated after leaving Bow Street several years ago, when he launched out on his own. The walls were a deep, rich blue and the Aubusson carpet was a dove gray with blue and plum woven through. The desk was a deep, polished oak and big enough for a fully grown man to sleep on. He knew this because he had actually done it on occasion. The chairs in front of it were the same dark blue as the walls, and one of them had a man sitting in it. Johnson—all brawn and bollocks—stood behind him.

The man stood as North closed the door behind him. Immediately North recognized him as Octavia's escort from the night before. He was the current Lord Spinton, heir to Octavia's grandfather. The man she was rumored to marry.

What the hell did he want? Slight of build and slight of hair, Spinton nevertheless had a kind, unthreatening air about him that made North want to like him despite his prejudices. Was Spinton there to warn him away from Octavia? He needn't bother. North had no intention of going near her.

"Lord Spinton," he greeted in a toneless voice. "What can I do for you?"

"Thank you for seeing me, Mr. Sheffield." Clutching a brown beaver hat in his hands, Spinton reclaimed his chair as North sunk into a similar, but more comfortable one, behind the desk.

North allowed himself a brief smile. "I do not think I had much choice."

Spinton colored. Well, damned if the man didn't seem to be as sincere as his unassuming nature.

"I have come to see you about a confidential matter concerning my betrothed, Lady Octavia Vaux-Daventry."

A claw sunk deep into North's heart and yanked. Even though he had heard the rumors, they had been just gossip until now. "Congratulations on your betrothal, my lord."

Another blush. "Oh, it is not official yet, but I hope that Lady Octavia will soon condescend to make me so happy."

As if North cared. He didn't. Really. "Where do I fit in?"

Spinton jerked a little at his abrupt tone. What did the man want, more felicitations? He couldn't help but be a little peevish that while he wasn't good enough in the old earl's eyes, this milksop—he didn't care if that was unfair—obviously had been. Of course, Spinton had a lot more to recommend him than North ever had—as far as society would be concerned at least.

"Lady Octavia has recently begun to receive strange letters." Spinton pulled several folded papers from his jacket and extended them across the desk. "She does not find them worrisome, but as her future husband, I find them greatly disturbing. I took these from the wastebasket in her parlor."

Frowning, North took the letters. Was someone threatening Octavia? Why? Blackmail, perhaps? Had they found out about her past? Is that why Spinton came to him? And why had Spinton resorted to rifling through his intended's garbage?

He opened one and set the rest on his desk.

My darling Lady,

I have watched you from afar these past months with a longing I can no longer contain . . .

North lifted his astonished gaze to Spinton's eager face. "These are love letters."

Spinton nodded. "From an anonymous admirer."

Still frowning, North gestured at him with the letter. "Are they all like this?"

"More or less."

North tossed them onto his desk. "So, why have you brought them to me?"

Spinton looked confused. "Because I know your reputation for solving mysteries and I want to know who is sending them. I am concerned about Octavia's safety."

I'd be more concerned about who was in her bed. That wasn't fair. Just because Vie was receiving love letters, didn't mean she actually had a lover. And as the man who had originally relieved her of her virginity, it wasn't his place to cast stones. This man didn't write like someone who knew her intimately—good thing, or North might actually be tempted to hunt the blighter down.

Quickly, he scanned the rest of the letters the earl offered him. As Spinton had said, they were all in the same vein. Nothing threatening, unless unfettered romanticism had become more dangerous than irritating.

He gave the letters back to Spinton. "I cannot help you, my lord."

Spinton blinked. "Whyever not?"

North regarded him for a moment. "Does Lady Octavia know you brought these to me?" As soon as he asked, he knew the answer.

"No." If Spinton got any redder, he'd look like a pomegranate. "As I told you, she does not believe there is any danger."

North smiled—a real one this time. No, Octavia wouldn't be threatened by mere words on paper. "You are a good man to be so . . . concerned, my lord. Your protective nature does much to recommend you, but if Lady Octavia is not concerned, I do not think you need be either."

The fair lord nodded, tucking the letters back inside his coat pocket. "I must seem foolish to you."

"Not at all." That was true, North realized as he rose to his feet. He seemed like a man very concerned about the woman he was going to marry. There was nothing foolish about that.

Spinton stood as well. "Have you ever been in love, Mr. Sheffield?"

North swallowed the lump in his throat. "Once."

"I do not know if you have ever met Lady Octavia, but she is the kind of lady—a rare and wonderful lady—that most men would count themselves lucky to possess."

Damnation, but he didn't have to tell North that. North *had* possessed her, for one brief and faraway night.

"You are a very fortunate man, my lord."

The earl left then, but not until he'd made North promise to reconsider taking the case should it take a more sinister turn. There was very little chance of that happening, so North consented.

"So you believe eventually these letters will stop?" Spinton asked, his hand on the door. "That this admirer of Lady Octavia's will move on and find someone else to pine for?"

Smiling, North nodded. He didn't bother to tell Spinton not to hold his breath waiting for that to happen.

He knew all too well how difficult it was to get over Octavia.

Evening cast a dark and moody gloom over the city as Octavia sat in her drawing room, sipping a glass of sherry. Spinton was going to be taking her and her cousin Beatrice to the social club Eden for dinner and socialization, but he had yet to arrive, and Beatrice was still above stairs. This was one of those rare moments of silence Octavia treasured above all else.

Growing up in the theater had accustomed her to noise of various natures and degrees, but there was nothing more soothing than the sound of silence so pure one could listen to the rhythm of one's own breathing. Of course, silence could be torture at times, as well. There were days—although few and far between—when she missed the excitement. Most of all, she missed sharing that commotion with North—or at least, she did now that she had seen him two nights before.

She sat alone, in the center of the salmon pink sofa, her wine silk skirts carefully arranged around her, a keepsake book balanced on her lap. Pasted onto the pages were letters, newspaper clippings . . . anything that marked some important moment in her life. Her grandfather hadn't known about her book. He wouldn't have liked her keeping it. There were notices about her mother, letters from Beatrice or other friends, but the newspaper clippings were about North and his daring adventures as a Bow Street Runner, and then running his own operation. He had made quite a reputation for himself over the years. It didn't surprise her, the degree of notoriety he had achieved. He'd always sworn he was going to change the world, and he was.

He no doubt hated all the attention. He never had been one for wanting to be the focus of a crowd—that had been her vanity. Odd how life twisted and turned. Here she was, the one who loved attention, living a quiet life of little import. And there was North, who was so content to stay in the background, who couldn't even leave his house without someone writing about it.

Then again, at one time he would have been happy to see her in a crowd. He would have held out his arms for her to run into. He wouldn't have shaken his head and pretended not to know her.

Glancing around the room, at the cream and golds used to offset the warm pinks, Octavia wondered—and not for the first time—what her life would have been like if her grandfather hadn't come for her, if she hadn't discovered that she was actually the legitimate daughter of the deceased youngest son of the Earl Spinton. Would she have ended up with no one to answer to but herself? Or would she have ended up dependent on a string of "protectors" for her well-being?

Such foolish thoughts were hardly worth entertaining. It

did not matter what might have been. All that mattered was reality, and the reality was that her grandfather had come for her, and he made her into a lady and gave her everything a young girl dreams of, except for the freedom to live as she wanted.

She was a bird in a cage—a gilt and pink cage, but a cage nonetheless. And she had entered it willingly. She promised her mother she would honor her memory by adhering to her wishes, and her mother wanted her to inherit her birthright. She made promises to her grandfather, out of gratitude and out of duty, and even though Mama and Grandpapa were both dead, Octavia was a woman of her word.

It was just another one of her many flaws.

She picked up a miniature watercolor tucked between two pages. Painted over a decade ago, it was of a grinning young man with pale blue eyes and unruly dark hair. Color bloomed high on his chiseled cheeks, and the painter had captured the mischief in his eyes. They'd each had a portrait done— Christmas gifts for each other. Did North still have the likeness of her? Did he ever look upon it?

"Oh, Norrie," she said with sigh. "I have missed you."

Several heartbeats passed as she stared at the tiny portrait, committing every detail to memory.

"What are you looking at?"

Shoving the watercolor between the pages once again, Octavia closed the book with a resounding snap. She forced a smile as Spinton entered the room. He was such a regular fixture in the house that the servants rarely bothered to announce him anymore. She was going to have to remedy that. The new earl he might be, but this was still *her* house. No doubt it was Spinton's imperious attitude that kept it from feeling like a home.

"Just some old keepsakes."

Her grandfather would no doubt have demanded to see it,

but Spinton was nothing like his predecessor. He merely smiled and nodded and seated himself in the dainty chair across from her.

He wanted to marry her, and they were alone. Wouldn't a normal man take this time to press his suit? Sit beside her on this fish-hued sofa and perhaps sneak in a few kisses? Not Spinton. He would never take such risks, such liberties. Perhaps if he did Octavia might be a bit warmer to the idea of marrying him. Their other incompatibilities she could overlook, but a lack of passion? She had been raised among people of volatile temperament—passion was an absolute must.

So was honor, so she would keep her promise to marry Spinton, but she just couldn't bring herself to accept his proposal—not now.

"Beatrice will be down shortly," she informed him, if for no other reason than to break the silence that a few moments ago had been so delicious.

Spinton seemed uncomfortable, shifting in his chair as though he had a rash in a most embarrassing place. His cravat and shirt points were perfect—not too starched, not too elaborate or too high. His buff pantaloons and blue jacket complemented the shades of the room, unlike her gown, which clashed in a most unflattering manner. Normally she liked this room and all the colors in it, but not tonight, it seemed.

"What is the matter?" If nothing else, she and Spinton had known each other long enough not to stand on ceremony. For that matter, they'd known each other long enough to use their Christian names, but she couldn't bring herself to do it on a regular basis.

He flushed. He colored as easily as a schoolgirl. "I have something to confess to you."

He was already secretly married. He preferred the company of men. These possibilities and more raced through Octavia's mind. It was not lost on her that every one of them was a reason that she and Spinton couldn't wed.

"We are old friends," she reminded him. "You may say anything to me."

He drew a deep breath. "I saw North Sheffield yesterday."

Nothing could have shocked her more—not even an announcement that he liked to dress up in women's clothing and sell oranges in Covent Garden. He had seen North? *Her* North? *She* had yet to see him for heaven's sake!

He flashed her a sheepish smile, and Octavia bit her tongue, waiting for him to continue. A lady, her grandfather had taught her, did not make demands of a gentleman unless he was her husband, and even then she must be careful not to seem like a fishmonger's wife.

Devil take it. "Why in the name of God did you visit him?" That was a fishwife if ever she heard one.

He was surprised by the ferocity of her outburst; it was written plainly in his eyes. "Well, I . . . er, wanted to discuss your . . . *admirer* with him."

She could strangle him, the stupid, well-meaning dolt. "After I asked you specifically not to investigate the letters?"

Another sheepish smile. "I am afraid so."

He was afraid so. What had happened? Had some invisible force pushed him to North? Had someone held a pistol to his head and made him do the one thing she'd asked him not to do?

"Why?" she managed to ask in a civil tone. "Why did you go to him?" *Of all people.*

"Because I am concerned for your welfare, and as your future husband it is my business to look after you."

Octavia couldn't stop herself; she leaped to her feet, tossing her book on the sofa. It bounced once and then lay silent. "You are not my husband yet, Spinton, and you never will be if you go against my wishes again."

His thin lips twitched, then parted, and finally his entire jaw dropped, creating a great gaping hole where his mouth once was. She'd shocked him, that was evident. In all the long years of their acquaintance, he had never seen her temper provoked, but he had crossed the line with her, and she was very tempted to say promise be damned, and tell him where to stick his marriage proposal.

Spinton's mouth worked, but nothing came out. Sighing, Octavia pressed the fingers of her right hand to her forehead. The left went to her hip. "Forgive me, Spinton. I forgot myself."

Speech eluded him for several more seconds before he finally nodded. "Of course, my dear. But it is I who should ask forgiveness. In my desire to protect you, I obviously ignored my promise to you, and I am sorry for it."

He had such a way of making her feel so horrible—as though she was the one in the wrong, not he.

Then again, he had gone to North out of some misguided gesture of affection. His intentions had been good, even if utterly stupid.

She was saved from having to apologize further, or from any questions her outburst might have raised in Spinton's mind, by the arrival of her cousin Beatrice.

Beatrice Henry was a few years younger than Octavia. However, where Octavia's wealth and position made her unmarried state pardonable, Beatrice's lower circumstances had the opposite effect.

Beatrice was an attractive woman, with dark hair and eyes and a beautiful English complexion. She was much shorter than Octavia, rounder in all the right places, and as softly spoken as a summer breeze. She looked lovely in a gown of soft rose silk—a perfect English rose. Ordinarily Octavia would hate her out of sheer spite, but they were family and, above all else, friends. Beatrice was the one family member—other than her late grandfather—who knew anything about her mother and her past.

Beatrice didn't know Octavia had seen North, however.

"Am I not the luckiest man in London," Spinton announced with a smile as he stood to greet Beatrice, "to escort the two loveliest ladies in the city this evening?"

Beatrice blushed under the praise while Octavia merely smiled. She was accustomed to the earl's lavish compliments, and perhaps a little spoiled by them now. It was nice to see someone appreciate them and take them for genuine praise rather than mere politeness.

"Let us go," Octavia said as she rose, shooing both of them toward the door. "I do not want to be late."

Spinton chuckled, but allowed himself to be herded like so much cattle. "I have never understood your fascination with punctuality, Octavia. We do not have to be there as soon as the club opens."

It took all of Octavia's resolve to not to remind Lord Spinton that she had sent word around days ago securing a special table for this evening. It would be rude not to arrive at the prearranged time. She merely smiled. "I suppose I am simply anxious to enjoy the diversions Eden has to offer."

"As am I," Beatrice spoke up, casting a supportive glance in Octavia's direction. "I find it all terribly exciting. I hear they have games of chance and all manner of exotic entertainments."

Spinton flashed an endearing smile—one that made Beatrice blush sweetly. "Yes, I can imagine such diversions would hold some fascination for ladies."

Octavia winced. She couldn't help it. Thankfully Spinton didn't see it. Here he was, the man she was expected to marry. A friendly, good-hearted dolt who obviously didn't realize just how ignorant he truly was when it came to "ladies" and the diversions they found entertaining.

Thank God she was so skilled at hiding her emotions when she wanted. It was a skill she was going to have to depend on from now on. From her wedding night onward, for the rest of her days, she was going to be concealing more than she could ever reveal.

What a suffocating thought.

Fortunately, there was no more talk of diversions or the minds of ladies. The trio—Spinton in the middle with Beatrice on one arm and Octavia on the other—left the house in lightweight outerwear and climbed into Spinton's well-appointed carriage. Octavia stared around the blind at the city drifting past as Spinton and Beatrice made small talk. How alike the two of them were. How much better suited than Spinton and herself. Wouldn't her grandfather rather his heir be happy? Did it matter which granddaughter Spinton married?

Yes, it did. She knew it did. She was the oldest, the daughter of the old earl's youngest son—his favorite—who had died before his time. He had decided Octavia would be the next countess, and he had made her promise to become so. She agreed because he was dying and it pained her to see him suffer. But why? Why did she condemn both herself and Spinton to a life of misery?

And why make herself even more miserable by dwelling on it? Marriage to Spinton would not be so bad. She was the stronger of the two of them. She would run their household, make all the decisions. She would live as she saw fit, and he would merely smile and find her "womanly ways" infuriatingly amusing. After she produced an heir he would no doubt take a mistress like other men to save her from the degradation of the marriage bed.

Poor Spinton. He probably wouldn't even notice that she wasn't a virgin bride. Her maidenhead had been taken—no, given—a lifetime ago, so it seemed. Even though her life had turned in a much different direction than the one she had feared, she never once regretted asking North to be her first lover. To this day, the memory of that sweet, awkward fumbling brought a lump of emotion to her throat.

"Do drop the blind, Octavia," Spinton requested. "We do not want to encourage footpads."

Octavia did as he bid, even though she thought it foolish. Footpads wouldn't be encouraged by an open blind any more than they'd be discouraged by a lowered one. Those who made their living from crime would attack whenever they felt like it. The only thing that discouraged them was a weapon— and a familiar face.

At one time she had run the streets around Covent Garden and its neighboring environs with North, safe in her familiarity with the people and the area. Safe with her champion by her side, even though there had been times when they were younger that he hadn't wanted her dogging his footsteps. She wouldn't be safe out there now—not with Spinton by her side.

They arrived at Eden shortly after eight o'clock. Octavia concealed her agitation as Spinton teased her about her hurry to get to inside. She couldn't tell him that her anxiety stemmed from the fact that tonight was about so much more than an evening out. She could go out into society whenever she wanted. No, tonight Eden was playing host to a party she wanted to visit. A party for a young woman she had known at the theater—Madeline DuBois, a young actress who recently made her debut and set London on its ear. Tonight Madeline and her fiancé were celebrating their engagement.

Octavia avoided the theater now, afraid that someone might recognize her and say something to make the gossips' tongues wag. There would be no one to be concerned about tonight, however. It was a private party in one of Eden's suites, arranged because the club's owner, Lady Lilith Warren, Countess Angelwood, was one of Madeline's biggest fans.

When Spinton and Beatrice were enjoying the assembly rooms or the games tables, she would sneak off on her own—if only for a few moments—to join Maddie's celebration.

Entering Eden was like entering another world. Lord and Lady Angelwood had designed the club to be the most elegant in all of London, and they had succeeded. Soothing colors and soft decor were set off by stunning works of art and muted lighting. Much of Octavia's anxiety melted away as soon as she stepped inside. The majordomo approached to direct them to the dining room.

Another man met them inside the large dining area. Tables set with pristine white cloths and sparkling crystal dotted the Italian marble floor. Candelabras on each table gave off a soft glow, but were small enough not to emit too much heat in the warmer weather. Wall sconces lined the soft yellow walls, adding more light were it was needed.

A few heads turned as they were shown to their table. Octavia waved to acquaintances and Spinton did the same. Thankfully there was no one in attendance that she felt it necessary to stop and speak to—not because she was feeling particularly unsocial, but because they might try to seize her attention later, and she wanted to spend as much time at Maddie's party as she could.

"What a lovely room," Beatrice remarked breathily.

Octavia made a mental note to take her cousin to Eden at least once a month from then on. Beatrice didn't get out of the house nearly as much as she should. That aside, Beatrice was right—it was a lovely room. And Octavia knew before the footman brought them their wine that the food would be just as impressive. She wasn't wrong.

Dinner was sumptuous—quail in a succulent wine sauce with buttered vegetables; warm breads; crisp salads; a sharp, sweet wine; and followed by sinfully decadent chocolate-covered fruits for dessert. Eden's chef was a master.

After eating, Octavia suggested that Spinton visit the gentlemen's section of the club while she and Beatrice visit the ladies'. Eden was designed so that the sexes could spend the evening segregated or together, with a male side, a female side, and then rooms in the center where the two could meet. It didn't take much prodding. Kind as Spinton was, he was still a man, and talking with his own kind would no doubt always be preferable to hanging about two ladies.

"I will not be long," he promised.

Octavia smiled. "Take your time."

Once he was gone, she turned to Beatrice. "I am going to one of the suites to see an old friend. Will you join me?"

Her cousin shook her head. "No, thank you. I see some acquaintances of my own here. But what do I do if Lord Spinton returns?"

Octavia shrugged. "Discreetly send one of the servants to find me. I am certain you can entertain Spinton until I return."

"But what do I talk to him about?"

Good Lord, did her cousin have no imagination? Octavia was giving her time alone with an attractive man; certainly Beatrice could think of *something*.

"Ask him about his new horse," Octavia replied, already inching out of her seat. "He will talk until your ears fall off."

Smiling at her cousin's dubious expression, Octavia waited until both Beatrice and Spinton had been swallowed up by the crowd, before slipping off on her own. She wasn't as familiar with the club as some of the other women there, but she didn't want to look as though she didn't know where she was going. Someone might think she was sneaking off for an assignation, and that was the last thing she needed the gossips to speculate about. Spinton might wonder as well.

A helpful footman discreetly pointed her in the right direction, and Octavia slipped through a doorway and up a flight of highly polished stairs that led to the party rooms above. Appropriately enough, Maddie's party was in the Green Room, no doubt in reference to her profession. The man at the door recognized her as soon as she gave her name—her old name—and let her inside without hesitation.

A few people recognized her as she entered the room— marvelously appointed in shades of sage and forest green. It wasn't a large crowd—but it would definitely grow as the evening wore on. Octavia would no doubt be gone by then. She would not be able to stay as long as she liked.

Madeline's eyes went wide as she saw her. Her little bow of a mouth dropped happily and she spread her arms wide. "Octavia!"

Grinning foolishly, Octavia allowed herself to be swept into the girl's exuberant embrace. She didn't care that they were being watched, that some onlookers even applauded. She was safe here. Her secret was safe here. These people would never betray her to the *ton*. They were more loyal than society could ever hope to be.

They laughed and chatted as they embraced, both gushing about how wonderful it was to see each other, and Octavia laughed in disbelief at just how lovely the young girl had grown up to be. A pudgy child, Madeline had blossomed into a full-figured, stunning woman.

"You look wonderful, Maddie!" Octavia took a step back and surveyed the younger woman head to toe. "Just wonderful."

"I could not agree more," came a voice from behind her.

Octavia didn't have to turn to recognize the voice. Deep, a little rough, and oh-so-musical, with a touch of Scottish accent still clinging to every vowel. The very sound of it twisted her heart into a tight knot.

Madeline threw herself at him, and he laughed as he

caught her in his long arms, the dark fabric of his coat pulling tautly across the broad width of his shoulders. Octavia watched, a strange, prickling cold-heat shaking her entire body. She drank in every inch of him, committing him to memory, so certain she was that this was a dream and any moment he'd fade away.

But it wasn't a dream. She realized that as Madeline released him and took both their hands, smiling happily as she stood between them, little and plump and oh-so-adorable.

"It is so wonderful to have both of you here with me," the girl enthused. "It means so very much."

Octavia's smile faded as she lifted her gaze from Maddie to the man beside her. It seemed his expression became more hesitant as well.

Somehow, she managed to speak around the lump in her throat. "Hello, Norrie."

Glacial blue eyes brightened, watching her with a nameless expression that made her knees quiver. And then he smiled—crooked and unsure.

"Hello, my sweet Vie."

Chapter 3

North found himself embraced in strong slender arms, engulfed by the heady scents of clean, warm skin and lavender. Soft hair brushed his cheek seconds before lips, feather-light, whispered a kiss against his jaw. He closed his eyes, afraid someone—*she*—might see the longing there.

His best friend. His sweet, sweet Vie.

Madeline was drawn away by other well-wishers, leaving the two of them standing alone, surrounded by bodies in their own little world.

Jewel-bright eyes watched him thoughtfully, searching his face as Octavia took a step backward, her hand sliding down to his. What did she look for? A glimpse of the boy he'd once been? At one time he would have thought that boy well hidden, as distant as a dream, but he knew he was there. All she had to do was gaze into his eyes and she'd see him, terribly afraid of just how happy he was to see her—touch her.

Her fingers tightened around his. "So you are not ashamed to know me after all."

Ashamed? Of her? "I would think you would not want to own to knowing me."

Her head tilted to the right, those brilliant eyes of hers refusing to release him. "Only because I made a promise to conceal my past. I have no shame of where I come from, Norrie. Nor am I ashamed of my friends."

His own eyes narrowed against the prickling there. "After all these years, what sort of friends are we, Octavia?"

Her thumb rubbed his, her skin velvet soft against the roughness of his own. "The dearest kind. The kind that cares not for how many years have passed or foolish promises made."

His smile was genuine, but bitterness twisted the curve of his lips. "The kind who would try to greet you in a crowded ballroom, regardless of what questions that association might raise?"

Some of the sparkle left her eyes, replaced by a deeper understanding that sent a trickle of discomfort down his spine. "The kind who would stop you from committing such a folly even though he longs for the reunion as much you."

He should have known she would see through him. She always could when they were younger, why should a dozen years change that?

A dozen years. She was thirty now, yet her features were unmarred by the passage of time. He had seen her a few years ago, at Garrick's funeral, but she had been veiled, hiding her face, and her grief, from those in attendance. A quiet maturity had sharpened the bones, deepened the hollows, but the face was still the same. It was her eyes that had changed. There was a darkness to her gaze that hadn't been there in her youth, a responsibility that weighed heavily. Despite the years that had passed between them, he wanted to take that burden from her and bear it as his own.

"You look wonderful," he blurted, cheeks heating. Compliments were never his strong suit.

Octavia smiled. "So do you."

North snorted. "My face has so many lines, I look like a map of London."

A soft chuckle escaped her lips as she raised her free hand—the other still held tight to his fingers—to his face. The pads of her fingers stroked the skin between his temple and cheek, where the lines fanned from the corner of his eyes.

"You look like a man, Norrie," she murmured, her gaze locking with his. "It suits you."

What could he say to that? Even if he was able to speak, her touch had robbed him of all ability to think of a suitable reply.

"You are not wearing gloves." Good Lord, now she was going to think he had become simple over the years as well.

Her lips curved in that mischievous smile he remembered from his dreams. "Neither are you, Mr. Sheffield. Mine are in my reticule. Where are yours?"

It didn't occur to him to lie. "Home."

Her laughter broke through the din around them, lighting her face with a glow that pinched at North's chest. "Of course they are!"

Seconds passed, years perhaps, as they stared into each other's eyes. Reaching down, he caught the hand that had touched his face just moments before, and held it tight in his own. The only parts of their bodies touching were their hands, and yet he felt her as surely as if he held her flush against him. Every fiber of his being was that aware of her presence.

"I've missed you," he confided in a low voice.

He watched her swallow, the delicate column of her throat constricting as though the action took great effort. "I know," she whispered. "I wish things could have been different."

His smile was kind, despite the hollowness in his chest. "But they are not, and now you must go before your fiancé starts to worry."

Was it his imagination, or did her fingers tighten around his? "You are right." Slowly, she stepped back, easing out of his grip as reluctantly as he let her go. "It was lovely seeing you again, Norrie."

Every time she called him by that nickname, the one that had driven him mad as a youngster, his heart squeezed painfully. She was breaking it, breaking it with nothing more than a reminder of what they once were to each other—and the regret that those days were so far behind them now.

"It was lovely seeing you as well." His voice was undeniably hoarse, betraying his regret.

Opening her reticule—the same deep burgundy as her dress—she withdrew long, ivory satin gloves. She drew them on slowly, silently, unknowingly giving North ample time to commit the graceful lines of her hands and arms to memory once more. He burned as much of her as he could into his mind's eye—the soft hollows of her neck, the gentle line of her collarbones, the smooth, unblemished flesh of her upper chest that gave way to the swell of a bosom more impressive than it had been when he last touched it. As a girl she had been sharp, lanky even, but now she was as elegant as a gazelle, as softly supple as a willow.

Her gloves on, she raised her gaze to his with a resolution that startled him. He couldn't help but assume she had decided to never see him again—or worse yet, that she *would* see him again.

"Good night, Norrie." Not the "good-bye" she owed him, not "farewell," but "good night," as though day might bring another meeting.

"Flights of angels, Vie."

She smiled. Had she realized that he hadn't said good-bye either?

She had taken but a few steps—almost to the door—when she turned as though a sudden thought struck her. Of course he was watching her, and their gazes locked once more.

"Spinton is not my fiancé," she informed him. "Not yet."

With that, she turned her back to him and left the room, her spine as straight and regal as a fine lady's should be. She was a lady now.

But underneath all that finery, she was still his Vie.

His Vie.

After congratulating young Madeline once more, North left the soirée himself. He needed to be alone—needed to play over his meeting with Octavia until it made sense. Twelve years since they'd last spoken and what had they discussed? How much they'd missed each other. It didn't seem possible. Didn't seem real. How could they still mean that much to each other after so much time? But it wasn't a lie. He had meant every word he said—and many that he hadn't. And he knew that Octavia had been honest when she told him how much she missed him, and that Spinton wasn't her fiancé.

Hadn't Spinton told him the same thing? So why did it mean so much more coming from Octavia? And why did it matter? As her "dearest" friend, her oldest friend, he should want to see her happily wed.

He did want to see her happily married, just not to Spinton.

A flash of movement caught his attention, and his gaze immediately followed. He saw a man disappearing into the crowd—an all-too-familiar man, even from behind. It was Harker.

What was he doing there? Certainly anyone with the means and proper attire could enter a public club, but Eden didn't seem the kind of place Harker would frequent. Had the bastard been spying on him? If so, for how long, and how much had he seen? Or was his mind, bent on revenge, simply playing tricks? It might not have been Harker at all.

Or his nemesis might already be trying to figure out the connection between North and Octavia Vaux-Daventry, especially if he saw their embrace. No matter, any attempt Harker made at blackmail would be easily brushed aside. No one would believe him over Octavia, or even North himself. No, Harker would not be a danger unless he found out the truth about Octavia's past, and he wouldn't put himself to that task unless North gave him reason. Harker had many flaws, but patience was his most prominent virtue. He wouldn't take action until he was certain it was the best action to take. Avoiding Octavia would keep her below Harker's notice.

How hard could it be to avoid her in this city? He'd been fairly successful at it these last dozen years.

North's brother Wynthrope was waiting for him in the gentlemen's club. North picked him out of the milling bodies easily. He simply looked for the haughtiest, the most impeccably dressed, bored-looking man there, and his gaze immediately fell upon Wyn. He was standing against the far wall, watching a game of cards with no more interest than he might watch dust settle.

Wynthrope Ryland was no more than an inch shorter than his illegitimate brother, and while their coloring was similar, Wyn's hair was darker and shorter, and his eyes were a deeper, darker blue. The only real resemblance between them was the Ryland lopsided smile, but on Wyn it was a cynical, cool expression, while his brothers tended toward amusement.

In fact, Wyn was smiling at him in just such a manner as he approached.

"I hope you were not dallying with some actress up there while I stood here like a dolt waiting for you?"

Dallying? Perhaps. With an actress? No.

"I met an old friend," he replied, nodding his head in the direction of the exit. "Ready?"

Wyn was obviously surprised as he shrugged away from the wall. "Not—?"

"Yes." North didn't even look at him as they walked through the club entrance and exited to the street. He and Wynthrope shared almost everything that happened in their lives. With only a few months separating their births, they had been friends as well as brothers. Wyn was the reason North left Bow Street, and never once did he regret the decision to put his brother ahead of his own career.

In fact, Wyn knew him so well, he didn't ask any more questions about Octavia and their meeting. He knew that if North wanted to talk, he would. Ryland men were very particular about discussing their emotions—especially Wynthrope. He wasn't very keen on discussing other people's feelings either, which was just as well, since North had no idea in hell what he would have said if his brother had asked.

They talked of other things as they walked to North's house. Wynthrope, from past associations, knew the market district almost as well as North did, and the darkened streets held little danger for two men whom the occupants recognized as men not to be trifled with.

They sat in North's office, each with a snifter of brandy. North never worried about developing the same dependency on spirits as his father and eldest brother had. Wynthrope never seemed especially worried either. Their youngest brother, Devlin, rarely drank at all, and he was the one among the four of them who would have the most reason to do so, after all he had seen in the war.

But Devlin was in Devonshire now, happily married to a woman who suited him perfectly. North missed Devlin. Even though Dev was much happier where he was, North missed his steadiness, his naive notions of right and wrong. Things were always much simpler with Dev around. Not so gray as with himself and the other two—in fact, with Wynthrope, things were sometimes just plain black.

But enough about his brothers. He had something much more pressing to think about at the moment.

"Let me ask you something."

Wyn eyed him suspiciously. "I despise it when you take that tone. It usually means I am about to incriminate myself in some way."

North smiled. His brother wasn't stupid—or gullible—enough to get himself involved in something unsavory again.

"If someone were to say to you, I have not read Shelley *yet*, would you take that to believe that they were planning to read his work, or that they had no intention of reading him?"

Wyn's eyes widened. Obviously North sounded as idiotic as he felt. But Octavia had said that Spinton wasn't her fiancé *yet*, and he needed to know what she had meant by that.

"I assume you mean other than the fact that this person is obviously a complete idiot, uneducated and unrefined?"

North nodded, fighting a grin. "Yes."

"Well," Wyn thought for a moment, swirling his brandy in the bowl of the snifter. "I suppose I would take that as an indication that reading Shelley was not that important to this person, else they would have already read one of his works."

"Exactly." How smug that sounded, but Wyn had confirmed North's own thoughts—that Octavia couldn't be that eager to marry Spinton, or she would have already. Why that satisfied him so, North wasn't quite prepared to investigate, other than he would hate to see such a dear friend unhappy in her marriage.

"On the other hand," Wyn added after a swallow of brandy. "The very use of the word 'yet' indicates that the person is simply waiting for the right moment."

"Yes, but if they have not read it *yet* there is some indecisiveness there, do not you think? They may not read it at all."

Wynthrope's brows rose at the peevishness in his tone. "What are we really talking about? Call me dubious, but I have a suspicion we are not talking about poetry."

"Nothing." He was surly and foul and really didn't want to discuss it anymore. Wyn would no doubt howl with laughter to discover that all these silly questions had to do with a woman whom he had not spoken to in over a decade.

Though when he finally had spoken to her, it didn't seem that many years had passed between them.

"Well, if we are discussing nothing, can we change the topic?" That was Wyn. He never asked questions, never pried. To some it would appear callous and uncaring, but it wasn't. He simply knew that if North wanted to talk about it, he would.

"What did you think of the play?" North asked, taking a drink. They had been to the theater before going to the club.

Wynthrope grinned. "I think you should introduce me to that charming little Juliet."

And that was how the rest of their conversation went—filled with jests and meaningless banter until North almost forgot about Octavia. Almost. Fate had brought her back into his life, and he wasn't ready to face the ramifications, or the feelings her appearance brought with it.

Not yet.

Guilt was not a stranger to Octavia. Over the thirty years of her life she had felt the stifling emotion many times. It usually accompanied the realization that she had done something wrong—either in her estimation or in someone else's.

As she sat beside Spinton in his carriage, silent in the dark as he and Beatrice discussed the evening, feelings of guilt tightened her chest.

And it wasn't because she had enjoyed seeing North. No, that was to be expected. After all, he had been her dearest friend at one time. Nor was it because she was unable to stop playing scenes from the meeting over and over in her head. No, it was because she had to hide her joy at seeing him from Spinton. He knew nothing about her mother and her vocation. He did not know that she had once adored North Sheffield.

And he never would know. She had promised her grandfather that she would do all she could to conceal her origins, even though she was legitimate by birth. Sometimes, it still angered her that she should be forced to live a lie when it was her grandfather's own fault that she was raised where she was. If he hadn't disowned his son for eloping with an actress, Octavia's life might have been very different.

She might not have known North. She might be one of those society women who simpered and flirted every time he came near, thinking him dangerous and fascinating, rather than knowing the truth.

Then again, if she had grown up in the world she had been born into, she might already be married to Spinton and be happy with the match because she would have nothing to compare it to. Or she might be miserable, and be sizing up North Sheffield for a possible affair.

Either way, it didn't matter. Her life had been very different at one time than it was now, and sometimes she missed it. *That* made the guilt all the worse, for why would she miss the past and the little house near Drury Lane when she now had everything her heart could ever wish for?

"—come in?"

Jerked from her thoughts, Octavia met Spinton's gaze with

a mixture of annoyance and embarrassment. "Forgive me. What did you say?"

His smile was kind, patient even. It should have made her feel even more guilty. Perhaps it did. Maybe that was why she had the sudden urge to slap it off his face. "I asked if you wanted me to come in?"

Oh, were they home then?

Beatrice would no doubt want him to come in. Beatrice always wanted him to come in.

"No," she replied, conscience-stricken for ruining not only Spinton's hopes, but Beatrice's as well. In fact, for one split second, she was tempted to tell him yes, come in, and then leave him and Beatrice to their own devices. Perhaps if she did that, the two of them would take the decision from her and elope to Gretna Green.

As if there was such a decision. She already knew the answer. She was going to marry Spinton. The only question was in regard to when the happy event was to take place.

Happy event indeed. Which of them would be the first to admit their misery? Right now Spinton professed a desire to marry her—a desire for her even, but what would happen when he came to know the real her? What would happen if he learned she had lied to him all these years? And he was bound to find out eventually; she couldn't keep it a secret forever, not when they were living under the same roof.

He looked disappointed, but he didn't press. "I will see you tomorrow then."

It was a statement, not a question, as though seeing her every day was the order of things, and his God-given right.

She had half a mind to be ill tomorrow, and stay abed.

"Good night," she said, as the footman opened the door to the carriage. She didn't wait for the customary kiss on the cheek, or press of her hand. She was too tired, too ill-tempered for either. This was a side of her Spinton saw but rarely. He did not like it, as he had said on several occasions, but it was something he would have to get used to. Sometimes she was cantankerous, nasty even. Sometimes she also took pleasure in it. What would her future husband think of that?

Spinton was never nasty. In fact, Spinton's emotions seemed to run the gamut of polite to convivial, and that was it. If he had a dark side, he was careful to never show it—something that Octavia's cynical side distrusted most heartily.

She stepped down into the dark night, followed by Beatrice, whose good-bye to Spinton was much sweeter and much more ladylike than her own. Her cousin remembered to thank the earl for taking them to Eden—a task that should have been Octavia's.

Heaven save her from agreeable people. She was spoiling for a fight, and there was no one who could give her one—no one who could match her and not leave her feeling terribly remorseful for tearing them apart when it was done.

Beatrice, God bless her, would give it a go, however. She waited until the butler had relieved both of them of their outerwear, and then followed on Octavia's heels, through the hall, to the stairs where she gave chase, finally catching up at the top.

"What in heaven's name is the matter with you?" she demanded in little more than a whisper as they neared Octavia's bedchamber.

"I have no idea what you mean." Deliberately obtuse, Octavia stripped off her gloves and tossed them on the carved oak chest at the foot of her bed. The lamps on the night tables were lit, the crystal shades sparkling prettily. The amber brocade coverlet was turned down, revealing soft sheets. Soon she would crawl between their lemon-scented freshness and forget all about this evening, waking up in the morning with a better attitude than the one she had now. All she had to do was ring for her maid.

And get rid of her cousin.

"I mean your behavior toward Lord Spinton." Beatrice might be timid in public, but alone with Octavia, she showed some of the spirit she kept hidden. "One would think you were trying to goad him."

Octavia plucked the pearl drops from her ears and tossed them onto her dressing table. "Would one?"

"Yes," her cousin replied, oblivious to her sarcasm. "I would think you would be a bit more civil in your addresses to him. He is your betrothed after all."

"Not yet." Strands of pearls landed near the earrings. Wasn't that what she had told North? That Spinton wasn't her fiancé *yet*. As if it actually made a difference.

"You say it as though there is a chance you might not marry him."

Was it her imagination, or was there a trace of hopefulness in Beatrice's tone?

Pulling the cord to summon her maid, Octavia shrugged. "I have not yet given him my answer."

Her cousins hands went to the fullness of her hips. How Octavia envied that tiny, round body of hers. "Do you not think perhaps you should give it to him? He will not wait forever, despite his promises. You are thirty years of age. Your chances of producing an heir grow slimmer, as do your chances of contracting a good marriage at all."

Octavia graced her cousin with a cool smile. "Perhaps I am merely less concerned with marriage than you are." That was low. Even for her. None of this was Beatrice's fault, but she was so damned tired of being told what she should do. What about what she *wanted*?

Beatrice's bow lips pursed. "And now you are trying to goad me. Why?"

Sighing, Octavia rubbed the heel of her hand against her forehead. "Forgive me, Bea. I am in a foul temper this evening. I should not take it out on you."

Her cousin's rigid stance relaxed somewhat. "You were fine at the club before we separated. What happened?"

There was no reason to conceal it. Beatrice already knew about her past. She had been Octavia's companion and confidante for years, and her loyalty to Spinton couldn't compare with her loyalty to Octavia herself.

"I saw North."

Beatrice's dark eyes widened into saucers. "Did you speak to him?"

Octavia nodded. "I did. It was as though only twelve days had passed rather than as many years."

All of the tension seemed to have drained from them both. Beatrice was solely focused on her cousin's well-being, and Octavia's peevishness disappeared once she revealed the origin of it—not that North was to blame. No, she could blame only herself for her behavior.

"Come sit and tell me about it." Beatrice seated herself on the thick softness of the bed and patted a spot beside her.

"Janie will be here soon. I just pulled the bell for her."

"Then talk quickly, but do not leave anything out."

Smiling, Octavia joined her cousin on the bed. "I went to a private suite to congratulate Madeline—"

Beatrice brows rose. "That actress you know?"

She knew more than one, but that was beside the point. "I cannot talk quickly if you keep interrupting me."

Her cousin nodded, duly chastised. "Continue."

"I was not there five minutes before he appeared. There was no reason for us not to speak as we were surrounded by old friends." Absently, she stroked the brocade counterpane. "It was good to see him again."

"And how did he react to meeting you?"

Poor Beatrice. Was the only excitement in her life what she could glom from Octavia's own? "He seemed pleased. He was pleased."

"Are you going to see him again?"

Her hand stilled on the bed. "No." And there it was, the reason for her ill temper. The next time she saw North Sheffield, he would no doubt pretend not to know her, and she him. It would be as though tonight never happened. As though the first half of her life with him no longer existed except in her own mind.

Beatrice's expression was sympathetic, as though she could read the direction of Octavia's thoughts. "Why do you not confide in Lord Spinton? I am certain he will understand."

Octavia was certain he would as well. Was there anything Spinton wouldn't understand, or at least try to? The man was all goodness—too good for the likes of her. "I promised my grandfather I would not."

A shrewdness came over Beatrice's smooth features, pinning Octavia where she sat. "You promised Grandfather you would marry Spinton also, but you have yet to keep that promise."

There was that word again. *Yet*. Such a little word to encompass so very much. So very much of nothing.

"But I will marry him," Octavia admitted. "I will marry him because I said I would, and if he finds out the truth after that, I will face the consequences, but I gave my word he would not hear it from me, and he will not."

Beatrice shook her head. "I used to envy your closeness to our grandfather, but no more. I am thankful he never made me make such promises. I am certain I could never keep them."

Octavia laughed softly. "Of course you could. You are by far the more honorable of the two of us. You would keep them and probably make Spinton a more suitable countess than I ever would."

Her cousin blushed softly in the dim light, so softly Octavia would have missed it if not for her sudden downcast gaze. Was it possible Beatrice's feelings for Spinton ran deeper than infatuation with a man who paid attention to her? Was her cousin in love with Spinton?

Or was Octavia simply hunting for reasons to put off her marriage even longer—perhaps indefinitely? What if Beatrice did love Spinton? More to the point, what if Spinton fell in love with Beatrice?

Lord, wouldn't that be a tangle! Wouldn't they all be wonderfully miserable then? Especially if Octavia kept her promise to marry Spinton. And she would keep her promise. Eventually.

It was at that moment that there came a knock on the door. At Octavia's command, her maid Janie entered the room. Janie was a pleasant girl; Octavia had never seen her ill, tired, or without a smile. Just the sight of her was enough to raise Octavia's spirits.

"Did you have a good evening, my lady?" she asked as she closed the door behind her.

"I did," Octavia replied as she stood. "But now I want nothing more than to climb into bed and sleep till noon tomorrow. Work your magic, Janie dear."

Beatrice slipped off the bed. "I should retire as well."

"Oh," Janie said, as though the thought suddenly occurred to her. "Something arrived for you earlier, Lady Octavia."

As she pulled a letter from her pocket, both Octavia and Beatrice stilled. Octavia had received enough similar missives to recognize it immediately—the way it was folded, the paper, the wax seal. It was another note from her secret admirer. She was becoming heartily sick of them. It was flattering to know someone held her in such high esteem, but not knowing who it was was vexing to say the least.

Taking the letter, Octavia was tempted to toss it in the

wastepaper basket without even opening it, but curiosity got the better of her. What would her admirer pay homage to this time? Her hair, her eyes, perhaps her bosom? There was always something, and it was always said in flowery language that would make even the most romantic of poets roll his eyes.

Beatrice came closer as she broke the seal and unfolded the heavy parchment.

I know your secret.

Octavia's heart faltered before falling heavily against her ribs. It was the same handwriting as before, the same signature—"*Yours Always*"—but while all the other notes had an air of lightness, this one had an ominous feel that could not be denied.

She had only one secret, and that was about her mother and her own past. How this person could have found out, she had no idea. But what concerned her most was what he planned to do with the information now. Extortion of some kind? What price would he attach to his silence? And would she be able to pay it?

Was this coincidence that such a note should arrive after her reunion with North? Was it possible that this person was someone she knew from the past? Someone who knew North as well? As much as she didn't want to believe it, she knew it was a logical conclusion.

Could it be that North was her admirer? It seemed too foolish to even contemplate. North would never do such a thing..Would he? And what purpose was he hoping to achieve by sending her such a missive now?

"My lady?" Janie's voice was heavy with concern. "Are you quite all right?"

Clearing her throat, Octavia nodded. "I am fine. Who delivered this, Janie?"

"A messenger, my lady. Naught but a lad."

As usual. It was always a young boy who delivered the notes, a different one each time, none of whom knew anything—or was prepared to tell anything—about his employer.

"What are you going to do?" Beatrice asked, her hand touching Octavia's arm.

"Nothing," Octavia replied, determined not to play along. Her admirer would *not* join the list of people she allowed to dictate her life. "I am not going to do a blessed thing."

And even if she did want to do something, what could she possibly do without revealing the details of her past to either Spinton or someone else? Whom could she trust? No one. Not even North.

Not *yet*.

Chapter 4

The offices of numbers three and four Bow Street were as unassuming as they possibly could be. They were sparsely furnished but clean, every inch of scarred wood gleaming with a highly buffed sheen. The early morning air was rich with the scents of polishes, waxes and lemon. An overlying whiff of tobacco hovered just above it all, followed by the rich aroma of freshly brewed coffee. Soon the smells of London would invade this surprisingly quiet space. Unwashed bodies, the stench of the underworld, would creep into the pores of the people working there, pollute their clothes and hair, but for now Bow Street had yet to be brought down to the same level as the criminals it captured.

This was how North preferred to remember the offices, and why he chose this hour to answer the summons sent to him by Duncan Reed, chief magistrate.

"What can I do for you, Duncan?"

Seated behind a massive oak desk that was rumored to have belonged to Henry Fielding himself, Duncan Reed regarded North over the rim of his coffee cup with the eyes of an old, wise wolf.

"Good morning to you too, North. Coffee?"

Flipping out the tails of his coat, North seated himself in one of the faded, but well-padded chairs in front of the desk. "Please."

Duncan took a battered pot from the tray on the table behind his desk and tipped it over a chipped china cup. If the brew in it tasted anything like it smelled, North would be awake well into the next week.

Once he had a cup of steaming, fragrant black coffee in his hand, North leaned back in his chair and waited for Duncan to speak. He didn't have to wait long.

The magistrate folded his long hands together on the surface of the desk. "I have heard that you have had dealings with an unfortunate by the name of Black Sally."

North nodded, trying not to grimace as he swallowed the coffee in his mouth. "She is helping me with a murder case I am working on. Why? Did your boys bring her in?"

Duncan's eyes were flat. "You could say that. One of my men was called in after she was found earlier this morning."

Horror clutched at North's chest. "Found?"

"In an alleyway in Whitechapel. Her throat had been cut." Duncan's voice was as void of emotion as his eyes, but he watched North carefully, weighing his reaction.

She was dead then. Poor Sally. North hung his head in benediction for the prostitute. These things were not uncommon on the streets, but that didn't mean he was any more accustomed to such violence than he had been ten years ago. Then realization overcame him. He had assigned his own men to watch Sally. Why had he not heard from the one designated to follow her last night?

He looked up. This time Duncan's eyes were bright with sympathy. "Your man was found not far away."

North squeezed his eyes shut, concentrating on the heat of the cup in his hands, willing that heat to flow through the ice in his veins. Harris was dead. He was only two and twenty and usually so careful. He took his job so very seriously.

"It appeared as though there had been a struggle," Duncan's voice cut through the numbness in North's mind. "He put up a fight."

Of course he had. But that didn't matter. What mattered was that Harris had lost the fight. Sally had lost the fight. North had failed them both. Both of them had been his responsibility, and he let them down. His fault. His to live with.

"Thank you for telling me."

Duncan nodded. "I wanted you to know before the rest of the city starts to hear about it. Do you have any idea who is behind it?"

North nodded. "Harker." The man he had been trying to build a murder case against for the last three months. Bastard. This was one of those times when North wanted to say to hell with the justice system and go after Harker himself—with a pistol. A ball of lead between the eyes would put an end to Harker's criminal career.

Duncan nodded. "We will be looking for him now as well."

North's gaze snapped to his former boss. "He is mine."

Again Duncan nodded. "Understood."

Setting aside his coffee, North raked both hands through his hair. "Goddamn. Poor Sally. Poor Harris." His gaze went unseeingly to the wall behind Duncan's head, and he sighed in sorrow and resignation. He would have to go to Harris's mother. He should be the one to tell her that her youngest son was dead.

"Why do you do this to yourself?" Duncan asked. "Why do you continue to trudge along like this? A man with your convictions could do so much more at a higher level."

Another sigh. This wasn't a new topic of conversation.

Duncan, along with Wynthrope and North's oldest brother, Brahm, had been trying for months—ever since he'd foiled an attempt on the regent's life—to convince him to go into politics. Brahm had even gone so far as to suggest North become MP for the riding that went with the Ryland holdings in Somerset. And with Brahm a peer, North would be sure to get his ideas and hopes for changes to Britain's criminal system heard. Changes such as a more organized countrywide police force.

But could he give up the satisfaction of being "hands on" to take a more behind-the-scenes approach?

Possibly. It wasn't as though his current methods were all that spectacular. One only had to look at Black Sally and Harris to see that. Why would anyone think he could make a difference? Right now he certainly didn't think he could.

He couldn't even keep a whore alive. What could he do for an entire country?

It would mean facing society again. It might mean being granted entrance. It might mean acceptance. It might mean rejection as well.

"I will think about it," he mumbled.

The expression on Duncan's lean face was dubious at best. "That is what you always say."

It was. North shrugged. What was he expected to say? He couldn't even think right now, let alone think of anything intelligent to say.

"I have to go," he said finally, rising to his feet. His legs were shaky—from the shock of hearing about Sally and Harris, no doubt. Over the years, North had seen plenty of death—victims, witnesses, criminals, and runners, but this was the first time he had ever lost one of his own men, and the first time he had failed to protect someone he'd sworn to keep safe. He felt the weight of their deaths as keenly as if he had run the blade across their throats himself.

"Do you need someone to take you home?"

North scowled. "I am not an invalid, Duncan. I believe I can survive the short walk back to my house."

If Duncan was taken aback by his sharp tone, he didn't show it. "Suit yourself. I will let you know what evidence we turn up."

North nodded. There wouldn't be any evidence. Harker would be certain of that. He would know that North would assume he was the culprit.

"And North?" Duncan's voice stopped him as he reached the door. He turned, saying nothing.

"Be careful," his friend and former employer urged, real concern coloring his tone. "If you press this investigation, Harker will eventually come after you."

North's hand turned the doorknob. He smiled bitterly. "I hope so." Right now, facing Harker was the one bright spot in his life—the one thing he had to truly look forward to. Catching criminals—the ones who honestly deserved to be caught—was what kept him going, what made his job worthwhile in the end. Putting an end to Harker's career would be the only way Sally and Harris's deaths would not be in vain.

Outside the day was off to a bright and sunny start. It had rained the night before, giving the air a slight, fresh chill that was already losing ground to the warmth of the sun. Usually he loved these kinds of mornings, but the drying puddles beneath his feet were merely reminders that any evidence with Harris and Sally's bodies would have been long lost, washed away with their blood, as insubstantial as their dying breaths.

God damn Harker. He would make him pay for this.

From Bow Street, it was a short walk back to his house. He walked slowly, his head filled with thoughts of Sally, Harris, and how he was going to nail Harker to the wall. His resolve grew with the warming of the sun, and by the time he took a right on Russell Street, into the heart of Covent Garden, he was still struck full of mourning for both dead, but his complete sense of loss had been replaced by sheer determination. He would let neither Sally nor Harris die for naught.

The market was bustling with activity, as it always was. A sense of joviality mixed with the frustration of poverty as business started for the day. As usual, the sight of it buoyed his heavy heart. He would mourn Harris and Sally, but he would not let the hate and anger cloud his perception. There was good in this world, and that was what he worked for.

He exchanged some coin for wares with an orange girl and removed the peel as he neared his house, tossing the discarded rind into the gutter. He was home by the time he finished, his hands full of ripe fruit and sticky from his efforts.

He had just taken a bite of the orange, spraying his face with the sweet juice, when someone called out his name.

Turning on the steps to his front door, he was already reaching for the pistol strapped beneath his coat when he realized it was Lord Spinton calling out to him. The hand reaching for his weapon changed course smoothly, tearing off another section of orange with the same efficiency as it would have lodged a ball in the earl's foolish skull. The man should know better than to sneak up on him like that!

But Spinton wasn't the kind of man who would know better. He no doubt rarely socialized with men like North. Aristocrats didn't have much reason to carry pistols on their persons, nor did they usually have reason to think of themselves as prey for a murderer.

Swallowing the pulp in his mouth, North graced Spinton with a forced smile. "Lord Spinton. You have returned. Why?" He hoped the earl didn't keep him long. He needed to find out what arrangements had been made for Harris and Sally. He wanted to attend the funerals and do whatever he could for their families. Right now that was more important than the earl's jealousy over a few love letters.

"I am sorry to bother you, Mr. Sheffield," Spinton apologized politely as he jogged up the steps toward North. "But you said I could come back if there were any developments in my case that might persuade you to look into Lady Octavia's letters."

If it had concerned anyone but Octavia, North would have told the earl in no uncertain terms to sod off. "I can spare you a few minutes. Come in."

As usual, Mrs. Bunting met them in the foyer. She took Spinton's hat and cane and offered them tea, which North refused with the added order that they were not to be disturbed. Inside the sanctuary of his office, he offered Spinton something stronger than tea.

Spinton shook his head. "Oh no. Too early for me."

North simply shrugged his brows and poured himself a glass of whiskey, which he downed in one swallow.

"Now then," he rasped, turning his attention to his guest. "What are these 'developments' you speak of?"

Turning his hat in his hands, Spinton graced him with an earnest gaze. "Last night, Octavia received another letter."

"Were you there when it arrived?" Was that where he was coming from now? Had he spent the night in Octavia's bed?

Spinton actually blushed. "I had returned home for the evening. No, I received word from Lady Octavia's cousin this morning about the letter."

"Not from Octavia herself?"

The earl blushed even darker. "I explained to you before that she does not see the letters as dastardly as I."

North resisted the urge to pour another drink. He resorted to sarcasm instead. Hardly professional behavior. "What did this one say? That her eyes were like sapphires? Her skin like ivory?"

Spinton looked as though he would like to ask how North knew the color of Lady Octavia's eyes and flesh, but he did not. "It said, 'I know your secret.'"

North froze. Setting his empty glass on the table, he turned to face the other man. "What secret?" The secret of Octavia's upbringing? That her mother had been an actress, a mistress to many men? Or that she and North had known each other—intimately—once upon a time?

"I do not know." Real frustration etched itself on the earl's face. "If Octavia has secrets, they are hidden from even myself. I can think of nothing that would be worthy of such a note, but I believe the author has blackmail in mind."

North was in agreement. Such a cryptic remark was usually the precursor to some kind of extortion—he had seen it before. He had sworn to protect Octavia's secret once before—promised deep within himself that he would do everything in his power to ensure she had the life she deserved. It was his duty to keep that promise. Perhaps he could do better by her than he had by Harris or Sally.

"I will have to see the letter," he instructed. "And I will need to interview Lady Octavia."

Spinton's sigh of relief was audible. "Oh, thank you, Mr. Sheffield. I will speak to Lady Octavia this very morning. Can you come for dinner tonight?"

Not a good idea. He knew that. "Where?"

"Lady Octavia's home in Berkeley Square." He gave the direction. "Say eight o'clock?"

North knew Octavia well enough to blink at Spinton's invitation. Normally he would check with her before accepting, but since Spinton was going to be heading to Octavia's after leaving there, he couldn't risk sending her a missive that the earl might see. It would raise too many questions.

"I will see you then."

Spinton grinned, shook North's hand, and took his leave. After he was gone, North sat at his desk, his boots propped up on the shiny surface, and contemplated what he had just done.

The decision to help Octavia—to at least determine whether the threat to her was real—had taken no consideration whatsoever. He would do anything for her, whether she asked it of him or not. No, for North the very real concern was whether she allowed him to help her.

He wasn't going to give her much of a choice. There wouldn't be much good in the world if Octavia wasn't in it.

"I spoke to North Sheffield again today."

Octavia froze, teacup poised halfway between her lips and its saucer. She couldn't have heard Spinton correctly. He couldn't have *that* little regard for her wishes, could he?

"I beg your pardon?" She added to the appearance of disinterestedness by taking a sip of tea. They were in her little parlor, facing the street. Sunshine streamed through the windows; the muffled clip-clop of horses went on almost continuously in the background. She might have napped if not for the ever-present shadow of Spinton.

The earl had the grace to look uncomfortable. He should, the blighter. "He said he would reconsider investigating the source of the letters."

"Did he?" Had that growl come from her own throat? It was a direct contradiction to her pleasant tone. "What made you believe I would want him to?"

Beatrice snapped to attention on the other sofa; a little yellow bee on a salmon pink blossom. She knew Octavia's mood was taking a dangerous turn. Her unease was palatable. Whose side would she choose if the situation escalated?

Spinton's, no doubt. Beatrice always sided with the underdog.

"Er, well . . ." Spinton met her gaze in a surprisingly bold manner. "I am *not* going to apologize for wanting to protect you."

Even Octavia blinked at his tone. Perhaps dear Fitzwilliam had a spine after all. "You might have informed me of your plans before you went behind my back."

His color rose. "And as my intended, you might have seen fit to share this so-called secret of yours with me."

Octavia's shoulders straightened. Backbone indeed. Unfortunately his show of audacity only served to strengthen her reluctance to cow. "While I appreciate your concern, Fitzwilliam, any secrets I have are my own, and I alone will ensure their protection."

"While those around you unwittingly share in the consequences."

She smiled—albeit bitterly—at his indignant tone. "So that is what truly worries you—not my safety, but what your involvement with me might mean for your own reputation."

He didn't deny it. "And for Miss Beatrice's reputation as well."

Ahh, there it was. Could it be that Spinton held her cousin in as high regard as Beatrice held him?

"Perhaps you should offer your hand to Beatrice instead, then neither of you would have to worry about my sordid past." Oh dear, her temper was running away with her. If she didn't keep her wits about her, she would reveal too much.

Both Beatrice and Spinton flushed a deep, dark red. Octavia was immediately contrite. She shouldn't have involved Bea in this. But before she could apologize, her cousin joined in.

"Octavia, that is not fair. Lord Spinton cares far more for your welfare than for mine. Although I do thank you for the consideration, my lord."

Octavia rolled her eyes as her cousin practically batted her eyelashes at Spinton. He puffed up like a peacock under her defense. It wasn't a surprise that the two of them were going to join sides against her. They usually did. One would think they would have learned by now that such tactics only made her more resolute to resist their arguments.

"So concern for one's welfare gives a person the right to interfere with one's business, does it?" She set her cup and saucer on the tray with a loud clink.

"Of course," Beatrice's tone never wavered. It was that same annoyingly soft cadence. "Genuine caring gives a person the right to do most anything to protect someone they care for."

Pretty words and a lovely sentiment, but hardly realistic. "You might feel differently were this your life being interfered with." Good Lord, she actually sounded petulant. There wasn't some part of her that actually *believed* Beatrice's naive notions, was there?

Her cousin lowered her gaze. "I would welcome that kind of devotion."

Devotion? *Devotion?* Was she completely mad? But then, perhaps Beatrice did see it that way. After all, she hadn't any secrets she'd sworn to protect.

"See, Octavia?" Spinton was positively haughty with Beatrice behind him. "Miss Beatrice knows I had nothing but your best interests at heart."

Unable to take any more, Octavia stood. "Beatrice would side with you even if you committed murder right in front of her and then denied it, Spinton. I am certain she will delight in telling you just how right you were to stick your face into my private affairs, but that will not change the fact that *I* believe you to have been wrong."

"But—"

She didn't let him continue, "I do not need, nor do I want

you trying to protect me. I am not some helpless female. Rather than endear you to me, all your refusal to abide by my wishes does is further convince me that we are totally unsuitable for one another. Now, if you will both excuse me, I believe I need to be alone."

Leaving the room with as much dignity as she could muster, Octavia was caught somewhere between righteous vindication and crippling guilt, but she stomped upstairs as though righteousness was her only emotion. Of course Spinton had acted out of what *he* believed to be her best interest. And of course Beatrice was only thinking of her happiness whenever she tried to smooth things over between Octavia and her would-be husband. Their intentions were good and honorable. They were *always* good and honorable, just as Beatrice and Spinton were themselves.

But after thirty years on this earth, shouldn't Octavia be able to make such decisions for herself? She was not a child, though at times she surely acted as one. She was a grown woman, with the means and intelligence to live her life as she wanted, yet here she was, still allowing others to dictate to her how she should act and live. No wonder Beatrice and Spinton found it so odd when she got angry—they weren't used to her noncompliance. Well, they would just have to *get* used to it. When it came to prying into her private life—digging into those things that she called hers and hers alone—Spinton would soon discover that the woman he wanted to be shackled to for the rest of his days was no meek miss. Much of her life had been decided for her by other people. She had allowed her mother and grandfather to dictate large aspects of her future, but Octavia was determined that the rest of her life would not always be ruled by others as her mother's had been.

For now she would try to swallow her anger and regain control of her emotions. It was either that or go back downstairs and tell Spinton there was no ruddy way she was going to marry him. Ever.

That would be breaking her promise—the one thing her grandfather had ever asked of her. And he had done so much for her. Hadn't he? She always thought so, but right now all she could think was that he had taken her from a place where she had been happy and turned her into a new person.

Oh, and there was the fact that he had most likely saved her from having to flit from man to man for "protection" as might have happened had she gone ahead and chosen a life on the stage.

Alone, in the solace of her bedroom, she fell onto her back on the bed, barely bouncing on the firm mattress. The bed was huge, the room spacious—everything she had dreamed of as a child. So why did it sometimes feel more like a prison than a haven? Perhaps because like everything else in her life, it had been given to her without anyone asking her opinion—not that she would have wanted any changes. She'd been too overwhelmed to ask for anything, and after that wore off, she simply felt too beholden.

Why had *she* been the one picked to marry Spinton? Was it really because of her grandfather's love for her father and his guilt for ignoring her and her mother all those years? He claimed not to have known where they were, but really, how hard had he looked? Not very. So why was she ruining her life to assuage a dead man's guilt? Why make her life—and Spinton's—miserable in the process?

And they would make each other miserable, of that there could be no doubt. Spinton would try to be a good husband, and Octavia would constantly find fault with him, just as he would constantly find fault with her. They were poorly suited, and it seemed only one of them knew it.

That made it all the worse. Spinton actually seemed to

want to marry her. It might be easier to break her promise to her grandfather if she didn't think she'd be breaking Spinton's heart as well.

Lord, she really was a piece of work. She sneered at Spinton behind his back and pitied him at the same time. He wasn't weak enough to earn her contempt, nor was he strong enough to garner her respect.

A knock sounded at the door. Octavia ignored it. It was followed by another—sharper this time.

"Please go away."

"Tavie, it is me."

Only one person could call her such a juvenile name as "Tavie" and not make her cringe.

Octavia groaned into a buttercup yellow cushion. "Bea, I am tired. I want to rest before dinner."

"I am coming in."

Octavia bolted upright on the bed. Damnation, she should have locked the door! "No, Bea—"

The door opened and Beatrice slipped inside, silently shutting it behind her.

"You do not listen very well," Octavia chided with a resigned sigh. She wasn't angry at Beatrice, not really, and even if she was, she couldn't stay that way for long.

"Of course I do not listen," her cousin replied with a smile. "I am related to you."

Octavia grinned in response. She patted a spot beside her on the bed. "Come sit then."

Beatrice did so. "I want to apologize." Meek and mild she might be, but Beatrice rarely beat around the bush when she had something she felt needed to be said.

Grasping her hand, Octavia squeezed gently. "So do I. I behaved unpardonably just now, stomping off like a spoiled child."

Her cousin's smile was one of patient understanding. "Perhaps, but it would not have happened had you not been provoked. I am sorry for siding with Spinton. I suppose as an outsider I find it easier to understand his motives."

Octavia arched a brow. "Nicely put." Let her cousin deny her favoritism. It didn't matter.

Blushing, Beatrice glanced away. "But as much as I believe his motives to be pure, his way of carrying them out certainly leaves much to be desired. He cares for you very much, you know."

Ah, so this was what it felt like to be stabbed. Remorse as sharp as a blade cut through Octavia's chest as her cousin's dark gaze once again met hers. Beatrice would no doubt give anything to have Spinton—or any man—care for her well-being to such an extreme. Unlike Octavia, she had never talked of wanting anything more than a husband and a family, the two things that seemed to be creeping further and further out of her reach the older she became.

"Why do you stay here with me, Bea? Why do you not find yourself an amiable man and get him to give you some lovely fat babies?"

Having finally regained her natural color, Beatrice flushed again. "Even the most amiable man wants a wife with *something* to recommend her. I have connections to be sure, but I am no beauty. Nor do I have an impressive figure or dowry."

Now, looks and build were two areas where Octavia believed her cousin to be very well endowed indeed.

"You are fair of face and form," she announced in a tone that brooked no argument. "And I will make it known that you will have a dowry."

The lower Beatrice's jaw fell, the wider her eyes became. "I cannot allow you to settle money upon me."

"You cannot stop me." Oh! It felt nice to be the one in control, the one deciding what was going to happen and ignoring all resistance. No wonder Spinton did it. It must make him feel very manly.

"Oh Tavie, thank you!"

Octavia was rocked by the force of her cousin's embrace. Beatrice squeezed her as though she thought she could force Octavia to accept her gratitude through her very pores.

She was also shamed and oddly touched. Why had she not thought to make such a gesture for Beatrice before this? Why had she not seen how unhappy her cousin was? Had she been that caught up in her own petty problems that she couldn't even see what was right in front of her face? How selfish she had been.

But then again, she was selfish by nature. Even her decision to *eventually* marry Spinton was tinged with a bit of self service. Yes, it was something she'd been talked into agreeing to, but she was not unaware of the benefits it would bring to her. She would be a countess, a very wealthy one. She would have all of London society at her beck and call, and all the freedom marriage allowed. Once she and Spinton were united and she produced the necessary heir, she would be able to do whatever she liked, with whomever she liked. It was perhaps a cold and harsh way of thinking, but there was no danger in admitting it—at least not to herself.

"Now that you are smiling and I am done sulking," Octavia said, gently pushing her cousin away. "We had better dress for dinner. Poor Spinton is probably ravenous."

Beatrice giggled. "Yes, of course." For a moment Octavia feared she might hug her again. Her ribs couldn't stand it. "Thank you again."

"You are welcome again." Smiling, Octavia watched her cousin skip from the room. She actually felt better than she had ten minutes ago. Amazing what thinking of someone else could do for one's mood.

She rose from the bed and rang the bell for her maid before

going to her dressing room to begin changing. Janie arrived a few moments later and set to work helping Octavia into a gown of rich blue satin and arranging her hair in a more elaborate style.

Somewhere between thirty and forty-five minutes later, Beatrice came to collect her to go downstairs. They would rejoin Spinton in the parlor for a drink before going on to the dining room. And of course Octavia would apologize to the earl for her outburst and hope that Spinton would cease in his investigation. The letters were nothing. She was certain of it. Just someone from her past playing a trick on her. Or someone thinking he knew a secret when really it was nothing at all—and nothing in any way related to her life before coming to live with her grandfather.

Beatrice was a cute little bud in a rose-colored gown that brought out the creamy perfection of her complexion. Yes, with a little money behind her she should have no trouble at all snaring a husband.

Mercenary lot.

What would Octavia do without her? It wasn't as though she had many friends. She had never been one to make friends easily. Perhaps that was something else she should apply herself to.

They heard voices as they approached the top of the stairs. One of them—the louder—was Spinton's. Naturally inquisitive when it came to visitors to her own home, Octavia stopped Beatrice with a gentle touch on her arm. She wanted to determine who was there before she went down. She was not one of those people who liked surprises.

Spinton spoke first. "Thank you for coming. I do appreciate having your attention on this matter."

"Thank you, Lord Spinton, for inviting me."

Oh dear God, she knew that voice! Spinton had invited North for dinner? To her house? Without her prior consent?

Ah yes, but he had to have known she never would have given her consent.

Breath coming in short, angry heaves, Octavia turned to Beatrice. Her cousin would know what to say to keep her from acting out her anger. Her cousin would keep her calm, make her remember her station as the granddaughter of an earl. Her cousin would discourage her from making a scene.

Beatrice's eyes were wide with astonishment as she met Octavia's gaze. "Oh dear," she murmured, "even *I* would want to flay him for this."

Chapter 5

She came down the stairs not like a graceful swan but like a vengeful hawk swooping down on its prey—magnificent in all her fury. Her eyes blazed and her cheeks were flushed high with color. It was all North could do not to smile at the sight. Spinton would undoubtedly die a slow and painful death later that night.

"I thought I heard voices. Forgive me for not greeting you properly, Mr. Sheffield, but Lord Spinton obviously forgot to tell me you would be joining us." The gaze she shot Spinton would have withered even the strongest of men, and poor Spinton was not that strong.

North sketched a bow. "A lady as lovely as yourself need not apologize for anything, Lady Octavia. It is my pleasure to meet you at last."

A visible change came over Octavia. All the anger seemed to drain from her, replaced by an effortless grace and charm. Her companion, North noticed, watched them both with a mixture of awe and incredulity as Octavia extended one gloved hand.

"The pleasure is all mine. It is not every day that one entertains the elusive Mr. Sheffield in one's home."

Her tone was all politeness, but she was teasing him, North could see it in her eyes. She might look as though she belonged in all this pale marble splendor, swathed in satin and laden with jewels, but underneath it all she was simply his Vie.

He took the hand she offered and brushed his lips across her knuckles. The fabric of her glove was thin enough that he could feel her warmth seeping through. Her fingers tightened—just for a second—around his before pulling away.

Straightening, North allowed himself one last glimpse before turning his attention elsewhere. In the golden light of fading day, Octavia was all peach and gold, the dark blue of her gown accentuating the brilliance of her eyes. Her rich, thick hair was piled artfully on top of her head, revealing the graceful column of her throat. Sweet and warm in the hollow between her neck and shoulder beat a pulse that had tasted like heaven on his tongue.

He licked his lips as a pulse in the vicinity of his groin jumped in response. How could his body remember a night from a dozen years ago? He'd had better, less embarrassing encounters since then, and yet he recalled very few details, even fewer sensations. He remembered every moment with Octavia—every sweet, aching, awkward moment.

And he was remembering these moments while her future husband stood not even two feet away from him.

"May I introduce my cousin, Miss Beatrice Henry?"

Ahh, the cousin. The companion. The confidante. How much did she know about Octavia's past? If the way she looked at him was any indication, she knew most of it.

"Beauty runs in the family I see," he remarked with a charming grin.

Beatrice blushed, but before she could reply, Spinton

clapped his hands together. "Well, shall we proceed to the parlor for a drink before dinner?"

North wondered at the edge of sharpness in the earl's tone. Was his disapproval because he thought North was flirting with Octavia or Beatrice? Or both? Obviously Spinton wasn't partial to sharing his hens with other cocks.

Spinton offered his arm to Octavia, which she took with only a second's hesitation. North offered to escort Beatrice, which she accepted with a happy smile. Rank was rank and if there had been more people in their party, North would have been shoved even farther down the line. So, he assumed, would Miss Henry.

"It is a pleasure to meet you at last, Mr. Sheffield," she whispered as they followed the other couple down the corridor at a discreet distance. "I have heard so *much* about you."

So she did know about his past association with Octavia. There was no denying the underlying message in her tone. "Then you have me at a distinct disadvantage, Miss Henry."

"Not for long, I suspect. If you are indeed in earnest about discovering the identity of my cousin's mysterious admirer, then I suspect you will make it your business to know everything about anyone who comes within a mile of Octavia."

This round little rose of a woman was more intuitive than he would have given her credit for. No doubt many people dismissed her as inconsequential, which was all the more reason for North to not only earn her confidence, but to keep a close watch on her as well. It was obvious from the way she watched Spinton's back that she had feelings for the man. Did these feelings run deep enough that she'd plot to ruin her cousin's plans to marry him?

Was there anything he could do to help her in that quarter?

Now why would he think such a thing? He might have his doubts about whether Spinton was husband material as far as Octavia was concerned, but he had no reason to plot against the man. He merely wanted to see his old friend happy. He wanted to see her living as she deserved—with a man smart enough to realize what a treasure he'd been given. Spinton did seem to realize his fortune in that respect, and he truly cared about Vie. Perhaps he would do after all.

In the parlor, a small but comfortable room decorated in shades of peachy pink and cream that made North think of the poached salmon his father's chef always used to make, Spinton poured brandy for the men and sherry for the women. Well, that was one point in his favor; at least Spinton wasn't one of those men who believed women incapable of handling spirits. Over the years North had seen women who could drink men three times their size under the table and ask for more.

Of course, if Spinton were truly open-minded, he would have offered the ladies brandy as well. Judging from the expression on Octavia's face, she would have preferred it to the weaker sherry. What was she thinking right now? Was she happy or upset to see him? Did she fear he would betray her secrets? Was she afraid her admirer would take his hint one step further and actually resort to blackmail? Did she wish they were alone, so they could talk openly and frankly?

And most importantly, did she have the strange, overwhelming desire to kiss him as he had to kiss her? What was this between them that made him feel as protective as a brother one minute, as defiant as a rival another, and then possessive as a lover the next? In his head he called Octavia a friend, but in his heart—in his soul—he knew her true function was something infinitely more complex.

Octavia forced herself to take small sips of her sherry, rather than downing it in one swallow and going back for the rest of the bottle. What did Spinton mean going behind her back—against her wishes—in this fashion? Perhaps it was meant with the best of intentions, but it didn't bode well for

Octavia's future. Until now Spinton had been relatively easy to control, but this strange defiance made her wonder. What else had she been deceived about where he was concerned? Would his personality deviate even further once they were wed?

And why was North looking at her as though he'd like to dip her in cream and lick her clean? He had to know it unsettled her, in a warm, sticky kind of way. It was hardly the kind of gaze one directed at an old friend. Of course, they were old friends who had shared a night of intimacy together— some of which had been quite pleasant if memory served. Perhaps that was why she felt that delicious tickle between her thighs whenever she glanced in his direction. Did he mean it? Or was it simply a ruse to make Spinton reconsider trying to hire him?

The frightening thing was, Octavia didn't know which she would prefer. In her youth she had loved North so dearly— not just as a boy, but as dearly as one could love another person. He had been everything to her, and later she had come to mean just as much to him. And was this what it was now reduced to, a tickle low in her body? A heated look? It was disappointing and exciting at the same time; as though something had changed between them and not necessarily for the worse, even though that old camaraderie was gone.

"Spinton, did you tell Cook to prepare enough for four?" Her tone was patently sweet, her question for no other purpose than to break the silence. Her kitchen staff always prepared more than enough food. It was as though the entire staff was on a mission to fatten her up. Either that or they were feeding orphans with the scraps.

As usual, Spinton pinkened at her reminder of his duplicity. Like most Englishmen, he flushed floridly. It made him look like a young boy. "Yes. Everything has been taken care of."

Her faced stretched with a false smile, Octavia set her empty glass on a nearby table. "Then shall we go in?"

Everyone murmured in agreement despite the fact that Octavia was the only one who had finished her drink. Once again she and Spinton led the way, with North and Beatrice behind. A spot between her shoulder blades itched and burned. Was it Beatrice staring a hole in her back or North? Her money was on North. He hadn't taken his eyes off her since his arrival, even though he'd made a good job of pretending to. Why? The annoying male-female awareness aside, was there something awkward about her appearance that made him stare? Or was he simply making up for all those years of not being able to look at her? God knew she wanted to look at him, but there were very few women who wouldn't want to gaze upon such unabashed male beauty.

He hadn't shaved before his arrival, that much was obvious from the shadow on his jaw. Most hostesses would be insulted, but Octavia couldn't bring herself to feel such a petty emotion where North was concerned. She couldn't even be certain that he had brushed his hair, though the unruly waves were considerably tamer than usual.

But what did it matter if he was well groomed or not? He had eyes that were like a glacial pond, cheeks that were usually rosy even if his mood was foul, and lips that seemed perpetually poised on the verge of a smile—albeit a sometimes sarcastic one. He had seen and undoubtedly done things that hardened the boy he once was, but she didn't mourn for that boy, not when the man he had grown into was so intriguing.

She wanted to get to know this man better and she couldn't, because she wasn't supposed to know him in the first place. It was not fair. And yet, she could say to perdition with it and break the promises she'd made to her mother and grandfather. She could toss their manufactured charade aside and be honest about who she was and her relationship with North. So why didn't she? Was it honor or duty that kept her silent? Or was it the fact that she was a coward, afraid to jeopardize the relative comfort she'd come to expect from her life?

Maybe it was easier just to go on pretending than to risk the consequences.

Regardless, she could carry on for this one evening. She had to. Just long enough to convince North that the letters were nothing to be concerned about, that she was in no danger whatsoever. That, she could do.

Dinner was hardly a grand affair. The walnut table was small compared to those in houses similar to Octavia's. The silverware was simple, the china plain, the crystal elegant, and the food delicious without being pretentious. Her mother had taught her to appreciate simple things, things that didn't go out of fashion as soon as one had paid for them. It was a practice that infuriated her grandfather, but one of the few things about herself she refused to change for him. Somehow he had managed to love her despite her many faults.

"May I ask what is so amusing?"

Octavia whipped her gaze around to Spinton's. "I beg your pardon?"

He smiled patiently. "You chuckled just now."

She glanced away as her lips tilted upward. "I was thinking of my grandfather."

"Ahh. Of course you would chuckle. He was such a jovial man."

Spinton's pleasantly caustic tone widened Octavia's grin. There were times when she enjoyed his company and liked him very much indeed. He was a good man, and sometimes— like right now—he made her smile. Perhaps they could make a good marriage together. Yes, he was very amiable indeed.

When he wasn't interfering in her life, of course. He clucked over her like he was her father rather than the man who wished to be her husband.

He held out her chair at the head of the table and took his customary seat at the other end. North and Beatrice were seated in the middle on either side. On a longer table it would have been ridiculous to seat a small party in such a manner, but around Octavia's modest setting, voices would be able to speak in moderate tones and everyone would have plenty of room.

Conversation was polite, concerning mostly the weather, as the meal began. Then, while slicing into the pink, juicy beef on her plate, Octavia decided to take the charade to its next, and expected, level.

"I am surprised that we have never met before this, Mr. Sheffield."

It was a good thing Spinton wasn't looking at Beatrice, or her cousin would have given away that Octavia was lying through her teeth. North, on the other hand, had the exact countenance one would expect from a stranger.

"I am not one for society, Lady Octavia."

"Oh?" she asked, lifting her wineglass. "Why is that?"

The briefest flicker of annoyance lit in his eyes before his mask slipped back into place. Was it not a question that someone who was in society might ask? Was it not something she herself had often wondered? She remembered a time when North very much wanted to be a member of the *ton*; now he seemed to avoid it as much as possible. Was it because of her?

"The Upper Ten Thousand does not look kindly on bastards."

"Mr. Sheffield!" Spinton looked as though he might suffer an apoplexy. "I realize you are not accustomed to being in society, but to use such language in front of ladies—"

North looked first at Beatrice and then at Octavia. His features were emotionless, his gaze unrepentant, but there was defiance in his tone. "Do you take offense to what I am, Lady Octavia?"

Offense? That he had made so much of himself was a marvel. Growing up in the area that they had, each of them had known numerous people born on the wrong side of the blanket. Few of them had gone on to make as much of themselves as North had—and to be so sought out by the very world that rejected him . . .

"No, Mr. Sheffield. I am not offended. Beatrice, dear?"

Her cousin flushed under the weight of their stares. She seemed torn between Spinton and Octavia. Poor thing. She really had no idea whom to give her loyalty to.

"While your choice of word may have been inappropriate Mr. Sheffield, I cannot say any offense I feel extends to your person."

Nicely put. Why couldn't Octavia have thought of something similar? A true lady would find North's choice of title objectionable. A *true* lady would be shocked.

One more reminder that she was not, nor would she ever be, a lady.

"My apologies, Mr. Sheffield," she murmured under Spinton's disapproving gaze. "I should not have asked." Of course she shouldn't have, not when she already knew the answer. Now Spinton was upset because of North's reply, and North was undoubtedly unimpressed with her question.

"Do not vex yourself, Lady Octavia," North replied, lifting his glass of wine. "I am not ashamed of what I am. Not any more."

She couldn't tear her gaze away from the ice blue of his. There was nothing damning in his tone, no censure in his features, and yet she couldn't help but feel that his remark was intentionally pointed—that he thought she was ashamed of her origins and he was disappointed in her for being so.

No, she wasn't ashamed. Never ashamed. It was her mother's shame and her grandfather's shame that kept her silent, not her own. Never her own.

"Nor should you be ashamed, Sheffield." Spinton cut into the beef on his plate. "There is nothing contemptible about a man who has carved his own destiny."

Try as she might, Octavia could not keep her brows from climbing high on her forehead. This was a side of Spinton she hadn't seen before. When had he, a man born with all the wealth and privilege anyone could covet, decided that anyone of a lower class was to be admired?

Perhaps there was more to Spinton than she ever allowed herself to believe. It was a suspicion that nagged at her throughout the rest of the meal.

"Lady Octavia," North said later, over dessert. "Perhaps when we are finished here you might show me the latest letter you have received."

Sighing, Octavia set down her fork. "Mr. Sheffield, I really do not believe that is necessary—"

She should have just kept her mouth shut. She shouldn't have said a word. If she'd simple smiled and nodded, Spinton and Beatrice, and even North himself, would never have jumped on her like fleas on a stray cat.

"Octavia, there is a very real chance that you might be in some kind of danger," Spinton announced. "If you do not show Mr. Sheffield the letter, I shall."

And there it was. Spinton, usually so affable and pliable, was giving her no choice. The one person in her life—other than Beatrice, of course—whom she thought wouldn't try to direct her life was doing just that.

Perhaps if she had just a bit more spine, she'd take back her control, but she wasn't certain she knew how to do that, or if she ever had it in the first place.

"Fine," she ground out. "If for no other reason than your

piece of mind, Spinton, but when Mr. Sheffield determines that these letters are indeed harmless, I hope that will be the end of this foolishness." Tossing down her napkin, she stood. "Shall we retire to the parlor once more?"

Once this evening was over with, she could have her life back. And she and Spinton were going to have to sit down and have a long, serious talk about what each expected from their marriage. She might have promised to marry him, but she hadn't promised to be ruled by him.

Damn her grandfather for guilting her into such a promise. She loved the old man dearly, but he knew exactly how to get what he wanted out of her. He knew how beholden she was to him for giving her a better life.

At least everyone *told* her she should be beholden.

Since Octavia didn't wait for any of them, North didn't bother standing on ceremony and offering his arm to Miss Henry. Charming as her cousin was, North's interest was firmly centered on the tall, slender redhead storming down the corridor ahead of him.

He had forgotten how easily her temper ignited. For a woman who looked as though she were carved from alabaster, Octavia was surprisingly passionate. Did Spinton appreciate that? Probably not. Poor old Spinton would no doubt learn to resent Octavia and her temperament someday. It was just one more reason that the two of them were so very obviously wrong for each other.

He'd wager ten quid Octavia knew it as well, but for some reason she seemed determined to keep up the charade. Why? The Octavia he'd known would never marry a man she did not love.

Her virginity had been another story. She had settled for a man—boy—she liked.

Back in the parlor—the room that didn't suit Octavia at all—North waited patiently while his friend collected the letters she'd saved. Beatrice and Spinton sat nearby as silent as statues. North turned his back on them. To be honest, the pair of them like that made the hair on the back of his neck stand on end. They seemed to be able to communicate with each other without speaking. It was disconcerting to watch.

"Here." Octavia shoved a stack of letters tied in a ribbon toward him.

"Pink?" He kept his voice low so the others couldn't hear the familiarity in his tone.

She actually flushed a bit, but her gaze never faltered from his. "The ribbon is Beatrice's. It was her idea to save the letters. I wanted to burn them."

No doubt she had. That was Octavia. Get rid of everything and anything she didn't need or want in her life. She kept only those things that were sacred to her.

Again, her virginity came to mind. She certainly hadn't wanted to hang on to that. He couldn't fault her for it, given the options available to her at the time. The fact that she chose to give it to him still astounded him. He had it still, tucked away somewhere among the cobwebs of his heart.

He took the letters, untying the delicate ribbon as he moved toward the small desk near the window. Such a dainty little room this was. So tiny and pretty and absolutely no good for anything but show. At least the desk chair didn't break when he sat down on it. It was stronger than it looked.

North unfolded a letter. Octavia hovered above him. Affecting an expression of disinterestedness, he raised his gaze. "Might I bother you for a little privacy, my lady?"

This time she didn't flush. In fact, she looked as though she would like very much to tell him just what he could do with his privacy. How would she explain that to her betrothed?

She shot him a glare that was for his benefit and his alone, out of sight of their companions. "Of course, Mr. Sheffield."

North wanted to watch her walk away, all stiff-shouldered

and petulant, but he denied himself the pleasure. Instead, he turned his attention to the letters, which appeared anything but sinister in their neat script and pink ribbon.

By the fifth mention of Octavia's "bright eyes" and "fine features" he was rolling his eyes and ready to arrest the culprit on a charge of abusing the English language. Good God, couldn't the man think of any other words? Perhaps other parts of Octavia to praise? She had much more to her worth praising than just her face.

Ahh, wait. Here was one celebrating the "swanlike column" of her throat. Rubbish. This person knew nothing of the woman he adored.

Perhaps Spinton was the man writing the letters.

No, that was foolish—almost as foolish as the letters themselves. From what North had seen, the earl didn't know Octavia as well as a fiancé should, but he knew better than to attempt such a stunt.

Quickly, he scanned the next three letters, pausing when the tone of voice seemed to change. It became more personal, the details more intimate. No longer did the author compliment just Octavia's features and form. On the third of last month—before Easter, but close enough that some of the season's entertainment would have already started—Octavia's admirer started noting specifics.

He watched her in public. Every note made some mention of something she had worn or done at a social event. Coincidence? Or was he following her?

The tightening in North's gut was all the answer he needed. The remainder of the missives only confirmed it. This person might have started out as nothing more than a harmless admirer—and might yet be simply that—but there was a chance that infatuation had turned to obsession, and that kind of attachment should not be dismissed as harmless.

Looking up, he found himself pinned by three unwavering

gazes. Unblinking, they watched him, waiting for his verdict. Good Lord, how long had they been staring like that? Judging from the thin set of Octavia's mouth, she believed they'd been kept waiting long enough. North had to agree.

"I will take the case."

Octavia jumped to her feet. "What?" She could *not* have heard him correctly.

North met her gaze directly. "I believe these letters merit investigation."

Oh, this was madness. The walls of the parlor seemed to close in around her. "You cannot be serious. Did you not read the letters? They are *harmless*, for pity's sake!"

Everyone was staring at her, Beatrice and Spinton flanking her like matching spaniels. North was the only one she concerned herself with. How could he, of all people, be so foolish?

"My dear, I think Mr. Sheffield is a better judge of these matters than the rest of us," Spinton spoke softly.

Meaning North was a better judge than *she* was, obviously. Luckily Spinton's judgment wasn't that good or he might start to wonder why a stranger had such an interest in his future wife's private life, or why that future wife reacted so strongly to said "stranger."

Not daring to take her gaze off North, not even for a second, Octavia replied, "Do not speak to me as though I were a child, Spinton. It is not a very attractive trait for a gentleman to possess."

She might have laughed at the surprise on North's face were she not so peevish with him. "Lady Octavia, may I speak to you privately?"

"No."

He froze her with a glacial stare. "Please?"

She would get no peace until she did what he wanted, that

she knew. Obviously he hadn't changed that much in the last
dozen years. In fact, he had probably gotten even better at
making people do what he wanted.

Now she favored her companions with a glance. "Beatrice,
Spinton, would you leave us, please?"

To her surprise, Spinton did not attempt to argue with her.
Perhaps he was still smarting over her previous set-down. He
simply nodded and gestured for Beatrice to precede him
from the room. Neither Octavia nor North watched them go.

"What the hell are you about?" she demanded as soon as
the door clicked shut. "I thought you were on my side."

He rose from the desk, coming around its delicate form toward her. "I am on your side. Vie, I think this person may be
serious."

Now that was just ludicrous. "Serious about what? Norrie,
they are just letters. Notes from an infatuated boy."

He folded his arms across his chest. His sleeves pulled
around the bulge of his biceps. When had he developed those?
"Perhaps, but a boy who claims to know your 'secret.' "

"Oh, that could be any manner of trivial things." She dismissed his concerns with a wave of her hand. "It is probably
nothing."

"What if it isn't? I thought you wanted to keep the secret
of your upbringing just that, a secret?"

Why did he make it sound so underhanded and dirty? She
wasn't ashamed of where she came from any more than he
was; she had just made a stupid promise to conceal it for the
sake of her family.

"I do."

"Then what if someone threatens to reveal the truth? Do
you want that to happen?"

"No." But she wouldn't have to get married if they did. She
wouldn't have to keep pretending . . .

His tone was pleading without sounding weak. "Then let

me help you. Let me find this person and determine what they know. If it is nothing, then fine. If it is simply a foolish youngster, we can silence him easily."

"You do not look convinced Norrie. Is your suspicious imagination having its way with you?" She couldn't help the slightly caustic tone that crept into her voice.

"I could not live with myself if I allowed something to happen to you, Vie. You must allow me to do this."

She frowned at the starkness of his expression, the entreaty in his eyes. "What happened?"

He shook his head. "Nothing you need worry about."

"No." He wasn't going to shut her out that easily. "Something has happened. Something you blame yourself for. What?"

He ran the flat of his palm over the stubble on his jaw. She had bought him a razor for his birthday years ago. Did he never use it?

"I failed someone I swore to protect. I let my guard down and that person paid for it. I will not make the same mistake twice."

"What happened to her?" Somehow she knew he spoke of a woman.

"She's dead."

Oh dear. Her poor sweet boy. She reached out for his hand. Surprisingly, he let her take it. "Norrie, no one's going to kill me."

"Damned right they're not." The conviction in his tone—in his eyes—sent a shiver down her spine, and it was just as pleasant as it was frightening. He would do anything in his power to protect her if he felt she needed to be protected. And obviously, he believed that she did.

"Let me do this, Vie. Please."

How could she tell him no? How could she ridicule his suspicions now that she knew how much it meant to him? Investigating these letters of hers was something he felt he needed to do—something he *wanted* to do for her. She would have to be both cruel and stupid to refuse him, and while sometimes she was both, right now she was neither. It would do her no harm to allow him to do this, but if she said no, there was a chance, however small, that he was right and she was wrong about the letters. Better safe than dead.

"All right. Investigate all you want."

She could practically feel the relief wafting from him as he squeezed her fingers. "You will not regret this. I will uncover the culprit as quickly as I can."

But not quickly enough. Mere minutes would be too long. How could she allow North into her life, even for a brief time, and then watch him walk out again? No, already she regretted her decision. Already she regretted letting him go.

Chapter 6

"**A**nother one?"

They were in her awful little parlor awaiting Lord Spinton. Did she never receive visitors in any other room? Perhaps she reserved this one for the callers she didn't want to stay long.

North had arrived five minutes prior to the scheduled time. Spinton was now five minutes late. Obviously, Octavia chose not to wait for her tardy almost-fiancé to share the newest development concerning her mysterious love letters.

Octavia smiled at his incredulous tone. "If nothing else my admirer is tenacious."

"Or obsessed," North muttered, scratching his jaw. At first he hadn't taken these notes seriously. Even when he agreed to investigate, he hadn't thought the author *that* dangerous. Now he wasn't so certain. The notes arrived with such frequency that the author surely must be plagued with thoughts of Octavia. Obsessed to be sure.

If he didn't know better, he might suspect himself of being the culprit.

"Not to mention suffering from ennui," Octavia added. "Sometimes I wonder if he has nothing else to do but write letters to me."

"What makes you so certain it is a he?" Not that he hadn't jumped to the same conclusion himself.

"A woman would have told me what she wanted by now."

Good point. He extended his hand. "Give it to me."

She held it to the bottle green muslin covering her breast, a patently sweet smile curving her lips. "Say please."

North's lips twitched at her provoking but he forced a scowl. "Do not bedevil me, woman." He snapped the fingers of the hand held out to her.

"I shall do whatever I please," she quipped, turning away.

"Why is it you only mean that when you say it to me?" *Damn*.

She stilled, her shoulders stiffening as she brought herself around to face him once again. All amusement was wiped from her cool features. "What do you mean?"

He had struck a nerve. Perhaps that had been his intention, but it was badly done. "Why do you give in so easily to others, yet fight me over the smallest detail?"

Her amber brows knitted. "I do not!"

"You do." Nothing like poking that nerve with a sharp stick. Twelve years had passed since they had last known each other, and yet their behavior was almost exactly the same. She did what everyone else—even dead people—expected of her and yet wouldn't allow him to see a bloody letter that he had been hired to find the author of. She even gave in to Spinton with less of a fight.

Slender arms folded beneath the softness of her bosom. "Perhaps because I know you will let me. You always let me win."

"Not always."

"Always when it mattered."

Was she referring to that night? He gave in so easily to her coaxing, the gentle, fumbling persuasion of her trembling fingers. But he wouldn't have caved so completely had it not been for the fact that he wanted to give in. She had to know that. He let her win because losing to Octavia didn't feel like defeat.

She offered him the letter. "I suppose it is time for me to allow you to have your way for once."

"Twice," he said before he could stop himself.

She stared at him. The slight tremor of the paper in her hand was the only indication that she knew what he meant. He took the letter, resisting the urge to touch her fingers with his own.

"We should talk about that night." Her tone was low and unsure.

North shook his head. "Not now, Vie. Not when the man who may or may not be your fiancé could walk in at any moment."

She didn't acknowledge his assessment of her relationship with Spinton. "Do you regret it?"

Did he not just tell her they would discuss this some other time? "No," he replied with a sigh. Then, pathetically, "Do you?"

"No."

"Then any discussion about it can wait." His tone was just as ruthless as his manner as he broke the seal on the missive. Red wax, embedded with the shape of a rose. Nothing special. He knew at least three abbesses and one opium den owner with the same seal—not to mention several ladies who had sent him invitations to very "private" meetings.

He does not deserve you. I am the only man for you.

Tenacious, and possibly a little unsound. "You might want to tell Spinton to be on his guard," he remarked as he handed the note back to her.

Octavia scanned the parchment quickly, her bright gaze wide. "Good Lord."

"Notice the fine script of the handwriting. It only solidifies my suspicion that our culprit is upper class, and obviously someone who is aware of your relationship with Spinton."

She met his gaze. "All of society knows of my relationship with Spinton."

He simply watched her, letting the implications of that sink in. When they did, Octavia sank to the sofa with a frustrated groan. "It could be anyone. Any member of the *ton*."

"Any male member," he quipped. He wanted to comfort her but didn't dare sit next to her in case Spinton chose that moment to arrive. "I will find him, Vie." He couldn't even keep Black Sally out of the way of a man whose identity he knew. How was he going to protect Octavia when anyone could be a suspect?

It didn't matter. He would protect her, or die trying.

Her expression was resigned, but not unconcerned. "I do not want Spinton to get hurt."

Oh, but he didn't matter, was that it? Of course it wasn't. He and Spinton were totally different people. He knew how to protect himself, what to do if he were attacked. Spinton did not. Perhaps he should have one of his men follow the earl just in case.

She nibbled on the edge of a fingernail. "I do not want you to get hurt either."

That would teach him to be jealous.

"Is someone injured?" It was Spinton, dressed in blue and smelling of soap—the quintessential gentleman. He matched this little parlor with his elegance and coloring. Thank God the man's timing was ludicrous, otherwise someone would have to explain why Octavia was so adamant about not wanting North to get hurt.

"Do not worry yourself, my lord," North said, turning his

attention to the shorter man. "Lady Octavia and I were just discussing her concern that you be kept from harm at all times during the investigation."

Spinton's expression was one of pure surprised pleasure. He gazed at Octavia in such wonder that North almost felt sorry for him. Whatever Octavia's feelings might be, Spinton wanted them to be more. North couldn't blame him. He'd wanted the same thing once.

"Tonight, you and I will meet at Lord and Lady Haversham's ball," he instructed the still slack-jawed earl. "Then you will introduce me to Lady Octavia."

"But what reason will we give for your continued presence?" Spinton asked as he regained himself.

North smiled calculatingly, his gaze slipping to Octavia's. "That is simple." Part of him wanted her to be shocked by his plan. Another part wanted her to rise to the challenge.

"I am going to try to steal your woman."

Pretending not to know Octavia had been easy, especially when she was so obviously sincere in her wariness of him. Dancing with her, however, was a tad more trying. Certainly he wanted to project interest in her, but if he wasn't careful the entire *ton* would figure out he knew what it was like to be inside her before poor Spinton had a chance to act the jealous suitor.

Holding Octavia felt like heaven. She was slender and warm in his arms, and he couldn't help but remember how it felt to hold her this way, lying on his rumpled bed, their bodies naked and entwined.

That night had changed everything between them, just as this night was going to change things.

She ceased to be just his friend that night. True, he had thought of her in a sexual nature prior to that—what young man didn't think that at least once of any young lady he knew? But with Octavia it had been different. It was more than merely physical. Somewhere along the line he had fallen in love with his best friend. And he suspected that she had fallen for him as well.

And now here he was, holding his first love, his first lover, in his arms once more. It was only natural that some of those old feelings resurface. This tenderness and possessiveness he felt for her was understandable as well. After all, he hadn't loved her just as a girl, he had loved her as a friend and a person. Aside from his brothers—and perhaps even more so in some ways—Octavia held the most special place in his heart. Even after all these years, he would give his life for her without a moment's hesitation. He would do anything to ensure her happiness.

Even watch her marry a good-humored man entirely unsuitable for her. Even pretend that he wanted to steal her away. Although right now, it didn't feel like pretending.

Worse yet was the guilt. What was he doing at this stupid ball when a killer walked free? What right did he have to dance and enjoy holding Octavia when Harker was out there laughing at him? Black Sally had been his best chance to nab the bastard, and now she was gone. Her death was North's fault. He should have had more men watching. He shouldn't have put poor Harris out there alone. He had thought the boy could handle it. He should have known he would be no match for Harker's henchmen. North should have been the one watching Sally. He should be trying to avenge her death right now, instead of chasing a lovestruck nobleman.

No one but a madman would give this case precedence over putting an end to Harker's criminal career. And yet here he was, dancing under the brilliant chandeliers while Harker enjoyed one more night of freedom. He told himself that Octavia's admirer could be dangerous, unsound, and a real threat. Did he believe it? Sometimes. His mind didn't always do what he wanted it to.

Had his reason and sense left him completely?

At least those present at the ball were reacting exactly as he wanted them to. They'd watched him meet Octavia and then witnessed his interest in her. If rumors hadn't started yet, they soon would. How could they not? In a gown of shimmering cinnamon silk, Octavia was stunning. How could he possibly look at any other woman? And Octavia, to her credit, seemed equally enraptured with him, although he did not allow himself to wonder why. It was just a ruse, nothing more.

"People are staring," he informed her, guiding her through a turn. Of course he had chosen the waltz for their dance. It was still scandalous enough to cause a stir.

She smiled up at him, as though he had said something particularly flattering. How easily she fell into the charade. "Is that not what you wanted?"

"Yes, but it makes it rather difficult to talk."

"Talk?" Her eyelashes fluttered. "What could we possibly have to talk about?"

She was teasing. She loved to tease him. Always had. "What are you going to tell Spinton when he realizes you are not a virgin?"

Shock registered in her eyes, but not her expression. "This is not the time nor place to ask such a question."

They glided through another turn, their steps perfectly matched. "You plan to conceal it from him then?"

Her expression remained pleasant, but her tone was pure ice. "Of course I do."

"What if he figures it out?" There he went with that stick again. Just as when they were children and he had that odd compulsion to pick on her until she either picked back or cried. He hated it when she cried.

"He will not."

"How do you know?"

Her cheeks flushed but her tone was even and low. "Because I am fairly certain he has no idea what is involved in taking a woman's virginity."

That could be possible. Not many men of North's acquaintance, unless they were married, had much experience with virgins. Debauchery wasn't looked upon very highly in most circles. Aside from Octavia, all of North's bedmates had been experienced women. Perhaps he was in a minority, but he wanted his lover to enjoy their time together, not fear it.

"If he does figure it out, are you going to tell him it was me?"

Her gaze brightened and a smug smile curved the voluptuous bow of her lips. "You are jealous."

"I am not!" Now who was being poked?

"You are. You are jealous of Spinton. Are you perhaps afraid he might prove the better lover?"

He scowled. She was so smug. He hated it when she picked back as well.

"Oh, Norrie," she said, shaking her head, "it is nothing to be ashamed of. I suppose it is only natural given our friendship and our history. I imagine I would feel much the same way if confronted with the woman you planned to marry."

The thought gave him some satisfaction. "I doubt you will ever experience such a meeting."

Her skirts fluttered around his legs as they twirled yet again. "Why not?"

"Because I have no plans to marry."

The delicate skin between her brows puckered. "Do not be silly."

Silly? It was plain common sense. Couldn't she see that? "Any woman who marries me will be putting herself in harm's way by nature of my work. What woman would do that?"

"One who loves you."

His heart tripped at her words. "But would a woman who loves me be content to sit back and watch me put myself in danger time and time again? I could not ask her to live that way."

"You could give up your career."

He smiled. It felt somewhat bitter. "Ah, but then I would have to love her more than I love my career, and I have yet to meet such a woman." His answer might have been different twelve years ago.

There was nothing but sympathy in her cobalt gaze, and he didn't like it. "You may someday."

He humored her. "Perhaps."

"You deserve to love and be loved, Norrie."

"So do you, Vie." He left the rest of his thought unspoken.

She sensed it anyway. Of course she did. She knew him better than anyone. "Spinton is a good man."

"But you do not love him." Poke. Poke.

Octavia shrugged. "That rarely matters in society. Besides, I like him very much."

"He might not find that a fair trade for his devotion." He couldn't keep the sarcasm from his tone. What man could content himself with "like?"

She sagged a little in his arms, as though she were suddenly very tired. It was a gesture of defeat, and he didn't like that either. "What do you want from me, North?"

"The truth. You can lie to everyone else, even yourself. But do not lie to me."

Her eyes shot daggers at him even as she smiled for those who might be watching. "I promised I would marry Spinton. I know he deserves better, but he does not seem to agree. He wants this marriage to happen as much as my grandfather did. I will be a countess and a lady, and then all my promises will be fulfilled."

She thought Spinton deserved better? Was there such a woman? Yes, there probably was a woman out there better suited for Spinton than Octavia. "You once promised me that we would always be friends."

"And so we will."

North swallowed against the lump in his throat. "You also promised me that you would always be my Vie."

Her gaze softened. "I still am."

"No, you are not. You are someone else. My Vie wanted to live on her own terms, and the rest of the world be damned. She did not play by the rules. You live by them."

He never believed himself capable of breaking a heart, but he could see in the dark blue depths of Octavia's eyes that he had smashed hers like a china cup tossed from a second-floor window.

"Perhaps I do, but is that any worse than making up your own? Your little world might be safe and comfortable for you, North, but sooner or later, you are going to have to join the rest of us in the real one."

Her words struck a chord. "Octavia—" but he never got a chance to finish. The music ended and she was pulling free of his embrace. He had no choice but to take her back to Spinton and walk away.

It was one of the hardest things he'd ever done.

For the next two nights, North was her constant shadow. Wherever Octavia went, whatever social function she attended, he was there. Sometimes he would speak, sometimes they would dance, but he was always watching—and no doubt aware that others noticed the direction of his stare as well.

They were never alone, yet she was as keenly aware of him

as she was of the clothes on her back. When she felt the warm brush of his breath against the back of her neck, she never knew if it was real or just her mind playing tricks on her.

Neither of them made mention of the words they'd exchanged at the Haversham ball. There was no point. Nothing had changed. Neither of them was going to revise his life just because the other didn't agree with the choices he'd made. But just because they didn't talk about it, that didn't mean she hadn't thought about that dance and all that was said. The foolishness about her virginity she dismissed as simple male jealousy. It meant nothing, save for the fact that North, like most men, didn't want another male marking what he considered to be part of his own territory—no matter that he had left it years ago.

No, it was his remarks about *his* Octavia, the one who didn't live by the rules, that affected her. He was right. At one time she flouted society's dictates like any other child of a student of Wollstonecraft and her modern sensibilities. *She* had decided who would be her first lover. *She* had decided how her life would play out. Then her mother died and everything changed. She found out she wasn't who she believed herself to be. She was the granddaughter of an earl, and it was the final wish of her mother—and the wish of her grandfather—that she live up to the expectations upon her.

And she had to be honest with herself, if no one else. She had *wanted* to be a lady. How often had she and North pretended to be those grand personages who seemed so exotic and wonderful in their finery and expensive perfume? She knew how much North wanted to be a part of that world, and a secret part of her had thought that perhaps if she was part of it also . . . Well, it didn't matter what she thought. North hadn't become part of that world. He'd remained in the one she left behind. She had changed. So had he. What right did either of them have to cast stones?

Still, he had his nerve—giving her such grief for living by the rules, and now here he was laying down some new ones.

"You are not to go anywhere alone. If you need to go out, either you will take Miss Henry with you or you will send for me."

Spinton, who was seated on the little brocade sofa in her parlor, suddenly sat up straighter. "I will take Lady Octavia wherever she needs to go."

"No." North pulled a pale imitation of a smile. "You are going to stay out of my way and away from O—Lady Octavia. The last thing I need is another person to worry about."

He was putting himself in possible danger for her and it didn't even seem to bother him. Was this what his life was now, gambling with his own personal safety time and time again? Yes. He had told her as much. What happened when his luck finally ran out?

No wonder he didn't want to marry. At least he had the grace not to ask a woman to go through that. She wouldn't be able to withstand such torture, of that she had no doubt.

Spinton was plainly affronted. "What about Beatrice's safety?"

On a first-name basis with her cousin now, was he? Octavia could barely keep her brow from raising at that.

North ran a hand along his jaw. There was some stubble there. He obviously couldn't be bothered to shave that morning, even though his unruly hair was damp from the bath. "I believe the person writing these letters is interested in Lady Octavia and any male admirers she has. Miss Henry is no threat to our boy and therefore in no danger."

"I do not like your plan." The earl's tone was churlish. "I do not like being made to look like a jilt."

North's brows lowered. "Not even for Lady Octavia's safety?"

Octavia was very interested in Spinton's answer to that. He flushed a dark red. "Of course she is my first concern."

Of *course* she was. His pride was his first concern, the little blighter.

North visibly rolled his eyes. He was the only man she had ever known who would so boldly poke fun at a peer of the realm. "You will not be a jilt. Lady Octavia's head will simply be temporarily turned by my attention and charm." He flashed her a conspiratorial grin, and Octavia had to hide her answering chuckle behind her hand as Spinton turned his indignation on her.

"No. I will not stand for such humiliation. Octavia, everyone knows we have an understanding. What will they say about you if they see you with Mr. Sheffield?"

"Exactly what we want them to say," North replied.

He wasn't helping things. He was intentionally teasing Spinton. Why? What satisfaction was there in tormenting an obviously weaker opponent? Unless North saw Spinton as having some sort of advantage over him. But what? Birth, perhaps? Her?

Spinton shot him an annoyed glance. "I will not have it."

"Lord Spinton," North's slight Scottish brogue was thick with aggravation as his lips twisted. "No one will truly believe there is anything between Lady Octavia and myself but a harmless flirtation. I may be considered a good catch by some mamas, but everyone knows being a countess is much preferable to a mere Mrs."

How could he say such a thing? Maybe to some women being a countess was the better deal, but any woman would be lucky indeed to snatch North as a husband.

A woman who wouldn't mind watching her husband go out almost every night trying to get himself killed.

"And since I have no interest in marrying, let alone marrying above my station, I can assure you that Lady Octavia and her reputation are perfectly safe with me. As soon as this is over, the two of you can pass it off as little more than a woman trying to make her long-time betrothed a little jealous."

His station. What did he consider that? He was the son of a viscount. She was the only daughter of an earl's son. The only thing separating them was the piece of paper that said her parents had been lawfully wed. It was rubbish, really.

Octavia sighed. "Spin—Fitzwilliam, I do not want you to get hurt. I could never forgive myself if something were to happen to you. Please, do as Mr. Sheffield says. If you want an end to these letters, it is the only way."

Spinton's jaw tightened. "I will agree on one condition."

"What is that?" She'd agree to just about anything to get him out of harm's way.

He fixed his gaze upon her with such earnestness it made her wary. "When this is over, we will set and publicly announce the date of our wedding."

Oh God.

"Fitzwilliam—"

He held up his hand. "I will not agree unless you give me your word, Octavia."

Octavia looked at North. His expression was perfectly impassive, just what one might expect from a stranger. But he wasn't a stranger. He was her friend, her first lover. Shouldn't he have *some* expression on his face? Happiness? Regret?

She looked away. That blank stare was unnerving. "All right," she murmured. "We will discuss it."

Spinton looked so happy he could burst. He didn't even seem to notice that his fiancée didn't share his enjoyment. He rushed toward her and caught her up in his arms. He hugged her so fiercely, Octavia could scarce draw breath. Only when he released her did she hazard a glance at North.

He was gazing out the window, his expression one of almost perfect disinterest, save for the ticking muscle of his jaw.

Then, as suddenly as a curtain lifting, he turned from the window and faced them with a gracious smile. "But for now, Lord Spinton, you must play the part of the rejected suitor. You must pretend to all society that Octavia has tossed you aside for another man—temporary as it might be. Can you do that?"

Spinton looked as though he was actually having fun now as he nodded. "But what if I need to speak to one of you, or you need to speak to me? We must assume the villain is watching Lady Octavia's every move."

Yes, how would they do that? Octavia turned her attention to North. His gaze was on Spinton, but she knew as surely as she drew breath that he was actually watching her.

"Miss Henry will be your link to Octavia and myself. She has already graciously agreed to act as a go-between, and no one will give any thought to you continuing an acquaintance with such an old friend, especially since she is a distant relation."

The earl seemed satisfied with that. Octavia's shoulders heaved with a sigh of relief. Could it be that they were finally all in agreement? And who else needed a drink?

"Then should we not include Miss Henry in this conversation?"

North nodded. "If you wish."

Octavia was already at the bar, pouring herself a glass of sherry. Something stronger would be preferable, but not while Spinton was around. "She is in the library, Fitzwilliam. Do be a dear and fetch her."

The door barely clicked shut behind Spinton when Octavia downed her sherry in one swallow and immediately went to North. She needed to know what he was thinking. Needed his opinion, his blessing—even his censure. She needed her friend, not this stranger.

"Norrie, I—"

He cut her off by placing his hands on her shoulders and leaning in to kiss her cheek. "Be happy, Vie. That is all I want for you."

The touch of his lips sent a tremor through her. "It is what I want for you as well."

"I am not certain we are all meant to be happy."

"You are." She meant it, and he knew it.

He only smiled. "Spinton is a lucky man."

She laughed. "You of all people should know the trials that await him."

"The only trial to marrying you would be the wait."

Like a stupid schoolgirl, she flushed under his flattery. "Liar."

His fingers flexed around her shoulders, warm and strong, kneading the tension from her muscles with such skill she almost moaned aloud. "I have never lied to you."

"Yes you have!" Laughter took the edge from her indignation.

"When?"

"The day you told me you knew firsthand what happens between a man and a woman."

His cheeks pinkened. "That was not a lie. I did know."

"Not from experience."

He shrugged. "No, but I did walk in on Mary Maguire and Jimmy Taylor one night in the wardrobe room."

She laughed. She couldn't help it. "A lot of good that did you!"

She'd shocked him. He couldn't stop the widening of his eyes. "It is not as though you were any great expert."

No, she hadn't been. "*I* never claimed to be."

His smile faded but did not disappear. "We seem to be coming back to that night rather often."

Her hunger evaporated. "We do."

They stared at each other, neither of them blinking. North

released her shoulder, as though he didn't want to be touching her when talking about that night. "I suppose we had better sit down in private someday and discuss it."

"I suppose so."

The fact that they were better off waiting for that moment was only accentuated by Spinton barging back into the room. He had Beatrice with him, ready to be told what she needed to know about their plan. Both of them looked like children teased with the promise of a grand adventure. Octavia almost envied them.

North gave Beatrice the details, with Spinton interrupting with his own remarks every few sentences. That North didn't tell him to be silent said much for his forbearance.

But then, he'd always been the more patient of the two of them. He had been so very patient that night they made love. She simply wanted it over with, but North had wanted to take his time—for her to take her time. Those slow, lazy moments had been the best part.

He had been so gentle and loving, arousing her with untutored yet knowing fingers. By the time he lowered his body to hers, she was begging for him. There was pleasure and then the discomfort of having her body parted by his. The discomfort was lasting, stiffening her limbs until he'd finally withdrawn after spending himself. Even though the irritation eased, even though her ache had long subsided under his body's invasion, she missed having him inside her.

Afterward, when she cried, he thought it was because it was so horrible, and he'd tried to make it up to her by bringing her to climax with his hand. He'd had no idea that the burning presence of his body meant more to her than the pleasure of his fingers. Having him inside her had been wonderful—a memory she cherished for the following years, because they had been as one and she had known, for a brief and magical moment, what it was to truly belong.

As she watched him talking with Spinton and Beatrice, Octavia smiled a little smugly. He had been her first and she had been his. The first woman to know what it was to belong to this beautiful, fiercely loyal man. No matter who else he was with, no matter whom she married, she would always be his.

And he would always—*always*—be hers.

Chapter 7

Hyde Park at five o'clock was *the* place to be if one was part of that great inner circle of the *ton*. That was precisely why North never went there.

"This is madness," he remarked, surveying the sea of horses, riders, and carriages swarming the track winding through the green grass. Despite the wide openness of the park, chatter buzzed all around them, as did flies, drawn as much to some of the aristocracy as to the horse manure dotting the path. Thank God there was a breeze—and that he and Octavia were upwind.

He heard Octavia's answering chuckle before her chestnut mare came up beside his own gray gelding. "It is rather overwhelming, but do not worry. You will get used to it."

North's eyes narrowed. "I have no wish to get used to it."

Her face was partially obscured by the broad straw brim of her hat. "Why? Because someone might think you are trying to rise above your station?"

Did his ears deceive him, or was that mockery in her tone?

He turned his gaze to hers, his brow knitting. "Are you not

concerned that some might think you are lowering yourself below yours?"

She scowled. "Do not be ridiculous. I am not ashamed to be seen with you."

That certainly seemed to be true. She sat straight in the saddle, her shoulders back and her chin raised, as though daring the crowd to notice them. Most obliged her quite quickly. "Your grandfather might disagree with that."

"My grandfather," she reminded him, "is dead."

He smiled. "I know. I sent flowers."

She looked as though she didn't know whether to laugh or chastise him. "Why are you so bitter toward a dead man?"

"He made you into a different person." And he didn't mean just socially either.

A scoffing sound drifted on the air between them. "I am not that different. I have merely matured."

He could argue that, but he wouldn't. "He made you promise too much."

She looked at him—really looked. He could see realization dawn in her eyes. "What did he make *you* promise?"

Damn. He looked away. "To stay away from you."

Her harsh gasp was little more than a whisper on the breeze. "Then it is not my promises that anger you. It is your own."

"No." He purposely wiped his face clean of all expression as he met her gaze. "I am angry because that old bastard thought he had the right to ask so much of either of us, and I am angry at myself for believing what he said about me." He still believed him. So far, every one of the old earl's predictions had turned out true—except for him not amounting to anything. He had amounted to something. He just wasn't sure what sometimes.

She stared at him with that relentless shrewd gaze. "He was very good to me. He could have left me to fend for myself, but instead he took me in. He changed my life."

Now it was his turn to scoff. "He kept you from doing what you really wanted."

She obviously saw it differently. Perhaps she'd ended up exactly where she wanted. "He saved me from being someone's mistress."

"You would *not* have had to be a mistress." He wouldn't allow her to give the old man credit for that.

She laughed then, bitter and mocking. "Oh, and what could I have been? A wife?"

That hurt. That was like a boot in the chest. Staring at the path between his mount's ears, North forced himself to breathe despite the pain.

"Oh, Norrie."

That sympathetic tone—the guilt and remorse—was even worse than her mockery. It was all he could do not to wince. He couldn't even bring himself to deny it.

Her gloved hand touched his arm. "North, I am sorry."

He shrugged her off. "Forget about it. It was a long time ago."

"Were you really going to—?"

He whipped her a glance meant to put an end to this stupid conversation. "I said forget about it. Be glad I never made an ass of myself by asking."

She was still so bloody sympathetic. "I never would have thought you an ass."

"I would have," he replied—more harshly than he intended. "Now, we're supposed to be relative strangers flirting with each other. Do you think we can leave the past where it belongs long enough to do that? And stop looking at me like that."

Instantly, her expression changed to that of a flirtatious coquette, and for a moment he was tempted to remark how that ability would come in handy on her wedding night, but he didn't. He didn't want to hurt Octavia. Any injury she had dealt him was unintentional. And she was right, it wasn't really her he was angry with—well, perhaps just a bit. It was himself, and her grandfather, and perhaps even fate itself, but not really her.

His reaction to having her back in his life was unsettling. It felt as though his entire world had been shaken. Every sense seemed sharper, every color brighter, when Octavia was near. It was as though a piece of him that had been missing for the last twelve years had finally been replaced.

She had taken the security of his world, the certainty of it, and turned it upside down by giving him something to care about. She made him long for things he couldn't have, a life that he thought he had given up dreaming about long ago. He wanted something better than what he had. He wanted her to be proud of him, rather than accusing him of hiding from the world.

She was his vulnerability, and if Harker discerned that fact, Octavia would be in more danger than either she or Spinton could ever imagine.

If it weren't for the fact that she would soon exit his life just as suddenly as she had reentered it, he might entertain Duncan's constant badgering to change his career, but what was the point of giving up all he was accustomed to when the reason for giving it up wouldn't be around to see it? Duncan was a fine one to talk; Bow Street was his life.

Then again, if he did pursue a career in politics, it would allow him entry into the higher circles even more than his current position. He could see Octavia whenever he wanted. No one would note the social difference between them then. Except that she would be a countess and as removed from him as she possibly could be. They could never be friends again after her marriage. She wouldn't want to risk Spinton finding out that her mother was an actress, little more than a courtesan. She would never let him know her origins, or that she had given what many would consider her most precious gift to the bastard of Viscount Creed—one of the most notorious drunkards and womanizers in the history of all England.

Spinton would believe he was the first man to lie between those softly quivering thighs. He would think he had it, but he would never truly know the awesome responsibility of holding Octavia's trust in his hand. He might be tender. He might be gentle, but he would never be as careful, as aware as North had been. She had been his first as well, and Spinton could never, ever have that.

"Am I to do all the flirting, Mr. Sheffield, or will you be joining me?"

The sound of her voice—not mocking, but softly teasing—drew him out of his thoughts. Fixing her with what he hoped was a charming smile, he replied, "I was merely trying to conjure the right words to praise your beauty, Lady Octavia."

She blinked, and for a moment, his Vie was there beside him. She never knew how to take compliments, but enjoyed hearing them all the same. A part of him enjoyed cracking the facade of poise she wore like armor. She tried so hard to be a lady.

He much preferred her as a woman.

"Do be careful, Mr. Sheffield," she replied, half coy, half droll. "You might turn my head."

Glancing around at the other riders teeming around them, North smiled. "I think we are turning enough of those already."

The tension dissipated between them as Octavia nonchalantly allowed her gaze to scan the park. She never could stay angry with him for long, nor he her. When they were younger they would keep talking—or arguing—until one of them began making fun of the situation. North always knew that if they could laugh about it, everything would be all right. If they couldn't laugh, they were in trouble.

Would they laugh about her grandfather later? Would they laugh about her marriage?

"Who would have thought all these people would have nothing to do but stare at me?" she remarked through a smile as she waved to an acquaintance passing in a barouche.

"Do not flatter yourself," he replied. "Those women are not looking at you, they are looking at me."

Her laughter was sweeter than the spring breeze. Sweeter than the grass shining rich and verdant under the late afternoon sun. Selfishly he took it, snatching it from the air with his mind and tucking it away where he might find it again whenever he wanted. At the same time, his motives hadn't been strictly pure in coaxing the sound from her. Laughter that pure, that rich and pleasureful, was bound to attract attention—and it did. It was just one more method of starting gossip about them. With that came the sobering thought that Octavia's "admirer" might own one of these faces turned toward them. He might, at that very moment, be seething with jealousy that it was North beside her and not himself.

Well, if it was one of these men, he wasn't anything to worry about. Not like Harker.

Christ, what was he doing in Hyde Park when he should be out looking for ways to catch Harker? Had Black Sally died in vain? Was he that weak-minded that he could be swayed from his task by Octavia's sudden reappearance in his life?

He was helping Octavia because she was his best friend other than Wyn, but he could not allow himself to forget what was really important. Once he saw her safely home he would check in with Francis and his other men. If not for his own sense of justice, he would do it for Sally.

Octavia's voice interrupted his thoughts. "Remember that time we snuck out to go to see that traveling menagerie?"

Brushing a lock of hair out of his eyes, North nodded. "They let us play with the monkeys."

Her leg brushed his as she brought her mare closer. "I rather feel like one of those animals."

North grinned. She was talking through her teeth again. "I thought you liked attention. You certainly could not get enough of it when you were younger."

"I wanted to be admired and complimented, not watched like a mouse by a hawk."

That was a strange analogy for her to use. "Who is looking at you like that?"

"Lord Hawthorne and his friends, over there to your left."

Slowly, North allowed his gaze to slide in that direction. Lord Hawthorne was a reasonably handsome man in his late thirties. His penchant for unpoetic language, and his rather coarse manners, made him an unlikely suspect for Octavia's admirer. That did not change the fact that he was indeed eyeing her as a predator eyes a tasty morsel. So were his companions. One of them might be his quarry, but more likely they were simply thinking that if Octavia had tossed Spinton over for him, that she might toss him for one of *them*. The rest of them being Lords Weston, Emmerson, and Powell.

As though he would ever allow that to happen—if she really had tossed Spinton for him, that was.

"I've had enough of this place," he growled when all four of the men tipped their hats in their direction.

Her reply was a gusty sigh. "Me too. Come back to my house and take tea with me."

He should say no, but Octavia's cook made the most delicious little cakes, and it wasn't often that he had a few moments alone with her without half of London watching.

"I cannot stay long. I have another investigation to attend to."

"This is news," she remarked curiously, the leering lords forgotten as they turned their horses toward the exit. "What manner of investigation?"

He debated whether to tell her. But if he couldn't tell his best friend . . . "A murder."

"Murder?" Her face went white. "Norrie, you will be careful, will you not?"

His chest pinched as he nodded. Really, her concern was touching, but unnecessary. And he wouldn't have her worrying about him. "I am always careful, Vie."

She was still pale. "But you could get hurt."

That was what his job was all about. Hadn't she realized that before now? "Have you not heard? I am the most feared of men among the villains of London. The very mention of my name strikes fear in the heart of even the most dastardly ruffian."

She stared at him as though he had sprouted wings. "Feed such rubbish to the pigs, not to me."

He laughed, but her manner warmed him. "I will be fine. I promise."

They continued out of the park in silence. When they were past the gate, the bustle and noise behind them, Octavia sighed again.

"That was the most amusement I have experienced in a long time."

He raised a brow. "You cannot be serious."

"I am," she insisted lightly. "Dinners and balls are usually quite stuffy, and I do not leave the house for much else other than visits or shopping."

He replied without thought. "That is pathetic."

Instead of reacting angrily, she laughed. "It is, isn't it?"

Words tumbled out of his mouth before he even finished the thought. "Tomorrow evening I am taking you out."

She feigned a yawn. "To a ball?"

"No."

"To a dinner party?" Her tone was a bit more interested now.

"Certainly not!" He would rather die.

She chuckled. "Where then?"

He wasn't too sure himself. "It is a surprise, but do not wear anything too fancy and leave your jewelry at home."

Her eyes widened. "You are going to take me somewhere dangerous?"

He grinned. "Of course."

A *real* lady would have quailed, but not Octavia. Of course, she wasn't a real lady. She was just pretending to be one. He should have known she couldn't change that much. His Vie could never be anything like these sour-faced gossip-mongers milling about them. And none of those silly society mavens could ever hope to be half the woman Octavia was.

He would take her someplace where she could let her hair down—literally if she desired. Where people wouldn't be so quick to judge. He would take her to a place where she could be herself again, and for one night, she would be his Vie and he could be her Norrie. One night. That was all he asked, and then he would solve the mystery of her faceless beau and walk out of her life for the last time.

Surely one night couldn't harm anything.

"You are going out?"

Octavia's smile was reflected in her mirror as Beatrice entered her bedroom. "I am."

Her cousin's dark eyes widened, one hand going to her mouth. "Dressed like that?"

Twisting her hair into a simple knot on her crown, Octavia slid around on her stool with a chuckle. "Yes."

Beatrice stared. "But you are not wearing any jewelry and your gown is—"

"Somewhat out of fashion. I know." Out of fashion by a couple of years at least, but it was still a nice dress.

Poor Beatrice looked as horrified as a heroine from a gothic novel. "You are not going out with Lord Spinton, are you?"

"I am not." Octavia rose to her feet, retrieving a worn shawl from the top of her oak dressing table. "And I trust you not to say a word about this to Spinton."

"What would I say?" Beatrice shrugged her plump shoulders. "I do not know anything save for the fact that you are going out dressed as a woman of much lower rank than you are."

"That is enough." Would Beatrice make the necessary connections anytime soon?

"You are going with Mr. Sheffield."

Dear Beatrice. She was a lot of things—terribly naive for one—but she wasn't stupid.

Octavia fought a smile. She hadn't felt this good—this *young*—in a long time. "Perhaps."

Her cousin's expression was one of fearful concern. What did Beatrice think she was doing, running away with North? Running out to commit some kind of criminal act? North was a former thief taker, for heaven's sake. He would no more break the law than Duncan Reed himself. Of course, that didn't mean North was incable of *bending* it.

Beatrice folded her arms across her chest. "Octavia, what are you up to?"

Rolling her eyes at the other woman's worried tone, Octavia sighed. "All right, I will tell you, but you have to promise not to tell Spinton."

Dark brown curls bounced as Beatrice gave her head a vigorous shake. "I cannot make that promise until I know what you are up to."

They stared each other down. Octavia knew she would be the victor in the contest of wills. Her cousin's curiosity was far stronger than any loyalty she might have to Spinton.

"Fine," Beatrice relented, churlishly. "I will not tell him."

Octavia grinned. She knew without reservation that Beatrice would never reveal the truth to Spinton. While Beatrice might have some loyalty to the earl, Octavia was still her cousin, and best friend.

"Yes. I am spending the evening with North."

Whatever battle raged in her cousin between adventure and propriety, adventure obviously won out—as did her naturally inquisitive nature. "Where are you going?"

"I do not know." And oddly enough, she didn't care.

"You do not know?" Well, maybe adventure hadn't won entirely. Poor Beatrice looked absolutely dumbfounded.

Octavia shook her head as she gave her appearance a second look in the cheval glass. The gown was a lovely muted blue and the shawl a rich plum. Yes, they were a little worn and outdated, but they still flattered her coloring. Dressing down did not mean her vanity had to suffer as well.

"Does that not worry you at all?" Obviously it would worry Beatrice. Beatrice had to know everything. She would never understand that part of the excitement was not knowing. Nor would she understand the kind of trust Octavia felt toward North. Of course she was not worried. Nothing ill would ever befall her while she was with North.

Octavia was honest. "Not really, no."

"He could take you anywhere!"

"I know." That was all part of the adventure. Really, could she and Beatrice possibly be any more dissimilar?

Her little cousin was scandalized to be sure. "For all you know, he could be planning to ravish you!"

She should be so fortunate. "He is not." If her tone wasn't convincing, the face she made should be.

"How do you know?" Beatrice sank onto the bed, apparently done in. One hand pressed against her impressive bosom while the other clutched weakly at the patchwork quilt at the foot of the mattress.

Oh good Lord, she was as bad as North with her prodding and poking. "Because, you twit, I know him! He would never behave so poorly."

Beatrice didn't seem to mind at all being called a twit. "You *used* to know him. He could have changed drastically in the last decade."

He had, but not in the ways that truly mattered. Of course, he avoided the real world as often as possible, but he was still her sweet Norrie. He would never hurt her, never compromise her, never put her in a dangerous position unless she asked him too.

And promises be damned, she was very tempted to ask. After all the years between them, North Sheffield was still the only man who ever made her feel quite so warm, quite so weak in the knees and shivery all over.

"Do not fret, Bea," she assured, going to the dressing table to dab a little more perfume behind her ears. "I am safe with North. Of that you can be certain."

Still dubious, Beatrice pursed her lips. "You are excited about it, aren't you?"

How easy it was to feign innocence. "About what?"

"Whatever it is he has planned. You are practically dancing in anticipation." She made that sound like a bad thing.

"I am not!" Why was she even bothering to deny it? She knew in her heart that it was true. Yes, in her heart she was dancing a jig at double time.

Beatrice was adamant, pointing a finger at her cousin. "You are, and I know what it means."

Octavia dabbed perfume on her wrists as well. "Then pray tell, enlighten me."

Beatrice rose from the bed, approaching her as cautiously

as a hunter to a fawn—every step wary and silent. "I remember what you were like when Grandfather took you in. I know how hard you worked to please him by changing yourself into something else, but you never changed, Octavia. People do not change like that. You are simply playing a part, something you have always done too well for your own good."

Fustian. "Do not talk so loose."

"It is true. I can see it in your eyes."

The perfume bottle hit the vanity surface with a loud thud. "Lord, Bea, you are a dog with a bone! Can you not gnaw in silence?" Why wouldn't the woman simply shut her mouth? Silence, that was all Octavia wanted.

But her cousin would not be moved from her course. "You can hardly wait for Mr. Sheffield to arrive. You are hoping he will take you someplace where you can be who you really are, with no one to tell on you when it is over. Tomorrow you will go back to being Lady Octavia, but tonight you are going to drop all pretenses, and I dearly hope both you and Mr. Sheffield are prepared for any and all consequences."

Beatrice was talking nonsense. "What consequences? For goodness' sake, Beatrice! We are simply going to a party, not an orgy!"

Blossom pink bloomed high on her cousin's cheeks. "Do not talk to me as though I do not know you, Octavia. It would not matter if Mr. Sheffield was taking you to church; if no one there knew you, the results would be the same. I have never met anyone who needs to have her own way as you do. It is not because you are selfish, it is just the way you are. You have denied your own nature for years, and if you expect to make up for it in one night, I pity all of London."

Octavia laughed; she couldn't help it. "You really must do something about that imagination of yours." Still, she couldn't deny certain truths in her cousin's words. Yes, she was looking forward to having a night as herself, when she didn't have to put on airs or watch what she said, but she wasn't hoping North would take her to a place where she knew no one. She wanted to go see old friends. She wanted to see people she used to know, people who used to know her. And for a night, she wanted to experience what it was like to be herself again.

Have her own way? By God, yes she would. She deserved it. Selfish or not, she planned to have it.

Some of the fight seemed to have drained from her cousin, replaced with nothing more than loving concern. That irked Octavia even more than the nagging. Dear Bea, she only wanted what was best for her. Could she not see that Octavia wanted the same thing? "You will be careful, will you not?"

"Of course. I am not naturally reckless." Not anymore, at any rate. No, not ever. Even her most foolish decisions had been the result of what she had believed at the time to be much serious contemplation.

Or at the urging of others.

Beatrice didn't look convinced. "Bea, I will have North with me. I will be perfectly safe, I assure you."

"It is with Mr. Sheffield that I fear for you the most."

Octavia rolled her eyes. Not this again. "With North? Why, it is his duty to protect me!"

"Who is going to protect you from him? Or for that matter, him from you?"

A bark of disbelieving laughter broke forth from Octavia's chest. "Neither of us need protecting from each other! Why can you not believe that?"

"I have seen the way you look at him, Octavia, the way he watches you when neither of you realize your masks have slipped. You look at him like a woman looks at a desirable man, and he gazes upon you like a thirsty man upon a cool stream."

"That's absurd!" But her heart tripped at it all the same.

Did North really look at her that way? And why did she want him to? Friends shouldn't behave in such a scandalous manner. But she and North were so much more than friends—what, she couldn't exactly say.

"Whatever existed between you all those years ago, even if it was nothing more than friendship, has grown. Neither of you are children anymore, Octavia. North Sheffield is a grown man, and he will not be easy for you to control—or control yourself around, I fear."

Such blunt speaking was astounding coming out of Beatrice's mouth—and vaguely insulting. "Your opinion of me is not so very flattering, Bea. I can control myself just fine, and so, I am certain, can North."

Beatrice's dark gaze was shrewd—too shrewd. "If you say so."

But Octavia wasn't ready to give up just yet. "Whatever it is you *perceive* exists between us is nothing more than joy at seeing each other again. You cannot imagine how lovely it is to have North in my life again, and now, thanks to his insinuating himself into my life, I may count on having him in my future as well."

Her cousin's expression was one of surprise. "My dear Octavia, you do realize that even this charade of Mr. Sheffield's will not enable you to see him again once he has captured your admirer."

No, she did not realize that. Why would she realize that? Now that she and North were known by the public to be acquaintances—even recent ones—there would be no reason that they could not be seen together at a later date. Was there? "Why not?"

"Because he is supposed to try to steal you away from Lord Spinton. It would hardly be seemly to ever be seen in public with him again."

She was right. Good God, why hadn't she thought of that herself? More than likely it hadn't occurred to her because she hadn't allowed it to. She had just found North again. She wasn't prepared to let him go.

It didn't matter whether Spinton discovered the truth about her past. Even if he knew she and North were old friends, she would never be able to spend time with North again, not without causing more than a few tongues to wag.

And no doubt North already knew this himself. No doubt he had known it from the very beginning. He never had any intention of being part of her future. He was going to walk out of her life yet again and expect her to pretend that he meant nothing to her. Worse yet, he was going to continue pretending that she meant nothing to him. Perhaps he could do that, but she didn't know if she could.

No, that wasn't true. She knew she could, because she would have to. There wouldn't be a choice—not if she was going to have the life laid out for her.

What was that North had said to her about living by the rules? There was a time when she would have sneered at a woman like herself, worried about what someone might say, what someone might think. But it wasn't for herself that she worried. She didn't want to do anything that might reflect badly upon Beatrice, Spinton, her grandfather, or even North. She really didn't care if people talked about her, but then she had promised her mother and grandfather that she would live up to their expectations of her.

"I know this must be difficult for you to accept," Beatrice was saying, "but you gave up all ties with your past for a reason—because they are a hindrance to the future you decided to pursue."

The future her grandfather chose for her. The future she agreed to because she hadn't known how much it would hurt to give up everything else. At the time she had wanted to be a lady, had jumped at the chance to have expensive things and socialize among London's finest.

What had she known? She'd been a stupid girl, too young to know that wealth wasn't everything and that London's finest didn't necessarily equate to London's best.

"Yes," she heard herself reply. "I know. North and I can never be anything but passing acquaintances at the most."

"The very most."

"Yes." The word was bitter on her tongue.

Beatrice's tone was kind. "I know you believe him to be the best of men, but you must promise me that you will be on your guard with him."

Still, Octavia persisted. "I do not need to be on guard with North."

Beatrice was not convinced. "He has attracted the notice of quite a few mamas with marriageable daughters. These women could guarantee him a spot in the lower orders of society, yet he has not married. Why is that?"

"Because all those girls are insipid and foolish." Or perhaps because he had never found anyone to compare to her . . . ? How could she even entertain such a vain notion?

"Or perhaps he is hoping to land a bigger fish—a bigger fortune."

If this did not stop soon, Octavia was going to do her cousin a violence. "Do not talk about him like that. You do not know him."

"Nor do you, not anymore." Ah, another well-placed jab. Well, she still knew North better than Beatrice ever thought to.

"I know him well enough to know he is no fortune hunter. He has his own fortune."

Beatrice ran her fingers over the edge of the vanity mirror, not meeting Octavia's gaze. "But what about rank? Surely he must envy his brothers' social standing."

He did—or rather he had. "No, I do not think he cares anymore. He is happy where he is."

Now Beatrice looked at her, driving her point home with her wide gaze. "Well, either way, it is just one more reason to make certain you do not form any attachments."

"Yes." One more reason not to form any attachments.

Too bad she was already attached. How fixedly, she had no idea.

Chapter 8

When North finally called to collect her later that evening, Octavia could scarce believe her eyes.

He stood in her parlor, dressed in a simply styled dark
gray coat and matching trousers that, while far from elegant,
fit and suited him perfectly. His waistcoat was a lighter gray,
a subtle contrast to the snowy white shirt beneath, which
was startling next to the tanned neck revealed by the open
collar. He wore no neckcloth, no intricately tied cravat that
so many gentlemen favored. His throat was completely bare,
followed by a wide V of chest. She could see the jut of one
collarbone and a teasing glimpse of the beginnings of his
chest hair.

It was, she realized, shocking to her now to see a man without a cravat, when she used to see it all the time in the Garden.

It was then that she knew that wherever he was taking her,
there was definitely no chance of them being spotted by any
member of the *ton*. In fact, he might very well be taking her
somewhere dark and dangerous—someplace where she
would be totally at his mercy.

Nonsense. Beatrice might believe him capable of such deceit, but Octavia wouldn't. She trusted him with her very life.

"Don't you look every inch the rakish scoundrel."

He grinned, a flash of straight, white teeth. "And you look like you should be selling cheese or something equally countryish."

It was true. She wore her hair in a simple knot, with just a few tendrils wisping about her cheeks. Her gown was a simple design of dark blue muslin without a hint of embellishment or trim. She wore no jewelry and a pair of slippers that she should have thrown out long ago, but were too comfortable to give up. She had a serviceable shawl in her hand in case the temperature dropped as the evening went on. She hadn't even bothered with gloves.

She felt sixteen again, and she and North were about to sneak out to somewhere they had no business going.

Yes, that was the reason for this tremor of excitement racing down her spine, the anticipation tightening her chest. It was that old feeling of being young and free. It had nothing to do with the way he was looking at her or the way she liked looking at him.

"Are you ready?" he asked.

She nodded, the butterflies in her stomach protesting fiercely. "I am."

Another grin as he held out his hand. "Then let us away."

Unable to keep herself from smiling, she took his hand and allowed those strong warm fingers to pull her out of the parlor, down the corridor, through the foyer, and outside into the mild evening.

A dusty black carriage waited for them.

"I hope you do not mind," North said, as he helped her down the steps. "I hired a hack. I thought someone might recognize yours."

"What about your own?" she asked as she climbed inside.

The hack's interior smelled of tobacco—a little stale, but it could have been much worse.

Leaping in behind her, North made a scoffing noise. "I do not own one." He rapped on the ceiling for the driver to move on.

Her eyes widened as the carriage lurched forward. He didn't own a carriage? Everyone she knew owned at least one, preferably several.

"Whyever not?"

He pulled a face. "What would I want with a carriage? I walk everywhere I can and I have a horse for those places I cannot. A carriage would only collect dust."

Not the words or attitude of a fortune hunter, she thought smugly. She would have to repeat his words to Beatrice later.

"Where are we going?"

"It is a surprise. You still like surprises, do you not?"

She rolled her eyes. "Yes. I have not changed as much as you seem to think, Norrie Sheffield."

The light of a street lamp shone through the window, illuminating his face as they rolled past. He was smiling, his eyes bright with mirth and something else—anticipation, perhaps?

"We shall soon find out. Within the hour I hope to know if you are still my dear girl."

She arched a brow. Cheeky blighter. "Girl? Girls grow up, my friend."

"What do they grow into, women or ladies?"

She frowned. "Can they not be both?"

"I suppose that is what we are about to find out."

Was she a lady or a woman? Or both? It was a question he would dearly love to know the answer to. The girl he had once known—once loved—would have grown into a fine woman. A lot like the one seated across from him now, he'd wager. But the other Octavia, the one she had lived as for the last dozen years, was a lady through and through. Perhaps it was possible to be both, but not in his experience. He had tried very hard to be a gentleman once upon a time, but eventually he realized what kind of man he wanted to be, and "gentle" wasn't it. So who was Octavia, really? Was she the lady she tried so hard to project, or was she the woman he hoped she would be?

Perhaps she was someone else entirely.

The point of this evening was his own selfish wishes and desires. He wanted to spend time with Octavia—*his* Octavia. He wanted to give them both the chance to be themselves, without the fear of anyone seeing. He wanted a chance to get to know her again—the real her—and he wanted her to know him. She seemed to think he was that same romantic, horribly naive boy, and he wasn't. Not anymore. Although sometimes he missed that young man. He used to think he could have whatever he wanted. Now he knew better. If that were true, Black Sally would still be alive and Harker would be locked up in Newgate instead of terrorizing what few people North knew had enough information to make certain Harker's jailers threw away the key.

But Harker didn't matter tonight. Tonight all that mattered was Vie and these few stolen hours. It was wrong, but he would absolve himself from the guilt for this one night. All too soon she would be gone from him again—for good this time. Lord Spinton would never allow his countess to socialize with someone of his ilk. It was only because he was useful that Spinton allowed him within twenty feet of Octavia now.

If Spinton only knew . . . but he never would.

"Will you tell me now where we are going?" They had been in the hack but a few moments and already she was asking questions, like a child on a long journey, eager to get to the final destination.

He smiled at her excitement. How young it made her seem. "Not yet. Soon."

The party was at an old friend's house on Half Moon Street—in the opposite corner of the Garden from where North lived. He would have hosted it at his own house if he hadn't known how difficult it would be to clear everyone out when he wanted them gone. This way, if Octavia wanted to leave, or they decided to go do something else, he wouldn't have to worry about all those people.

Octavia addressed him, her face bright with curiosity. "Will there be dancing?"

He nodded. "I suspect there will be."

"And drinking?"

"Without a doubt."

"And music and laughter and conversation about things that truly matter?"

Laughing, North rubbed his jaw. He should have shaved earlier. "Yes, yes, and yes. Are you happy now?"

"Oh yes!" She even went so far as to clap her hands, dear thing. "You have no idea how long it has been since I've had real fun. Will we have fun tonight, do you think, Norrie?"

Good Lord, what kind of life had she been living in that ivory tower of hers? The hopeful exuberance in her face and tone damned near broke his heart. "I will make sure of it."

She bestowed a smile on him so bright it was almost blinding in the darkness. "I know you will. We always used to have so much fun. Do you remember those times?"

"Yes." With painful clarity. He remembered being young and happy and free of any cares when he and Octavia were together. And although many years had passed and he had become a jaded and cynical man, there was an element of that feeling to this night. Even though the hack smelled and had seen better days, and was certainly too low for a countess, and their clothes were far from the height of fashion, North was already having the best evening he'd had in the last, oh, eleven or twelve years.

Octavia sighed, leaning back against the dusty squabs, oblivious to the damage they could do to her gown. "I miss those times. Do you ever miss them?"

"I miss the good."

"I do not remember the bad." Her smile was saucy.

He raised a brow. "What about the time Jonesy tried to court you?"

She laughed. "He lit so many candles in the parlor, he almost caught his pantaloons on fire!" Her laughter faded to a smile. "Poor Jonesy. If it were not for the fact that he was already dead I might have suspected *him* of being my admirer."

North smiled too, remembering the old man who fancied himself quite a Lothario.

"He was a good man." So many of the men who hung about Covent Garden hadn't been, but he didn't have to say that. Octavia knew firsthand. She had seen her mother take lovers, seen some of them treat her badly. A few had even tried to take Octavia as their own, but somehow she avoided them all. Her mother managed to protect her, but then her mother died.

She had come to him that night, so sure of how her life was going to be. She was resigned to being a mistress, she said, but he saw the doubt and fear in her eyes. She wanted him to be her first lover, didn't want some dirty aristocrat to have that satisfaction.

Dirty aristocrat. Those were her words, not his. Now she was one of them.

They talked more about the past and the people they had known. She surprised him by knowing details about many of them. Obviously she had kept in touch with some old friends. Odd, he thought she would have given up that part of her life with all the others.

The carriage finally rolled to a stop a little while later. Before he could stop her, Octavia had her face close to the dirty window, peering out into the darkness.

"We are in the Garden." She turned to him with an expression of dazed wonder. "We are in Half Moon."

Opening the door, North stepped out and offered her his hand. "Come."

Octavia's mouth gaped slightly as she accepted his help down. She glanced around at the familiar setting, her eyes bright in the moonlight. "This is Margaret's house."

So she did remember. "Yes. Shall we go in?"

"I have not seen Margaret in years." Dear Lord, was she going to cry? She certainly looked as though she was.

"If you do not want to—"

"No." She squeezed his fingers hard with her own. "I want to. I want to."

Holding her hand, North walked beside her up the low steps and knocked on the door. Perhaps he had made a mistake bringing her here. Perhaps too much time had passed. Perhaps the past was all they had.

Perhaps there really wasn't much of his Octavia left at all.

She was amazing.

Leaning against the wall, a glass of punch in hand, North watched as Octavia whirled about the floor with yet another partner, kicking up her heels and twirling her skirts as the band played a lively reel.

Sometime during the course of the evening—after several glasses of punch—her hair had come loose, great chunks falling around her face until she'd finally yanked the pins from the heavy strands and let it fall down her back in a great, wonderful mess.

Her gown was dark between her shoulder blades from perspiration. Her cheeks glowed warm peach from her exertions, and yet she looked perfectly content. No, she looked *happy*. So happy that just watching her made him happy—happier than he'd been in some time.

Wouldn't Wyn have something to say about that? Wouldn't Devlin? Wyn might be caustic, but Devlin was still in the early stages of marriage and believed a good woman to be the perfect source of happiness for any man.

And Octavia was a good woman, of that there could be no doubt. There was no hint of the lady about her at all as she skipped and whirled to the music. She was very close to being the Vie he remembered.

But there was more. She wasn't that girl anymore than he was still that boy. The essence was the same, but she had grown, blossomed. There was no denying she was fully mature—her figure was as ripe as a midsummer peach, though all willowy grace. There were years in her face, though child-like joy shone in her eyes.

She was more beautiful now than she had ever been, even more so than the night he had given her his heart, his soul, his innocence. He had traded his for hers. And at this moment, his heart was so light, so content that he allowed himself to think that perhaps he retained some of that innocence still. Just a drop—not enough to matter, just enough to hurt.

It was lovely to watch her, but hell knowing that eventually this night would end and he would have to take her back to Mayfair. Eventually he would find out who was sending her those damned letters and then there would be no reason to see her again. This might be the only time he got to see her so unfettered, so alive.

So what was he doing standing against the bloody wall while some other bloke danced with her?

Tossing back the rest of his punch, he set the empty glass on a nearby table and walked out into the middle of the floor where Octavia danced with her young swain.

"My turn, Posenby," he told the young man, tapping him

on the shoulder. Posenby merely grinned, bowed to Octavia, and went in search of another partner.

"Norrie!" Octavia threw her arms around him.

"No more punch for you," he admonished with a grin, peeling her arms from his neck.

She grinned. "You think I have had too much to drink, but I haven't. I've had just enough."

"Enough for what?"

"Enough to have fun and not care about tomorrow!" She grabbed his hands in hers. "Dance with me."

"With pleasure." He didn't bother telling her that had been his intention in the first place. It didn't matter.

The music was lively and played with rural zeal. Some of the tunes they played were Scottish. North recognized them as melodies his mother used to hum. It had been a long time since he'd danced to such music, but that didn't matter. All he had to do was be quick on his feet and he was as good as dancing.

"Are you having a good time?" he asked as he twirled her around.

She gasped and laughed. "I am having a lovely time, thank you!"

Her words brought him more pleasure than they ought to have. "I am glad."

"You should be." Her smile was blinding. "It is all because of you, you know. If not for you I would be at a ball somewhere, listening to ladies gossip about each other."

Grabbing her about the waist, he whirled her around the floor to the rousing music. "Sounds dreadfully dull."

"Oh it is, it is. Not like this. Spinton would hate this."

"Yes, he probably would."

"But I adore it. I adore you. Always have."

"Me too." Had she any idea how deeply her words touched him? Obviously not, or she would not toss them about so carelessly.

"I have seen so many old friends tonight. I cannot believe it. Did you arrange this just for me?"

He could lie, but what would be the point? He wanted nothing more than to see her smile again. "I did."

He was not disappointed. Her smile was like a beacon in the dark. "Thank you!" Pulling from his embrace, she wrapped her arms about his neck. Laughing, North wrapped his around her waist and lifted her off her feet, swinging her around as though she weighed no more than a child. She squealed and clung to him all the tighter, but her laughter was pure delight.

The music ended as he set her down. She swayed visibly on her feet. Then her gaze locked with his.

"It is time to leave, Norrie."

So soon? Was she ill? "Do you want to go back to Mayfair?"

"No. Not yet." Her gaze was dark and intent. "Take me to your house. Take me home."

Octavia knew going to North's was a mistake, but she couldn't bring herself to care. Ever since he'd revealed that he had engineered that party just for her, all she wanted was to be alone with him. Just a little more time with just the two of them before she had to return to reality.

"Oh! You have turned the parlor into an office!"

He tossed his coat onto a chair. "I do not have much use for a parlor."

"I like it." She twirled around on the carpet. "Is this where you keep your wine?"

"No," he replied with a patient smile. "I think you have had enough to drink."

She stopped twirling. Thought she was foxed, did he? "Not yet. Not until you have a glass with me."

He smiled. "All right. Claret?"

"Please."

She watched him cross the carpet to a cupboard on the far wall, his shoulders swaying with masculine grace, his trousers caressing his buttocks and thighs. Her body hummed at the mere sight of him. Oh, but he had always had that effect on her. He was the finest, most handsome, physically perfect man she had ever seen.

And to think she had been his first lover. The first woman to ever touch that chest, that glorious back. No matter how many other women he had lain with, she would always have the pleasure of knowing that somewhere, in the back of his mind, he had compared them all to her.

God help her, she hoped it wasn't she who came up lacking.

He came back to her. Brazenly, she admired his front as well. He handed her a glass. There wasn't much wine in it.

"I am not drunk, Norrie." No, if she were drunk, she would be numb and wouldn't feel this fire burning inside her. If she were drunk, she could excuse her thoughts, but she was just sober enough to know that what she was thinking was wrong.

But not sober enough to stop thinking them.

He swallowed his claret in one gulp. The tilt of his head allowed her to watch his Adam's apple bob as he swallowed. What a lovely throat. Did all men have such nice throats? It seemed a shame to cover them with stocks and such if they did. There was something about North's neck that made her want to bury her face in the crook between it and his shoulder.

"Do you want more?" He asked.

"Oh *yes*." Then she realized he was talking about the wine. "No, thank you. I think you are right. I have had enough."

He frowned. "Are you not feeling well?"

She ought to tell him not to come any closer, but she couldn't convince her tongue to form the words.

"N-no. I am fine." *Not nearly as fine as you.*

"Are you certain?" He rubbed his hand over his jaw. He hadn't shaved earlier. She liked it.

"You looked lovely tonight."

He chuckled, his eyes lighting with amusement. "Customarily the man says such flattery to the lady."

Octavia shrugged, her muscles as wine-loosened as her tongue. "One day you shall make the face of heaven fine, Norrie."

He took her empty glass, and set it, along with his own, on the desk behind him. "You are foxed, Vie."

"Perhaps. Perhaps I have lost some of my reason, but that does not stop me from wanting to kiss you, dear friend."

"Octavia," he said, backing away. "This is folly."

"Too rash, too unadvised. Yes, I know. Kiss me, North. Just this once. I want to taste you again. I miss your taste."

He would have backed away if not for the desk preventing his escape. Never in her life had Octavia been so thankful for a piece of furniture.

Well, except for North's bed twelve years ago, of course.

Running her hand up his chest, Octavia rubbed the crisp hair peeking out of his open shirt. Her other hand came up behind his neck, holding him with all her strength as she lifted herself up on her toes to press her lips against his.

He was as immobile as a statue, as unyielding as rock, and yet he still felt better than anything she'd felt in a long, long time. Was he truly that immune to her? No, he wasn't. She could feel the evidence of her effect on him hard against her hip. He wanted her and yet he resisted. Why? She was offering him whatever he wanted to take and was asking nothing in return, save that he give her exactly what her body—what *she*—demanded.

Finally, she pulled away. "It is different. You do not taste as you did that night."

"It is the absence of tears."

"Ahh yes." She remembered now. "We both cried that night, didn't we?"

He nodded. "We did."

Her fingers traced the lines bracketing his mouth. "You were so sweet, so gentle."

"I was foolish and fumbling and I made an idiot of myself."

"You were perfect. Do not ever think otherwise."

Before he could argue further with her, she pressed herself against the solid warmth of him, feeling his heart beating against her chest, the heat of him seeping through the thin fabric of her gown. Lifting herself on her toes, she placed her mouth on his—without hesitancy, without regret.

Oh, but he tasted divine! All man and sweetness. Mindlessly, she devoured him, licking at him with her tongue, nipping with her teeth. And when the muscles in his arms tightened beneath her hands, when she felt the hardness of his erection press into her hip, she groaned in triumph. Such power came in the knowledge that his body responded to her.

But instead of holding her as she wanted, he pushed her away.

His breathing was shallow, his eyes bright. "Do not tempt me, Vie."

Wantonly, she shifted her hips against his. "Are you tempted, Norrie?"

He growled low in his throat—she was certain she heard him growl. "Hell, yes."

"By what?" She trailed her fingers up his arm. "The chance for a tumble, or by me?"

"By you. Only you."

Then his fingers were in her hair, pulling and massaging at her scalp, and it was she who now ran the risk of being devoured. She didn't care.

Her fingers—far less nimble than she would have liked—

fumbled with the fastenings on his waistcoat, stripping the offensive garment from him in quick, jerky tugs. No sooner had she dispensed with it than her hands seized the soft linen of his shirt, pulling it free of his trousers, plowing her hands underneath, caressing the silky flesh of his back and ribs as she shoved the fabric upward. Still he did not stop her. In fact, he broke their kiss so that she could pull the shirt over his head, and then he balled it up and tossed it to the floor.

He was so beautiful, so overwhelmingly male, so vibrantly sensual. The sight of him made her tremble, the sound of his breathing raised the delicate hairs on her limbs, and the look in his eyes tightened the tips of her breasts.

"So very fine." Her lips pressed against his shoulder, her tongue snaking out to lick the salty flesh there. "Dear Lord, who would ever think a man could taste as good as you?" And he did taste good. He was tangy sweet, warm and firm beneath her hands and mouth. That skinny boy was gone, replaced by a man all muck and muscle, as her mother used to say. But he was still her boy, her Norrie, and he filled her senses like no spirit or opiate ever could—twice as potent and ever more addictive.

And she, unrepentant wanton that she was, wanted to twine herself around him, take him into herself until she tumbled into the darkness of oblivion.

"Ach," she whispered in a Scottish lilt, pressing his mouth to his throat. The pulse there beat heavily against her lips. "You are bonny and fine, Norrie Sheffield."

His arms stiffened, putting distance between them. "Do not mock me, Vie."

"Mock you?" She reached for him, unable to keep herself away from that golden flesh. "I love the sound of your voice. I always have, especially now that you do not try to hide your accent."

His eyes were pale stones in the rigid set of his face. Anyone else might mistake his expression for one of anger, but not Octavia. He was trying to fight the attraction between them—trying to fight *her*.

"I adore almost everything about you." Her hands slid up the solid wall of his chest, the crisp hair tickling her palms. "I adore *you*, North. I always have. You are and always will be one of my dearest—"

"Memories," he cut her off. "Promise me after we find this admirer of yours you will make me a memory, Vie. It is the way it has to be, we both know that."

"Why?" She winced at the whine in her voice. "We cannot be friends because I had the advantage of being born legitimate? That is stupid!"

He held her at arm's length, despite how she struggled to free herself from the forced separation. "Maybe so, but that is the way I want it. Nothing good will come of our association— not for you."

"*You* are good, Norrie. Regardless of everything else, you are still the only person who knows the real me, whom I can trust with all my secrets and know that you will never turn your back."

His expression was resolute as he relaxed his arms. She took advantage and stepped closer. "Not when you need me, no. But I will turn my back on you when this is over, and unless you are in danger I won't ever come back."

He meant it, and it hurt her beyond his knowing to hear him say it.

She lifted her face to his, her fingers kneading deep into the muscles of his shoulders. "Then give me something to hold on to. Something to remember you by." She couldn't— wouldn't—let go of him. Not yet. Not when she had just found him again. She didn't know if this was lust or desperation or something else entirely, but the need to hang on to him, hang on to the one thing in her life that had ever been good and pure and hers alone, was all-consuming.

She slid her hands up to his neck, his jaw, his face, cupping his head with her hands, twining her fingers in the glossy curls of his hair. Her body she pressed to his, feeling the heat of him through the fabric of her gown.

"Kiss me. Kiss me and then I will let you go." Begging, blackmail, coercion, she didn't care. She had no pride, no shame where North was concerned. She never had.

She didn't have to beg twice. He did kiss her, and when his lips touched hers, she opened herself to his plunder, matching every lash of his tongue, every taste with one of her own. If she could climb up him, she would. If she could merge their two bodies into one whole, she would—that was how desperate she was to have him. The control she prized above all else was ready to snap, and she did not care.

In fact, she wanted to lose control. She wanted this man— her Norrie—in a most violent fashion. She wanted his possession, wanted to possess him, and if it left her bruised and tender, aching with reminders of his passion, then so much the better.

Again he pushed her away. Why couldn't he give up his control as well? It hadn't been this difficult to seduce him before.

"God, Vie, this has got to stop."

"Not yet." She raised her gaze to his. "It has been so long since I felt this way, Norrie. Not since that night."

His eyes burned with icy fire as raw as the low timbre of his voice. "There has been no one else?"

"No one." The room seemed to shrink around them as she raised her fingers yet again to his cheek. "Just you, my dearest friend."

Something changed then. The air thickened, becoming more difficult to breathe. The temperature soared, damping her hairline with perspiration. Everything swam out of focus save for the harsh male beauty of North. He stared at her as though he could sense the direction of her thoughts, the tingling deep inside. And she knew that if he made love to her this night, he would not be foolish and fumbling.

Desperately, North tried to collect himself, but to no avail. He hauled her flush against him, bruising her lips with his own, his tongue ravaging the sweet confines of her mouth. He wanted her with a desperation he had never felt before. Wanted to plunge inside her warm wetness, wanted to feel her wrapped around him until this torment inside him ceased. It had been a mistake to bring her here. He knew that before they left the party, but he couldn't bring himself to feel sorry for it, not even now, knowing she was another man's fiancée.

No, technically, she wasn't Spinton's fiancée. She had agreed to discuss marriage with him after this investigation was over. She wore no ring. Not yet.

And a good thing that was too, as she was clawing at his clothes like a cat trying to get to a mouse. Lucky for him, he enjoyed being mauled.

But this wasn't how he wanted things to be between them. He didn't want to make love to her when her judgment was so impaired. Oh, perhaps she knew what she was doing, but he didn't want to give her the opportunity to hide behind her drunkenness once he returned her to her own world. If they made love again, it would be when both of them had clear minds, were aware of the consequences, and there could be no recriminations between them.

Groaning, he broke the contact between their mouths, caught her insistent hands in his, and shoved her—gently—away. God give him strength, he would not be able to refuse her again, not with his control stretched so thinly.

"Octavia, no."

Her lips red, her eyes wide, she stared at him. "Why not?"

"Because I do not take advantage of foxed women."

She stomped her foot. "I am not foxed!"

Her blatant lie made him want to smile. He resisted the urge. "You are close enough."

"I do not care."

"You will care in the morning, when you wake up in my bed." Just the thought of it made him throb. "You know I am right."

Dark, slightly unfocused eyes blazed. "No, I will not. I am tired of doing the right thing all the time. I want to do what I want. I want to have my own way. Give me my own way!"

He shouldn't, but he couldn't help but laugh at her petulant tone. How ironic. The one time she was prepared to not care about what others thought, or the consequences of her actions, and he couldn't take advantage. "Not when I know you will regret it later."

Her fingers tightened around his as her expression softened. "I do not regret making love to you twelve years ago, North. I would not regret doing so again tonight."

North swallowed hard. He believed her. Drunk or not, she would not regret lying with him. Maybe she wouldn't regret the act, but she might regret the consequences.

Warm, liquor-sweet breath fanned his face. "Do you know why I promised my mother I would become a lady, North?"

He wasn't sure he wanted to hear this. "No."

Suddenly her gaze seemed infinitely clear. "I knew how much you wanted to belong to society. I thought that if I became a lady that you might . . . but you never did."

He stared at her. There were so many things that she could be alluding to, but in his heart he knew exactly what she meant.

"I did." Pulling one of his hands free of hers, he lifted it to her cheek. "Oh, Vie, I did and I wanted to, but—"

"But you knew my grandfather wanted you to stay away."

"Yes." Of course he knew. The old man had told him in no uncertain terms.

Her mouth tightened as her chin trembled the slightest bit. "You found it easy enough to do that."

How could he explain so that she would understand? It was for the best. What kind of life would they have had?

"It was a fantasy, Vie. It wasn't real."

"No, Norrie." She pulled free of his grasp. "What we are doing now, the lives we live, *those* are not real. Our friendship was as real and true as anything you or I have ever experienced. The rest has all been lying, something we both are entirely too good at."

What could he possibly say to that? He wanted to deny it, to tell her she was fooling herself, that they had been living in a dream world back then and *this* was reality, but he couldn't.

"And what is the most sad," she continued, her voice hoarse with what he feared might be tears, "is that we have been lying for so long, we no longer know how to be ourselves. It is so much safer to be someone else."

"Vie—"

"Thank you for a lovely evening, North, but I think it is time that I returned to Mayfair."

She still hadn't referred to her house as home. Only his house had that distinction. Right now he didn't want to entertain the meaning behind it.

He didn't even bother to straighten his shirt as he shrugged on his coat. He'd paid the hackney driver to wait outside. He'd see her back to her house and then he'd go around to Wyn's and see what he was up to. He couldn't come back here right away, not with the scent of her still lingering.

Because for the brief time she'd spent there, the house actually felt like home.

Chapter 9

North was either the noblest man in England, or the stupidest. One thing for certain, Fitzwilliam Markham, Lord Spinton, was without a doubt the luckiest. North hoped the earl's luck would hold out and Octavia wouldn't kill Spinton on their wedding night.

Lying in the middle of his bed among rumpled, sun-dappled sheets, North rubbed his palm over his stubbled cheek. God knew Octavia was going to be the death of *him*. He couldn't survive another interlude like last night's. He wouldn't be able to stand against her. It was only the fact that she hadn't had all her wits about her that stopped him. Thankfully she hadn't been sober.

Even sober she was a temptress of mythical proportions.

What would Spinton think of that? His lady bride was *not* going to be very ladylike in the bedroom. In fact, she was going to be all woman, with all the needs, desires, and demands that came with that soft, luscious flesh. She would be wasted on a proper dolt like Spinton.

North would make certain none of her went to waste.

Christ, if last night was any indication, there would be nothing left of either of them by the time they were done. The want—nay, *need*—for her had been so intense, so incredibly strong, it scared the shite out of him. Never before had he ever experienced such a sensation. He'd actually thought he might die if he didn't have her. It had taken all his strength to refuse her.

Too bad he couldn't take comfort in his noble gesture. He should have screwed her. That would teach her to get foxed and tempt poor defenseless men. Weak, randy men.

But he didn't want to simply "screw" Octavia. *That* was what saved her. He wanted her in his bed, completely aware of what was happening to her. He wanted clarity in her gaze when he buried himself inside her. God knew he would be acutely aware of every inch of her wrapped around every inch of him. He wanted no less from her—and he wanted her to come to him fully prepared to face the consequences of letting him possess her.

And there would be consequences. There always were. Consequences were what made a difference between simple screwing and what the poets called "making love." How apt that was. Love was often one of those consequences. He had faced that one with Octavia once before. Could he risk facing it again?

No, the risk was just too great. To give her his heart once more and then let her walk out of his life was beyond him. Letting her go once was noble. Twice would be the height of stupidity.

She hadn't been with anyone else. The knowledge was staggering. Twelve years, and the only man to have ever touched her—to have ever been inside her—was he. What he had done to deserve such an honor, he had no idea. He knew only that Spinton would soon rob him of it, and that he would rather saw off his own arm than see that happen.

North pushed the sheets down around his hips. He was too warm, too hard, and a little too late for such jealousy. Spinton would be good to Octavia. His insistence that North investigate these mysterious letters was proof enough of that. He even risked Octavia's wrath to ensure her safety. He was wealthy and powerful and well liked among the *ton*, and he had the benefit of having been handpicked by Octavia's grandfather. North, of course, had been decidedly unwanted as far as marrying into the family was concerned.

He doubted the old curmudgeon even told Octavia that North had come to visit the morning her grandfather took her. And he would bet money that the old man certainly never told her that North had been prepared to propose marriage. Of course he hadn't. Octavia had been so surprised by his admission that day in Hyde Park.

Her grandfather had smiled, told him he was a good boy, and then asked him to never come near his granddaughter again.

She deserves better. I am sure you can understand that.

Sadly enough, he could.

No, Spinton would be a good husband to Octavia. More importantly, they belonged to the same world. Spinton would never bring lowlifes or criminal types into their house.

Spinton probably wouldn't play at foolish games with her either. Spinton wouldn't make an ass of himself just to see Octavia smile. And Spinton wouldn't have to watch her marry another man, knowing someone else was going to kiss those lips, stroke that skin . . .

And she had the nerve to tell him he was living a lie. That they both were. He had little doubt that her life was nothing more than a series of scenes and acts, but *his* was real. Black Sally's grave was proof of that.

Although Octavia had been correct when she said that their friendship had been real. The most treasured friend of his life, she was. She always would be. A part of him would always adore her, always want her. But he could never, ever make the mistake of having her. If he made love to her again, he would never want to let her go. And he had to let her go. It was what was best, for both of them. She wasn't safe in his world, and he would die of boredom in hers.

Still, it might be worth it to have her in his bed again.

"Frig it all!" Tossing back the covers, North swung his feet over the side of the bed and stood. He wasn't accomplishing anything lying in bed daydreaming about his first lover. That had to be why he was feeling this way. Octavia was his first, just as he had been hers; that was why he felt this strange possessiveness where she was concerned. There was nothing else to explain it.

The door to his bedroom burst open just as he was reaching for his dressing gown. Wynthrope strode in as though he owned the place, a cup and saucer in one hand.

"Good morning, brother—dear God, tell me *that* is not for me."

Scowling, North pulled on his gown and tried to ignore the very pointed stare his brother leveled at his groin. "How did you ever guess?"

Wyn merely grinned. "I brought you coffee to get your blood flowing, but I see you are quite awake as it is."

North inhaled the scent of freshly brewed coffee deep into his lungs. He was in no mood for Wyn's teasing. "Just drop it, Wyn."

"You first."

Turning his back on his brother with a grunt of frustration, North willed his erection to wilt before his brother made anymore of a mockery out of him than he already had. "Isn't it a little early for you to be out and about?"

There was the sound of Wynthrope setting the coffee cup on the nightstand. "Yes, but seeing as how I was done sleeping, I thought I would get up and come see my dear brother."

Either flippant or caustic, that was Wyn. There were very few in-betweens.

"Mrs. Bunting gave me this to give to you. Good thing she did not decide to deliver it herself. You might very well have given the old girl a seizure."

North turned. Wyn held out his hand. In it was a note. From the spidery handwriting on the outside, he could tell it was from Francis. He broke the seal.

His brother watched with what appeared to be perfect boredom. "I take it is from one of your associates?"

North nodded. "Francis. I gave him one of the notes Octavia's admirer sent. The paper had a watermark on it. He has found the shop that makes it."

"Well, let's have breakfast and head over there."

North stared at his brother. "You want to come with me?"

A frown marred Wynthrope's otherwise cool countenance. "Yes, why not?"

Shrugging, North collected the cooled cup of coffee and took a drink. "Nothing, just that you've never had an interest in my work before."

"That is not true."

He took another swallow of the hot brew. "I hardly think the one time you were directly involved in the case I was investigating counts."

"It should. I consider that one your most important investigations to date."

Wynthrope might sound blasé, but North knew better. His brother had never forgiven himself for being duped into a life of crime, nor had he forgiven himself for the fact that North left Bow Street rather than turn him in. North, however, was just glad he had been the one to uncover Wyn's involvement and that he managed to get him out of harm's way before he could be arrested.

Wouldn't Harker like to get his hands on that bit of information? It was one more reason for North to tread carefully where the villain was concerned. Normally no one would believe a man of Harker's reputation, but if Harker whispered in the right ears . . .

There was no point in worrying about that now. "There must be some other reason you want to have breakfast and accompany me on business. What is it?"

Wyn rolled his shoulders in a lazy shrug. "Do I have to have a reason?"

"You never do anything without a reason."

The Ryland lopsided smile became a smirk on Wyn's lips. "Feed me and I shall tell you."

"Fine." He was used to his brother's secrecy. "Just let me dress." Setting the cup on its saucer, North turned toward his wardrobe.

"Please do, we cannot have you frightening innocent bystanders with your *turgid* display of virility."

He didn't so much as glance at his brother. "Get out."

Wynthrope chuckled—a sound that made North smile in return—and left the room.

Fifteen minutes later, washed and dressed in buff breeches, dark gray coat, and black hessians, North met his brother downstairs in his office. Wyn was seated at the table, drinking a cup of coffee and staring out the window at the sunny morning.

"What an interesting neighborhood you live in, brother. I just saw some nob relieved of his purse."

Served the "nob" right if he came into the Garden carrying a lot of blunt. "I like it."

Wyn sipped his coffee. "You would."

"What is that supposed to mean?" North demanded, pouring himself a cup from the silver pot. He needed at least two cups just to feel alive some mornings.

Wyn lifted his dark blue gaze. He was almost completely devoid of expression. "Only that from here you have no place to go but up."

North smiled. "I could go down."

"No." Wyn turned his attention back to the window. "I do not think so."

"Don't you start in on me as well." Seating himself on the opposite side of the table, North shot a glance at the view that seemed to so captivate his brother. "There is nothing wrong with my life."

This time there was plenty of expression on Wynthrope's face. He was not impressed. "Of course not, if one considers living among the same criminals you hunt a good way to live."

North took no offense. His brother had a point. "Not everyone that lives here is a criminal. And do not forget that I grew up here. This is my home."

"Then why does it seem more like a mausoleum?"

He looked around. A mausoleum? "It does not."

"Let me give you some advice." Turning in his chair, Wyn lazily crossed one leg over the other. "Those numerous sheets draped in almost every room of this house? They actually have furniture underneath them. If you take the covers off, you can use the furniture to do things on, like eat, sit, or screw."

North rolled his eyes. "Charming, Wyn." But his brother's words cut deeper than he would ever know.

Mrs. Bunting appeared in the doorway with a cart. "Here's your breakfast, Mr. Sheffield. Mr. Ryland, I made poached eggs just for you."

Wynthrope flashed a charming—and surprisingly genuine— grin. "Bunting, my darling, I adore you."

The older woman blushed a charming pink. "You and your sweet talk."

North rolled his eyes. His brother was the only man alive who could use food as an implement of flirtation. Wyn's charm was his holland covers, covering everything he didn't want to face, just like the furniture in North's house.

Wyn didn't understand—or perhaps he did—that taking the covers off would be North's final commitment to staying in Covent Garden and giving up his childhood dreams of leaving it all behind. And that didn't mean leaving it behind for society either. It meant letting go of the past completely. As much as he didn't want to give up the house, he wasn't quite ready to give up those dreams, or his past.

Perhaps when all this was over with Octavia, he'd take the covers off. Perhaps.

Halfway through their meal, North looked up from his sausage and eggs to find his brother watching him.

Wyn's gaze narrowed. "You did not shave."

How very astute. Was he just now noticing? "No, I did not."

A frown appeared. "And you plan to go out in public?"

North let just the right amount of sarcasm creep into his voice. "I do." Even though he had allowed Octavia's investigation to take most of his time, he wasn't about to let up on his pursuit of Harker. He was going to talk to some of his informants throughout the day—uncover Harker's latest movements, discover if anyone else felt like telling what they knew. Then he'd meet with Francis and hear what he had found out about the paper Octavia's admirer used. That watermark should tell them something.

"You do not give a fig what you look like, do you?"

"Not a one." And it was true. He didn't care what he looked like. No, that was untrue. Sometimes he cared when Octavia was around. He wanted her to like how he looked. Oddly enough, she never seemed to care either.

Wynthrope shook his head. "So, what's this I hear about

you and Lady Octavia Vaux-Daventry being seen together about town?"

He should have known this was coming. Wynthrope was the only one of his brothers who knew the whole story about himself and Octavia. Even in their youth he and Wyn had been close; the few months separating their births only added to it.

"It is true."

There was real interest—and surprising concern—in his gaze. "You are not swiving her, are you?"

In addition to charm, Wynthrope was also gifted with the ability to be remarkably crass.

North set down his fork and knife. "What makes you think that is any business of yours?"

"I am your brother." He said as though it were explanation enough. Usually, it was.

"You are nosy."

"That too." Wyn's expression changed. It hardened. "I do not want to see you hurt again."

"I was not hurt." *Liar.*

"No?" Wynthrope arched a dark brow. "It must have been an imbalance of the spleen that made you prone to melancholy and bouts of ungentlemanly weeping."

Oh Christ, he knew about the weeping?

North wiped his mouth with his serviette and tossed it on the table. "It does not concern you."

Now Wyn was scowling. "Do not be stupid. Everything in your life concerns me. You are my brother."

Their gazes locked. North would be damned if he'd look away first. "Then be concerned with something else."

Wyn's mask slipped back into place. Suddenly, he was uncaring again. "Don't want to discuss her, eh? Sounds serious to me, but then again, perhaps it is just your spleen again."

"*Wyn.*"

Shrugging, Wyn leaned back in his chair. "Fine. I will say no more on the subject."

"Thank God." It was all he could do not to sigh in relief.

Wyn glanced out the window before settling his gaze on North again. "How about His Highness's offer to assist you in becoming an MP? Have you given much more thought to that?"

Good God, did his brother have no other purpose in life but to vex North and occasionally endear himself?

"By 'His Highness' I assume you mean Brahm?"

Wynthrope poured himself another cup of coffee. "Have I ever meant anyone else?"

North smiled. "Oddly enough, you have used the title to refer to our king."

Wynthrope lifted his cup. "But my inflection holds a tad more respect when I speak of Farmer George."

True enough. And the king didn't generally warrant a sneer either. "No. I have not given any thought to Brahm's offer."

It was only a partial lie. North had given more thought to becoming the member of Parliament for the Creed riding of Hewbury in Surrey. He simply hadn't reached any kind of decision. The thought of being able to affect law and legislation at such a level was certainly tempting, but there was still so much he had to do where he was. Catch Harker, for one. Perhaps after he had done that, he'd *think* about considering his brother's—and Duncan's—suggestion that he direct his passions elsewhere.

Him, a member of Parliament. People might think he was trying to rise above his station.

Did that really matter? Octavia had reminded him that even if he was illegitimate, he was still the son of a viscount. His blood was half noble, and thanks to his mother, he knew in his heart that he was just as good as any aristocrat. He just didn't like spending time among them. And a career in politics would mean a lot of time among the *ton*.

Time with Octavia. A chance to be almost equal with her socially. He could see her, dance with her even. No one would think anything of it.

Except for the fact that he was now pretending to try to steal her from Spinton.

He could watch her in her role as Spinton's countess. Spinton's wife. Spinton's *lady*.

He met his brother's gaze over the rim of his cup as he lifted the hot coffee to his lips. "I do not think I am suited to a life in politics."

"No?"

"No. I think I'm better off exactly where I am."

Do not tempt me.

The words echoed in Octavia's head as she stared unseeing at the page before her. North's words from the night before. Had he truly considered himself tempted, even in all his restraint? If it were true, what did he consider her? Surely by that measure, her own actions went far beyond the reaches of mere temptation.

Sheer desperation would be a good start.

Oh, if only she had been too intoxicated to remember, but she hadn't been. In fact, she had been shamefully sober. Certainly her judgment had been impaired to a degree, but not to the point where her actions could be easily dismissed.

She had practically thrown herself at North and he refused her. It should be lowering. She should feel ashamed, dirty, and more than a little relieved.

She felt none of it—not really.

What kind of man refused such an offering? North was not stupid, nor did he find her unattractive, that was obvious. It was because they were friends. That was the only thing that saved her from making what she knew she should consider a horrible mistake.

Unfortunately, she couldn't quite bring herself to believe that giving herself to North would be that much of a mistake. It would only be a mistake if people found out. If Spinton found out.

Yes. Spinton. Her soon-to-be-fiancé. Her future husband. She should be heartily ashamed of herself for even contemplating such a sin as to couple with another man behind his back, and yet she couldn't bring herself to feel one ounce of guilt. In fact, she would have felt much more remorse had she tried to seduce Spinton. What did that say about her?

Nothing good, of that she was certain.

There was a soft knock on the door. Slipping a piece of ribbon between the pages to mark her place, Octavia closed the book and bade whoever it was to enter.

The door opened, revealing Beatrice, looking pretty and sunny in pale green speckled muslin.

Octavia's mood instantly improved at the sight of her friend and cousin. "Do not you look pretty!"

Beatrice flushed, her gaze dropping bashfully. "Thank you. Lord Spinton offered to take me to Gunther's for an ice this afternoon. Would you care to join us?"

An ice would be divine, but she had no desire to ruin Beatrice's outing, which was exactly what would happen. Spinton would demand to know what was going on with North's investigation, and Octavia would not have much to tell him, and then they would argue. Plus it would cast doubt on their charade that the two of them were temporarily estranged.

"No thank you, dear. Enjoy yourself and give Fitzwilliam my best, will you?"

Was it her imagination, or did Beatrice look relieved? "All right. Oh, Mr. Sheffield is here. Should I send him in?"

It was on the tip of Octavia's tongue to say that telling her of North's arrival should have preceded an invitation to Gunther's, but she resisted the urge. "Yes, please."

Her cousin nodded and ducked out of the room. Glad that she actually seemed suited to this room for once, Octavia rose to her feet and smoothed the skirts of her cream morning gown. If only she could smooth the trembling in her stomach as well.

North appeared before her a few moments later. He was dressed in a charcoal gray coat and pale, buff-colored breeches that hugged his thighs. His cravat was tied in a simple but elegant knot, and his boots gleamed with a high polish. He had obviously taken extra time getting dressed this morning. Not *that* extra however—he was still unshaven and his hair was mused.

She smiled, despite the buzzing in her stomach. "Good morning, Norrie."

Her smile seemed to relieve him as well, for he visibly relaxed before her eyes. "Hello, Vie."

"Shut the door."

He did as she bid, coming deeper into the room. Every step brought him closer to her. Every step intensified this new— no, not new. Heightened. Every step intensified this heightened awareness she had of him. Her nerves tingled, her skin tightened.

She gathered her courage. "I suppose you wish to discuss last night?"

He stopped in the middle of the blue and cream carpet. "Do we need to discuss it?"

Well, perhaps not, but she felt as though they *should*. "I am sorry if I made you uncomfortable."

His gaze was bright, clear, and unflinching. "You made me deuced uncomfortable. Fortunately, erections eventually wilt."

Oh. *Oh*. Heat flooded her veins. A shiver eased down her spine. "That is not what I meant."

"I know."

She couldn't tear her gaze away from his, even as she burned under the weight of his clear stare. His will tugged at her, urging her to reveal her own reaction.

"I . . ." She swallowed, her heart thumping wildly. "I was *uncomfortable* as well."

North's eyes darkened to a smoky blue. He understood her meaning. He moved closer, his steps slower, more purposeful.

"Did you later find *release* from your discomfort?"

Was he asking what she thought he was asking? Oh yes, he was. Octavia's face flamed with a mixture of shame and arousal. This was madness, dangerous.

"Did you?" Was that croaking sound actually her voice?

He stood directly in front of her now. All she had to do was reach out, and she could touch him, cling to him. Her Norrie. Her friend. Her lover. Her strength.

"Yes." His voice was low, a silky, lilting caress that sent a shiver of longing down her spine. "But it did little to satisfy the torment."

"No," she admitted, lifting her gaze to his. "It did not." Good Lord, what was she to reveal such wanton things? And to revel in his admissions as well? They had each pleasured themselves while thinking of the other, and yet it had not been enough. Not nearly enough.

Surely friends did not behave in such a way. But if they were not friends, what were they?

"This is folly," she whispered.

He nodded, the fire banking in his eyes. "I know."

For what seemed like eternity they stared at each other. He was not going to release her willingly, she understood that. It was up to her to put an end to what she had started last night. He had wanted her then. Regardless of why he had stopped, she now knew that he hadn't wanted to. He had wanted to make love to her. For now that was enough.

"What did Mr. Francis find out?"

Instantly North was all business. He took several steps backward. Suddenly she could breathe again. "The paper your boy uses is expensive and somewhat unusual."

"We already knew that."

He crossed his arms over his chest. The sleeves of his coat strained as his muscles pushed against them. "Yes, but now we know who sells it. It is exclusive to a shop on Bond Street."

"Wonderful!" And so were those arms of his.

"Do not get your hopes up just yet," he cautioned. "While he is the only papery in the city to sell this particular watermark, it is apparently a favorite with his clients."

Then they were really no closer to finding the culprit. For some reason, the realization didn't disappoint her. "So what do we do now?"

"I asked him for a record of everyone who has purchased the paper in the last six months."

"Did he agree?"

North's smile was cool. "It took a little convincing."

How ruthless could North be when he wanted? "You reminded him of how difficult you could make life for him."

The smile faded. "Something like that."

She wanted to disapprove. She didn't. "That was very naughty of you, Norrie."

He shrugged. "It worked. He said it would take some time, but he will have it for me as soon as possible."

"Do you always get what you want?" Did she not know better than to ask him such questions?

He had a way of looking at her that made her think he could see deep inside her, past all the lies and pretending. "Usually, but not always."

She shook her head, blushing despite herself. Did he think of her at all when he answered that?

"You are spoiled, I think, Mr. Sheffield."

"You should know, Lady Octavia." This time his grin was genuine.

"What is that supposed to mean?"

His eyes were bright with mirth. "It means you should not criticize my will when yours is just as strong if not stronger."

"Stronger?" She snorted.

"Who seduced whom twelve years ago?"

Breath caught in her throat—any more tangible and she would have choked on it. "I cannot believe you brought that up!"

Scratching his unshaven jaw, he shrugged again. "You are the one who always wants to discuss it."

He had her there. "Not like that!"

"Not the actual mechanics, you mean? What was done, what was said?"

"No." Oh, he seemed to delight in tormenting her this way. She just cooled down and now he wanted to heat her up again. "You remember what we said?"

"Every word."

Their gazes met with an impact that shook her right down to her toes and scratched her throat with hot, itchy dryness. "Oh."

"What do you want to discuss, if not that night's events?"

She swallowed. "What it meant—to both of us." It had changed her—changed her feelings for him. Had it changed things for him as well? That was what she really wanted to know. Had it meant as much to him as it had to her?

"I think the events would be more interesting."

She was too flustered to hide it by the time she realized he was teasing her. "You ass!"

He chuckled, his expression slowly giving way from mirth

to tenderness. "It was the most significant night of my life, and I will never forget it or you as long as I live."

It was? He wouldn't? Oh, how long she had waited to hear that! So why did it fill her with more sadness than joy? "I feel the same."

A tiny smile curved one side of his mouth. "Then there is nothing else to discuss."

Yes there was. She couldn't let it go, even though she knew she should. "Norrie, about last night—"

"Blame it on the drink, Vie. Pretend you were not yourself, and I will pretend to believe it, and we can put it behind us."

That sounded good. It also sounded incredibly callous. "But—"

He cut her off, but it was his expression that silenced her more than anything. "You are my best friend and I would do anything for you, but if we take this any further, I will forget everything except that I am a man and you are a woman. You do not want that to happen. Not here. Not now."

It was a struggle just to swallow. All the moisture in her body seemed to have pooled in one spot, and it was much, much lower than her mouth. "All right."

He sighed, his relief obvious. "I need a list of your mother's lovers. Do you think you can get one for me?"

"Possibly." Her brow puckered. "Why?"

He scratched his jaw again. If it itched, why didn't he simply shave in the morning? "I want to compare them to the list I get from our shopkeeper. If your admirer really does know the truth about your past, there is a very good chance he either was one of her protectors or somehow related to one."

The need to defend arose. "It will not be much of a list. My mother was very particular, not to mention discreet."

"I know." Was that sympathy in his tone? He knew how much she'd hated her mother's "companions." He knew how envious she had been of the fact that his mother was with only one man. "Most men, however, are not."

"Are you?" She couldn't help but ask it. The need to strike out in retaliation for his damned understanding was too powerful.

He tilted his head ever so slightly, regarding her with pale eyes that saw everything and revealed nothing. "What do you think?"

She didn't have to think. She knew—just as she knew how patently unfair it had been to even ask.

She glanced away. "Mama kept several journals during her life. I will consult those and have a list for you as soon as I can."

"Thank you."

Not looking at him was even more discomfitting than being pinned by that glacial gaze. She turned back to him. "I am sorry to have questioned your integrity, Norrie."

"I know." His hand brushed her cheek. The sensation was so acute it hurt. "I understand the thoughts you are thinking, Vie."

"You do?" She didn't even understand.

He dropped his hand. "I have them myself. Is this attraction between us built on memories of a sweet and awkward night, our pleasure in seeing each other again, or is it something different?"

He did know. He did understand. "I do not know."

"Neither do I." His smile was sad. "But it does not change anything between us. You are still my dear Vie, and even if you were not bound to another, I would never forgive myself for taking something you might not know the full consequences of giving."

Consequences. Oh yes, she was well acquainted with those. Her life seemed to be full of them.

The consequence was that she had fallen in love with him.

The consequence was that she had never wanted another man since. The consequence was that she wanted more. That one time had not been enough. It only served to whet her appetite. She wanted him again and again until this awful yearning for him went away. Surely it would go away.

"I have to go," he announced suddenly, jarring her out of her sinful thoughts. "I will see you later."

Where was he going? And why did he have to leave so soon? "Very well."

Halfway across the room he turned with a thoughtful expression. "You might want to find something different to read, Vie." He nodded at the book on the table.

Octavia tilted her head. "Why? I thought you liked Shakespeare."

"I do, but something a little happier perhaps."

What would be his idea of "happier"? If anything, he seemed more hell-bent on self-punishment than she ever was. What did he know about being happy? How long had it been since he'd had any joy in his life? "I believe Romeo and Juliet are united in the end."

His smile was almost patronizing in its sympathy. "People from different worlds never end up together, Vie. Not even in heaven."

Her heart crumpled in her chest. "What if they started out in the same world?"

There was no answer. He was already gone.

Chapter 10

Octavia awoke the next morning, vexed and restless. She hadn't seen North again after he left her yesterday, despite his promise that he would see her "later." And she had spent the remainder of the day thinking about all they had said to each other. Even as she drifted off to sleep, his words swam through her mind, as did memories from other days—memories not conducive to sleep. Thus, she did not feel very well rested.

Coffee did nothing to improve her mood, nor did a large breakfast with Beatrice. All her cousin could seem to talk about was the lovely time she had with Spinton at the park with their ices. The mention of her future betrothed needled Octavia in a manner she couldn't quite explain.

"Oh, Octavia!" Beatrice trilled, "You never told me how amusing Lord Spinton is!"

Amusing? Spinton? Just thinking the two words together made her head spin.

Octavia spread strawberry jam on a bun. "It must have slipped my mind."

Her sarcasm was lost on her cousin. Beatrice looked positively sympathetic as she returned her delicate china cup to its saucer. "Of course it did. You have had much more pressing issues to think about."

Oh wonderful. Now she felt guilty. Perhaps if she remained silent Beatrice would take the hint and be quiet as well.

She did—at least for a little while. But after a few precious minutes, Beatrice spoke again, "You will be attending the charity event at Vauxhall tomorrow evening, will you not?"

Sighing, Octavia reached for more jam. It was either that or stuff a buttered roll in Beatrice's ever-flapping mouth. "Truth be told, I had not given it a thought either way."

Her cousin's eyes widened. "But Lord Spinton will be there! It will be the perfect opportunity for the two of you to meet without jeopardizing Mr. Sheffield's investigation."

Octavia smeared the jam on another warm bun. "Well, that is reason enough in itself to attend, is it not?" She stuffed the roll into her own mouth instead.

This time Beatrice picked up on her tone. "You are very peevish this morning."

Still chewing, Octavia merely smiled—insincerely.

Her cousin seemed not to mind the lapse in her table manners. "Has something happened? Is there something vexing you?"

She could hardly tell her cousin she was jealous, could she? Not jealous of her *amusing* afternoon with Spinton, but jealous of the fact that Beatrice managed to have fun with a member of the opposite sex without turning it into a lesson in rejection and wanton behavior.

"North wants a list of my mother's protectors. He think it might lead to a clue."

Beatrice nodded as if she somehow understood everything, which was, of course, impossible. "I understand that might be difficult for you, given the fact that you have tried so hard to put that unfortunate business of your past behind you."

Octavia frowned. "I am not ashamed of my mother or my past."

"Of course not! I never meant to imply otherwise."

Her cousin's tone *did* imply otherwise, however. Octavia chose to ignore it. If she denied it any more, Beatrice might begin to suspect the truth; that Octavia sometimes envied her mother's sexual liberation. She chose her lovers carefully, picking one man at a time from a sea of admirers who routinely vied for her favors. Whether she loved any of them remained a mystery, but as far as Octavia knew they were all very good to her mother—and even to her. Yes, it was embarrassing knowing that a man basically "kept" her and her mother in return for her mother's companionship, but it was far preferable to going hungry. Still, she had envied North's almost "typical" home. He had known his father—something she could never have. And he'd had his mother's undivided attention—something else she'd wanted.

Not only did Octavia envy her mother in some ways, but she also respected her. She did what was necessary to provide for herself and her daughter. She made sure Octavia had the best of everything, including a tutor so she wouldn't live her life ignorant of the world around her.

No, she was not ashamed. Any shame she felt came from her own inadequacies. How could she judge her mother when she was essentially whoring herself out to Spinton? He got her body to produce his heir, and she became the countess to a very wealthy earl. It was an exchange of goods and services, not a marriage. Not a real one.

"Well," she said, unwilling to dwell on such thoughts any longer. "I had best get started. The day is wasting."

Beatrice's brow pinched. "Would you like some help?"

God no! "Thank you, but I prefer to do this alone." Was it her imagination or did Beatrice look relieved? Octavia was curious.

"By the way, what are your plans for the day?"

Beatrice blushed. "Oh. Uh . . . I have been invited out for tea later this afternoon."

By Spinton, no doubt. Perhaps Beatrice was going to meet his mama. She hoped the old bat would be a little kinder to her cousin than she had been to Octavia herself. Maybe she'd try to talk her son into marrying Beatrice instead.

After telling her cousin to have a lovely afternoon, Octavia turned on her heel and left the dining room.

How long had it been since Spinton invited her to take tea with him and his mama? Perhaps a week or so, no more. She usually made certain she had a convenient excuse to avoid the meeting. The old woman was a viper coiled in a nest of silks and lilac-scented powder.

Lifting her skirts as she climbed the stairs, Octavia realized that Beatrice was quite possibly the only person cut out to handle Spinton's mother. Beatrice was so good and so sweet, there was no way anyone could find fault with her—not even Octavia's future mama-in-law.

On the top floor of the main part of the house, Octavia opened the door to the attic and began to climb the narrow stairs. Taking a kerchief from the pocket of her apron, she placed the square of fabric over her head, knotting it below the bun at her nape. Her gown was old and faded, her apron borrowed from one of the maids, as was the kerchief. The maid had been more than happy to lend them to her. Octavia prided herself on the way she treated her servants. It was the people close to her that she treated badly.

Look how she treated North. He was her friend, her dearest friend, and he was interrupting his own life to fix hers.

How did she repay him? By throwing herself at him, challenging his integrity by offering him a sexual relationship with no strings attached.

Oh, but there had to be strings. There were always strings—strings that she would twine around him deep inside, binding him to her no matter what the future held for either of them.

Regardless of what the future held, of how impossible it was for them to have any kind of relationship, she would make certain he never forgot her. God knew she wouldn't be lucky enough to forget him. He would be the measure against which she judged every other man.

Would they all be found lacking?

Octavia knew exactly where her mother's trunk was located, and she wasted no time in finding the journals—anything to keep herself from thinking about North. She hadn't time to sort through the various belongings, nor did she feel like confronting the feelings and memories they might bring. Melancholy would just make things worse.

Balancing each journal on her knee, Octavia flipped through the pages until she found the entry where her mother talked about first joining the theater. Every man that was mentioned in a romantic context she wrote down the name of. Thankfully, there weren't that many. Still, it took her some time to read through the books, her attention being snared here and there by thoughts and reflections that soon had her reading in an effort to feel closer to her mother rather than just for information.

Her poor dear mother. Selling herself so that she and her daughter might have a better life. Had her pride been worth not asking her father-in-law—Octavia's grandfather—for assistance? And would the old earl have given it if she'd asked? As much as Octavia loved her grandfather, he hadn't been a saint of a man. Perhaps her mother worried that he might have tried to separate her and Octavia. Certainly he might have, and being a peer, he would have succeeded.

There were footsteps on the attic stairs, followed by a knock and one of the maids poking her head through the open door. "Begging your pardon, my lady, but Lord Spinton is here."

Ah, he must be there to collect Beatrice. Had so much time passed already? That would mean she had been in the attic for at least two hours. "Thank you. Please tell him I will be right down."

Smiling, the maid bobbed a curtsy and disappeared. Octavia waited until the footsteps faded before folding the list and standing.

The paper and pencil tucked inside her apron, Octavia replaced her mother's journals and closed the heavy trunk lid. Later perhaps, she would return for the journals. Despite the wish to respect her mother's privacy, and despite her own wish to avoid depressed spirits, she had a need to feel close to her mother again. Reading her journals would ease the loneliness.

Spinton was in the parlor, waiting—either for her or for Beatrice, or both. He was dressed impeccably in biscuit-colored breeches and a dark blue morning coat. His sandy hair was artfully curled, his cravat perfect, his jaw smoothly shaven.

She had never seen Spinton looking anything but his best. He would certainly never be caught with stubble on his jaw. Perhaps he didn't ever have stubble. Hair wouldn't dare grow on his face—it was too barbaric.

My, wasn't she in fine form today?

"Good morning, Spinton."

He turned, his expression of pleasure turning to one of distasteful surprise. "You look like a scullery maid."

Octavia shrugged. "I have been cleaning." She didn't want

to tell him the truth. Perhaps she was ashamed of her mother after all.

Or perhaps she didn't feel like defending her mother to this man who had never known her and had no right to judge her.

He seemed surprised. "You have servants to do that for you."

"Sometimes I like to do things for myself." Could he understand that? "Do not you like to do things for yourself, Spinton?"

He stared at her as though she had two heads. "You are not saying you enjoy being dirty, are you?"

Sometimes she very much liked being dirty. What would he say to that? Down and dirty, foul and filthy. She liked to sweat, liked to feel her body heat with exertion.

"When we make love, are you going to insist on doing it in the dark with my nightgown hiked up to my waist and the blankets over your head?"

Poor Spinton looked as though he might collapse. He actually sputtered. "Dear God, what kind of question is that?"

She shrugged. "An honest one."

"This is Sheffield's influence isn't it?" His face was flushed as he spoke. "He can be very crass and blunt at times."

"Nor—Mr. Sheffield has nothing to do with our marriage, Fitzwilliam. Did you know the prefix 'fitz' implies illegitimacy?"

His expression was comical in its bewilderment. "What has that to do with anything?"

Another shrug. "Nothing. I just think it is very interesting. It is a family name, is it not?"

"My mother's maiden." He straightened his coat. "You know that."

"Ahh, so someone way back in your mother's lineage was a bastard then." She nodded.

"Octavia!"

She pulled a face, waving her hand at him. "Oh hush, I meant no offense." But she had, hadn't she? Else why say such things to a man unaccustomed to such language from a "lady"?

He was visibly flushed and flustered. "I vow I do not know you sometimes."

And you never will. "I never would have pegged you for being such a prude, Fitzwilliam." Now, that was a lie if she ever told one.

His jaw lifted, tightened. "And I never would have thought you capable of such speech, Octavia."

Oh yes, she'd astounded him. Completely thrown him off guard. What else could she do?

Slowly, she prowled toward him. "I am capable of much more than speech, my dear."

Spinton's Adam's apple bobbed as she approached. Was it her imagination, or did he actually take a step backward?

"What are you doing?" he demanded as she drew closer.

"I just realized it has been forever since I kissed you. Do you mind if I kiss you?"

It took him a moment. "Wh-why, no."

She made him nervous. She could see the uncertainty and anticipation in his eyes. She was a very sexual creature to him, and for all his quirks and eccentricities, Spinton was a man like any other. He found her attractive, wanted to claim her as his, even though he must know as well as she how ill-suited they were.

Did she want to bed him? Not really. She could, but she didn't want him as she wanted North. Then again, North had an unfair advantage over Spinton. She'd had him before, and she wanted to have him again.

But more importantly, she wanted to compare kissing Spinton to kissing North. She wanted—no, *needed*—to know if anyone could ignite these feelings within her or if it was only her first lover that made her hotter than a crowded the-ater in the middle of an August thunderstorm.

And she wanted to make him regret telling her she looked like a scullery maid.

Her hands were dusty and grimy. The dandy in him would surely shrink from her touch, so she didn't touch him. She simply lifted herself up on her toes, closing the distance be-tween them, and touched her lips to his.

He was the one who seized her and pulled her to him. He was the one who shocked her by sliding his tongue between her lips. He kissed her as he had never kissed her before—with more passion than she had ever experienced from him.

And yet it did very little for her. In fact, he kissed her with such desperation that Octavia couldn't help but wonder at the reason behind it. It felt as though he was trying to prove something. Whatever his point was, his tongue made it.

"Sorry to keep you—oh."

Octavia jerked free of Spinton's grasp, embarrassed, but oddly relieved that it was Beatrice who caught them rather than North. Of course, given her cousin's hero worship of Spinton, it was unfortunate that Beatrice had to catch him at such a completely human moment.

Poor Spinton was so chagrined, he flashed Beatrice an apologetic expression, and Beatrice was so discomfitted that she stared at them both with something that looked very much like horror.

And jealousy. And hurt.

"Forgive me," she said hoarsely. "The door was open."

"It is all right, Beatrice," Octavia said soothingly. Why did she feel so guilty for kissing her own fiancé? Because she feared her cousin felt more than just friendship for Spinton? Good Lord, how was she going to feel after the wedding night? If her suspicions about Beatrice's growing regard for

Spinton were true, she wouldn't be able to look her cousin in the eye after sharing Spinton's bed.

How perfect it would be if her foolish attempt to feel something—anything—for her betrothed had injured her cousin. It would be just one more wonderfully awful thing she had done this day. Right up there with pouncing on poor Spinton.

"I will not delay the two of you any longer." She purposely kept her tone light. "Enjoy the afternoon. Now, if you will excuse me, I must change."

She swept from the room dramatically. But despite all her hauteur, she had the strangest feeling of being an intruder in her own home. And she couldn't shake the feeling that she had somehow been unfaithful by kissing Spinton. But had she been unfaithful to herself, or to someone else?

It was like looking for a shadow in a bucket of tar.

Sitting at his desk, a steaming cup of coffee near his hand, North studied the list Octavia had sent to him via messenger the previous afternoon. It was a good place to start, but really wouldn't do him much good until he had the list from the paper seller to compare it to. He had to accept the idea that there might not be any connection between the two, just as he had to prepare himself for the fact that there just might be a connection. There was a very good chance that Octavia's admirer—what a stupid term to use for such a man—was someone who knew far more about her past—and North's—than either of them would like.

Certainly more than Spinton would like.

Of course, what Spinton would or would not like didn't matter to North. He didn't care if Spinton found out about Octavia's past. In fact, he thought it would be for the best if he did. Marriage built upon deceit might be a regular occurrence among the *ton*, but it didn't bode well if one wished for a happy union.

But Octavia cared whether her fiancé learned the truth, and so he cared as well. Even more than that, he cared about the fact that someone out there might mean her harm. He could allow her to marry a man she didn't trust—didn't love—but he would not allow anyone to hurt her. Not while he still breathed.

But he would be glad when he tracked down this letter writer of hers and put the entire business to rest. He had let his hunt for Harker lag during this new investigation. He had given Francis much responsibility that should have been his own, and the realization of it weighed heavily upon his shoulders.

It wasn't that he was letting his duties slide because of another case. He was letting his duties slide because of Octavia. Since her reappearance in his life, everything else paled in comparison. That wasn't right. It *shouldn't* be right.

He wasn't even all that concerned that many of his informants had told him that Harker was preparing for all-out war with him. Apparently, Harker wasn't as bright as North gave him credit for. Harker had believed that killing Sally and Harris would make North back off. He couldn't have been more wrong. Every experienced man North had in his employ was working on building evidence against Harker, hindering Harker's business, making Harker's life harder. They weren't to be reckless, however. North didn't want to have any more blood on his hands.

There was a knock on the door of his office. Mrs. Bunting stuck her head inside the room at his command.

"Pardon the intrusion, Mr. Sheffield, but the Earl Spinton is here to see you."

Speak of the devil. Spinton knew their plan. He knew he

wasn't to make physical contact with North unless it was an emergency. "Send him in."

A few moments later, Lord Spinton swept into the room, splendidly dressed and fashionably coiffed. North ran a hand over his own unshaven jaw, all too aware of his own sagging cravat and disheveled hair. He wasn't wearing a coat either, and his sleeves were creased and bunched from being rucked and rolled during the course of the morning. He no doubt looked like a rangy mutt next to purebred Spinton.

What did that matter anyway? He didn't need to impress Spinton with his sense of style. He didn't need to impress Spinton at all.

No, but he wouldn't mind feeling superior.

I screwed your betrothed, you starchy bastard. What do you say to that?

Oh yes, he felt superior now.

One look at the expression on Spinton's sculpted face wiped away all traces of victory. "What has happened?"

"I demand to know your intentions toward Lady Octavia."

He didn't bother to hide his surprise. "You demand?"

"Yes."

North kept his expression bland. "I intend to discover the identity of the man sending her letters and I intend to protect her if necessary. That is what you are paying me for." Money that was going directly to a nearby house dedicated to the care of unmarried mothers and their children, but Spinton didn't need to know that. Spinton didn't need to know that he had accepted this commission for Octavia rather than money.

"I was referring to your personal intentions."

Of course he was. Did he think North such a simpleton that he couldn't detect the jealousy in his tone? A better man—or perhaps a better liar—would assure the earl that his intentions were nothing but noble. North couldn't do that.

"What do you think?" Why needle the man? Why not just lie and tell him he had no intentions?

The earl stiffened. "I suspect they may be less than honorable."

It didn't matter if it were true; North didn't like the other man's tone. "Many men have been called out for attacking another's honor."

Spinton didn't look as though he liked that thought very much, but North should have known better than to tease him. Spinton might not be as tough, or as street savvy, but the one thing he and North had in common was their determination to defend what each considered his.

Unfortunately, both of them had their own claim to Octavia. Was it North's fault that he had staked his first?

"Forgive me, Mr. Sheffield, but with few exceptions, your family has not exhibited a great fondness for acting within the bounds of dignity."

If Spinton wanted to piss him off, he'd chosen the right avenue. "You have not earned the right to speak of my family, Spinton, earl or not."

The earl colored, but did not back down. "Even your youngest brother the war hero has drawn attention to himself upon occasion, and the exploits of you father and other brothers are public knowledge."

Not all of them, but Spinton would never know that either. "When I agreed to this investigation, I did a little delving into your family, my lord. Would you care to know what I uncovered?"

Spinton shrugged. "Nothing nefarious, I am sure."

North chuckled mockingly. "I discovered all manner of interesting facts—such as the story about your uncle Theodore and his desire for a certain twelve-year-old girl from Yorkshire."

This time Spinton went positively white. North was fairly

certain Spinton didn't know all the details about his uncle, but he had heard enough to know it was not a story that Spinton wanted all of society to hear.

"Are you trying to blackmail me?"

North scowled. "Do not be an idiot. Of course not."

Spinton did not look convinced. "Then why did you mention my uncle?"

"Because you should not be so quick to judge others based on their relations." No wonder Octavia didn't want him to know about her mother. Spinton would probably have a seizure if he learned his dearly departed mama-in-law was a lowly actress.

Looking somewhat relieved, the earl relaxed a bit. "Then you do not have designs on Lady Octavia?"

"I swear to you that I have not taken any liberties where she is concerned." Luckily, it didn't occur to Spinton to ask if Octavia had taken any liberties with *him*.

The earl's relief was obvious, but there was something else. Was it guilt? Unease? Perhaps he didn't believe North's claims. Or perhaps the earl had hoped to lay a little blame at North's feet to cover up his own indiscretions? But why? As an unmarried peer, Spinton was practically expected to dip his wick wherever he wanted. In fact, it was considered a bit of an oddity that he didn't have a mistress. So why would he feel any remorse from acting as he was expected to act?

Unless he was developing feelings for whomever he was dipping his wick into.

Interesting.

"Do you love her?"

Spinton jerked. "I beg your pardon?"

"Lady Octavia. Do you love her?" And what answer would North be satisfied with, yes or no?

Spinton looked as though he might suffer a fit. "That is none of your business!"

He couldn't help but twist the knife. "How do you expect to declare it in front of God and all those witnesses if you cannot even declare it to me?"

Spinton fidgeted under his stare. "I care for and respect Octavia very much."

North noticed Spinton had neglected to refer to Octavia by her title. "I care for and respect my housekeeper, but I have no intention of marrying her."

"That is hardly the same!" If Spinton got any hotter under the collar, the whites of his eyes would turn pink.

North scratched his jaw. "You reckon?"

"My feelings for Octavia go far beyond your regard for your housekeeper!" Spinton was so enraged he actually spat the words.

"Ah, so you *do* love her?" Somehow, it would make losing Vie much easier knowing Spinton would give her the love she deserved.

"Love is very good, but it is not the only foundation for marriage."

The little cretin didn't love her at all then. "It is supposed to be."

Spinton straightened. Defensive, was he? "Not among the *ton*."

Shrugging, North fought to keep his temper at bay. "Most of the *ton* are money-grubbing idiots."

"I beg your pardon!"

Another shrug. "Perhaps you esteem Octavia's fortune. Perhaps you respect her lands or the matched grays that lead her carriage."

"Mr. Sheffield!" The earl was positively purple with indignation.

"But let me tell you something about women, Spinton." North spoke as though he were about to impart great wisdom to a very close friend. "Every last one of them wants to be loved just as we do. Maybe you can fool her and maybe you can fool yourself that love is not necessary, but eventually she will resent you for it. And one thing you do not want to be on the receiving end of, my friend, is the wrath of a resentful woman."

Spinton smirked. He actually smirked. North never would have thought him capable of it. "Speaking from experience?"

"Of course." It was pride that made him admit it. "I have known quite a few women in my life."

"No doubt."

North smiled. It was hardly an insult. He had known a few women, and he had adored them all in his way. "A woman like Lady Octavia—a woman with backbone and intelligence and spirit—she deserves to be loved the way she wants to be. She deserves passion and devotion."

"How would you know what she deserves?"

North pinned him with his gaze. "It is what every woman deserves, Spinton. Is there any creature in the world that deserves less?"

"Even criminals?"

If Spinton thought to bait or trap him, he was choosing the wrong route. "Of course. Love can change a man."

"I never would have pegged you for a romantic." The earl's tone dripped with condescension.

North didn't miss a beat. "I never would have pegged you for an idiot."

Obviously fed up with being insulted, Spinton scowled. "If it were not for my concern for Lady Octavia, I would relieve you of your duties."

North shrugged. "If it were not for my concern for Lady Octavia, I would let you."

Finally understanding each other, Spinton simply nodded. "Then perhaps you will do all in your power to finish this assignment quickly?"

Now it was North's turn to smirk. "You may be assured." He'd take as much time as he wanted, frigging blighter.

Spinton didn't bother to make the usual niceties as he took his leave, for which North was grateful. He was just a hair's breadth away from telling the earl to go swive himself—something that Octavia would undoubtedly take him to task for.

And speak of the devil, she walked into the room not five minutes after Spinton walked out.

"What the hell are you doing here?" Good Christ she looked good—like a willowy bit of cinnamon dipped in sugar in her slender russet and white skirts. One taste would only lead to wanting more.

Her only reaction was a subtle lift of her coppery brows. "It is lovely to see you as well."

He ignored her sarcasm. "Did you see Spinton?"

"Yes." She began stripping off her gloves. "I waited until I was certain he was gone to come in."

"Did he see you?" Could she tell he was spoiling for a fight?

She slipped her gloves into the foolish little bag dangling from her wrist. "No. I took a hack."

"Unescorted?"

"Yes."

Obviously she couldn't tell at all. "Into this part of town?"

She shot him a quizzical look. "Of course, I am here, am I not?"

"You are a nervy, foolish baggage. That is what you are."

She scowled. "I am going to assume that your bowels are distressed, and that is the reason for this undeserved rude-ness."

"My bowels are just fine, thank you. In fact, your fiancé's visit made me want to empty them." It was crude talk—too crude for a lady, but strangely comfortable between friends.

She nodded, her posture relaxing. "Ah. It is not me you are angry at, but rather Spinton. What did he want?"

Some of the fight left him. "To make certain we are not swiving under his nose."

"No!" Her expression was one of genuine horror.

"Yes." He folded his arms over his chest. "He is very concerned for your virtue. Prepared to fight a duel over it, in fact."

Octavia's cobalt eyes blazed. "The idiot!"

"He is merely concerned for you." How did he come to defend Spinton?

"Concerned about dictating my life, you mean." Balled fists rested defiantly on her delicately rounded hips. "I am heartily sick of everyone deciding how I should and should not be living my life."

"He has some right," North reminded her. "He is your fiancé."

"Not yet, he is not."

"Close enough."

She flashed him an annoyed glance. "No closer than a mistress is a wife—and you and I both know how that normally works out."

North's heart skipped a beat. "Are you saying you are considering not marrying him?"

She sighed, dropping her arms to her sides. "No. I owe it to my grandfather and mother."

He had a pretty good idea where her grandfather could go—if he wasn't there already. "What about what you owe yourself?"

"Spinton is a good and honorable man. He will make a fine husband." Which one of them was she trying to convince?

"He'd make a fine duck hound as well."

She didn't even crack a smile. "It was decided a long time ago that he and I would marry, and I will hold to my end of the promise."

"So, you will not tolerate being told what to do, but you will tolerate being told who to marry?" He should just drop it. It was none of his business, he knew that, but that didn't stop him from *feeling* differently.

"It is hardly the same thing. Marrying Spinton will combine our fortunes and ensure the continuance of the family. I am certain we will get on very well together. Marriages built on less have lasted decades." Again, for whose benefit did she speak?

"Purebreds," he muttered, rubbing his palm over his eyes.

"What?"

"Never mind." He shrugged "It is none of my concern who you marry."

Up went those sharp brows again. "It is not?"

"I only want to see you happy." That was true at least. "If you believe Spinton can do that, then I wish you well."

She stared at him, searching him with her bright blue gaze. What she was looking for he didn't know, but he heartily hoped she didn't find it.

"Why are you here, Vie?" After his bizarre hot and cold behavior yesterday he would have thought she'd wipe her hands of him.

"I came to bring you this." She handed him a folded slip of paper from her reticule.

"What is it?"

"Another letter. It arrived this morning. I thought you might want to see it."

He snatched it from her hand. "I do."

"You are welcome."

Quickly, North scanned the paper. *Sheffield's not good enough for you either. Cannot you see you deserve so much better?* The words, no matter how true they might be, brought a familiar tightening to his chest. He wasn't good enough. He knew it, everyone knew it. Probably even Octavia knew it, but sometimes she didn't seem to care. For that matter, sometimes neither did he.

He closed the note. "He has noticed us then."

Octavia was watching him. Could she really see inside him as he sometimes suspected? Christ, he hoped not. "What do we do now?"

"We rub his face in it," he replied decisively. "We flaunt ourselves a bit more."

"Where? When?"

"The charity event at Vauxhall tomorrow evening. We will attend it together. That ought to do for a start."

She didn't look convinced. "You think he will be there?"

"Everyone who is anyone is going to be there. The regent himself planned this event to showcase some of his favorite artists. Even if your admirer does not go, he will hear about our appearance from the gossips."

She tilted her head as she regarded him. "Do you know your eyes light up when you scheme and plot?"

He blinked. "They do?"

She smiled. "They do. Like two diamonds on pale blue velvet."

His lips twisted. "How very poetic."

She swatted his arm. "Do not make fun. Shall we take my carriage tomorrow night, or do you want to walk?"

"Now who is making fun?" He smiled despite her remarks, and himself. "I will borrow one from Brahm. I do not want people thinking you brought me instead of the other way around."

She nodded, grinning. "Ahh yes, masculine pride."

"I do have some, you know." How easily they fell back into such comfort with each other.

"I know." She eyed him as only someone who knew him inside and out could. "Obviously, Spinton knows now as well."

"Obviously." He wasn't going to give her details. It wasn't his place. "Now, do you have to leave immediately, or would you like to join me for luncheon?"

"That depends on what you are having."

He rang the bell for Mrs. Bunting. "Since when did that matter? You ate anything that was not moving as a child."

Removing the reticule from her wrist, she chuckled. "How impertinent of you to remember."

He smiled as the bag landed on the desk with a heavy thump. God only knew what she had in there. "I remember everything about you."

She stilled, then turned toward him, laying her hand upon his arm. "No matter what happens, you will always know me better than anyone, Norrie. You know that, do you not?"

He nodded, his throat suddenly tight. "I do."

"Good." It came out as a sigh, so blatant was her relief.

But what good would knowing her better do when he would have to spend the rest of his days pretending not to know her at all?

Chapter 11

When North went round to collect Octavia for their next excursion, he made certain he borrowed a carriage from Brahm rather than resorting to hiring another hack. Octavia's roots might have taken hold in the same soil as his, but they had blossomed into something much different. She was used to having a fine conveyance, and even if he wasn't, the least he could do was ensure her comfort.

It was what a gentleman should do, he reminded himself. Besides, that remark she had made about them walking to the event still stung. That was no doubt the reason for the strange sensation of having his guts tied into knots. He was doing his best gentleman impersonation that evening—a part he hadn't wanted to play for quite some time.

Would Octavia, damn her eyes, notice that his jaw was freshly shaved? Or that his hair was newly trimmed and somewhat tamed by a tiny amount of pomade pilfered from Brahm's valet? And if Octavia did notice, would she care?

Not that it should matter one bit if she did. In fact, it would be easier if she didn't give a rat's ass about his appearance.

He was no smarter than any other man when it came to the fairer sex, but even he understood what was happening between him and his childhood friend. The attraction between them was obvious—to each of them if not to anyone else.

The question was, how much more could he—or she— take before they gave in? It wouldn't be as though she were being unfaithful to Spinton. Technically they weren't yet betrothed. But it wasn't so simple as that. Physical intimacy would make it that much harder to walk away when this was over. To entertain the idea that they might have a future was folly—and indicated a deeper commitment than he wanted to entertain. They were from different worlds now—she didn't belong in his and he could never truly live in hers.

Sex would make the situation all the more complicated— and neither one of them needed *that*. But need and want didn't necessarily always agree. He had wanted to be a part of his brothers' world, but he didn't *need* it. Not anymore. At least, he didn't think he did.

Octavia met him at the door in a gown of bronze satin. It matched the shimmering depths of her hair and made her skin look like the purest alabaster, accentuating the delicate rise of her breasts. He took her gold silk shawl from her hand and placed it over her shoulders. Beneath his gloves, his fingers itched to touch the warm softness of her flesh.

"You look lovely, Vie." Lovely didn't even begin to describe it, but he had to at least try to tame his wild enthusiasm for her. He could feel it, but giving it voice was unwise and dangerous.

She gazed at him as though he had told her she was the most beautiful woman in the world, which he supposed he had. He wasn't much on physical appearance, or complimenting it. She knew that, and she knew that if he noticed, she looked better than lovely.

"Thank you, Norrie. So do you."

Inwardly he preened. He felt a little too starched, but it was worth Octavia's praise.

A footman held the carriage door for them as they climbed inside, shutting them in once they were situated. North rapped on the ceiling and they were off. A little while later they were in a boat bound for Vauxhall Gardens.

Vauxhall at night was a sight to behold, and this night was even more replete than others. Tonight the regent played host to all London citizens who could afford the price of entry. Tonight the music would be that much better, the ham that much thicker, the punch sweeter, but no less strong. There would be acrobats, trained horses, exotic animals, and dancing.

And somewhere in the throng, North hoped Octavia's admirer would be watching.

Entering the gardens was like entering another world. They passed the statue of Handel as they entered Vauxhall through the river gate, and North kept his eye sharp for anyone who might be paying them undue attention. He also searched for the men he had stationed nearby. Vauxhall was large—covering nearly twelve acres. There was no way he could watch it all by himself—especially not when the lady on his arm was such a delicious distraction.

Tonight the Grand Walk, with its bordering elms, sparkled like a crystal stream beneath the torch light as ladies and gentlemen, richly dressed and heavily jeweled, strolled along the path. This walk was always well lit, as were most, but there were a few that were deliberately kept dark. He would have to ensure Octavia didn't happen upon them without him.

Then again, it might be safer for them to avoid such places altogether.

"I hear Prinny has arranged for a reenactment of Waterloo to take place this evening."

Octavia's breath was warm against his face as she turned her head to whisper to him. Fighting a shiver, North smiled grimly. "War is always so entertaining for those who were not affected by it."

She stopped walking, and he had no choice but to stop as well. "You sound so grave. Was your brother Devlin not declared a national hero after his performance at Waterloo?"

North nodded, urging her into motion again. "He was, but the war changed him. I refuse to celebrate that."

She said nothing, but he could feel the weight of her stare upon him for the next few beats of his heart.

"There is Brahm," he remarked, itching under her gaze. "Let us say hello."

Brahm seemed surprised to see them, which made North smile. Brahm had known they were going to be there—he had lent North his carriage, after all.

"Perhaps you can help me with something, Lady Octavia."

North's brows shot up as Octavia's own rose delicately. "What would that be, Lord Creed?"

Brahm gestured at his younger brother with the head of his cane. "Help me convince this one to give up a life of chasing criminals for a career in politics."

North kept his features perfectly blank as he met Octavia's questioning stare. "Politics, Norrie? Do you think you could sit still long enough?"

Was that laughter in her tone? "I can sit still just fine, thank you."

Brahm appeared amused as well—damn him. "I keep trying to tell him he could do more to reform our criminal laws from a higher position than he could running down the alleys of Covent Garden."

"So he could," Octavia agreed, an unreadable brightness in her eyes. It was as though she was seeing him differently. North didn't know if he liked it or not.

They talked to Brahm for a few moments more—on a different topic, thankfully—before moving onward. Many people stopped to talk. They were more Octavia's acquaintances than his own—just further proof of how different their lives were now. While his companion chatted about the inane topics that somehow seemed so compelling to the Upper Ten Thousand, North scanned the masses for anything, or anyone, unusual. When they began walking again, he paid little attention to where Octavia was leading him as he picked out his own men in the crowd. They nodded at him—the signal that all seemed well.

Then his men were gone, as were the other guests—and the lanterns that made it easy for him to search for predators. They were on one of the unlit paths. Not just any path, either. Unless he was mistaken, this was the Lovers Walk

It was dark here, in the infinite shadows between torches. Too dark. Too quiet. The breeze was warm as a caress, soft as a sigh. This was not a place they should be alone together—not if Octavia wanted Spinton to renew their understanding once this was all over.

Perhaps they weren't alone. It was too dark to tell—another reason that they should not be there. How had they ended up there anyway?

"We should not be here," he murmured. "It is too dark."

Octavia's fingers twined with his. "It is nice to have you to myself."

His head turned. Her features were barely discernible in the murky light. "You always have me."

"Usually we have an audience."

They might have one now as well, but he wasn't about to remind her of that. They should return to the relative safety of the crowd. They should keep to the light. It was safer where there were people. Being here made it too easy to forget what he was doing. It would be far too easy for someone to launch an attack against one of them. Harker would love to find him in just such a situation. Unfortunately, where there was safety, it was also very public. Octavia was right, it was nice to be alone. Too nice.

He was supposed to be hunting the man bothering Octavia. He was supposed to protect her—at the request of her fiancé. Instead, all he could think of was the feel of her skin, the scent of her hair.

What was wrong with him? Had he learned nothing from Black Sally's murder? He had become too arrogant, too relaxed in his methods. He didn't believe Octavia's admirer to be dangerous, but what evidence had he seen to that effect? None. He couldn't make assumptions. Assumptions got people killed.

If he were responsible for Octavia's death he could never forgive himself. He wouldn't be able to go on with her blood on his hands. He'd rather go straight to hell and rot there.

"We should go back."

She turned to him, so close that their torsos were almost touching. Her face—softly kissed by silver moonlight—was just inches from his own. For a moment, North's heart ceased to beat. He ceased to breathe. This was death and he wasn't afraid at all.

"In a minute." Her voice was lower, huskier. She wanted to kiss him. It was as though the thought leaped from her mind to his, so certain he was of her desire.

What harm could one kiss do? Spinton never needed to know about a kiss. There was no harm in a kiss between friends.

His lips hovered just above hers. A little lower and they would touch. A little lower and he risked losing himself in her kiss.

But before he could claim the prize offered to him, a loud

cracking sound split the night. Instinctively, North shoved Octavia into the shadows as pain exploded in his bicep. It felt as though someone had shoved a hot poker through his flesh.

Rifle shot. He'd been hit. If he hadn't moved his arm . . .

Suddenly Francis and two others were there with them. How much had they heard? How much had they seen? He'd never know unless he asked. And they would never tell either.

"Did you see him?" North demanded, ignoring the burning in his arm.

Francis's eyes narrowed as he scanned the darkness. He pointed into the trees. "There."

North stopped the burly man before he could pursue. "Take her to my house." He shoved Octavia toward him. "Stay with her. No one gets near her."

"Norrie!" Octavia's frightened voice cut through him like a blade, but he ignored her. There was a man with a rifle out there. A man who would have shot her had North not moved, and by God he was going to catch the bastard—one way or another.

With one of his men hot on his heels, North tore off through the night, chasing the shadowy form threatening to outdistance him. His arm was bleeding heavily. Blood oozed down his skin in warm, sticky rivulets. He'd been shot at many times in his career, but this was the first time he'd actually been hit. It didn't feel as though the ball was lodged in his arm, but it still hurt. No doubt it would hurt even more later, when the heightened emotions of the evening wore off.

He ran faster, leaping over rocks and bushes that impeded his pursuit. He was closing in, but not close enough. Soon, the culprit would reach the entrance, where he could easily blend into the crowd, and then he would either hide in plain sight or make his getaway in one of the many boats waiting at the dock. Either way, if North didn't catch him now, he never would.

Having narrowed the distance between them considerably, North stopped and drew the pistol from his belt. He took aim—thank God it had been his left arm hit—and fired. His quarry staggered, but kept running.

An eye for an eye. He'd winged his prey.

Lungs burning and straining, North forced his legs to pump faster. He almost tripped over something. Dimly, it registered. The rifle. His quarry had dropped his weapon. North ran faster.

The entrance was near. The edge of the crowd was thickening, beginning to swallow the man ahead of him. The spectators seemed to pay little attention to the heavyset fellow pushing his way through them, but unfortunately they noticed North all too easily. His frantic pursuit and bloodied appearance alarmed them, and instead of clearing a path for him as he hoped, they closed in with expressions of fear and concern.

"Out of the way!" he shouted, wincing as someone collided with his injured arm. "For Christ's sake, *move!*" He shoved the butt of his pistol into a man's shoulder, thrusting him out of his path.

How many precious seconds he'd lost reaching the gate, he couldn't count, but it had been enough. Obviously his shooter had friends waiting, because he was in a boat being rowed with great speed across the river. There was no way North could catch them on his own, not with an injured arm.

He'd lost him. Shoulders sagging, North gasped for breath, sweat trickling down his face in the warm night. He shoved his pistol into his pocket and wrapped his fingers around his left arm. He was still bleeding—bad enough that he could smell it.

But he had shot his opponent as well. And as soon as he could, he'd have Francis and the others questioning every quack and surgeon in the city. Someone would have to tend to the man's wound, and if North had been accurate enough to plant a ball in his arm, it would be easy to identify as his own. He marked all his shot.

He would catch him. It was a promise. And God help him when he did. The bastard would consider himself lucky the bullet hadn't hit Octavia. But the intent had been there, of that North was certain, and for that, the shooter would suffer.

Suffer badly.

There was a lot of blood. North's blood. North was hurt.

It was all her fault. Rationally, she knew better than to blame herself, but her heart refused to listen to reason. He had been shot in her company, possibly because of her or instead of her. Who else could be to blame?

Blast it all, where were his many minions when they were needed? They'd been crawling all over Vauxhall, dogging their every step. They'd no doubt been watching them on the Lovers Walk as well. If North hadn't been shot, they would have watched them kiss.

Stupid of her to try to kiss him like that. Stupid of her to lead him away from safety. Stupid and foolish, and it could have cost North more than a lot of blood. It could have cost him his life.

"Take your coat and shirt off," she commanded, her voice hoarse as she stopped pacing the carpet in his office. They had been in his house mere minutes. Mrs. Bunting was fetching supplies to treat his wound, but no one had arrived to tend it.

He held his hand over his injured arm. "I am all right. Francis will look after it."

He most certainly was *not* all right. Being shot was far from all right. "You could bleed to death before Mr. Francis returns."

"It is not that bad."

"Damn it, North!" Her voice was shaking. *She* was shaking. "Take off your coat and shirt!"

Surprisingly, he did as she commanded. Or rather he attempted to do as she commanded. The fingers of his right hand were covered with blood—fresh and dried. They fumbled with the fastenings of his coat, slipping on the metal and staining the soft wool.

"Let me do it. At the rate you are going, you *will* bleed to death." Perhaps she shouldn't be so short with him, but seeing him shot had scared her, and then for him to take off as he had . . .

The buttons on his coat were wet and sticky as she slipped them through their holes, and she could smell a salty, copper scent about him. *Blood.* Her stomach rolled.

He managed to pull his right arm out on his own, but she had to help him with the left. Carefully, she tugged the sleeve, drawing it down so the fabric avoided his wound. She tossed the coat on the floor. It landed with a thud. He had something heavy in one of his pockets. A pistol, probably, but she didn't want to think about that.

"I liked that coat," he remarked with enough regret that it would have been comical were she not still so very much concerned about him.

With the darkness of his coat gone, the wound looked much worse. His shirtsleeve was saturated and glued to his flesh with shades of deep and bright crimson. The tear where the lead sliced through the fabric was almost black with blood. Octavia swallowed.

"You are very pale," he told her. "Really, it is not so bad. Let Francis look at it."

Her trembling fingers went to his cravat. "Be quiet." Untying the knot, she unwound the starched linen, tossing the strip on top of his coat when she was done.

She tugged his shirt free of his waistband, catching a glimpse of brown flesh beneath.

God, the sight of his skin was more troublesome than his blood. Shame on her.

"Lift your arm." She didn't have to tell him which one. No doubt he couldn't lift the other. Up the shirt slid, and he pulled his right arm free as she lifted. The neckline came over his head—he had to duck a bit—and then, very gingerly, she peeled the destroyed linen down over his left arm.

She tossed the shirt in the hearth.

North smiled. How he managed it, she didn't know. His face was pale beneath his tan, but he still wasn't as white as she was. And now she was all the paler because of this wound. He had to be in pain, but he hid it well.

"You seem to have a penchant for throwing my clothes around, my lady."

She actually blushed. How could she not when his tone was so flirtatious? The rush of blood warmed her cold cheeks. Now if only it would spread to her—

"Christ, those are cold!"

—hands.

She jerked back. "Sorry."

He was scowling now. "Warm those things before you touch me again."

As if on cue, Mrs. Bunting bustled into the room carrying a tray with a basin of hot water, a bottle of amber liquid, and a pile of cloths on it.

"Here you are, my lady. Are you sure you do not want me to tend to Mr. Sheffield?"

Octavia shook her head. It was her fault North had been shot in the first place. She would look after him.

"It is going to need stitches," North said softly, drawing her gaze to his. He was giving her the opportunity to change her mind about playing surgeon.

"Thank you, Mrs. Bunting." Her gaze never left North's. "That will be all."

North sighed, but said nothing. When the door closed, he seated himself on the corner of his desk and stared at her. "Go ahead then."

Dipping one of the many cloths in the basin of water, Octavia hissed as the heat scorched her numb fingers. It was too hot, but it felt good—a strange mixture of pain and pleasure as the feeling returned to her hands. She wrung out the cloth and turned to her patient.

God, but he was lovely—even with bloody arm and a frown on his face. The last time she had seen his naked torso she'd had too much to drink, and her memory of the sight was clouded by that fact. The sight of him now was a vision she would carry for quite some time—and not just because of the blood.

Mounds of taut, golden-rose skin, dipping into lines of sinew before rising again in smooth lines of muscle. Jutting bones, deep hollows, he would be a challenge for any painter to recreate. And how could any brush capture the ropey strength beneath the hair on his chest?

"You are damned lucky I'm bleeding, looking at me like that."

The low timbre of his voice jerked her back to reality—and to the fact that he was indeed bleeding. Here he was injured and she was ogling him like a prize bull at market! She should be slapped—hard.

"A woman would have to be dead not to look," she replied, wetting the cloth again to warm it. "You do not need me to tell you how fine you look, Norrie. I am sure you already know."

"I know how fine you looked with your clothes off, Vie."

Her hands shook as she brought the cloth to his wound,

and it wasn't because of the shock of the evening. "This might hurt a bit."

"Just looking at you hurts."

"You should not say such things." She pressed the damp linen to the gash in his arm. He sucked in a breath, but did not tell her to stop. She dabbed at the wound and surrounding flesh until the cloth was dark with blood and then wet another, wiping the blood from the rest of his arm.

"You realize that by tomorrow morning I could have this son of a bitch in custody and there will be no reason for us to see each other again."

"Please do not say such things."

"I will miss you."

Tears stung her eyes. "Stop it. I cannot tend to your injury with eyes full of tears." She wiped at her eyes with the back of her hand, feeling something sticky smudge on her cheek. Blood, no doubt.

"Hold this against the wound while I clean the rest of your arm."

He took the cloth in his good hand and did as she ordered. "I never meant to make you cry."

"I know." That was all she could say.

After cleaning the rest of his arm, she stitched the wound shut, wincing every time the needle slipped through his flesh. How could he stand it? He hardly made a noise and yet she knew it must hurt like the blazes.

Finally she tied off the end of the thread and snipped it with a pair of scissors. If only she had given more attention to her needlework as a girl.

North glanced down at her handiwork, the whiteness around his mouth easing. "You would make a lousy seamstress, Vie. Luckily I do not care if it is pretty or not so long as it's not bleeding."

"You were right. It was not as bad as I thought." She didn't bother to respond to his comments about her stitches.

He nodded at the bottle of amber liquid on the tray. "Pour some whiskey on it."

"I beg your pardon?" Never had she heard such a ridiculous notion!

"Devlin claims it works better than water for cleaning wounds."

"And you believe him?"

"He would know better than you or I."

Good point. She uncorked the bottle, and placing a wad of cloths underneath his arm, poured a liberal amount of whiskey on the newly stitched flesh.

"God damn!"

Eager to have this whole situation over with, Octavia hurriedly bound his arm with the leftover cloths, wrapping the wound with a thick, protective covering.

She could have sunk to the floor and wept when it was all over.

"Thank you."

She stared at him, tears threatening again. "For what? My God, Norrie, it was my fault!"

"Your fault? Oh, Vie, it was not. Come here. Let me wipe your face."

She stepped closer, into the V of his legs as he wet the one last cloth and wiped the smudge on her cheek.

"I am sorry." She sniffed. "I cannot stop thinking that you were shot protecting me."

He caught her beneath the chin with his finger, tilting her head upward so she was forced to meet his gaze.

"And I would do it all over again. If anything ever happened to you—"

He didn't finish. He didn't have to. She knew exactly what he meant, because it was exactly how she felt. How close they had come to losing each other that night. How empty her world would be without North somewhere in it. It would be like someone killing her twin, her other self.

"I do not want to lose you," she whispered.

"You won't." His hand slid up to cup her cheek. "No matter what else, I will always be there if you need me."

And she knew he meant it. Despite all their other promises, all their decisions over the years, Octavia knew North would betray every promise and vow for her if she asked him to, as would she for him. She would even risk Spinton learning the truth—risk the entire *ton* learning the truth—if North asked it of her.

But he would never ask it, nor would she. They both knew that as well.

"Norrie—" How could she possibly put what she was feeling into words?

He pulled her closer, his hand now curving around the back of her neck. "I know. I know."

And then his mouth was on hers and her arms wrapped around his ribs, her fingers digging into the firm warmth of his back.

His tongue parted her lips, sweeping inside with a forcefulness that made her knees quiver.

There was desperation in their kiss—desperation, longing, and a sweetness that made Octavia's heart ache. How could he want her? How could she want him, knowing it would only lead to sadness and hurt? This attraction between them would only serve to make saying good-bye all the more difficult.

Even if things were different, even if Spinton were not in her life, North would not be comfortable in the world she now lived in, and she wasn't all that certain she would be comfortable in his. She certainly couldn't sit by and watch him put his life in jeopardy time and time again, not if tonight was any indication of how dangerous his work was. And yet that did not stop her from clinging to him like ivy to stone. It did not stop her from wanting this moment to last forever. She could have lost him, but she didn't. And now she refused to let him go.

"Come to bed with me, Vie," he whispered roughly against her mouth. "Be mine one last time."

She would be his for all time, but she didn't say it. She simply nodded, her gaze held by the blue heat of his.

He took her left hand in his right and led her to the door of the office. Outside, the house was dimly lit and quiet. Had the servants all gone to bed? Did it matter? No. Right now she didn't care if anyone saw her follow North upstairs. She was not ashamed of wanting him, even though she knew others would expect her to be. How could any woman in her right mind be ashamed of such a man's desire? North Sheffield wanted *her*. It was something to be proud of.

North's bedroom was at the far end of the upstairs corridor, at the back of the house. Here the noise outside was muted—nothing more than a low hum.

A lit lamp sat on the bedside table, casting the room in a warm, inviting glow. The last time she had entered this room, she'd been so nervous her palms dripped and her knees knocked. Tonight she was perfectly calm. Perhaps it was the shock of the evening numbing her. Perhaps it was the feeling that spending the night with North was the first *right* thing she had done for quite some time.

He toed off his boots, but when it came to removing his trousers and stockings, his fingers fumbled. His injured arm made him awkward.

"Let me." Pushing his hands away, she released the buttons on his falls. She was terribly aware of his gaze upon her, hot and predatory. She glanced up, saw the stark want, saw the *need* in his expression, and then dropped her gaze to her hands, trembling.

Slowly, she peeled the fabric down his legs and over his feet. When he was completely bare before her, she slid her palms up the solid, hairy curves of his calves, the dip of his knees, the strength of his thighs. He was golden and warm and beautiful beneath her hands. And when she reached the rigid length of flesh jutting from his groin, she touched it with tentative wonder.

North hissed, but it was a pleasureful sound. "Easy. It has been a while."

Smiling, filled with a sense of womanly power, she gazed up at him as she continued to stroke the satiny flesh. "Twelve years?"

"No."

She could be jealous but she had no right, and it wasn't as though his other lovers mattered. She had been the first. She was the now. And he would always be hers no matter whose bed he was in.

"Then you do not know what it is to suffer," she informed him softly. "For more than a decade I have remembered the pleasure you gave me but have been unable to ever duplicate the sensation. You have."

His fingers closed around the ones holding him, stilling her caress. "No, I haven't."

The words struck her, and for one brief moment Octavia feared she might cry. Leaning forward, her knees digging into the carpet, she placed light kisses on the hand holding hers, and then she ran the flat of her tongue over the head of his erection.

"Jesus." His hand released hers, cupping the back of her head instead. He didn't push, but neither could she move away—not that she wanted to.

She licked him, kissed him, opened her mouth and took him inside, savoring the feel, the musky salt of his skin. His fingers tightened in her hair as she worked him with her tongue and lips, the desperate feeling blossoming again low in her belly. Her hands clutched at his flanks, holding him exactly where she wanted him.

"Stop," he ordered hoarsely, the muscles beneath her palms flexing. "Stop now."

She did. Knowing she could have sent him over the edge was satisfaction enough, and while she enjoyed pleasuring him, her mouth was not where she wanted him.

His eyes were diamond bright in the lamplight, burning with desire. He tugged the pins from her hair even though it must have pained his injured arm to do so, and when he had the long, heavy mass streaming around her shoulders, he ordered her to turn around so that he could unfasten her gown. It took a while—long enough that Octavia's nerves were fairly frayed by the time he finished, but eventually the neckline sagged and the gown slipped from her arms.

She turned, giving him access to the ribbons on her shift. He untied them, flicking the flimsy gauze to the floor. She stood before him, naked save for her stockings and garters.

He pulled her against him, and she gasped as her naked flesh met his. Rough yet smooth, hard yet supple, he was like nothing she had ever felt before. The years had made him bigger, more muscled. And he was hotter than she remembered, his skin like a brand against her own.

"You are even more beautiful than I remembered," he whispered against her ear. "You have no idea how often I've thought of you this way."

She shivered as his warm breath caressed the side of her face and neck, closing her eyes in pleasure as his lips followed the same path.

His fingers combed through her hair, massaging her scalp and neck until her muscles felt limp and rubbery, she was so relaxed, and yet filled with a coiling tension that increased with his touch rather than eased. Between her legs she was already throbbing with anticipation. Warm and moist, she was ready for him, even though she had no idea whether the invasion of his body would be more welcome than it had been that first night a lifetime ago.

He lowered her to the bed, propping himself up on one elbow so he could look at her.

"You look like an angel," she whispered. Backlit by the candlelight, his entire form was cast with a warm, golden halo.

Gently, he smoothed the hair back from her face, fanning it out around her on the pillows. There was not a flaw to be found on him anywhere. The loose waves of his hair gave him a boyish look, the lines of his face were softened by the soft light. Only the bandage on his arm marred his perfection.

He was perfection to her.

North smiled tenderly. "I look at you and I lose all rational thought. You are a temptress, dear Vie."

Her gaze locked with his. "And you are pure sin."

His hand slid up her thigh. The muscle there quivered at his touch, and she shifted beneath him. She wanted him to touch her, stroke her. He brushed his lips across the taut peak of one breast, sending a delicious thrill shooting through her. "You are so beautiful. So perfect in every way."

She wanted to argue, but he robbed her of speech as he eased the tip of his tongue around her nipple. It puckered and tightened, aching for more.

"Everything about you is beautiful," he murmured, his breath hot and moist and oh-so-tormenting.

"Stop talking," she demanded, her fingers tangling in his hair, pushing his head to her breast.

He chuckled softly before taking her hardened flesh into his mouth. He suckled gently as his fingers stroked her waist and hip.

Octavia moaned and arched her hips against him. His fingers trailed down her belly to the juncture of her shivering thighs. She parted her legs for him, anxious for his touch.

Her body jerked when he slid a finger into the damp valley there. Her muscles clutched at him as her fingernails dug into his shoulders. It was too much. It was too good, too intense. And yet she wanted more. She writhed against his hand, unsure whether she wanted more or wanted to escape.

"Are you all right?" he asked softly, his breath warm against her cheek.

"I want you inside me," she panted, staring unabashedly into the fiery blue of his eyes. "I need you inside me. Please, North."

He didn't answer, but she felt his hardness pulsate against her thigh, and she gasped as he slipped another finger inside her.

"You're so wet, I won't last more than a minute inside you. I want more than a minute Vie. I want you begging and sobbing and coming so hard your bones will turn to butter."

She closed her eyes as his words and fingers lifted her to another plane. The sweet ache between her legs intensified with every whispered caress. When she could stand it no more, she reached down and wrapped her hand around him.

"Ahh, Vie, no."

"So smooth and hot," she teased, using his own tactics against him. "Are you ready to beg, Norrie?"

"You're going to end up with me all over your hand," he warned through clenched teeth.

Laughing, Octavia pushed him onto his back, rolling after him, careful of his injured arm. She felt no modesty with him, no need to allow him to dictate how their coupling would proceed. There was just want and need, and something else. Something so strong she didn't want to even try to identify it.

North stopped her only for as long as it took him to withdraw a sheath from the drawer in his bedside table. Guiding her hands, he showed her how to put it on him, securing it at the base of the engorged sex that strained against her hands.

She straddled his hips, rocking back and forth so that the moist folds of her sex rubbed against the rock-hard length of him. The ache inside her intensified. She wanted him now.

Gazing at the body beneath her, she marveled at how his form, once boyish and smooth, was now knotted muscle and sinew. She ran her hands along the firm ridge of his ribs into the dark hair that covered his chest.

"You are so beautiful," she murmured, leaning down to kiss him.

North wrapped one arm about her waist as their lips met, holding her tightly. Boldly, Octavia reached between them, guiding him to the entrance of her body. North arched his pelvis as the blunt head slid inside her.

Both of them gasped as her body engulfed him completely. The sensation was almost too much to bear. There was no discomfort as there had been that first time. There was nothing but a delicious, full, stretched feeling that made her want to move on top of him until both of them were dripping with sweat.

This was not going to be a slow and tender union like their first one. This was going to be fast and wild and overwhelmingly intense. After finding each other they had come dangerously close to losing each other again, and their coming together wasn't about all the affection and desire they felt for each other. It was about the fear. Fear of living in a world where one of them no longer existed.

Octavia fell forward, grasping the headboard as if she was trying to tear it from its base. One of her breasts brushed against his mouth, and he caught the nipple between his lips, sucking hard enough to make her gasp in pleasure-pain.

His tongue against her nipple as he slid in and out of her sent Octavia over the edge. She brought her knees up to flank his torso, opening herself for even deeper penetration. Using the headboard for leverage, she began lifting and lowering her entire body, tensing every muscle so that she could feel a trickle of sweat between her shoulder blades and breasts. Her hair fell around them like a thick curtain, brushing against his face and chest as she rode him as if she were trying to break him.

His hips arched up to meet her every thrust and the pressure, the demanding ache between her legs grew—a sweet, desperate torment that she craved release from but wanted to go on forever at the same time. North was almost vicious as he drove his body into hers. She could feel him tensing beneath her, and her own movements quickened.

"Oh God," he cried, arching against the pillows.

Octavia lost complete control as she felt his release. She tossed her head back and cried out as wave after wave of intense pleasure crashed throughout her body. She continued to writhe against him until the intensity began to ebb, wanting to hold on to the incredible sensation for as long as she could.

Finally, she collapsed on top of him. They lay in silence with only the sound and rhythm of their breathing between them.

"Vie," North whispered after what felt like forever.

"Don't." Pressing her fingers against his lips, she shushed him. "Please. Don't say anything that might ruin it."

He nodded, wrapping his arms around her. They were silent for a long time.

There wasn't anything to say.

Chapter 12

He watched her while she slept.

It was late—very late. The hour, the tiredness of his body, and the potency of their lovemaking should have had him snuffed out like a candle but it didn't. He was afraid—afraid to close his own eyes for fear she would be gone when he woke. Somebody might take her away, or worse, she might leave on her own.

So he lay on his side, quiet and still in the gloomy darkness, not daring to move despite the ache in his injured arm and the increasing numbness in the arm beneath his head. Let it fall asleep. Right now that was preferable to having her wake up. In the morning he would be able to deal with her regrets, but not now.

"Norrie?"

Damn.

"What is wrong?"

He rolled over onto his back, distancing himself from her gaze. It would be so much easier to hear whatever she might say if he wasn't looking at her.

"Nothing. Nothing is wrong."

"Then why are you behaving so?"

Was that hurt in her voice or accusation? And just how the hell did she think he should act? Tonight changed everything. Complicated everything. Could she not see that?

He glanced at her. "I screwed you, Vie. Or was it so disappointing you forgot?" It hadn't sounded like she'd been disappointed.

Her eyes widened and he thought maybe she paled, but it was impossible to tell in the dim light. "Do not be so vulgar."

Vulgar? She thought that was *vulgar* ? She really had been away from the Garden too long. Mincing around in that gilded little world of hers had changed her after all. To think he had once wanted to be part of that world as well. He was lucky he wasn't.

So why was this bitter taste in the back of his throat?

"What would you have me call it? Swiving, frigging, slapping skin, a bit of in and out, hide the willy, fornication, ride the wet pony, rutting, f—"

"Stop!" Ahh, he had made her angry. That was good. He could accept her anger. If she told him to bugger off now it wouldn't hurt so much.

Silently, he stared into eyes so blue they seemed black in the dark, finding some satisfaction in the distaste he saw there. But there was hurt as well, and there could be no satisfaction in that.

Sheffield, you are an ass.

Tension drained from his muscles. "I am sorry, Vie. It was vulgar of me, you are right."

Her hand was soft on his arm. "Do you regret last night?"

"I regret being shot at, if that's what you mean."

She actually smiled a bit. Could she see through all his surliness? Did she know that he was only acting this way because the only thing that scared him more than losing Octavia was having her?

"It is not."

No, he'd known it wasn't. He did not want her to think he regretted bedding her, but masculine pride—and common sense—wouldn't allow him to admit just how much it meant to him either. "This changes everything."

Octavia looked stricken. "I do not want things between us to change."

How did she mean that? How did she view their relationship as it was? Did she want to remain friends and nothing more? She must. She obviously could not be feeling the same confusion he was.

If she didn't want things to change, that meant she wanted to carry on with her engagement to Spinton. She wanted to go back to her little world and leave him behind. It was for the best, he knew that. Honestly, he did.

"Fine," he murmured. "Things will not change."

She looked so relieved it broke his heart. "Good. I just want to enjoy being with you again. I want to savor every moment."

So she'd have something to think about when Spinton was huffing and puffing on top of her? Or because she actually felt something deeper than friendship toward him? He didn't know, and he was too much of a bloody coward to ask.

Her marrying Spinton would be for the best. She deserved that life. How many times would he have to tell himself that before his heart believed?

Instead he covered her hand with his own. "Me too."

Silence, awkward and heavy, passed between them. Eventually, Octavia's gaze flitted away as her fingers slid free of his. "I should return home. Beatrice is no doubt beside herself."

Maybe she was beside Spinton, but North didn't bother to give voice to his thoughts. He very much doubted the earl would make such advances, nor did he believe prim and proper Beatrice would accept them—no matter how much either of them might want to.

No, he and Octavia were the only ones in the wrong. Odd how something so wrong, so scandalous and sinful, could feel so right.

She wanted to go and he knew he should let her, but as she sat up in the bed, not bothering to hide her nudity from him, he caught her by the arm. He kept his gaze riveted on her face. Her body was beautiful and he had committed to memory just how wonderful every inch of it had felt against his, but he wanted to see her—see the emotions on her face.

"Is that what you want?" Never mind that, who was going to protect her if she left him? Spinton? He doubted it. If she truly wanted to go, he'd let her, but he'd stand guard night and day in front of her house himself to make sure she was safe.

She smiled sadly over her shoulder at him. "You have distanced yourself from me so much over the past few minutes that I think it must be what you want."

God, he hadn't meant to hurt her, only to protect himself. Could it be that she didn't want to leave him? She should, yes, he knew that. But what if she wanted to stay? Could either of them dare take that chance?

"It does not matter what I want." He had to allow her to decide this for herself, no matter how much he wanted to force her to remain in his bed.

She watched him with a little frown. "Of course it matters. This is your house. I will go."

He refused to release her wrist, pushing himself upright so that he sat beside her, the sheet pooling around his hips.

"Damn it, Vie! Just this once, do not think about what I

want, or what anyone else wants. What do you want?" Did she even know?

She stared at him.

"Do you want to return home to your empty bed, to Spinton and Beatrice and society, or do you want stay with me, here in my bed—my house?"

"I . . ." Her mouth worked, but no sound came out.

So that was it then. North released her arm. "Then you had better go. I will have Brahm's carriage brought round for you."

This time it was he who was stopped. Octavia placed the flat of her hand full on the center of his chest.

"I do not want to go." Her voice was raw and husky. "I want to stay. In your bed."

Her words aroused him more than any touch, any erotic image ever could have.

"Then stay."

Their gazes locked and North knew she wanted more than to simply stay with him. She wanted him. She didn't understand the attraction between them any more than he did, didn't want to question the depths of her feelings, but one thing was for certain—he was as much in her soul as she was in his. For years she had been the most important person in his life, surpassing even his brothers. He had been the most important person in hers as well. No one knew more about him than Octavia, and no one would ever know her better than he.

She lowered herself to the mattress and held her open arms up to him. Her long, smooth legs parted easily as he slid between them. Her nipples brushed his chest as her torso pressed against the length of his. She was warm and damp against his cock, moving against him although he had yet to touch her. This time it wasn't going to be about physical arousal, it was strictly emotional.

There were things neither of them knew how to put into words, but their bodies knew how much they cared. Her affection for him was in the trembling of her thighs, the desperation of her fingers. She clutched at his arms, arching against him, her body begging him to fill her, possess her. She wanted as much as he could give her, wanted as much as she could possibly have, and he knew it was so she would have something of him with her later.

He'd give her something she'd never forget.

He slid down the slender length of her, kissing her breasts with their swollen pink tips and the delicate flare of her hips.

Sliding between her firm thighs, he kissed the warm flesh there, parting the moist curls with his fingers. His tongue probed the salty-sweet pinkness, seeking and finding the small, hard pearl that brought a moan of pleasure to Octavia's lips when he licked it.

Ruthlessly he made love to her with his mouth and fingers. Without mercy he stroked and tasted, tormenting her with the promise of satisfaction until he finally gave it to her. When she came in a shuddering, keening symphony of rapture, North raised himself above her, thrusting his eager erection into the welcome wetness of her body. It didn't occur to him until he was inside that he hadn't gotten another sheath. He didn't care about the consequences. Right now he was mindless, concerned with nothing more than the joy of Octavia's body, Octavia's soul.

A long time ago he'd promised himself that he would never father a bastard, and he meant it. If Octavia ended up pregnant with his child, she would marry him—not Spinton. He would see to it.

Muscles straining, North thrust himself deep within her, as deep as she could take him. Her legs locked around him, her hands gripped the trembling length of his forearms. The wound in his arm throbbed in protest. He ignored it. Her breathing nothing more than shallow gasps, Octavia arched against him, whimpering. He thrust harder. Faster. Then everything stopped. He ceased to breathe, to think, to live, as his orgasm was wrenched from him by the hot, demanding flesh clenching his.

Panting, he collapsed onto her, his arms quaking as he tried to shield her from the brunt of his weight. Christ. It felt as though she had taken ten years off his life—or added them.

This was not fair. Sex with his best friend should not be the most incredible he had ever experienced. It was wrong for it to feel so right. Perhaps he and Octavia were simply living proof that men and women could not be simply friends. Attraction would always complicate things.

And Christ, were things ever complicated now. She didn't want things to change, but how the hell could they possibly remain the same? Maybe she could pretend that sharing his bed hadn't reset the rules, but he couldn't. No, he could—but it wouldn't be easy.

And it certainly wasn't going to be easy to hand her back to Spinton. She was his, damn it. Spinton couldn't have her. But Spinton would have her. That was how it had to be.

"What are you thinking about?"

He brushed the pad of his finger along the tip of her pert little nose. "You."

She smiled. "Good things I hope."

"After tonight how could they not be?" As he spoke the words, his left arm twinged, reminding him that not everything that had happened that evening had been as good as being inside Octavia.

The expression on her face told him her thoughts were in the same place. "Do you truly believe his intent was to kill you?"

There was no need to define who "he" was. "I don't know. It may have been meant as a warning."

Obviously something of his suspicions managed to find its

way into his voice or his expression because she finished his thoughts, "Or it was not intended for you at all."

"We do not know that.'

"No, but it is your job to consider it."

She wasn't stupid, his Vie. He might try to conceal things from her, but she hadn't always lived in a gilded cage. She knew how the underside of the world worked. She knew just as well as he that things weren't always as they appeared.

"I will not allow anyone to harm you."

"I know that." Her gaze locked with his. "And I will tear apart anyone that hurts you."

She meant it. Anyone else and he might have laughed, but he knew better. This was not an empty promise. She would exact revenge for any harm that befell him—or she would try. The consequences of what might happen if she tried and failed were not something he wanted to talk about.

"Leave the law to me, Vie." He rolled to his back, relieving her and his injured arm of his weight.

But she wasn't going to let him distance himself again, that was obvious when she rolled after him, propping herself up on her elbow to face him once again. "Why do you put yourself in such danger?"

He tucked his good arm behind his head. "It is my profession."

Her lips brushed his cheek. How glad he was that he had shaved earlier—just so he could feel that tender touch of her mouth. "You could change professions."

"What else would could I do? Trod the boards, become an actor?" He laughed—harshly. "Think I could give old Kean a little competition?"

She trailed her fingers through the hair on his chest. It was nice. "You could enter politics."

He scowled. "You do not believe that shite Brahm was spewing tonight, do you?"

She scowled back. "As a matter of fact, I thought he was correct. It would be a safer occupation."

And one he had already considered, yet now he rebelled. "A boring one."

Dawn was coming. He knew because he could see clearly as she rolled her eyes. "I do not believe that is your real reason for objecting."

Let her believe whatever she wanted. He replied lightly, "I detest being bored, you know that."

"You also detest society." The fingers stroking his chest stilled. "Is that not your true reason for dismissing the prospect?"

She knew him far too well. He looked away. "You do not know what you are talking about."

Octavia tugged at his chest hair, drawing his gaze back to hers. "I know and you know I know."

"I know you think you know." Despite his annoyance with the conversation, North could not stop the smile that curved his lips as he rubbed the spot where the hair had pulled. Octavia grinned back.

"I refuse to jump whenever some nob commands it." There was an honest answer if ever he gave one.

Her fingers were down around his navel now. "Just do what you always do, Norrie. Ignore him and do what you want."

Suddenly the direction of her fingers didn't matter. She'd struck a nerve. "That sounds a little hypocritical coming from someone who lives strictly by the rules."

Octavia tossed her hair. One thick chunk slid forward to curve down around one partially exposed breast. "Is that less hypocritical than changing them to suit as you go along? I made promises. And I beg your pardon, but my face is somewhat above where you are staring."

Caught. "I know." Not just where her face was, but what

she was saying. "You promised me you would always be there if I needed you."

She pulled the sheet up to cover herself. How could she conceal herself from him, of all people? She could try to hide it all she wanted, but her body was as familiar to him now as his own.

"So did you," she reminded him. "Looks like we both lied."

What the hell . . . ? "I never lied." He was scowling again.

"Neither did I, but we were children. Neither of our lives is that simple anymore." She lifted her chin, as if daring him to disagree. "Nothing is simple."

"No," he agreed. "If things were that simple, you and I would not be in this bed."

"Or I would at least have the decency to feel remorse for being here."

If she had hit him with his own shoe he wouldn't have been more stupefied. "You don't?"

Octavia sighed. Her fingers came up to touch his cheek. It was a light caress at best, but it tightened an invisible band around his chest so fiercely, it was difficult to breathe. "I do not. I have many regrets in my life, Norrie. This will not be one of them."

She had a way of knowing what to say that completely drained all of the fight out of him. He couldn't be angry at her—at circumstances, at her grandfather, at the whole world, even—but not at her.

"Come here."

She did, moving into his embrace without hesitation.

"I was always there for you in my heart," he admitted when her head was safely tucked in the crook of his arm, her gaze averted.

Soft lips brushed his throat. "So was I."

They fell asleep with those words, and all their possible implications, hanging above them.

There was something incredibly intimate about wearing a man's clothing, Octavia realized later that morning as she and North took their breakfast. She sat across from him at the little table in his office, clad in his dressing gown. The dark blue brocade was soft and well worn and smelled distinctly of soap and North. The next time he donned it, the gown would smell of soap and her. Would he like that? Would he even notice?

Yes, of course he would notice. He was every bit as attuned to her as she to him, though sometimes in entirely different ways.

Silently sipping her coffee, she studied him as he read through the various reports his officers sent him. He wore trousers and a shirt and that was it. His feet were bare, and the open collar of his shirt revealed the strong column of his throat and the golden upper expanse of his chest. The stubble on his jaw, and the disheveled curls on his head, only added to his piratelike appearance.

How the upper classes would tsk-tsk over him. He would never be a polished gentleman. No matter what he did he would never truly be accepted in that—her—world. No wonder he created his own then. He lived in a world that was neither lower nor upper class. A world where he alone made the rules and reigned as he saw fit.

How she envied that. The only expectations placed on North were the ones he alone orchestrated. He wasn't bound by promises or the fear of besmirching his family name. Of course, it wasn't as though the Ryland name was all that pure to begin with. He was fortunate that way, even though he probably wouldn't see it. He didn't have to pretend to be something he wasn't just so his past wouldn't taint his relations. He didn't have the guilt of leaving friends and loved ones behind to start a life that he both enjoyed and despised. She didn't mind admitting that while she liked the comforts money and consequence afforded, she could do without all the posturing.

But North was just North. The lines around his eyes and mouth, the unfashionable tan and stubble, were the things that set him even further apart from her world. And they were the things that made her heart ache every time she noticed them.

"I love you, Norrie."

He looked up from his papers. Reaching across the table, he gave her hand a gentle squeeze. "I love you too."

There was nothing different in his inflection, nothing in his expression that gave her any indication that the love he spoke of was as deep and terrible as hers. He loved her as he had always loved her—as a friend. A dear and special friend, of that there was no doubt, but a friend all the same. She knew he would do whatever she asked, would do whatever he could for her.

Anything except love her as she wanted him to. And she did want him to love her, she realized that now. She had never forgotten her girlish love for him, and being with him again had allowed it to blossom into something more mature and painful. He was her best friend, her lover, her only. He was the most important person in her life—the one person who had seen her at her best and at her worst. The one person who knew all her secrets—well, all except for how she truly felt about him. He was the one person she trusted above all else. If North claimed he could stop the sun from rising she would believe him.

So she believed that he loved her, even though she knew he did not. Not in the way she wanted. This was one time when Beatrice would be wrong. Octavia would not get her way.

It was for the best. She knew that. And yet that foolish young girl within her wept a little bit. For years she had entertained the notion that he had felt the same about her all those years ago, and maybe he had. But he didn't now, and now was what mattered.

Still, he was her Norrie, and she would always be his Vie. Surely there was some satisfaction to be had in that. She simply had to look.

"Do you suppose it is usual for friends to make love?" God, why do this to herself? He was not going to give her the answers she wanted.

He choked on a mouthful of coffee. "Good Lord, Vie. Wait for me to swallow before you ask something like that."

"Sorry." She wasn't sorry at all. "Well, do you?"

Wiping his mouth with his hand, he had the grace to look uncomfortable. "I do not know. It seems to be usual for us at any rate."

"Do you think others have a friendship like ours?" She toyed with the serviette beside her plate. *Do you think other women set themselves up for heartbreak as I do?*

"A man and woman cannot be friends without it leading to something physical."

That was just *wrong*, but she didn't want to argue with him when he so obviously did not want to discuss it. Instead of upsetting her, his dancing around the subject gave her hope. The only time North avoided a discussion was when he feared making himself vulnerable. And he was the kind of man who was only vulnerable to people he cared about.

Of course, she knew he cared about her. She just didn't know how much.

"I like to think our friendship is special." Why could she not just leave it alone?

He met her gaze. "The most special of my life."

Her heart skipped a beat.

His expression changed to one of deep sadness for a split second before being engulfed in blankness. "I regret that I will not be there to see you marry Spinton."

Oh he knew how to turn the knife! Regardless of his own feelings for her, he wasn't going to let them get out of hand, nor was he about to allow her to entertain any romantic notions. No doubt he thought that sex instantly changed things for a woman. How like a man. The only thing sex did was let a woman know she had some control over a man. Her feelings were the same as they always had been.

North Sheffield was still her favorite man in the whole world, despite the fact that he was sometimes purposely stupid.

God love him, he was doing all he could to make leaving him behind easier for her. It was she who made it so very difficult.

But for now, they were together, and she refused to accept that in a few hours they might never see each other again.

Time for a change of subject. Drawing the neck of the dressing gown closer around her like armor, she asked, "When are you going to the paper shop?"

He folded the last of his letters and set it aside with the others. "As soon as Francis reports in. If he found our shooter, then I won't need to go the shop."

Octavia sipped her coffee. "You could go anyway. The man with the gun might have been hired."

North's hand curved around his own cup, not bothering with the delicate handle. He scowled at her. "I am not leaving you here alone."

"I will not be alone." There were servants there, for heaven's sake!

"Unprotected."

"You cannot protect me forever."

"Not forever, no." His cup hit the saucer with a loud clank. "That will be your husband's job."

Another twist. "Yes."

"But for now it is mine."

And so was she. He didn't have to say it aloud; she could hear the possession in his tone. It unsettled her—thrilled her.

Her gaze fell to the table. "There is the problem of my reputation."

That threw him off—she could hear it in his voice. "What?"

"If people find out I am here alone with you, my reputation will be ruined."

He made a scoffing noise. "I often bring people here for protection. Everyone knows that."

Octavia traced the gilt edging on her cup with the tip of her finger, purposely avoiding his gaze. "Yes, but you have been seen flirting with me in public, remember? People will assume the worst."

He hadn't considered that. His only thought had been her safety. She smiled inside.

"Until I find the culprit, you are not safe at home."

She didn't want to go home. She shamelessly wanted to stay with him, but she didn't want her reputation—and those of Beatrice and Spinton—to suffer for it.

"You could have Beatrice come here to act as a chaperone." Holding her breath, she raised her gaze to his once more.

His expression was dubious at best. "She might suspect we've been . . . intimate."

"I think we could convince her otherwise." That was true. Beatrice would believe what she told her because Beatrice would want to believe it. And even if she didn't, who cared? Octavia wanted to stay with North, and to be honest, she didn't give a fig how she managed to accomplish it.

He still did not seem convinced himself. Could it be that he did not want Beatrice around because he wanted Octavia all to himself? And was it awful of her to wish it?

In the end, he must have seen that it was the only solution. "Fine," he growled. "Send for your cousin."

Victory! She had managed to keep herself in his life for at least a little while longer. "I will do so directly. How is your arm?"

"The same as it was when you asked ten minutes ago. It is fine."

It had been much longer than ten minutes, and obviously something *wasn't* fine because his mood was quickly deteriorating.

He didn't want anyone else to intrude upon their world. He didn't want to share her.

He filled his cup from the silver coffee pot and offered to do the same for her. She shook her head. "You might also want to send a note round to Spinton."

"Oh?" Why would she want to do that? Beatrice was their go-between.

"Yes." Now it was he who avoided her gaze. "He is your betrothed."

Who was he trying to remind, her or himself? It didn't matter; it was a sharp reminder for both of them.

"You are right." She chuckled feebly. "Although he may decide he does not want me after this."

North's gaze pinned her to her chair. "Spinton will still want you. Any man would."

Octavia's chest tightened. Did he include himself in that statement? "You have a higher opinion of me than I deserve."

"That is not possible."

"Stop it, Norrie." She was blushing now, and thoroughly uncomfortable. She was engaged to one man and sharing the bed of another. Could he not see just how undeserving she was?

"You are a good person, Vie. You are loyal to a fault. If you make a promise you keep it. Spinton will never want a better countess than the one you will be."

"Yes," she agreed, a tad more bitterly than she intended. "Because I will remind myself daily how things might have been had I followed in my mother's footsteps."

He squeezed her hand again, this time more forcibly. "Because you *are* a lady, Vie. You are honorable and loyal, and your being here with me does not change that."

Oh but it did. Could he not see that? Being with him made her *want* to be dishonorable and disloyal. One word—actually three words—from him and she would be seriously tempted to toss all those promises to the wind and say to hell with being a lady.

But hadn't she been the one to say she didn't want things to change between them? Stupid, stupid. At the time she'd been afraid that he had meant they couldn't be friends anymore, that they couldn't be anything. But now . . . Now she wondered if perhaps he hadn't been referring to a change for the better. A change to something more intimate than just friends.

Whatever he had meant, it didn't matter now. He would never tell her, just as she would probably never tell him. For all their blustering, they were both cowards beneath it all, scared of losing their friendship, scared of being rejected because their lives had been full of loss and feeling unwanted.

And now their lives were so different. He wouldn't want to be part of the world she lived in, and she didn't know if she could live in his. Watching him put himself in danger time and time again was not something she could do. But could he be happy doing anything else? And would hearing about his exploits be any easier than living through them with him?

She was giving herself a headache. Why did she insist on dwelling on these things?

"Promise me you will be careful today if you find the man who shot you."

The glacial gleam in his pale eyes told her he would not make any such promise. "I am going to make certain he never bothers you or anyone else again."

Could he hear himself? "For God's sake, North, it was you who got shot, not me!"

Her outburst seemed to startle him almost as much as it had her. Wonderful, now she was going to cry on top of it.

"Just promise me you will be careful." Her voice cracked as her eyes burned. If anything happened to him . . . She couldn't live in a world without him in it, no matter whose world it was.

North seized her free hand in his, all the ice melting from his gaze as it met hers. "I will be careful, Vie. I promise."

Such sweet relief his words brought. He would be careful, she knew it. She nodded.

He didn't move to hold her or comfort her. They both knew how dangerous it would be, what the outcome would be. They would end up back in his bed, or on the floor, and the emotions between them would become even more heightened, when what they needed right now was to bring them down a level—or seven.

Releasing her hands, North smiled encouragingly. "Why don't I send a messenger round to your house for Miss Henry. Would you like that?"

Ignoring the fact that he was talking to her as if she were a child, Octavia nodded. North obviously did not know how to react to her overwrought state. That was all right; she didn't know how to react to it either.

He rose from the table and left the room, giving her a few moments alone to collect herself. Regardless of his not knowing how to handle her emotions, he still knew exactly what she needed to regain control of them.

Sniffing, Octavia inhaled a deep breath. It had an instant calming effect, and she turned toward the window as she exhaled.

What she saw robbed the breath from her lungs.

Out on the street, across from the window where she sat, stood a rough-looking man in surprisingly neat clothing, smoking a cigar. For a second, his gaze locked with hers and he smiled—a smile that sent a shiver down her spine. He tossed his cigar to the ground and turned away, exhaling a thin stream of smoke as he strolled down the street.

Octavia watched him go, her heart pounding against her ribs. Who was he? Had he been watching her and North?

And if he had, how much had he seen? And why was he watching?

Chapter 13

Was Octavia genuinely trying to make him insane, or was she ignorant of the delicate balance of his reason? First she said she didn't want things to change, then when he agreed to that, she acted as if she *did* want things to be different between them. What did she want from him? If he knew what she wanted he could at least act accordingly. One minute it seemed all she wanted was to be with him, the next as if she couldn't wait to get back to Spinton.

And just why was she marrying someone she did not love? Out of duty? Because of a promise? Regardless, she'd better not think that he would still be there whenever she wanted a bed partner, because he'd seen what that kind of arrangement had done to his mother. If Octavia decided to be his, she would have to be all his, and that was final.

But for now he'd take what she was willing to give, because that was better than nothing at all. She would never fully be his. That was impossible.

He wanted her. Damnation, but he wanted all of her. In his life, in his bed, everywhere. Unfortunately, she didn't want to stay in his world. She seemed to like parties and society, and what woman in her right mind would give up the chance to be a countess? Not very many. Only the deepest love could persuade someone to make such a decision, and even then that person would have to be slightly insane.

Still, he would be lying if he said he didn't want Octavia's love as well. He did. He thought he'd outgrown all that foolishness, but apparently he hadn't. He wanted her love, and he was too much of a coward to go after it.

She'd almost killed him that morning when she told him she loved him. How much he wanted to believe she meant it in a way other than platonic, but he knew better than that. If Octavia truly loved him he would know it, because that would make him the luckiest man on the face of the earth.

And his luck just wasn't that good.

His own feelings were almost as hard to pin down as Octavia's. One minute he needed her as he needed air, and the next he was more than prepared to send her back to Spinton. Spinton could give her so much that he couldn't—a life that she was born to. A life that she deserved. All he could give her was himself. It didn't seem like that good of a trade. All he wanted was to see her happy. Spinton stood a better chance of doing that. Which was why he wasn't going to try to make her stay.

That and the fear that she'd turn her back on him and walk out of his life again.

"Mr. Sheffield?"

Giving himself a mental shake, North came back to the real world. He was with Francis in the paper shop, and the man behind the counter was staring at him expectantly.

"Hmm?" How relaxed he sounded, as though the thoughts that distracted him from his mission weren't tearing him apart.

The proprietor, Mr. Jones, handed North a list. "These are

all the people who have bought the paper you inquired after."

Flashing the man an easy smile, North fought the urge to compare the list to the one Octavia had given him. He didn't want the man to see how important this was to him. He didn't want anyone else to know.

He flipped the man a guinea. "Thank you."

Jones looked disappointed. Obviously he had been expecting more remuneration. He could keep expecting. He wasn't going to get it.

Outside, North pulled Octavia's list from his pocket. His gaze scanned the different handwriting as he quickly compared names. His heart jumped. There was one. One match. All he needed was one, provided it was the right one. In his gut, he knew this was it.

Lord Alexander Merton.

Of course it would be a lord. An earl, as it were. North had heard of him before. Merton was a regular at the theater when he was growing up. It wasn't surprising that Octavia's mother had had a relationship with him. Merton liked beautiful women, and Octavia's mother had been very beautiful.

Elation, mixed with a large dose of rage, filled him. He was going to catch Merton. He was going to prove the bastard was harassing Octavia, and he was going to see him pay for it.

And then what? Then he was going to step back and allow the woman for whom he would gladly risk more than a bullet in the arm to marry another man. How stupid was he?

No, not stupid. Stupid had nothing to do with it. He didn't have a name to give her—not a "good" one as far as society was concerned. She was part of a world that might want him now but could decide it didn't want him tomorrow, and even if she didn't care about that, he did.

Then there were those damned promises of hers. She had

made promises to her mother and her grandfather, and while the dead couldn't enforce such vows, Spinton could. Octavia had agreed to marry him; North had heard her. Octavia didn't make or break promises easily. She would marry Spinton unless he tried his damnedest to talk her out of it.

He wasn't going to do that, not when the nature of his job could put her in danger. Even if they could have a future, what if someone tried to use her to get to him?

And why was he thinking of them having a future? Octavia was his friend, his dearest friend. For a while he had thought of her as so much more, but he had no idea what she thought of him. For that matter, he had no idea what his feelings for her were now. He didn't want to lose her but the idea of spending the rest of his life with her . . .

It was a little frightening. And exciting. And impossible. Better to stop thinking about it. It would only make it hurt more when she was gone.

He didn't want to let her go, but continuing her acquaintance with him would only increase the chance of someone uncovering her past. It was flimsily concealed as it was. If anyone found out about her mother, Octavia would lose much of her footing in society. Only marriage to Spinton could save her from whatever damage her past had wrought.

That was the end of the story.

Good Christ, what was he doing? Harker was still on the loose, and here he was, standing on the street, once again mooning over a woman he couldn't have! Wouldn't the boys at Bow Street have a laugh if they could see him now? They would no doubt think he had taken complete leave of his senses.

Perhaps he had. And it was all because of Octavia. He couldn't think of anything but her. It was damned annoying.

And it could be dangerous as well. What if Harker were

lurking around, waiting to make a move? North was a prime
target standing out in the open with his head in the clouds.
Black Sally and Harris were dead because of Harker, and
North wouldn't be able to make their deaths worth something if he was dead as well.

Tucking both lists into his pocket, he bid farewell to Francis, who was off to watch Harker, walked to where his horse
stood, and hoisted himself into the saddle. He was going to
collect a couple of his men, and then he was going to con-
front Merton and make certain the bastard never came near
Octavia again. Then he was going to return home to tell Octavia she was safe. Then he'd take her home.

And say good-bye.

"I came as soon as I could. Why are you dressed like that?"

Octavia embraced her cousin as she entered the inviting,
manly room North used as office, dining room, and parlor.

"I am so happy to see you. I found it in the attic. Do you
not like it?" She twirled around, wrinkled skirts floating
about her ankles.

Beatrice's pert little nose wrinkled. "You smell as though
you have spent the last twenty years packed in an old trunk."

Octavia chuckled. "I have not, but this gown has. It was
North's mother's." It was a serviceable gown, a tad too big
and a shade too short, but it would suit her purpose. It was far
from fashionable—even at the turn of the century—and Octavia supposed Nell Sheffield had worn it for the very same
reason she was—to clean house.

Her cousin, who was dressed very prettily in a gown of
pale blue muslin, handed her a valise. "I brought you some of
your own clothing. The gowns will need to be pressed, but at
least you will not be forced to wear *that*."

Still smiling, Octavia set the bag aside and draped an old

kerchief over her head, knotting it at her nape. "I am wearing this because I am going to make this house livable. And you are going to help me."

Beatrice's gaze drifted about the room. "It looks livable enough."

"This is the only room he lives in." Other than his bedroom, of course, but she needn't mention that to Beatrice.

"Perhaps he likes it that way. I am certain the servants must. Why are the servants not doing the cleaning?"

"Because I remember what this house used to look like, how it used to smell and feel. It was much warmer than this, I assure you." In fact, seeing the house as it was disturbed her. It was eerie, seeing everything covered so.

"Trying to recapture the past, Tavie? It cannot be done, you know."

"I know." Her tone was surlier than she intended. "But this used to be a home. North deserves to have that again."

Beatrice looked dubious as she cast another glance around. "If he wanted that, surely he would have done it himself."

Octavia balled her right hand into a fist, rubbing it against the palm of her left. "He is afraid."

"Afraid?" Her tone alone said just how ludicrous Beatrice thought that was. "Of what? I have always thought him the kind of man who fears nothing."

Octavia turned away only to start pacing a small expanse of the blue and wine carpet. "He is afraid of being happy because he believes it will not last."

"And you want to make him happy."

For moment Octavia thought her cousin was mocking her, but there was no sarcasm in her words. "Exactly."

"Even though you are betrothed to another and will eventually have to leave this house?"

"Yes."

"You love him."

"Yes." There was no point in lying. None at all. Beatrice already knew the truth.

"Spinton deserves better."

Octavia stopped pacing and faced her cousin. There was no judgment in Beatrice's dark gaze, only sympathy. She would have preferred judgment. "I know."

"*You* deserve better."

"Perhaps." Right now she didn't know what she deserved. She wouldn't even face what she *wanted*, for pity's sake.

Beatrice folded soft, plump arms over her impressive bosom. "If you love Mr. Sheffield you should not marry Fitzwilliam. It is wrong."

Fitzwilliam? Octavia crossed her own longer arms likewise over her less impressive chest. "It is not that simple."

A dark brow arched. "Whyever not?"

Octavia mirrored her expression by raising a brow of her own. Why had she never noticed how similar she and Beatrice were before this? "Because Spinton and I both made promises. There are certain things expected of us."

"Expected?" Now her cousin was openly scowling, her opinion of these promises obvious. "By whom?"

"My grandfather for one."

"He is dead."

Oh yes, they were very similar indeed, perhaps not in looks, but definitely in attitude. Beatrice could be downright blunt when she so desired. "Spinton's father."

This time both of her cousin's brows lifted. "Dead."

"My mother." If it was a list Beatrice wanted, Octavia could certainly give it to her.

"Again, dead."

Octavia threw her arms into the arm. Was her cousin unable to utter another word? "It does not matter if they are dead or not!"

"Of course it does!" Beatrice jabbed her finger in the air. "If they are dead they do not care if you keep your promises."

Octavia splayed a hand across her own breastbone. "*I* care. And I am very much alive."

Beatrice actually laughed at that. Who would have thought that such a mocking guffaw could come out of her prim little cousin? "Yes, you are. More alive than I have ever seen you. Odd that your 'aliveness' seems to coincide with Mr. Sheffield's reappearance in your life."

"He was my best friend." She was *not* going to justify her pleasure at seeing North again.

All traces of mockery were gone, replaced by that sympathetic gaze again. "And your lover."

Octavia looked away.

"Dear heaven, he still is your"—Beatrice's voice dropped to an accusatory whisper—"lover."

A flush of guilt crept up Octavia's cheeks. "Last night, after he was shot. We were carried away . . ."

"I know you. You do not get 'carried away' by anything." Forget mocking. Forget sympathy, Beatrice was downright incensed now. "You are betrothed to another man!"

Octavia cringed. She deserved this. "I know."

"You have to tell Spinton."

What? "I most certainly do not! What good would that do?"

Hands on her muslin-clad hips, Beatrice faced her like a mother berating a child. "He is being true to you. He deserves to know."

He most certainly did not! How could she tell him such a thing? And how did Beatrice know whether he was being true to her? Spinton was a young man; surely his natural "urges" drove him to find companionship now and then. "It is none of his concern."

"He is going to know." Beatrice's tone was haughty, condescending even.

"Not if I pretend to be a virgin," Octavia replied in a similar manner. She would make Spinton believe she was inexperienced. It was as much for his protection as her own.

"How are you going to pretend a maidenhead, Octavia?" Beatrice demanded. "Tell me that!"

Octavia stared at her cousin, her mouth gaping. Never had she seen Beatrice so emotional about anything before. Never had she heard such direct language come out of her cousin's mouth before either.

Her shoulders sagged. She had driven Beatrice to this point with her blatant refusal to face reality. Beatrice was right. She did try to control things, even other people, just so circumstances would turn out the way she wanted. She always told herself she could accept the consequences of her actions, but then she tried to control the consequences as well.

She wanted to fulfill her promises, but she wanted to have her own way as well. And part of her was afraid what might happen if people found out the truth. She wanted North, but she was afraid to have him—afraid of the changes it would mean. And yet the thought of being without him was infinitely worse.

"Oh Bea. I've made such a mess of things."

Beatrice crossed the carpet to her, gripping her by the upper arms. "Yes you have, but you can fix them, you know."

Raising her gaze, Octavia stared into her cousin's kind, dark gaze. "How?"

Beatrice's lips tilted at the corners, as though she found it amusing that Octavia didn't know the answer already. "By being honest with yourself and with Spinton and Mr. Sheffield."

Oh God. That meant telling Spinton the truth. That meant telling North the truth. "I do not wish to injure Spinton."

"I think we both know you are more concerned with yourself than any injury to Fitzwilliam."

So Beatrice was not as naive as Octavia had once thought. "Ever since my grandfather brought me to live with him, I have known Spinton was intended for me. He has always been there. Someone has always been there. If I lose Spinton I will be alone."

Beatrice rubbed her hands on Octavia's arms. "You have Mr. Sheffield."

"No," Octavia shook her head. Her heart hurt. "I do not believe I do."

Beatrice's gaze was sympathetic, as though she understood, although Octavia didn't know how she could. "Then you will still have me."

A rush of emotion, powerful and raw, swept over Octavia. She seized her cousin in another embrace. For the first time she felt the strength in Beatrice's arms, the steel in her spine, and she knew that no matter what happened to either of them, the other would always be there.

"Thank you," she whispered.

Beatrice patted her back. "You are welcome." Then, pulling away, she smiled. "All right. Find me another one of those awful gowns and let us get to work. It is going to take the both of us to make this place happy again."

As she and her cousin and Mrs. Bunting worked side by side cleaning the downstairs rooms of North's house, Octavia wondered if perhaps she shouldn't be honest with Spinton.

Perhaps he would decide he didn't want to marry her after all, she thought, as she gathered the holland covers draped over a sofa in the parlor. She would be free to tell North how she truly felt about him.

But she had told North how she truly felt about him and he either hadn't understood or he'd purposely pretended not to. Either way, she wasn't so certain she wanted to attempt it again in the near future.

Still, wouldn't being rejected by North be preferable to wondering what might have been for the rest of her life?

Not really, no.

And what kind of future could they possibly have? She liked to go to parties once in a while. He seemed to despise them. Most days he couldn't even be bothered to shave. How would he feel about having to pretty himself up on a regular basis?

More importantly, how would he feel about the fact that society would always accept her more readily than they would accept him? That the *ton* would always consider her a lady while he couldn't aspire to gentleman without at least one meanspirited person saying he was trying to ape his betters?

Was she a good enough person that the gossips wouldn't bother her? Was she a good enough woman that she could leave her house in Mayfair and return to this piazza where she'd spent so much of her childhood, dreaming of a better life?

"Well la, would you look at this?"

Mrs. Bunting's voice jerked Octavia from her thoughts. The older woman had found something beneath one of the many protective linen veils draped through the room.

Setting her own bundle of dusty cloth aside, Octavia drew closer, curious to see what treasure the housekeeper had found. As she peered over Mrs. Bunting's round shoulder, her heart skipped a beat.

It was a cushion. Bright and garish, it stood out like a wound against the subtle colors in the room. Shades of violet, wine, and russet velvet, embroidered with gold thread, sewn with uneven, painstaking stitches.

"Good heavens, that is awful!" Beatrice remarked. "Whoever could have made such a thing?"

"I did," Octavia whispered. "I made it."

Her cousin was instantly contrite, not that Octavia paid much notice. Mrs. Bunting turned to her with a sweet smile. "You were a wee girl of ten I believe."

"Eleven," Octavia corrected, her voice still damnably hoarse. "It was a birthday present for Nell."

Her fingers trembled as she reached out and took the cushion from the older woman's hands. The velvet was soft to the touch, the irregularities in the stitches distinct. Beatrice was right. It was awful.

But that wasn't why it made her feel like weeping.

"I cannot believe she kept it." She could not believe North kept it. He'd had no compunctions about telling her just how ugly it was at the time. Nell had cuffed him upside the ear and told him to mind his manners. Then she gave Octavia a hug that smelled of powder and roses.

It is lovely, darling. I shall treasure it always.

Fourteen-year-old North had snorted. *That's the kind of treasure that should be buried.*

His mother raised her hand again and he ducked, grinning.

Nell hadn't lived to see her next birthday. By that time Octavia and North had started to become friends, and after his mother's death, he'd gone to live with his father and brothers. He returned to the Garden often, however, just to make sure Octavia was all right. He had appointed himself her protector. Maybe being there with her made him feel as though his mother was still nearby. Maybe he had known even then that his father's world wouldn't accept him.

Maybe he simply couldn't bring himself to say good-bye.

"Would you like to have it, my dear?" Mrs. Bunting inquired. "I am sure the master would not miss it."

That is where the old woman was wrong. North would miss it. She'd wager ten shillings that even though this room had been hidden from view for years, North knew exactly where everything—including this cushion—was.

God, was there nothing about him that didn't have the power to break her stupid heart?

"No. Leave it where it was."

She had envied North having a father. Envied him a mother who only had one lover. Envied him his oh-so-close-to-perfect family life. It never occurred to her how much it must have hurt him to have that taken away. He'd gone from that loving world—his mother, father, and the theater fold—to one that didn't want him no matter how hard he tried to fit in. No wonder he'd eventually fashioned his own. It must have been so much easier than constantly fighting for acceptance.

No, she could never ask him to live in her world. It would be too cruel to expect him to make himself so vulnerable again. How could she even ask it of him? She couldn't. And if she did, he wouldn't do it. Not for her, not for anyone.

"Do not change anything," she instructed, handing the cushion to Mrs. Bunting. "Put everything back exactly as it was after you have cleaned." She wanted North to see that she did not expect anything of him, that all she wanted was to give him a little bit of that world back again. It wouldn't be easy for him to accept, not after hiding from it for so long.

Mrs. Bunting regarded her with watery eyes. The old woman understood.

"Aye, dearie. Don't you worry."

Her throat and chest tight, Octavia glanced around the room as Beatrice and Mrs. Bunting resumed their work. With a little effort, the house could be almost exactly as it once had been, with bright, open windows, gleaming furniture, and the scent of beeswax in the air.

Perhaps then North could remember the love he'd been given in this house. Perhaps it would feel like home again.

And maybe, just maybe, Octavia herself would remember that old longing, remember the things that had once been so important to her. All she had ever wanted was a family, to feel as though she belonged—that she wasn't alone. Her mother had been too busy, too popular with her admirers and her protectors to give her the attention she craved. Her grandfather had tried, but the old man had thought gifts and expectations were adequate ways of showing affection. And Spinton—dear Spinton—he had so much affection to give, in his smothering, condescending manner. None of it was want she wanted—what she still so desperately needed.

The only place she'd ever felt that acceptance, that love, had been in this house, when Nell would try to teach her how to sew, or when North pulled her hair or teased her. This house felt like home to her.

North felt like home to her. And if her time with him was running out, she was going to enjoy it as much as she could.

For as long as she was able, she was going to pretend this was her house—hers and North's. That this was their home. And when it was time to leave, she would go with a heart full of memories, and the realization that she had found where she belonged.

North wasted no time getting to the point when Merton's butler showed him into the earl's study. He refused to sit and he refused a drink, and when Merton fixed him with a haughty, yet curious stare, North refused to back down.

"I know you have been sending letters to Octavia Vaux-Daventry."

Whatever Merton had been expecting, this obviously was not it. "I beg your pardon?"

"The lady has been getting annoying letters from a lovestruck swain. You."

Merton looked outraged. The earl was one of London's wealthiest and most highly respected citizens. He was certainly not accustomed to people accusing him of anything. "I most certainly am not! Why, I knew her when she was but a child."

Aha! "So you admit to knowing her mother."

"Of course I do." There would be no point in denying it, Merton had to know that. "Her mother and I were together for some time. I was very fond of Octavia—not that I saw her very often."

No. It wasn't very romantic having a child about.

"I knew your mother as well, Sheffield."

The best way to piss a man off was to insult his manhood or his mother. Merton knew this as well as any other man. "But not in the biblical sense."

"Of course not." The earl affected a shudder. "Creed would have called me out."

North's lips curved, but not in amusement. "He was funny that way."

Straightening his shoulders, Merton rose to his full height. He was a tall man and impressively built for a man of his station. No doubt he'd "known" many women in his day. "I do not like your attitude."

North shrugged. He was hardly intimidated. "And I do not like men who try to kill my friends."

Merton's jaw dropped. "I beg your pardon?"

He'd had enough of this dancing around. North went straight to the point. "Who pulled the trigger at Vauxhall last night, Merton? Was it you, or did you hire someone to do it?"

Shaking his head, Merton looked every inch the indignant peer. "I have no idea what you are talking about."

North struck him in the left shoulder with the flat of his hand. The earl grunted in surprise—not pain as he had expected. He wasn't the man North had shot.

He didn't bother to apologize for his assault. "You hired someone then."

"What the devil are you talking about?" Merton rubbed his shoulder. "I didn't shoot you!"

"How did you know I was the one shot?"

"Everyone knows!" Merton backed away as though he were nervous. "Half the *ton* saw you after it happened."

Right. Christ, he was losing his touch.

"And you claim to have nothing to do with it?" He didn't want to believe, but there was nothing guilty in the earl's demeanor.

The earl stared at him, his eyes wide. "Of course I did not. Why would I?"

North tilted his head to one side. It was time to call Merton's bluff. "Because you use the same writing paper as the person who has been sending threatening notes to Octavia. Because you are the only person with that writing paper who knows about her past. Because you had the mother and now you want the daughter. You want her badly enough that you would have me shot just to get to her."

Merton's face turned bright red. "By God, you have a lot of nerve coming into my house and making such allegations."

The earl had no idea just how much nerve he had. If he proved that Merton was behind the letters—and the shot—North was going to make him suffer like no man had suffered before. "Or perhaps she was your target. Couldn't have her so you decided no one else could either?"

"You are mad! I would never hurt Octavia!"

North actually believed him. "But you would hurt those who do not 'deserve' her. Is that it?"

Merton was furious now. He took a step forward. "Get out of my house."

North moved to meet him in the middle of the floor. "Not until you tell me the truth. I can make you tell me the truth."

"He is telling you the truth."

Both North and Merton turned toward the door. There stood Merton's oldest son and heir, Robert.

"This does not concern you, son," Merton growled.

Young Robert stepped into the room, his boyish face pale. "Yes it does. My father did not write any letters to Lady Octavia, Mr. Sheffield. I did."

North's jaw dropped before he could stop it. "*You?* But you are just a boy!" Hadn't Octavia herself maintained that the letters were written by a lovestruck youth?

"I am not. I shall be nineteen soon."

North knew what it was like to be nineteen and under Octavia's spell. Something told him the boy was telling the truth. Still, he had a lot to answer for.

Were it not for the boy's father being present, North would have grabbed him and slammed him against the wall. He settled for prowling closer, backing the young man into a corner instead.

"You could have killed someone, you little bounder."

"I did not try to kill anyone!" Robert's expression was one of panic. "I swear! It was not me!"

The boy was so afraid, North could practically smell it. It was the terror of confusion, and it told North he was not lying.

"You had Lady Octavia's fiancé very concerned."

Robert snorted at that. North raised his brows.

"So you do not believe Lord Spinton good enough for her, eh?"

Robert stiffened. "Of course not. Neither are you."

"You are right. I am not." The boy seemed surprised that he didn't argue that fact. "You insinuated knowing a secret of Lady Octavia's. What is it?"

Young Robert glanced nervously at his father. "I know about her mother and my father. I know her mother was a whore."

Lord Merton scowled. "Maggie Marsh was not a whore."

Robert glared at his father with his fists clenched tightly at his sides. "Yes she was!"

"The two of you can argue about that later," North interrupted. He focused his attention on the younger man. "Is that all you referred to when you mentioned a secret?"

Robert nodded. His disdain for North was obvious, but he was also obviously intimidated by him. For once North was glad the *ton* blabbered about him as they did.

"That is all, not that it is any of *your* business."

"Boy," Merton warned. "You are in enough trouble. Do not add rudeness to the list of your crimes. Apologize to Mr. Sheffield."

The boy's eyes dropped to the floor. "Sorry."

"No you're not," North retorted matter of factly. "And I do not care. However, I do want you to know that your letters have not earned you Lady Octavia's admiration. In fact, if she were here right now, she'd give you a set-down that would make your ears blister."

Robert flushed. "Oh."

"What do you intend to do about it?" North demanded of the boy. At almost nineteen he was more than accountable for his actions.

Merton folded his arms over his chest. "I will make certain my son is adequately punished, of that you can be certain. First, he is going to apologize to the lady."

To the boy's credit, Robert didn't argue. "Yes. I never intended to upset Lady Octavia."

"And you swear you had nothing to do with the shooting?" What he wanted was young Robert's balls on a platter, but he knew just how hotheaded and stupid boys could be. His brother Wynthrope was proof of that.

The boy shook his head. "I sent the letters, but I did not have anyone shot."

There was no pretending the boy's alarm, not unless Robert was a better actor than North himself. But if Robert didn't shoot at them, who did?

Harker.

Oh Christ. Octavia was at his house. Alone.

Chapter 14

"I will answer the door, Johnson. You attend to the emergency below stairs."

The large butler paused in the middle of the foyer, scratching his shiny bald head. The frown on his face demonstrated how he was torn between his duty to the staff and his duty to protect Octavia from whomever might be standing on the other side of the door.

"It will be all right." Smiling patiently, Octavia pushed him on his way. "Miss Henry will call you if you are needed. Go now. Go."

Reluctantly, Johnson did as she bid. Shaking her head, Octavia immediately went to the door. She doubted their caller would mind that she greeted him personally. Besides, Beatrice was abed with a headache, and she was eager for someone to talk to, even though it undoubtedly was someone calling for North.

She opened the door to find herself face-to-face with a man caught somewhere between attractive and ugly. His features were so strong and fierce, his eyes so piercing, that it was almost impossible not to be captivated by the sheer power of him. His presence was overwhelming, the lines of his face unyielding and unforgiving.

And there was something oddly familiar about him.

His gaze met hers, and he smiled. Octavia shivered. There was something very predatory about that smile. It was as though she were a helpless fly and he a hungry spider.

"Good morning," he greeted politely. "I am looking for Sheffield. Is he about?"

Ah, he was a friend of North's then. That explained his somewhat frightening countenance. "I am afraid Mr. Sheffield is not at home right now, Mr. . . . . ?"

"Harker. James Harker." He flashed another smile. He had good teeth for a man of dubious origins. He had better teeth than most aristocrats, for that matter. They seemed sharp and prime to take a bite out of her. "Might I ask when you expect him to return? I am rather anxious to speak with him."

His accent was good as well, but it was obvious this man had been taught to speak this way. It took effort.

"I expect him shortly." It was awful of her to be suspicious of a man just because he wanted to project himself as a higher class. Who was she to judge? She had been raised in a theater.

She stood back to allow him entrance. "Would you care to wait?"

He stepped inside. He wasn't much taller than she was, but he was heavily muscled and had an air about him that made him seem much, much bigger.

Power. This man had an abundance and he knew it.

"You may wait with me in the parlor, if you like. I just rang for tea." Regardless of how silly she believed her suspicions to be, she wasn't about to allow him entrance into North's private office.

Of course, she wasn't so certain she wanted to be alone with him either, but she'd rather have him where she could watch him than turn her back on him.

"I would be delighted," he replied. His sincerity was obvious, but there was something odd about the gleam in his dark eyes—as though he was laughing at a private joke she wouldn't understand.

She led the way to the parlor, the short walk seeming like a mile. The flesh between her shoulder blades burned and itched. He was watching her, staring. If the burning sensation dropped any lower, she didn't care if he was a friend of North's or not—he was leaving.

"You have a lovely home, ma'am," Mr. Harker remarked as they entered the little parlor.

Yes, it was lovely. Very lovely. Just not hers.

"Oh, it is n—" She knew as soon as she looked at him that he was well aware she didn't live there. Of course he did. A friend of North's would know that he wasn't married. He was simply being polite. Obviously he believed her to be North's mistress.

Octavia flushed. She was North's mistress. For now.

"Thank you, Mr. Harker." She was saved from having to say anything further on the subject by the arrival of Mrs. Bunting with the tea. The elderly housekeeper flashed a suspicious glance at Harker, but said nothing. No doubt she would mention the visitor to Johnson as soon as she had a chance.

"Tea?"

Harker nodded. "Please. Black."

"How do you know North, Mr. Harker?" Octavia asked once they each had a cup of tea in hand.

Obviously unused to such delicate china cups, Harker hunched in a dismissive shrug. "We go way back. Years."

Hmm. Did that mean they once worked together at Bow Street? Or had North once arrested him?

"Are you involved in law enforcement as well?"

Harker smiled. "You could say that."

She could also say the man wasn't much of a conversationalist.

While Octavia tried to think of something to talk about, Harker didn't seem to mind the silence at all. He sat quietly relaxed, drinking his tea, gazing around the newly cleaned and aired parlor with all the interest of a man who hadn't seen it before.

That didn't mean anything. Of course he hadn't seen it before. Until recently it had been covered and closed.

A few moments later, he set his empty cup on the tray. "I have to go."

She raised her brows. He had been there only ten minutes. "May I tell Mr. Sheffield to what your visit pertained?"

"It is nothing of great importance," Harker replied as he stood. "I sent Sheffield a message the other night. I was wondering if he got it."

A message? He called in person to inquire after a message, but he wasn't willing to wait? "Will he know how to get in touch with you should he want to respond?"

Another smile. "He'll want to respond, and yes, he knows where to find me."

Octavia accompanied Harker to the door and wished him a pleasant day.

Harker bowed. "It was a pleasure to meet you, Lady Octavia."

She stiffened. So he did know who she was. "You as well, Mr. Harker."

As soon as he was through it, she shut the door. After a moment's hesitation, she locked it as well. Then she went to North's office and curled up in a chair by one of the windows with a book, arranging the curtains so anyone outside looking in could not see her.

It was then that she realized where she had seen Harker before. He was the man she caught watching them through the window the other day. Perhaps North had hired him to watch the house. Perhaps that was why he sent North a message rather than come himself—he hadn't wanted to talk business in front of her. It also explained how he knew who she was.

More than likely that was all there was to it. Her strange misgivings and suspicions were nothing more than her frayed nerves playing games with her. That was all.

By the time North came tearing into the room, she was engrossed in her reading.

"Whatever is the matter?" He looked as though he'd had the very life scared out of him.

"Are you all right?"

Good Lord, was his voice shaking? "Of course I am."

"Did anything happen while I was gone?" he demanded, raking his hand through his unruly hair.

Worried about her, was he? "Nothing unusual."

He visibly sagged in relief.

"Oh, wait. Your friend Mr. Harker was here." How could she have forgotten after all the foolishness she'd put herself through during and after the poor man's visit?

He stiffened, the color draining from his face. "Did he talk to you?"

"Of course." Setting her book aside, she rose to her feet. North obviously wasn't going to sit. "He wanted to wait for you, but he had another appointment. We had tea in the parlor."

"Parlor?" He scowled, his brows knitting into a deep V. "What parlor?"

"*Your* parlor." His tone and expression made her nervous. "Show me."

It was very tempting to point out that having grown up in this house, he should know where the parlor was, but she held her tongue. North was more tense than a leading lady on opening night, and she didn't want to be the person he unleashed his tension on—even though the odds were against her.

"Why didn't Johnson answer the door?" he asked as they walked across the hall.

She glanced at him over her shoulder. His face was as dark as a thunder cloud. "There was an emergency below stairs."

"Emergency, my arse. An emergency of Harker's making."

Could that be? The "emergency" and Harker's arrival had happened simultaneously. Had Harker engineered the situation so that he could avoid Johnson and have Octavia to himself? But why? Aside from being a little unnerving, he hadn't done anything improper at all.

North stopped in the parlor doorway. "Where are the holland covers?"

"I took them off." Now was not the time to be looking for his praise, but she did so anyway, turning to him with a hopeful smile.

If she was looking for more enthusiasm on his part, she wasn't going to get it. "Where did Harker sit?"

She pointed to the settee. She would not pout; she wouldn't. The ungrateful cur. "There."

To her surprise, North crossed to the small sofa and ran his hands along it. From between the back and seat cushions he withdrew a small card. Octavia frowned. That hadn't been there when she cleaned earlier.

"What is that?"

"Harker's card."

Harker's card? When had he left it? Why, she'd been watching him the entire time. Hadn't she?

North scanned the small ivory card. His fingers trembled as he slipped it inside his coat. "Are you certain he didn't touch you? Didn't frighten you?"

"He seemed a little odd, but no. He was nothing but gentlemanly in his behavior. Why?"

"Oh my God, Vie." Octavia found herself crushed against him in a fierce embrace, his lips plundering hers.

Instinct told her to follow his lead, and so she didn't argue or protest when he guided her around the back of the sofa, shoving at her skirts with anxious hands. Pinned between him and the settee, Octavia allowed him to lift her so that her bottom rested on the carved back. She wrapped her legs around his waist for balancing, never once breaking their kiss, trusting whatever he had planned.

He fumbled between them, and then the hard, insistent length of his sex shoved against the entrance to her body. She accepted him readily, her body moist and willing despite her own lack of arousal. This was something North needed, she knew that. He needed to take from her, possess her, and she didn't need to climax to appreciate or enjoy having him inside her.

She held him tightly, with her arms and legs, trying to stop the trembling of his body with sheer force of will. He was frantic in his movements, unsteady and forceful. There was no rhythm, just thrust after thrust until he spent himself inside her, groaning into her mouth as he came.

Octavia continued to hold him after the shuddering stopped, after his mouth left hers. Still joined, she rested her chin on top of his head as he buried his face in the crook of her neck, his breath hot and moist against her skin. One arm remained wrapped around her waist, while the hand of the other gripped the sofa for support. He trembled still, and she smoothed his hair with her fingers, rubbed his back as well, trying to soothe the quivering within him.

She was not frustrated. She did not long for her own release. She was strangely content, knowing that she had given him whatever it was he sought. It was oddly satisfying to have remained in control while he so obviously tossed his aside.

Slowly, he withdrew from her—emotionally as well as physically. "I am taking you home."

"What?" Surely she could not have heard him correctly.

Fastening his falls, he turned away from her, his tone flat. "You are going back to your own house. I will have Francis and some of my other men on guard at all times."

Standing on her own, Octavia straightened her skirts, all too aware of the dampness between her thighs. This must be what it felt like to be a whore. "I do not understand."

"Make sure Spinton is there as often as possible. Beatrice as well." He faced her, but did not look at her. "Do not go anywhere alone."

"North, you are frightening me." What the devil was going on? Why was he acting this way? Had he uncovered something about the man who shot at them? About her so-called admirer?

He laughed. It was a shaky, uncertain sound—and it scared her all the more. "I am frightening myself."

This wasn't like him to admit fear. Wasn't like him to admit to weakness at all. Then realization sunk in.

"Dear Lord. Those shots really were intended for you, weren't they?" Now she was trembling as well. "But not because of me."

"No. Not because of you. You were correct." Now he met her gaze. He was ashamed of himself, she could see it in his eyes. "Your admirer turned out to be nothing more than a harmless boy whose father once knew your mother. He will not bother you again."

She couldn't believe it. She should be relieved that it was all over, but she wasn't.

"You are in danger." The idea of anything happening to him was worse than any peril that might befall her.

"Yes."

She didn't need to ask, but she did anyway. "From Harker?"

"Yes."

Damn him for sounding so nonchalant now—when he should be concerned. He had been more worried about her safety than he ever would be for his own. "How much danger?"

For a moment she thought he wasn't going to tell her. "He murdered a woman I was trying to protect and one of my men in the process."

Oh no. She wanted to hug him, wanted to comfort him, but she knew it would not be welcome. He would not make himself vulnerable to her again so soon. "You are afraid he will hurt me to get to you."

North's eyes hardened to shards of ice. "I could kill him just for speaking to you."

"He wants to kill you as well." If only she could sound as unconcerned as he, but she couldn't! Her voice trembled on every word.

He simply nodded, his expression matter-of-fact. "If I do not drop my investigation, he will try."

By God, she'd see him in hell first. "I am not leaving you."

"You do not have a choice." He had his hard and uncaring face on again. He turned his back on her.

What was it about her that made others so determined to dictate her life? Was she not as strong as she believed herself to be? "I want to stay with you."

He glanced over his shoulder. "I do not want you."

Had he struck her, it would have hurt less. "Why not?" Had that whiny sound truly come from her?

Sighing, he turned, running his palm over the stubble on

his jaw. "I've enough blood on my hands without adding yours to it. You will be safer in your own house."

"Do not make me go, Norrie. I will be so worried about you if we are apart." Wonderful, now she had lowered herself to begging. What next? Where was her pride, her resolve? She didn't truly believe she could do anything to protect him, did she?

"I will worry about you if we are together. You are going, Vie. Gather your things."

"But—"

"Must I do it for you?" He didn't bother trying to hide the pain and resolution in his expression. "You are going, and that is all there is to it."

He would not be refused, she knew that. If he had to he would truss her up and physically remove her from his house. This was the end. Their brief reunion was over.

"Fine," she replied, willing strength into her voice. "I will go." In her mind, Octavia knew he was right, and she was anything but stupid.

But in her heart, she wanted to stay, wanted to be reckless and rebellious and risk it all to be with him.

Someday she was going to give in and listen to her heart. Someday.

She is lovely.

The card crumpled in North's fist, the corners digging into his palm. Rage coursed through his veins. Fear trickled down his spine. The thought of Harker visiting Octavia—speaking to Octavia—filled him with such emotions, he didn't know where to begin trying to name them all.

He could kill Harker. Kill him and not feel one ounce of remorse. In fact, he *wanted* to kill him. He'd watch the bastard dance on the wind at the end of a hangman's noose and laugh.

If Harker ever came near Octavia again, he'd string the bastard up himself.

Octavia.

Thank Christ she was all right. Harker hadn't come there to hurt her—not this time. This was simply a warning. A message to North to back off or she would get hurt. Harker would never get that chance. Little did he know that his threat had the opposite effect. North was *not* going to back off. In fact, he was more determined than ever to bring Harker down—by any means necessary.

"We are ready."

North whirled around. How had she managed to sneak up on him like that? Never mind that she was carrying luggage, or that she had Beatrice with her, normally he could sense her the moment she stepped into a room. It was just another reminder that Harker had found the perfect way to rattle him.

She stood just inside the doorway, her petite cousin behind her. Beatrice's expression was one of bewildered concern. How much did she know about the situation? Did she know he and Octavia had been lovers? Did she know Harker was more of a threat than any foolish "admirer" could have been? Did she know just how incredibly stupid he had been? Allowing his feelings for Octavia to cloud his judgment, his senses?

Christ, he was not a stupid man, but Octavia made him feel like one.

And now she had the nerve to look at him as though she were the only one suffering. Did she think he wanted to let her go? He *never* wanted to let her go. The fact that she wanted to stay made it all the more difficult. Things never should have gotten this complicated between them. He never should have made love to her. And what about that fiasco earlier here in the parlor? He'd taken her with less finesse than a green boy, not caring about her pleasure, wanting only to assuage the desperate fear in his soul.

"As soon as I have briefed my men I will escort the two of you home."

Octavia straightened her shoulders. "That is not necessary."

She was so proud and defiant in her rumpled gown, her jaw still faintly pink from the rasp of his beard. Had she washed when she went upstairs to collect her things from his room? Had she wiped all traces of him from between her legs? Had she rinsed her mouth to rid herself of his taste?

She would never be rid of him. Did she not know that? She thought he was abandoning her, rejecting her. He didn't have to be a genius to know that she'd felt cast aside by almost everyone in her life—including him. Only he knew the truth, that he had never truly abandoned her, and never would. He would know every aspect of her life right up until the day he died. He would never be free of her hold over him. And he would never let go of her. Never.

"It is necessary," he informed her, his voice and face void of emotion. "You are my responsibility."

"Not anymore. You have fulfilled your obligation to my fiancé. You are no longer required, nor being paid, to protect me."

Christ, she knew just where to hit. So did he. "You are my friend. And more important than any amount of money."

Octavia paled. Beatrice stared at him with something that looked very much like respect.

But Octavia wasn't done with him yet. "As soon as we have reached my home, I will pay you for your services."

"You already have." As she flushed that bright pink that only redheads could flush, he continued, "I am all the richer for it."

She obviously did not know how to take that, which was just as well because he wasn't quite certain how he meant it. It was romantic in a flowery and pathetic kind of way.

Octavia opened her mouth, and he cut her off with a lift of his palm. No more. No more trading these foolish barbs and thinly veiled admissions of feelings. Right now he had to be at his sharpest, and he couldn't be with her around.

"If you ladies would not mind waiting for me in the parlor, I see that my man has arrived."

Sure enough, Francis walked by the study window just then, bounding up the front steps with his usual and odd grace for a man of his stature.

Johnson didn't bother to announce him, nor did Mrs. Bunting. The entire household was used to Francis coming and going at all hours.

Octavia flashed a North a glance that told him she was far from being done with him before exiting his office with all the rigidity and poise of a queen. Beatrice followed. Francis bowed to both of them at the door as they swept by.

"Shut the door," North instructed, not caring if Octavia was out of earshot. "I do not trust her not to listen."

Grinning, Francis closed the door. "I take it she is not pleased that you are sending her back to her fiancé?"

As much as he liked Francis, what did and did not please Octavia was none of his business.

"I want you and Barnes to watch her house. Be on your guard, Harker's men might be around. I don't want either of you ending up like Harris."

"Neither do I."

"And have some of the boys keep an eye on Harker and his lads. If Harker takes a shite I want to know about it."

Francis's brow furrowed. "What are you going to do?"

"What I should have done a long time ago," he replied bluntly. "I am going to bring the bastard down."

"What about the law?"

North shrugged. "What of it?"

"We generally tend to follow it, remember?"

"You go ahead and follow it. I have other plans."

Francis appeared genuinely concerned. "Do not be stupid. That is what Harker wants."

"I don't intend to give him what he wants. I intend to give him what he deserves. Now do me a favor and go fetch the women. The sooner they are out of my house, the better I'll feel."

Francis didn't look as though he believed that for a second, but he was wise enough to keep his opinions to himself. He nodded sharply and exited the room.

A little while later, Francis sat up top with the coachman while North sat inside the carriage with Octavia and Beatrice. Despite the fact that Brahm's carriage was comfortable and well appointed, North was convinced Francis got the better arrangement. Sitting outside in the light rain would definitely be preferable to ending the daggers Octavia was shooting at him with her stormy blue gaze. She was angry and hurt, and she blamed him—that was obvious. He tried not to look at her, but it was difficult, since the only thing he wanted to look at was she.

Christ, how long did it take to drive to Mayfair?

Finally the carriage rolled to a halt, and the awkward silence of the drive was broken by the opening of the door by a footman and the lowering of the steps.

Octavia surprised him by actually speaking. "I would like a moment with Mr. Sheffield, if you do not mind, Bea."

Beatrice nodded, shooting North a look that was meant either as encouragement or a warning; he couldn't tell. Usually he was good at reading expressions, but the Vaux-Daventry women were a mystery.

Once her cousin had exited the carriage, Octavia beckoned for the footman to close the door once more. The latch had barely clicked before she moved to sit beside him. The bonnet she held in her hand bumped against his knee.

Gone was her expression of recrimination, replaced by stark fear—and concern.

"Will you promise me something, Norrie?"

"Only if it is a promise I can keep," he answered honestly.

A slender, gloved hand wrapped around his own. "Will you be careful?"

He nodded. "Yes."

Naked pain shone in her dark eyes. "Will I see you again?"

No. Never again. That was what he should tell her. "If you send for me, I will come."

It was not quite the answer she was looking for, he knew that, but it was all he could give. She nodded, her hand reaching for the door.

"Merton's son—the boy who wrote you the letters—will be calling on you to apologize."

"All right." Her hand curled around the handle.

"Tell Spinton I will call on him tomorrow."

Another nod.

Christ, this was hard. "Vie?"

Something in his tone must have reached her, must have given him away, because she whirled around at the sound of her name. He reached for her just as she reached for him, and they seized each other in a fierce embrace, their lips meeting in a desperate kiss that seemed to last for hours.

Finally, breathless and gasping, they broke apart, their foreheads resting against each other, their hands clasped around each other's necks.

"Be happy," he whispered.

She stroked the stubble on his jaw with her thumbs. "Knowing you are alive and safe is all I will ever need to make me happy."

And then she was gone, leaving him alone with a heart so full of her it was slowly breaking.

But not slowly enough.

"I want your help."

North stood in his father's house, in the room where he and his father used to talk. Where he and his brothers always used to talk.

"My help?" Setting his cane nearby, Brahm lowered himself into a brown brocade wing chair, stretching his lame leg out in front of him. "You have never asked for my assistance before."

North shrugged, scratching his jaw. He was going to have to shave again. "I never needed it."

His brother rubbed his own smooth jaw thoughtfully. "Why now?"

Brahm obviously knew something was amiss, so there was no point skirting the issue. "I want Harker out of business. Permanently."

Brahm smiled. "Why not just have Dev shoot him?" The smile faded. "You are serious."

"I am."

Sitting as straight as his lame leg would allow, Brahm was all seriousness. "What has happened?"

"He came to my house. He spoke to Octavia." To North that was explanation enough.

Brahm frowned, massaging his leg with his left hand. "Vaux-Daventry?"

"Yes."

"What was she doing at your house?"

What did that have to do with anything? There was no need explaining. Brahm was perfectly capable of drawing his own conclusions. "We were shot at. I thought she was the target."

"Now you know it was you."

"Yes." Shite, and now Brahm did too. Brahm might not have been a perfect elder brother—not in the eyes of the *ton*—but he was loyal and protective. North wouldn't put it past him to go after Harker himself.

Brahm kept his expression carefully disinterested. It wasn't a good sign when Brahm put on his card-playing face. "Where is Lady Octavia now?"

"I returned her to her own home." He hoped she would stay there.

Brahm's dark eyes narrowed. "For her protection."

Meeting his brother's gaze, North kept his own shuttered. "Of course."

"I thought perhaps it might have been for your own."

His patience fraying, North rose from his own chair. "I haven't the time for your insights. Will you help me or not?"

Brahm was in no way intimidated by having to look up at his younger brother. Nothing intimidated Brahm—nothing human, that was. "Of course I will, but not when it comes to breaking the law."

"Christ, you're a peer," North reminded him, shoving a hand through the messy curls of his hair. "You are above the law."

"True." Brahm's tone was calm. "But you are the law."

It was tempting to confess all about Wynthrope's involvement with the thieves and how North risked his career to save him. Let his brother toss such nonsense in his face after that. But Wyn would never speak to him again if he imparted such information to their eldest brother.

Instead he murmured, "You and I both know the law does not always work."

Gripping his cane, Brahm pulled himself to his feet again, grimacing as his weight settled on his bad leg. "But it is still the law. You cannot bend and change it to suit yourself."

Now was not the time for a brotherly lecture. "Can't I?"

Right now he didn't give a rat's arse how petulant he sounded. He was *this* close to throwing a tantrum.

"That makes you no better than the scoundrels you pursue."

North folded his arms across his chest. How very sanctimonious and damnably *right* his brother sounded. "You never preached like this when you were foxed."

Both hands braced on the head of his cane, Brahm shrugged. "I never cared."

"You were also much easier to anger." If only that were the case now. He was spoiling for a fight, and usually his brothers were very good about indulging him.

"Not now. What would you like me to do, North?" His tone said that he would do whatever was in his power. "I have very few friends left among the *ton*."

"But you still know more nobs than I do. You know who to talk to. Someone must owe you a favor or two." Never had he felt so powerless before. It wasn't just Harker who had that effect on him, it was Octavia. The problem of Harker he could eventually solve, but not at the risk of Octavia's safety.

Brahm shook his head, regret etched in the lines around his mouth. "Why do you not talk to Duncan Reed? I would think Bow Street would be more helpful."

Duncan would tell him the same thing. Duncan was less likely to go beyond the bounds of the law than Brahm was. "I need people with power. People who can change the law."

"If you were an MP you could be one of those people."

Not this again. But this time, the full implication of the position sunk in. If he went into politics as his brother and Duncan pestered him to, he could become one of those men who influenced parliament, a man who had the power to change the law.

He might not be a peer of the realm, but he was popular in their circles. They just might support him, especially if he reminded them of all he had done to protect their way of life.

He, the bastard of the late Viscount Creed, just might become a person of importance. It would be a way into the world he thought he no longer wanted to be part of. His brothers' world. Octavia's world.

Bollocks. Had he ever truly stopped wanting to belong? Perhaps society had ceased to matter, but finding his own corner of the world was still something his soul craved. Only being with Octavia satisfied that craving. Perhaps that was the answer. He belonged wherever she belonged. His corner of the world was whatever one had her in it.

He couldn't be with her when his job brought danger to himself and those he loved. Every assignment he took set him up as a target, but if he were behind the scenes, so to speak, he could still effect change without putting those he cared about in harm's way.

It was tempting. More tempting than ever before.

Meeting his older brother's dark gaze, he smiled gravely. "I need your help."

Chapter 15

She couldn't live like this.

Two days after being returned to her house by North, Octavia had yet to feel as though she was home.

Seated at the head of the table, she picked at the food on her plate and tried to ignore the fact that Spinton and Beatrice seemed to be ignoring her. Of course, they weren't *truly* ignoring her; both were far too polite for that. No, it was simply that they were so caught up in their own conversation that neither thought to include her in it.

Which was just as well, she admitted, raising her wineglass to her lips. She didn't feel much like talking. She didn't feel like much of anything. It would be too difficult to pretend that everything was all right tonight. Too hard to be that person she tried so hard to be.

Never before had she felt *this* out of place in her own house. Never had she felt as though she truly didn't belong. Before there had been a sense that this life was her *right*, a privilege of her birth. Now it simply felt wrong. But this *was* her life. This was her house (with its ill-suited decor), her cousin, her betrothed—although Spinton had yet to offer her a ring, or a date for their wedding.

And outside, in the fading light of day, her guardians sat watching. North might be one of the best in his line of work, but he had so many men stationed outside her house at all hours that even she was aware of being watched. Thankfully, neither Beatrice nor Spinton seemed to notice.

She turned her attention to her fiancé. Though Spinton had seemed relieved that the mystery of her "admirer" had been solved, he didn't act like a man who had just discovered that the woman he planned to marry was out of harm's way. In fact, he seemed very much on edge. Perhaps he wasn't as oblivious to the men outside as she thought. Perhaps on some level, Spinton sensed that she wasn't completely out of danger.

Or perhaps his awkwardness stemmed from the woman seated across from him farther down the table. He and Beatrice had eyes for no one but each other as they chattered like magpies. What did they find to talk about? Spinton didn't chat like that with *her*. Then again, perhaps if she had shown more interest in what he had to say . . .

Dear God, was that what the rest of her life was destined to be? Pretending to be interested in what Spinton had to say? How could she share a bed with a man who bored her? Granted, they would share that bed only for the purpose of achieving an heir. The mere thought had her stomach clenching. Spinton was an attractive man. A good and kind man, but she did not want him to touch her. Not after North.

"Pass the wine please, Bea."

Her cousin appeared not to have heard her. She was too deeply engrossed in what Spinton was expounding on. Sighing, Octavia half rose from her chair and reached down the table for the bottle. If she ended up with gravy on the front of her gown, it would be all Beatrice's fault.

How could her mother have made her promise to do as her

grandfather wanted, to be a true lady? How could her grand-father have made her promise to marry Spinton? And why did she feel so duty-bound to keep her word to two people who were both dead and never had the slightest inkling of what she really wanted out of her life?

Her mother had tried to be a good mother, but she was rarely around, and very few of her beaux had wanted a child around—unless their interest in Octavia was something con-siderably darker than paternal. Her grandfather had been generous and kind despite his gruffness, but he'd never had much interest in her as a person. He'd never once asked what she wanted or what she would like to do, and as a girl she wasn't much use to him as an heir.

So why were these vows to them so very important? Why did they bind her like chains to Spinton and this farce of a life?

What about her promises to North? She had promised to always be there for him, just as he had promised her. Only in true North fashion, he had made it impossible for her to keep that promise by shutting her out and turning her away. He thought he was protecting her from danger. Perhaps he was, but he was also hurting her.

And what about those promises she should be making to herself? Didn't she owe herself something more than a life of disinterestedness? Her future, her marriage, and her children should not be something she looked upon as a penance or a duty—or even a punishment. These were things she dreamed about as a young girl, things she once longed for. She had vowed to marry for love, to carve her own destiny, far re-moved from her mother's.

How could she consider herself different from her mother when she was basically selling herself? Paying a debt to the man who had taken her in by marrying the man he had cho-sen for her.

Wouldn't her grandfather and mother much rather she be

happy? Surely they had each loved her enough to want her happiness to come first? Surely she loved herself enough to decide for herself what she would and would not do with the years left to her?

What was she going to do? She had to make a decision, and soon. This wasn't fair to anyone involved. It wasn't fair to North—even though he, like her mother and grandfather, was trying make these decisions for her. It certainly wasn't fair to Beatrice, who stared at Spinton as though he hung the moon in the sky, nor was it fair to Spinton himself, who was a good enough man that he deserved to be loved and respected by his wife.

Nor was it fair to herself. And it was time she started thinking of herself. She was done wishing for something or someone to come along and decide her future for her. Call her selfish, but surely it wasn't a sin to want a little joy out of life, and to give joy to others in the process.

She could not spend the rest of her life with Spinton without knowing she had at least tried to grasp her own happiness. In fact, she wasn't certain she could spend the rest of her life with Spinton at all, but that was something else she had to decide soon. She didn't know if she could spend the rest of her years worrying about North and his safety either. These past days with no word from him had been difficult enough. Could she stand by and watch him put himself in danger day after day? Could she be content to hear about it from a distance and wonder as an alternative? Which would be worse?

Wouldn't five minutes of something wonderful be preferable to a lifetime of nothing? No. She would rather have North than mere memories any day.

That solved it. It was time to sort out her future. She had to decide her fate, and much of that decision rested on North.

Pushing back her chair, she stood. "If the two of you will excuse me, I have some urgent business to attend to."

Both Spinton and Beatrice regarded her with startled expressions, but she gave neither of them time to respond or protest. She swept from the room with strides as long as the confining skirts of her gown would allow, resisting the urge to hike it up around her knees and run.

She was going to take action. No more would she sit by and let life drift past. The time had come for her to make good on some of her promises.

But which ones?

"What are you doing here?" Octavia demanded, hands on her hips, a scowl wrinkling her brow.

He had hoped for a better reaction than that. True, the hour was late and he hadn't been expected, but was that reason enough for such a lackluster reception?

Maybe not, but making love—and very badly at that—to her and then sending her home probably had been.

"Good evening to you also, Vie."

If he'd hoped to guilt her into being more friendly, he was going to fail miserably. She didn't give an inch.

"I have not seen nor heard from you in two days and now you expect me to welcome you with open arms? It does not work that way, Norrie."

Ahh, but she still called him Norrie. She hadn't totally given up on him. Although they would probably both be better off if she did.

"You could offer me a drink."

Her tongue swept the inside of her cheek, bulging the skin there—no doubt in an effort to keep from telling him to go to hell. "Would you like a drink?"

"No thank you."

He'd hoped to get a smile out of her, but she only fisted her hands on her hips and glared at him.

He scratched his beard. They were alone in her parlor, the

door shut against the outside world. They should be able to speak plainly to each other, but Spinton was only a few rooms away, still having his dinner, if he had heard correctly.

"Did the Merton brat apologize?"

She gave a sharp nod. "Yesterday."

That was it? No details, no thank yous?

"What do you want from me, Vie?" Why bother trying to guess? He never would.

"An apology, to start," she informed him haughtily.

Ahh, so she was upset about his sloppy seduction. He didn't blame her. "I am sorry for being so selfish and base in my lovemaking—"

"Not for that!" Was it his imagination or had she actually stomped her foot?

He blinked. All right, so he still hadn't guessed correctly. "For what then?"

"For deciding my life for me. For making decisions that are not yours to make and tossing me aside, and then thinking you can waltz in here whenever you want. I am not one of your men, or your brothers. I will not be treated with such assumptive behavior."

Assumptive? Christ, where had she learned to speak like that? She sounded like Spinton, or worse, her grandfather.

"I only wanted to keep you safe." Why was he defending himself? He shouldn't have to explain the situation to her. She knew why he had done what he did. He wanted her protected— and as far away from Harker as possible. Christ, she let everyone else dictate her life, why not him as well? He was the one who wanted what was truly best for her.

Her expression was mulish. "You mean you wanted to keep me out of your way."

There was that too. "I cannot concentrate on catching Harker if I'm worried about you."

She came at him like a harpy—a beautifully furious one—

swooping down on her prey. "Never mind that I might be worrying about you. Did you ever consider how worried *I* might have been these past two days?"

Honestly? "No."

She didn't seem surprised by his answer, and that peeved him. Did she think that his mind hadn't been filled with thoughts of her regardless? He'd done very little without thinking of her before, during, or after. He missed her before breakfast, during the afternoon, and after going to bed. Never mind all the times in between.

"Of course you have not thought of it. All you've thought about is what you want. My wants you dismissed."

"Damned right," he growled, the blackness of his mood quickly escalating. "I have always given in to you. Whatever you wanted, if it was within my power I gave it, but not when it could put you in harm's way, Vie. So stop pouting and accept that I have acted in your best interest."

He thought that would mollify her, take her down a notch. If anything it only made her angrier.

"My best interest!" She seethed, finger pointed at her own chest. "You have not been a part of my life for twelve years, what could you possibly know of my best interests?"

"I know enough." He wasn't about to explain himself to her, not when the answer should be so completely obvious.

Crimson blossomed high on her cheeks. "I am heartily sick of people claiming to know what is best for me, people making decisions for me. I am the only person who knows where my interests lie, best or otherwise."

Fine time for her to realize what a puppet she was. Still, he couldn't help but be a little relieved. This wasn't about just him, or the two of them for that matter. This was about something far deeper.

That didn't mean she didn't hold him somewhat responsible, however.

"Who has ever made decisions for you other than your-self?" he demanded. As if he needed to be told. He knew who they were. He was the kind of man who liked to hold a grudge.

"You," she fired back. No surprise there. "My mother, my grandfather, Spinton . . ." she trailed off, as though too tired to continue.

"How?"

Octavia flopped onto the sofa like a marionette with cut strings. "Spinton hired you against my wishes. My grand-father decided marrying Spinton was best for me. My mother decided being a lady was best for me."

He leaned his hip against the chair next to him. "Perhaps you didn't agree with Spinton, but what of your mother and grandfather? You went along with them, did you not?"

Rubbing her forehead, she nodded. "Because I wanted to please them, because I felt I owed it to them."

Ah, guilt. It was a wonderful motivator. That and duty were the only things that could force Octavia onto a path she didn't necessarily want to take. She was so very loyal to those she loved. She would do anything they asked, even if she hated it.

Like leave when she wanted to stay.

Like marry a man she did not love.

"I could tell you to break your word, but I don't think that would make you feel any better."

She smiled. She looked so frail, so tired. "Probably not."

Crossing the Aubusson carpet, he seated himself beside her, careful to keep from touching her. If he touched her, what little restraint he had would crumble. He wanted nothing more than to take her into his arms, kiss and comfort her. Make love to her, take all her fears and doubts away. But it wasn't his place. Wasn't his right. And if Spinton happened to walk in, it would call for an awful lot of explaining—explaining that would reveal Octavia's past.

Why did he care? He'd made the promise to conceal her origins to her grandfather. The old bugger was dead, pleasantly so. So why did he bother to keep his word to a dead man after questioning Octavia for doing the same thing?

Because he had made his promise to protect Octavia, not to please the old earl. He would rather die than see anything happen to her, which was why it had scared him so to come home and find out Harker had been there. That same fear was why he had sent her home, and why he could not hold her as he wanted to now.

"I wish I could help you, Vie."

She nodded, knowing he spoke the truth. They were both bound by so many oaths, conventions, and expectations. And fear. Both of them were ruled by their individual fears of disappointing someone, not living up to expectations, not being good enough to achieve their goals.

He was terrified he wouldn't be able to stop Harker. And now his greatest enemy knew his greatest weakness. Only Octavia's upper-class status, something even Harker would think twice about challenging, kept her reasonably safe. The one thing North resented her for was the one thing he was most thankful for at this moment.

"Might we talk as friends, Norrie?"

His brow furrowed. "You can always speak to me. About anything."

She smiled. There was such an expression of hopefulness in her eyes that it pained him to look upon it, yet he could not look away.

"I would like to ask your counsel."

Counsel. Not opinion, not advice. Such a proper, detached term to use with such a friend.

Because he was her friend. Everything else aside, the aching of his heart not withstanding, she would never know another friendship like his, and vice versa.

"Of course." He clenched his fingers into fists to keep from touching her. "You may ask me anything."

"It is of a very personal nature."

Oh God. She was pregnant and didn't know if he or Spinton was the father. No, that couldn't be. She had told him she hadn't been with Spinton, or anyone else for that matter.

Christ. She was pregnant and *he* was the father.

"I do not love the man I am supposed to marry."

The sigh of relief that threatened to blow him apart at the seams was as much from learning that she wasn't with child as it was to hear her acknowledge she didn't have feelings for Spinton.

"That is not uncommon among your class." It was also not news to him. Octavia never would have shared his bed if she loved another. Strange how that made him want to thump his fists against his chest.

She scowled at the world "class." "It is not uncommon among yours either."

Touché.

"But"—she sighed—"that is not my problem."

Rubbing his jaw, North nodded. She was quickly losing him. "What is?"

She met his gaze with a direct and level one of her own. "I am in love with someone else."

It was as though someone had punched him, sucking all the air out of his lungs. He couldn't breathe, couldn't think. Octavia was in love. In love.

"You see my predicament now," she continued, as though he wasn't dying beside her. "I love this man, but am pledged to marry another. What should I do?"

Call for a surgeon, was his first thought, but as air slowly seeped back into his lungs, common sense returned. "Tell me about this man you love." His voice was little more than a hoarse croak.

She smiled, her gaze falling to her feet. "He is a man without equal. He makes me laugh and he makes me so very angry . . ." She looked up. "But he has a very dangerous profession and I worry about him."

A dangerous profession. God, dare he believe . . . ? Did she mean what he hoped/feared she meant? Christ, how stupid could he be not to realize?

"It kills me to think of anything happening to him, and I know living with him wouldn't be easy, but I fear living without him will prove even more difficult. I promised him I would always be there for him and I will be, but I do not know how he feels for me."

North stared at her, mouth slightly agape. He must look every inch the idiot, and yet he was powerless to stop it.

Then Octavia took his hand and he knew he was done for. "Norrie," she began, her eyes wide and pleading. "What should I do? Should I follow my heart and hope that he loves me as well, or should I give up hope and marry Spinton?"

She was his. His for the taking. All he had to do was say the word, and she would be his forever. His friend, his wife, his darling Vie.

A pawn for Harker and other enemies to use against him. A target for all those who wished to destroy him.

A lady. Too good, too much above him. She deserved better than the life he could give her.

But he could give her his love. He could give her his heart. He could do that.

Swallowing hard, North met her gaze. His heart hurt, as though a huge hand was squeezing the very life out of it. His throat was tight, and his eyes burned with tears he simply refused to shed. Not in front of her.

"Marry Spinton," he rasped. "Marry the man who can give you what you deserve and give up on the other. If he isn't trying to hold on to you for all he is worth he either doesn't want or doesn't deserve you. Either way, Spinton is the better man. A gentleman in every sense of the word. And for God's mercy, stop looking at me like that!"

Her damnable gaze followed him as he leaped to his feet and turned his back on her.

"Norrie, please."

She would break him yet, by God. Tears brimming hot and unwanted in his eyes, he half turned to face her one last time.

"Marry the man who belongs in your world, Vie. Marry the man who stands an outside chance of growing old. The man who can give your children a better life than what we had. Do it for me."

She swallowed, staring at him with eyes that were as wet as his own. "Telling me what to do again, Norrie?"

He would have laughed if he wasn't so frigging heartbroken. "Begging actually."

A tear trickled down her cheek. "You have never begged for anything."

That wasn't true. He had begged *her* for so many things.

"Marry Spinton," he commanded with as much finality as he could muster as he strode toward the door.

"And then what?"

Christ, could she not let it go?

He paused on the threshold and turned his face toward her. If he didn't leave now he was going to turn into a bawling idiot.

"And then never come near me again."

"Thank you for taking the time to see me."

Clad in a black cloak, Octavia removed her veiled hat as she stepped into the somewhat shabby but surprisingly clean back room.

Harker regarded her with a mixture of amusement and wariness, his large form lounging like a tensing lion on a blue velvet divan. Clad only in his shirtsleeves, trousers, and boots, he looked every inch the dangerous villain. "You intrigue me, Lady Octavia. How did you manage to do the one thing your lover cannot?"

Her hat clenched in her cold fingers, Octavia allowed a questioning expression to pass over her otherwise blank features. "You mean find you?"

Harker nodded. "He has been trying for days. Your luck makes me suspicious."

Octavia feigned a careless shrug. "North will determine your whereabouts eventually, Mr. Harker, if he has not already." Saying North's name brought a rush of pain fresh and sharp with it. But it also brought hope. He wouldn't have said all those things to her last night if he didn't love her. All she had to do was take away his reasons to deny it.

Lazily rising to his feet, Harker grinned—a baring of teeth much like a snarl. "You and I know better than that. If Sheffield knew where I was, he would have been here by now. He would not let me get away with approaching his woman."

Octavia was silent, allowing the far too predatory man before her to follow through to the next obvious fact.

Harker's gaze narrowed as realization dawned. "Nor would he send that woman here to trick me. He doesn't know you are here."

Those words should have been ominous, and would have sent her knees knocking in terror were it not for one simple thing.

"But he will know shortly," she replied. "His men followed me here." At least she hoped they had. She might be beyond foolish for coming after Harker on her own, but she wasn't *completely* without sense.

Harker didn't seem too concerned about his nemesis's unavoidable arrival. "Would you like a drink?"

A drink? How very civilized! "No, thank you."

"Then why don't you get to the point of this social call?" His tone was mocking, dismissing her as a nuisance, nothing more.

Fine, he wanted her to get to the point, then she would. "I want you to remove your business from London."

His reaction to that was exactly what she expected. He laughed. "No."

Of course he wouldn't say yes. She'd question his wits if he had, and Harker hadn't made it as far as he had by being stupid.

Twirling her hat on her finger, she casually strode toward the mantel and examined a porcelain sheep there. Inside, she was as coiled as a spring, watching Harker from the corner of her eye.

"Then stay out of North's way." She made it sound more like a suggestion than a command.

"I have an idea," Harker made his own proposal, moving closer on silent feet. "Tell your lover to stay out of *my* way."

Octavia turned slowly. She wanted him to know she was aware of his approach, but not that he made her the least bit uneasy. Men like Harker were like dogs. They could smell fear and knew how to use that fear to their advantage.

"You and I both know he will not do that."

Harker folded his arms across his impressive chest. "Then we're done talking."

"Do you have a mistress, Mr. Harker?"

That brought him up short. He eyed her warily. "You already know I do."

How empowering to have this man look at her with the realization that she was not some insignificant twit.

"Cassie Crocker is a lovely girl. A truly fine actress."

No, he didn't think her a twit at all. Not now. And ten

pounds said he was beginning to see her as a lot more than simply North's "woman."

"Surely she wasn't fool enough to direct you to me."

Octavia shook her head. "No, another girl at the theater who knows one of your men told me that. I have known Cassie since she was a girl. Did you know that?"

The frown on his face told her that he hadn't. It also told him he didn't like the idea of his men blabbering such details to their bed partners.

"The theater crowd is a lot like a band of criminals, Mr. Harker. They are very close-knit, and close mouthed. They tend to be a tad more loyal to their own, however." Let him stew on that for a bit.

He made a scoffing sound. "Actresses are little more than whores."

He was trying to bait her, or maybe he truly meant it. Whatever his reasoning, she wasn't about to let a man so low on the human ladder make her second guess herself.

"A whore is still leagues above a thief or a murderer."

The face he made told her what he thought of that. "You think a slag who sells herself is worth more than a man who takes what he wants?"

"You may take everything else you want in life, Mr. Harker, but I know Cassie makes you pay for it."

Harker's face flushed dark red. "How does Sheffield pay you?"

His calling her a whore should have been offensive, and maybe it might have been, had there been any truth in his words. If Harker wanted a verbal duel, he'd picked the wrong woman.

"I give myself to North for free." She tilted her head thoughtfully. "To whom do you suppose Cassie gives herself freely?"

She had pushed him too far. His eyes were as hard as granite, his jaw so tightly clenched it pulsed. Like most men, he didn't like the idea of someone else having what he thought of as solely his. Never mind that he probably had several women whom he considered his own private property.

"Cassie will do as I tell her." But there was a hint of doubt in his bravado. "She knows what's good for her."

Octavia couldn't resist the opening. The only way this man could hurt her was physically, and even Harker would pause before harming the granddaughter of an earl. "Do you truly believe that a woman who knows how to make you beg would be afraid of you?"

Cassie would be smart to be wary of this man, but afraid? No, she probably had enough blackmail material on Harker and more than enough ways of safeguarding it to keep herself alive for a long time.

Much to her surprise, Harker smiled. "Perhaps you are not as much of a lady as I first thought." He said it as though it were a compliment.

Face impassive, Octavia tilted her head. "I wager I am many things that would never occur to you, Mr. Harker."

"I usually don't like mouthy women, but you've got a tongue like a whip, my lady. It can cut a man clear down to the bone. Makes me wonder what else it can do."

Good God, was he going to try to force himself on her? Octavia's heart almost stopped at the thought. But no, she could tell that wasn't his intention. Harker wouldn't want to force her, he would want to conquer her. Despite his distinct advantage over her, he still regarded her as his social better. Years of living by his own rules hadn't completely erased the ingrained sense of social hierarchy instilled in every English citizen from lowest birth to highest.

"You keep wondering," she tossed back calmly. "That is all you will ever get." Turning on her heel, she strode toward the exit. "If you will not agree to leave London, then our business is at an end, Mr. Harker."

"I'll tell you what."

Blood drumming hard in her ears, Octavia paused, glancing over her shoulder at the massive man behind her. "What?"

"I won't kill him." Both tone and expression were sincere. "Not unless he gives me reason."

It must be a large concession for him, but how she couldn't figure. How did a person go about killing another? She supposed she would find out if Harker ever did kill North, because she would hunt the bastard to the ends of the earth herself.

But his words gave her little solace. "He will give you a reason."

Harker nodded. "But I will wait for it. That I will promise you."

Well, that was all she could ask from a murderer and soulless animal. "Thank you." The words were like sawdust in her mouth.

"If you ever decide to toss Sheffield over, feel free to come find me again."

She turned the doorknob, fingers trembling. "You could not afford me, Mr. Harker."

"I thought you gave it away for free." His mocking tone drifted over her shoulder, raising the hairs on her neck.

"I do. To North Sheffield." With that hanging in the air between them, she let herself out of the back room, put on her hat, and didn't stop until she reached her carriage. Once there, shaking in relief, she ordered her coachman to take her home as soon as possible.

It wouldn't be long before North came calling. This would bring him back to her.

Chapter 16

⟅◦◦⟆

"She did what?"

The young man before him visibly quaked under the onslaught of North's rage. "She snuck out in the middle of the night—"

"I heard you the first time." Scowling, North raked a hand through his hair. Christ on a playbill, what had she hoped to prove? If she wanted to terrify him, anger him beyond his limits, then she had succeeded. It had been incredibly stupid of her to go to Harker.

Yet, furious as he was, he had to admire her for finding the bastard. How had she managed it? North himself had searched that club and found nothing. He would ask her that very question after he shook her even more senseless than she already was.

Had his words not gotten through that thick skull of hers? He had told her to stay away from him—out of his business. To most women that would have been sufficient enough good-bye, but obviously not for his Vie. No doubt she thought she was doing him some great service, proving her loyalty to him by putting herself in harm's way.

Or perhaps she had done it for revenge—a spiteful way of making him worry about her the way she claimed to have worried about him. Or better yet, she had done it to make him suffer for rejecting her, for telling her to take her love and give it to someone else.

She loved him. *Him.* It was his most secret dream and darkest fear. Octavia loved him not just as a friend but as a man, but she belonged to another. Belonged *with* another. Spinton would give her a good life, keep her as she was accustomed. Granted, North had ample fortune—enough that, coupled with Octavia's inheritance, they could live quite comfortably for the rest of their days and leave enough behind for their children as well.

But society would never accept him, would they? He hadn't been wanted all those years ago, why would they want him now? And he would not have his children suffer as he suffered. Octavia's children should be allowed into society, not sneered at because their father had the misfortune to be born a bastard.

Misfortune. Had it been? If he had been legitimate, he might never have known Octavia. He wouldn't trade that for all the legitimacy in the world.

And yet, had he been a true Ryland, he might have met Octavia at a ball or a party and fallen in love with her there. There would be no objection to their marriage. But then he wouldn't know the truth about her past. They wouldn't have the connection they had now. No, things were the way they were meant to be. *He* was as he was meant to be. Born to neither world, he'd been content to make his own. But now . . . Now, it was perhaps time to choose.

Octavia loved him. And he—he would never admit, not even to himself, how deep his own feelings went. They were better locked away deep inside, where he didn't have to name or face them. It would be folly to act any other way.

"Sir?"

He looked up, meeting the questioning gazes of those select few of his men who were present. How long had he been distracted by thoughts of Octavia? He should be thinking of Harker and how to finally capture the bastard, not allowing his emotions to run away with him.

"What is it, Morris?" he asked more peevishly than he intended.

The young man's eyes widened. "We were wondering what you would have us do."

Ah yes, they expected orders, his being their leader and all that. Maybe he should turn control of the operation over to Francis. He wouldn't be so distracted.

"Is Harker still at the club?"

Morris nodded, forelock tumbling over his shiny brow. "Unless he has some secret exit that we don't know about."

Which was entirely possible, knowing Harker.

The coat he pulled from the back of the chair was the same deep blue as the upholstery. "If I am not back in two hours, alert Bow Street and storm the club."

Francis scowled at him. "You plan to go alone?"

Shrugging into his coat, North nodded. "I do."

"In God's name, why?"

Facing the brawny man, North schooled his features into a blank mask. If his eyes held any of the rage he felt, Francis would know for certain what his intentions were. "As it stands, we have nothing on Harker—nothing that will send him to the hangman. The worst he will face is deportation. I want him dead."

Something must have shown in his gaze because Francis's gaze narrowed. "That does not explain why you are going after him alone."

"The minute he knows I brought reinforcements, he'll bolt. If I go alone, he'll see it as bravado and retaliate. He'll want to rub my face in the fact that so far he's gotten away with everything. That arrogance is what will get him caught."

Francis nodded, his expression revealing his lingering doubt. "So we will be watching him round the clock after this?"

"Exactly. He doesn't take a shite without us knowing how big it was." It was a good plan. Too bad he didn't intend to stick to it. He was through with planning. Through with waiting.

Francis was obviously satisfied now. "What about Lady Octavia?"

North faced the rest of his gathered men. "Those of you who have been watching the Vaux-Daventry household will continue to do so until further notice. I want to know who comes and who leaves. Keep yourselves hidden. I don't want O—Lady Octavia to know you are there."

One of the men chuckled and nudged Morris in the side. "No more peeking in her bedroom window then, Morris old man."

It was most likely an innocent jest, but it sent a fresh rush of rage coursing through North's veins. He glared at Tommy Fields, who made the remark, and at Morris, who flushed in embarrassment as the men around him laughed at his expense. Then he turned his glare on the others.

"Anyone who cannot behave in a professional manner or doesn't think he wants to follow my orders is free to leave now."

Eyes downcast, the men shuffled their feet. No one moved.

North nodded sharply. "Good. Now get out of here."

Once the men emptied out, Francis closed the door and turned to North. "Do you think it was necessary to be so hard on them? They were only having a bit of fun?"

North fixed him with an uncaring stare. "At Octavia's expense."

The broad, hairy man nodded as though he understood, which of course he didn't. "Ah, of course. What do *you* plan to do about Lady Octavia?"

North didn't even pretend to misunderstand him. "Nothing at all." But that wasn't true. If things went the way he planned, he was going to see Octavia when this was over and give her the tongue-lashing of her life—and not in a pleasureful way either.

But dealing with Octavia would have to wait. He had something more important to do first.

He was going to kill Harker.

Octavia was still in bed when Beatrice came bustling into her room late that morning.

"Stop it!" she growled, pulling the blankets over her head as her cousin flung open the heavy cream brocade drapes.

"What in heaven's name are you doing still in bed?" came the muffled demand.

Lowering the bedclothes, Octavia squinted at the bright sunlight. Of course Beatrice would find it strange that she was still in bed. Beatrice hadn't been up visiting one of London's most notorious criminals in the middle of the night.

"I *was* sleeping, no thanks to you."

Fresh-faced, dressed, and glowing with energy, Beatrice flounced onto the bed, the skirts of her lemon yellow gown spreading around her like the petals of a flower. "Well, it is far too nice a day to spend it sleeping. Get up!"

Brow furrowed, Octavia leaned back against the pillows. "Get out." At her cousin's giggle she added, "I am serious."

"I know you are." Smiling, Beatrice braced a palm by Octavia's hip. "And you do not frighten me, Miss Grumpy Face."

Grumpy Face? "Why are you so blasted happy?"

Beatrice shrugged. "Why are you so grouchy?"

A tight smile pulled her lips. "I did not sleep well last night."

Her cousin's smile faded into an expression of genuine concern. "Are you unwell?"

Sighing, Octavia closed her eyes. "I believe so, yes." She had to be to pull the stunt she'd pulled.

Warm fingers touched her brow. "You do not feel feverish."

Octavia opened her eyes, her gaze locking with her cousin's. "That is not where I am unwell."

Beatrice's eyes widened into saucers as a flush crept up the smooth flesh of her cheeks. "You are not . . . ?" She made a vague gesture around her stomach with her hand.

Octavia's scowl returned with renewed exasperation. "Of course not!" And she wasn't, thank the Lord. Her menses had come after North sent her home and lasted but two brief days, as though her bodily functions didn't want her either.

And she ought to be thankful. Pregnancy was one complication she didn't need in her life. Although a baby might be just the thing to bring North to his senses. He wouldn't want his child to be born a bastard . . .

How could she entertain such an awful idea? She would never try to trap North like that.

Beatrice breathed a heavy sigh of relief. "Oh thank heaven."

Yes, that and North's fairly regular use of sheaths, but her innocent cousin didn't need to hear about those.

Wide doe eyes gazed at her in sympathy. "You miss him."

Why bother deny it? "Yes." She also wanted to throttle him for his oh-so-noble rejection of her those few days ago. It felt like years.

"Is that why you have been so miserable ever since you returned home?"

Octavia nodded. God, she was tired.

"What are you going to do, Tavie?"

She shrugged. "What my mother and grandfather expect of me, I suppose."

Beatrice must have found her mournful tone somewhat amusing because she smiled sympathetically. "Do you truly believe either of them would want you to go against your own desires?"

Octavia stared at her. "Perhaps not my mother, but Grandfather . . . yes, I think perhaps he would. I do not think my happiness was a consideration. Contentment, maybe."

Beatrice tilted her head, her sable curls bobbing about her ears. "And do you think that was his hope for Spinton as well?"

"I think his only hope was that between Spinton and myself we would have enough Vaux-Daventry blood to purify the family line." Perhaps it was wrong of her to speak so ill of the dead, but she had secretly thought it for years.

Beatrice looked horrified. "That is awful!"

Octavia shrugged. "It is the way of the *ton*."

"Well, it is wrong. People should marry for love."

A bitter smile curved her lips. "That is very romantic of you, Bea, but not very realistic."

Beatrice's stare was shrewd and piercing. "I remember, years ago, when you and I first became friends, you told me that only love would induce you to marry. You wanted to marry Norrie Sheffield and live happily ever after."

God help her, that was what she still wanted. "I grew up."

"You mean you gave up."

"Take your pick."

Sighing, Beatrice lowered herself onto the bed, stretching herself out beside Octavia and laying her head on another pillow, so that their faces were no more than a foot apart.

"I do not believe your mother would want you to give up your dream."

What did it matter now? "I do not believe I have a choice."

Beatrice blinked. "Whyever not?"

Her throat tightening, Octavia fought the urge to cry. "Because Norrie Sheffield does not want me."

She expected her cousin's sympathy, not the scowl that occurred instead. "Have you taken complete leave of your senses?"

Now it was Octavia's turn to blink. "I beg your pardon?"

"If that man does not love you, then he is a very good actor."

And a liar. And a friend. And a lover. "He is."

Beatrice's scowl deepened. "Not that good. Maybe he can fool Spinton and maybe he can fool the rest of the world, but I have seen the way he looks at you when he thinks no one will notice. I have heard how his voice changes when he speaks to you, how it softens and sounds more Scottish. The only reason he would reject you is if he believes it is in your best interest."

There was that damnable phrase again. Her *best interest*. Had she not told him that he had no idea what her best interests were? Obviously he hadn't been listening because Beatrice was right. He might have rejected her, but he had done it because he cared about her. Even she was smart enough to decipher that—at least when she stopped feeling sorry for herself long enough to think clearly.

Blinking back the tears, she met Beatrice's soft gaze. "He loves me." Realizing it, embracing it, was almost as wonderful as hearing him say the words himself.

Beatrice nodded, smiling serenely. "Yes, although I doubt he has accepted it himself."

Knowing North, he hadn't. He was so good at explaining things away, making them fit where he wanted, or avoiding them all together. After all, what was this determination to not be a part of society when it was obvious society wanted him? They had rejected him once; he wasn't about to give them a second chance.

And she had left him once for a "better life." No doubt he was afraid to give her a second chance as well.

Stupid idiot, she would have gladly left that "better life" if he had just asked her to.

But he wouldn't ask her to. He was too afraid. Afraid of being turned away. Afraid of rejection.

What did he know of rejection? At least he had known his father. At least his mother hadn't brushed him aside every time she took a new lover. He had known he was loved. And now he knew that she loved him as well because she had told him as much.

What had he given her? His martyred version of love—giving her up because he didn't think he was good enough, didn't believe she could be happy staying with him for the rest of her life when she could have everything he had ever wanted but hadn't been allowed.

Oh, he was infuriating! Stupid, silly man! How could he willingly do this to both of them? How could she have hung on to duty and responsibility so very long? It seemed so foolish to her now, keeping to a vow that she knew was wrong. What an idiot she had been. How afraid. She'd been hiding behind her promises to her mother and grandfather, just as North had hidden behind his own stupid notions. Only because they had thought it was the right thing for them to do. She believed she owed it to the two people who looked after her, and he believed he owed it to her to stay way.

They had both forgotten what they owed themselves.

"What do I do?" she whispered, wiping at her eyes with the back of one hand.

Beatrice's own eyes were a little wet. "What do you want to do?"

"I am not certain."

"Let me help you." Her cousin's expression turned earnest. "How do you feel about North?"

As if that required an answer. "I love him."

"How do you feel about Spinton?"

"I do not love him." What wonderful release that was!

Tears spilled from Beatrice's doelike eyes. "I do."

Octavia's own vision blurred, but she fought it. "I know."

"Please do not marry him, Vie." Beatrice's voice broke. "If you feel you must keep a promise, then make this one to me. Do not take him away."

Any doubts, any reservations or misgivings Octavia could have possibly retained about her future melted at her cousin's heartfelt plea. Choosing a course that might make herself unhappy was one thing, but choosing a path that would bring so much misery to so many undeserving people was unthinkable. She could not do it.

"I will not," she promised, finally giving in to her own tears. "I will not take him away from you."

"Oh, thank you!" Openly sobbing, Beatrice threw her arm over Octavia, seizing her in an awkward and tight embrace. Octavia hugged back, both of them laughing and crying at the same time.

As she embraced her cousin, Octavia hoped that wherever her mother and grandfather were, they could accept her decision and wish her happiness. Because from now on, she truly believed it was in her own best interest only to make promises she thought she could keep—the most important of which would be those she made to herself.

The first step Octavia took in her new life was to stop hiding her past. Perhaps it should have been setting Spinton free of their engagement, but he wasn't home when she went to call on him. She decided to stop by Covent Garden instead—

not to visit North, however. She wasn't quite ready to face him, and she wanted all other obstacles out of her way first. Besides, he was not going to be pleased with her for going to see Harker. That was why she went to the theater, to make certain Cassie Crocker hadn't suffered for her association with Octavia.

She found Cassie at home, in her spacious apartments on King Street, sipping a cup of tea in a lacy peach peignoir set that had obviously been a gift from a protector.

The pretty blond actress ushered her in with a smile. "Whatever did you say to Harker?"

Instantly filled with dread, Octavia grasped her arm. "He did not hurt you, did he?"

Cassie laughed—a deep, throaty sound. "Hell, no! He cut me loose. Ended our arrangement yesterday."

Caught somewhere between relief and surprise, Octavia sank into the offered chair. "Why?"

Shrugging, Cassie sat down across from her and poured tea for them both. "I do not know and I do not care. I am just glad to be rid of the brute."

She was? "Then you are not angry with me?"

A slender hand cut through the air in a dismissive wave. "I am thankful, darling. Unbelievably thankful. Harker was brutish, unrefined, and had no taste whatsoever. I was stuck with him, however, because no other man would come near me so long as Harker staked his claim. Why, I have already found myself a *much* better protector."

The leading tone of the other woman's voice cued Octavia to ask, "Oh? Who?"

It was obviously just what Cassie wanted her to ask. The actress positively squirmed in her eagerness to tell. "Viscount Creed."

Octavia's jaw dropped. "Brahm Ryland?"

Cassie nodded, grinning with delight. "The same. And let

me tell you, sweetie, that man can do things I have never experienced before. He certainly knows how to please a woman. But then, I think you understand the effect the Ryland boys can have on a girl, do you not?"

Octavia flushed under her friend's knowing gaze. "That was a long time ago."

"Umm hmm." Cassie didn't look convinced. "Not that long. He was here earlier this morning, you know."

"Creed?"

Cassie rolled her wide hazel eyes. "Playing dumb does not suit you, Octavia. North Sheffield was here."

Blast his hide, but her heart jumped every time she heard his name! "What did he want at such an hour? To inquire after your intentions toward his brother?"

It was a weak joke and didn't provoke Cassie to burst into further raptures about the eldest Ryland as she had hoped.

"He was asking about Harker." Cassie paused to sip her tea. "And he asked about you."

Octavia froze, her cup clattering against the saucer as she tried to lift it. "Me?" Oh dear, he had already found out about her visit to Harker then, if he was asking Cassie questions.

"Yes." The actress's gaze was thoughtful. "You. He wanted to know if you had come to see me about Harker. Seems his brother told him that Harker and I had ended our agreement, and North thought that was a bit of coincidence given the fact that you and I are old friends."

Coincidence her foot. North's men would have told him that she visited Cassie shortly before her nighttime excursion to Harker's lair. In fact, she wouldn't be surprised if North had sent Brahm after Cassie, but that was too much, even for him. That part was a coincidence, but little else was, of that she was certain.

"And he gave me a message to pass on if I saw you again."

This time Octavia didn't bother trying to hide her surprise. "Oh? What did he say?"

Cassie smiled. "He said to tell you he was going to wring your foolish neck."

Laughter welled up inside her, bursting forth like water from a dam. She couldn't help it, his message thrilled her.

He loved her. He really loved her.

Shortly after eleven, North entered the small gentlemen's club and coffee house on Russell Street and seated himself at one of the tables. He was such an idiot. Harker had been hiding within walking distance of him and he hadn't known—hadn't sensed it—because he'd been too busy shagging Octavia to use his other, less base, instincts. True, he had searched the coffee house before, but obviously not well enough, because Harker had managed to elude him.

The bastard wouldn't elude him this time. In fact, he meant what he had said to Francis and the others. He was counting on Harker's arrogance to bring him into the open. And normally he would count on that same arrogance to push Harker into making a move, but not today. Today he was going to end this. Once and for all.

He hadn't been able to protect Black Sally or Harris, and obviously he hadn't been able to keep Octavia safe either, but he was going to fix that now. Harker had crossed the line when he called on Octavia, and Octavia had foolishly called more attention to herself by visiting Harker. He would know for certain that she was the best way to get to North, and he wouldn't hesitate to use her.

North was going to have to kill him. It was madness, but it was the only option. He couldn't risk anything happening to Octavia—not because of him.

He hadn't been sitting for long when a waiter approached

him. "Coffee," he said. "Bring two cups. And tell Harker to get his arse out here. I'm tired of waiting."

Obviously he had caught the man off guard, because he didn't bother trying to deny Harker's presence in the building. He simply blinked, nodded, and rushed off as though his bowels were about to explode.

North waited, aware of the curious glances his appearance had attracted, lazily drumming his fingers on the tabletop. He lounged in his chair, turned so that his left arm sprawled across the back, his right ankle resting on his left knee. His boots, he noticed, could use a good polishing. He focused on the leather, channeling his anger into a feeling of icy calm, quelling his anxiety with the certainty that he was doing the world a favor by taking Harker out of it.

The waiter reappeared with a tray bearing two cups, a pot of coffee, cream and sugar. One cup he set in front of North, the other on the opposite side of the table. Harker had obviously gotten his invitation.

Without having said a word, the waiter scuttled away. North watched him go, void of expression. He could feel the tension in the club mounting so acutely that he knew the exact moment Harker came up behind him.

"Have a seat," he said, not bothering to turn around.

There was stillness for a moment. He could almost feel Harker's indecision. That was good. He wanted the bastard confused. It would make everything so much easier.

Color appeared to his right, a flash of Harker's coat as he rounded the table to seat himself on the opposite side. His posture was just as falsely relaxed as North's.

"Am I paying for this, or are you?" he asked with deceptive lightness.

North poured them both a cup of hot, rich coffee. "It is your club. I think it only right that you pay the bill."

Harker nodded agreeably. "Yes. You have paid for much lately. All deserved, of course."

North refused to give him the pleasure of seeing his anger. "Your turn is coming."

The criminal's expression turned mockingly smug. "Do you think so? I don't see it that way."

North shrugged, lifting his cup to his lips. "I don't care how you see it. It is true."

Harker laughed. "You are a sad little man, Sheffield. What your Lady Octavia sees in you, I have no idea."

"Leave her out of this."

Leaning forward onto the table, Harker fixed him with a bright and sparkling gaze. "Where would the fun be in that? After all, she just walked right into it, like a rabbit into a snare."

North leaned over the table as well, one hand on the scuffed surface, the other on his right thigh. "There's a rabbit in the snare all right, but it isn't her."

Harker simply smiled.

North's hand crept down into his boot. "How many men do you have watching me, Harker?"

Harker's gaze never wavered. "Three."

Swiftly, silently, North pulled the blade from his boot and set the razor-sharp tip against Harker's thigh under the table. "Do you think any of them will be able to bring me down before I slice your bollocks to ribbons?"

Harker's eyes widened. "You wouldn't."

North raised his brows. "Why wouldn't I? You would. You never hesitate to kill, why should it surprise you that someone else might not either?"

All traces of humor were gone from the other man's face. "Not anyone else, just you. You are not a killer."

"You don't know what I am. If you did, you never would have brought her into this."

Harker's lips curved slightly. "Careful, Sheffield. You're revealing your throat."

North exerted just enough pressure on the knife that the tip pierced Harker's flesh. The criminal hissed, but was careful not to draw attention. "I'm preparing to slit yours."

"My men will kill you." Gone was the congenial criminal, replaced by the gutter rat North knew he was. Harker was seething evil, nothing more.

"Not before I kill you."

"What about your precious Lady Octavia, what do you think they'll do to her?"

North remained silent. The thought of anything happening to Octavia sickened him, but he refused to let it show.

Harker's gaze narrowed, searching North's face for some sign of weakness. Silently, North prayed he would find none.

"What do you want?" Harker demanded finally.

North smiled. Let those watching think they were reaching some kind of friendly agreement. Let them think Harker was buying North off. Let them think he was going to finally bring Harker in. He didn't care what they thought. It didn't matter. The only person whose opinion he cared about was Octavia's.

"I want you gone," he replied honestly.

"Your bitch asked me the same thing. I'll tell you what I told her. No swiving way."

The knife dug a little deeper. "I wasn't asking, you son of a bitch. I am telling you."

Sweat beaded on Harker's brow. His leg had to hurt. A drop of blood landed on the back of North's hand. "How do you plan to get rid of me? You've got nothing on me."

"I figure I'll just kill you. How does that sound?"

He might have laughed at the expression on Harker's face were he not so coiled, so ready to drive the knife into his belly and welcome the death that was sure to follow—Harker's and his own.

"You don't have the stones," Harker taunted.

North turned the blade. Harker's jaw clenched in pain. "Stones do not matter. I have a knife. That's all I need. You'll be the one lacking stones."

"Am I that important to you, Sheffield, that you would die just to bring me down?"

North shook his head. "You're not, but she is."

Understanding dawned in Harker's eyes. "And if you somehow manage to make it out of here alive, if your rich brother keeps you from the noose, what then? Do you honestly believe a *lady* like her would let a murderer in her bed?"

This was a new tactic, especially for Harker. Obviously he knew North better than North thought. Honestly, he hadn't given any thought to what Octavia might think of him for killing a man. His only thought had been keeping her safe.

She knew he had killed before, but those killings had always been in the line of duty. What would she think of him taking a man's life in cold blood, especially when she was his reason for doing so? She would be horrified, possibly even disgusted. Above all, she would be so very disappointed.

He didn't want to die with her thinking she was the reason. Didn't want to die with her despising him. And if he killed Harker here and now, there was a very real chance he wouldn't make it out of the club alive.

He couldn't do it. He couldn't let it end this way, no matter how badly he wanted to stop Harker forever.

But now what? If he let Harker go, Harker might very well have his men fire on him anyway, and then he would die an idiot and Harker would go on his merry way—and probably take revenge on Octavia.

Damn. How could he have been so stupid as to let his emotions drive him to this impasse?

Harker knew he was caught as well. The vermin could probably smell North's indecision.

Just then, a familiar figure appeared behind Harker's chair. It was Francis. He did not look impressed to find his friend and employer sitting in public with one of the most dangerous men in London.

"Time to leave," Francis said softly. "Mr. Harker, I am afraid your men have fallen asleep on the job. You might want to speak to them about that."

Never had North been so pleased to have Francis follow him in all his life. Slowly, he withdrew the blade from Harker's thigh and wiped it clean on the criminal's trousers. Then he slid it into the sheath in his boot and slowly rose from the table.

"We are not finished, Sheffield," Harker snarled, shoving a wadded napkin into his lap.

North smiled as he backed toward the door. "We might not be, but you certainly are."

Chapter 17

It was the next morning before Octavia summoned the courage to call upon Spinton. She had missed him the day before when she went to visit Cassie, and he hadn't joined her and Beatrice for dinner that night. The time for procrastination was past, however. This wasn't merely her life affected by her decision, it was Beatrice's and Spinton's as well. The time to hesitate was over.

Dressed in a lovely new gown of gray-blue, a darker blue pelisse, and matching bonnet, Octavia stepped into the carriage and rapped on the roof with her umbrella for the driver to be on his way. Her stomach was twisted into knots and her neck was stiff with tension. Why was she so nervous about this? If Spinton returned Beatrice's feelings, then this could only be a happy occasion. But if he didn't return her cousin's regard . . . Well, that wasn't something she should consider. She had to let him go. It was in both their best interests.

A weak chuckle escaped her. Now she was the one thinking she knew what was in someone's *best interest*.

Spinton resided in the same house where Octavia had

spent the years leading up to her grandfather's death. It still seemed strange to take the carriage to Grosvenor Square and enter that house as a guest, especially since Spinton hadn't changed a single thing.

It was a warm morning, with bouts of bright sunshine periodically breaking through the cover of clouds. Spinton was strolling through the garden, looking very cool and fashionable in a pale blue coat and biscuit-colored trousers. He was a handsome man in a very English sort of way. Too bad she liked her men—man—a little rougher around the edges, a little less polished.

Her heart thumped with dread as she approached him, her damp fingers clutching at the blue muslin of her skirts. She did not want to do this. Did not want to hurt him or offend him in any way, but how could she possibly avoid it? How could a man not be hurt when the woman he planned to marry told him she simply couldn't go through with the wedding? Even if he loved Beatrice, it was bound to wound him to know that Octavia didn't want him.

Gravel crunched beneath her slippers; a pebble stabbed the delicate skin of her right arch, making her hiss in pain.

Spinton, who had paused to admire a bush of roses, looked up. He smiled.

It was not, Octavia noticed, the kind of smile a man gave to the woman he hoped to marry. While Spinton certainly looked pleased to see her, he did not look overjoyed to see her, which was how a bridegroom should look. It was how North usually looked—when he didn't want to throttle her.

"Octavia. What a pleasure."

If this was his idea of pleasure, she would hate to see what happened if he ended up with a rock stuck in his foot. "How are you, Fitzwilliam?"

They exchanged the necessary pleasantries before touring the garden together. Octavia was going to miss this garden.

Today might very well be the last time she ever had to enjoy the many colors and fragrances it afforded.

"How is Miss Henry?" he asked as he plucked a red holly-hock from its vine.

Not even five minutes into their visit and he inquired after Beatrice's well-being before he asked after Octavia's own.

"She is well. She sends her regards."

He brightened at that, adding to her suspicions. In fact, he looked more pleased by that remark than he had been to see Octavia in person. That settled it. She was bringing this melodrama to its close. Curtain call, final bow, exit to the greenroom.

"We need to talk," she blurted, wincing at her own bluntness.

Stopping on the path, his golden hair lightened by a sudden burst of sunshine, Spinton regarded her with uncensored concern. He really was a good man. "About?"

"About our marriage."

Was it her imagination or did he pale somewhat? He started walking again, the gravel crunching beneath his feet. "What about it?"

How to put this? She should be delicate, considerate. There was a right way and a wrong way to do this. "I do not think we should go through with it."

He froze again, and this time she knew it was *not* her imagination. He was pleased. Startled, but far more pleased than dismayed. The bounder didn't want to marry her either!

He was, however, still a gentleman and managed to contain himself. "Might I ask why?"

Turning, she faced him with an earnest and open expression. "Does it matter?"

Flushing, Spinton shook his head. "Not really."

She answered him anyway—he deserved that much at least. "I do not believe we suit one another." There, that was a bit more delicate than her earlier admissions.

He nodded. "Perhaps you are right."

Octavia placed her gloved hand on his arm and met his kind gaze from beneath the brim of her bonnet. There was no censure in his gaze—nothing but understanding, acceptance, and yes, that little spark of happiness he couldn't quite hide.

"Somehow, I do not think you are injured by my decision. Are you, Fitzwilliam?"

He placed his other hand over hers, the red hollyhock fluttering in the breeze. "My dear Octavia, while it grieves me to discover that you do not think of me as a pleasing candidate for your husband, I cannot pretend that I do not share your misgivings."

Now *that* was the right way to tell someone you didn't want to marry them. Trust Spinton to be a true gentleman in every situation.

She smiled and dropped her hand. "I thought you might be suffering from a change of heart."

"It has nothing to do with you," he assured her as they began walking once more. "Please do not think otherwise."

Linking her hands in front of her, Octavia continued to smile. It felt as though a huge weight had been lifted off her shoulders. "I would not dream of it. I believe it has more to do with Beatrice than with myself."

Again he blushed—she watched him color out of the corner of her eye. "You are right again. Am I that transparent?"

"On the contrary," she replied, bending to smell a bright yellow bloom. "How could a man as good as yourself help falling in love with a woman equally as good?"

He shot her a startled glance. "But you are good as well, Octavia!"

Chuckling, she shook her head. What an odd conversation this was! "Not like you and Beatrice. You two are much better suited to each other. You have similar likes and dislikes. You were even born into similar situations."

Now he frowned. "But you were born into the same sphere as Beatrice and I. Better in fact than Beatrice, for she is but your distant relation."

She noticed he had stopped referring to her cousin as Miss Henry. "Spinton, I am going to tell you something I swore to my grandfather I would never tell another soul. In fact, only a few other people know this secret."

His expression was somewhere between concern and trepidation, as though he wanted to know but feared what she might say. "Go on."

Octavia linked her fingers again, staring straight ahead at the pale gravel and green grass spread out before her. "I was not born into the same sphere as you and Beatrice. Not truly. I was raised in Covent Garden by my mother, Maggie Marsh."

She cast a glance at him, eager to see his reaction to her confession. It was as she expected—his eyes were round and his jaw slack with disbelief. "The actress?"

Octavia nodded. "The same. She and my father eloped when they were very young. My grandfather disapproved of the match, and when my father died, he blamed my mother and refused to support her. She was a very proud sort and was determined to make it on her own. By then she already knew she was carrying me, so she stayed with friends until after I was born and then she went back to work."

Spinton's cheeks flushed. Did he find her distasteful now? It didn't truly matter, but after all they had been through, she would like to think they might still be friends of a sort. "I cannot believe your grandfather told you to keep such a secret from me," he said at last.

What a relief. He didn't see her as a pariah.

"Not just from you," she reminded him, in an effort to soothe his wounded pride. "From everyone. He was heartily ashamed of his actress daughter-in-law, but when he found out he had a granddaughter—a little reminder of his dead son—well, he decided to take me in and make me the lady he and my mother thought I should be."

His expression still tinged with incredulity, Spinton smiled. "But not the lady you thought you should be?"

Octavia returned his grin. "Something like that."

Spinton's gaze turned thoughtful. "That was why you did not want me to hire Sheffield, was it not? You knew him from your past."

The Earl Spinton might be a lot of things, but stupid was not one of them. "Yes."

His eyes narrowed. "There is more to your relationship than simply sharing a similar background, isn't there?"

Her cheeks warming, Octavia nodded. "Yes. Much more, I am afraid."

His eyes lighting as though he had just solved a baffling mystery, Spinton snapped his fingers. "I knew it! He tried to deny it, but I knew he had designs on you." Then, as the thought occurred to him, "If I had not brought him back into your life you would have gone through with our marriage, would you not?"

The fire in her cheeks burned even hotter. "Yes."

Stopping once more, Spinton flashed her a grin more roguish than she had ever seen grace his features. "Then are you not pleased that I stuck my nose into your business?"

Octavia laughed. How could she not? "Yes! And I am sorry for giving you such a tongue-lashing for it."

They rounded a curve in the path in comfortable silence, turning back toward the main house.

"Does he know you love him?"

Spinton's question caught her off guard. She never would have expected such a personal inquiry from him. "Yes."

"And he returns the feeling?"

She frowned. "I believe so. I hope so."

"How could a man as difficult as Sheffield not love a woman as difficult as you?" Spinton asked with a wink.

Openmouthed, Octavia stared at him. "You were never this amusing or smart-mouthed as a fiancé."

He shrugged. "You were much more intimidating as my betrothed than you are now."

Flabbergasted, she couldn't think of a suitable reply. Still smiling smugly, Spinton handed her the hollyhock. "Tell Beatrice that I will be joining the two of you for dinner tonight, would you?" He climbed the steps to the house. "And feel free to roam around the garden some more if you wish. I am afraid I have business to attend to."

That was it? He was dismissing her? Just because she'd jilted him was no reason to be rude!

On the top of the stone steps, he turned and smiled. "Thank you for not marrying me, Octavia. I would have hated making you miserable."

She smiled. That was better. That was almost sweet. "And I you, Fitzwilliam."

How long she stood there after he disappeared through the French doors into the house was a mystery. She was like a statue—trying to make sense of what had just happened.

She was free. Totally and without restriction. No one was in control of her destiny now but herself. It was a heady feeling. And more than a little frightening. Where did she start?

She could start by leaving her erstwhile betrothed's home.

She was drifting lazily down the corridor, gazing at the portraits of her ancestors with a lingering feeling of giddiness when she collided with something hard and strangely familiar-smelling.

"Christ!" The something growled.

North. If she never saw him again for the rest of her life, she would recognize his voice in heaven.

She looked up—into glacial blue eyes that stared at her as though they had never seen a face like hers before.

Does he know you love him?

Yes.

And does he return the feeling?

I believe so. I hope so. The conversation she and Spinton had shared rang in her mind.

She smiled, her heart pounding wildly in her throat. It was so very good to see him again. "Hello, Norrie."

He did not smile. In fact, he looked rather pained. "Vie."

Well, just because he looked as though he'd rather be anywhere but there with her didn't mean she was going to be as rude. "What are you doing here?"

He took a step backward, robbing her of his heat and strength. "I am here to see Spinton."

And was that all the explanation she was to expect? Probably. "I see."

His gaze dropped and then shuttered. "What is that?"

Octavia followed his line of vision. It was the hollyhock. Somewhat bedraggled from having been crushed between them, the delicate flower was still pretty if not a little lopsided.

"It was a flower." She couldn't help but smile a little. "Now I believe it is little more than a mess."

He nodded, not sharing her humor. "A gift from your fiancé?"

How wonderfully, stupidly jealous he sounded! He was the one who told her to marry Spinton. He was the one who rejected her love when she offered it to him. What amazing nerve to now look at her as though she were somehow betraying him.

"It was a gift from Spinton, yes." She could tell him the truth, but a part of her wanted him to suffer just a little while longer. Now was not the time or the place to have this conversation. When North admitted his feelings for her—whatever they might be—it would not be in her grandfather's house.

He stared at her, the muscle in his left jaw twitching. "How thoughtful."

Octavia couldn't resist raising a brow at that. "Sarcasm does not suit you, Norrie."

"Reckless stupidity does not suit you, Vie," he shot back, eyes narrow.

"Reckless stupidity?" How dare he! Her good humor fled as though snatched by the wind. "What the devil are you talking about?"

His expression was just as acrimonious as his tone. "Your little visit to a certain coffee house on Russell Street."

"Oh." So he knew then. Well, she had known that he would find out eventually. Hadn't she hoped he would find out? After all, she had counted on it bringing him back to her. So far her gamble was a huge loss.

He scowled. "Is that all you have to say?"

She nodded, lifting her chin defiantly. "For now, yes."

The naturally rosy hue of his cheeks grew even darker. "God help me, Vie—"

"We will talk about it later, Norrie," she interrupted. "Now is not the time or place."

He glanced around, as though he had forgotten where they were. Perhaps he had. They seemed to have that effect on each other—the ability to erase all other people and surroundings until just the two of them existed.

He obviously wanted to continue. "Will you be at home later today?"

She would be, but she wasn't about to deal with him when he was in *this* dark a mood. "No. You may come by this evening if you wish. Come for dinner. Spinton will be there."

His face tightened. "I would rather not, thank you."

She shrugged, biting her tongue to keep from chuckling. Oh, she should be ashamed of herself for taunting him so, but she wasn't. After all he'd put her through, he deserved to suffer a little bit. Lord knew he was going to make her suffer for going to Harker!

"Come by later then," she suggested. "You can join me for a glass of brandy."

"Fine." Was that his neck she heard snap when he nodded so stiffly?

She plastered a huge, overly bright smile on her face. "Wonderful! I shall look forward to it."

His smile was nowhere near as large but just as false. "You do that."

She couldn't plague him anymore, not when she knew how much hearing about her visit to Harker must have scared him.

Gracing him with a more natural, and repentant, gaze, she lifted herself up onto her tiptoes and brushed her lips across his cheek. "Try not to be too angry with me, Norrie."

He visibly relaxed, the tension seeming to leave his spine. But his expression was still one of disapproval and distrust.

"Be careful on your way home," was his gruff response.

Somehow, she managed to smile. What she really wanted to do was kiss him silly. "I am certain you have enough men still following me that I do not have to worry about my safety."

His eyes widened and she chuckled. Had he thought she hadn't noticed that his men dogged her every step? Maybe they were able to follow some people without being noticed, but a big burly man with a beard was sure to stand out in a ladies' dress shop.

She tucked the flower into the topmost buttonhole of his coat, fluffing its battered petals into some semblance of beauty.

"Until tonight, Norrie. Do not keep me waiting."

And as she left him there, Octavia allowed a smug smile to curve her lips. He would not keep her waiting. Of that she was certain.

Do not keep her waiting. Impertinent baggage. She knew very well he would not keep her waiting—but not because he was so concerned with her wants. He wouldn't keep her waiting because he'd stewed far too long already and needed release from the emotions tormenting him before they swallowed him whole.

Seeing her had not helped, not at all. Those big blue eyes, tiny tilted nose, and sweetly mocking lips only served to sharpen the blade picking at his heart. What right had he to be jealous when he was the one who sent her running into the arms of another man? She was only doing what he told her to do. He should be glad that his life would soon return to normal, but he wasn't. And *that* only made him all the angrier.

Once he finally had Harker—and he would have him, make no mistake—he would turn his thoughts to something else. A new cause, a new villain to chase. Brahm and Duncan's urging to pursue a career in politics haunted his thoughts more than normally. Perhaps it was time for a change. Perhaps he would be better suited trying to change the laws than ridding the world of criminals one by one.

But a political career meant spending more time in society, offering himself up for the approval of others—his betters, so to speak. Certainly the *ton* seemed to harbor a certain liking for him now, but only because he took care of their sometimes dirty little secrets and scandals.

Or maybe this change of heart, this indecision about his future, came from the fact that he had received an invitation to Lady Amelia's wedding that morning. She was marrying her young lord. Seems her father had claimed her after all—

even settled a large portion on her. She had done what North never could, but then she'd had the guts to try and take it. He hadn't.

And what the hell was he doing thinking of all of this while standing outside Spinton's study? Christ, he must look like some kind of dolt, standing there, lost in his own thoughts.

He had turned into an idiot. If he thought about it long enough, he knew he could trace this loss of his mind directly to Octavia's reentry into his life. Things seemed so much more complicated when she was around, and yet he never felt life was so simple as he did when she was there beside him.

Sighing, he raised his fist to the heavy oak door and rapped sharply. Facing the man who would have Octavia in his bed for the rest of his life was only marginally easier than facing Octavia herself. What would it take for both of them to leave him alone?

Lord Spinton answered the door with a convivial smile. North returned it easily while noting how fine the earl's attire was, how smooth his jaw, how neat his hair. It made him that much more aware of his own clothing—his usual austere gray—and his own unshaven jaw and unruly hair. How could Octavia say she preferred him over a man like Spinton?

Yes, there was something he would do well to remember. Octavia might marry Spinton, but it was he who had her heart—for all the good it did him.

"Mr. Sheffield," the fairer man greeted, gesturing for him to come in. "Thank you for coming so quickly."

"I had nothing else to do," North replied honestly and without petulance. Had Spinton arranged this meeting so that North would run into Octavia? Did Spinton want to rub North's face in his victory?

No, he didn't think so. Spinton wasn't that kind of man. Meeting Octavia was a coincidence, nothing more.

The blond man nodded at his chest. "I see you met up with Octavia on your way in."

North glanced down. The abused hollyhock stood out against the pale fabric of his coat like blood. "Yes." What else could he say?

Spinton didn't look the least bit perturbed that his betrothed had given his gift to another man. "Brandy?"

"No. Thank you." He would be having brandy with Octavia that evening. What would Spinton think of that? Perhaps that would drive this frozen stick to show a little emotion.

"I will get right to the point," Spinton spoke as he poured himself a drink at the sideboard. "I know you must have business of your own to get back to."

"Yes." Being angry, feeling sorry for himself, trying to find sufficient evidence against Harker—those were the most pressing issues in his life, and in that order.

With that infuriatingly pleasant expression still gracing his features, Spinton took a swallow of his brandy and crossed the brief expanse of blue, green, and gold carpet to his polished oak desk.

He offered North a bank draft. "Your payment for solving the mystery of Octavia's admirer."

North stared at the paper. It didn't even waver in the earl's grasp. He didn't need the money—didn't want the money. Taking it would be like rubbing salt in a wound, but he could hardly tell Spinton that.

"Keep it," he said, raising his gaze to Spinton's. "Consider it my wedding gift to you and Lady Octavia." The words choked him like sawdust.

Finally the kindness disappeared from Spinton's face, replaced by sheer astonishment. "Wedding gift? She did not tell you?"

His heart tripping against his ribs, North took a deep breath before asking, "Tell me what?"

Taking another drink of brandy, Spinton leaned back against his desk, bank draft hanging at his side. "There is not going to be a wedding—not between Octavia and myself. She ended our understanding just before your arrival."

Ended their arrangement. No wedding. North's head spun. Could the damned woman not do anything he told her to do?

God, he . . . adored her. No, not adored. Loved. He loved her. He could admit that, if to no one but himself. He loved her and it scared him. She was his one and only weakness. She would be the route every villain ever took to get to him if they were to be together while he was still in this line of work. She would be in danger until he finally caught Harker and anyone else he decided he needed to rid the world of. But she wouldn't understand that, not when it kept him from loving her the way he wanted.

And if he pushed her away, if he dictated the rules of their relationship, then he never had to worry about her leaving him—or being taken from him. Because the one thing North feared more than rejection was being left behind.

He had gotten so used to being alone, what if he opened himself up to someone else? What if he gave himself to Octavia, let her into his heart and soul and then he lost her? Or worse, she saw just how little worth he truly had and she turned her back on him? What if he wasn't the prize she thought him to be?

"Your silence is answer enough," Spinton remarked kindly. "Obviously she wanted to tell you later. My apologies for upsetting you."

"You didn't upset me." Was that his voice? It sound strange and muffled in his head.

He thought he heard Spinton chuckle at that. "No, I should think this news would be anything *but* upsetting for you."

That snapped North back to reality, and back on his guard. He met the earl's gaze. "What do you mean?"

Spinton smiled. "Oh come now, Mr. Sheffield. For whom do you think Octavia ended our betrothal? It was not me, I assure you."

Him? Had Octavia jilted Spinton for him? Had she turned her back on the wishes of her mother and her grandfather—willfully ignored North's own advice—because of her love for him?

What had he ever done to deserve such devotion?

"I—" Words refused to come.

"Forgive my impertinence, Mr. Sheffield, but do you love her?"

North glared at the other man. "You're right. You are impertinent."

Spinton shrugged. "Octavia and I have known each other for a long time. Regardless of the present change in our circumstances, I still hold a very high opinion of her. I would hate to see her injured in anyway."

"So would I." That was why he told her to marry Spinton, for Christ's sake!

"If you love her, you should tell her. She deserves nothing less."

"What she deserves," North bit out, "is a man who is not going to put her in danger every time he takes a new assignment. She deserves someone of her own sphere, someone who can keep and treat her as she is accustomed."

"Do you really think such trivial things matter to her? She is the granddaughter of an earl, she will always have rank and connections. What she *deserves*, Mr. Sheffield, is to be loved and respected by the man she loves, and that, I am sorry to inform you, is you. None of your excuses and arguments can change that."

North stared at Spinton. He wasn't as foolish and foppish as North first thought. "My career makes me many enemies. They would love to use her to get to me."

Spinton finished his drink. "Then you do your damnedest to protect her and reconsider your choice of profession."

He shook his head. "It is not that simple."

"Of course it is not. It never is. What you have to decide is if it is worth taking a chance on. Ask yourself this question: What would you prefer, a life alone chasing criminals, or the chance to spend as much time as you can with the woman who loves you enough to break several vows to have you?"

He was right, of course. What would he rather have? As terrifying as losing Octavia might be, the idea of not having her at all was infinitely more frightening. But he had to dispose of Harker first. Had to decide what he was going to do next before he could give her that kind of commitment. He could not go to her a failure, could not ride her name and connections to a position in society. He had to do it on his own.

"I have been considering a career in politics," he admitted. "My brother wants me to run MP for his borough. The people there like him and have known me for years. Winning there should not be a problem, but garnering support here in London for reform may be. Brahm's reputation here may do me more harm than good."

Spinton chuckled. "I can certainly understand that. Perhaps I can help you a bit. You are certainly popular among the *ton* in your own right. Capitalize on that. Remind people of what you have done for them and others like them. Those who have been victimized will be certain to support whatever reforms you wish to push."

North eyed him carefully. "I am a bastard, Spinton. Won't that damage my chances of winning peer support?"

Another chuckle escaped the earl's mouth. "My dear Mr. Sheffield. You talk as though you are the only person to ever have been born on the wrong side of the blanket. Do you have any idea how many members of society have fathers different from those whose surname they share? At least you have the advantage of knowing the man who raised you actually was your sire."

He made it sound so simple, so easy. Was it? Could it be?

Swallowing his pride, North met the earl's gaze evenly. "And you would be willing to help me, even though I am the reason Octavia ended your betrothal?"

Spinton nodded. "Of course! Octavia knows that my heart has belonged to another for some time now."

Comprehension dawned. "Miss Henry."

A grin curved the earl's lips and brightened his eyes. "The very same. So you see, you actually did me a service, Sheffield. Now it is my turn to do one for you."

That sounded fair. "All right. Thank you."

Spinton thrust the bank draft at him. "First, however, you must take this and promise me one thing."

North took the payment. "What is that?"

"Hire yourself a valet. We cannot have you entering society looking like a wildman."

For the first time in days, North laughed—really laughed. It felt good. It gave him hope.

Maybe he could have everything he ever wanted. Maybe he could find where he truly belonged.

And maybe, just maybe, he and Octavia could finally be together.

Chapter 18

He was keeping her waiting.

Staring at the clock on the mantel, Octavia sipped at her second glass of brandy. Dinner had long since been finished, and Spinton had whisked Beatrice off to the parlor to tell her the happy news. They were still in there, doing God only knew what.

At least someone was happy.

"Mr. Sheffield is here to see you, my lady."

God, she hadn't even heard the butler knock. "Show him in."

A few seconds later, North sauntered into the room. He seemed totally unconcerned that he was late. It didn't matter that they hadn't agreed on a particular time, he was still late—and he knew it.

"Took you long enough," she remarked once the door closed behind him.

He raised a brow, totally unrepentant. "I had business to attend to."

"You always do." She tossed back the rest of her drink.

"How much have you had?" he asked when she went to pour herself another.

She didn't look at him, but instead concentrated on pouring her drink. "Two. Would you like one?"

"I think I had better."

A drink in either hand, she turned to join him, only to find him sitting in one of the chairs near the center of the room. He seemed so large, so masculine—too big for the dainty frame.

She handed him a drink and seated herself in the chair opposite him, where she waited in silence for him to speak, even though she seethed inside with impatience.

At least he didn't keep her waiting much later. "Why did you not tell me that you had ended your engagement to Spinton?"

Ah, so Spinton had let the cat out of the bag, had he? She would have much rather told North herself—or at least have been there to see the expression on his face when he learned she had denied him of what he considered her "best interest."

She affected a careless shrug. "I did not think you would be interested."

His eyes widened, then narrowed over the rim of his snifter as he raised it to his lips. Slowly, he lowered it, his throat constricting as he swallowed. "Why would you think that?"

He sounded so calm, but she knew the truth. She knew *him*. His knuckles were white as he gripped the fine crystal. No, he wasn't unaffected at all.

"You told me you wanted me to marry him." Her tone was syrupy sweet—innocent.

North's expression didn't change. "I never said I wanted you to."

She rolled her eyes. "You told me to marry him. You also told me to get out of your life. I thought you meant it."

"I am an ass."

Octavia almost choked on her drink. "I will not argue with you there."

His gaze was level, clear and pale as a summer sky. "And you are a brainless, reckless twit for going to see Harker."

She smiled at him. "I cannot argue with that either."

For a moment they simply sat there, watching each other in silence, sipping their drinks, waiting.

She gave in first. That was no surprise. It was amazing she held out as long as she did. "I only wanted to help you, Norrie. I wanted to show you that you are not alone."

He closed his eyes briefly, an expression of exquisite longing tightening his features. "Thank you," he whispered.

No matter what she might have expected—yelling, anger—this wasn't it.

There was only one thing she could think to say. "You are welcome."

He rose from his chair, leaving his half-finished brandy on the side table. She had almost finished her drink, and she was beginning to feel the effects of so much liquor.

Slightly unfocused, she watched as he crossed the inconsequential distance between them and lowered himself to his knees before her. Gripping the arms of her chair, he pulled her closer, nudging her knees as far apart as her skirts would allow so he could slide between.

"But if you ever scare me like that again, I will lock you in the attic until you are a frail old woman, do I make myself clear?"

She grinned despite the gravity in his tone. "Yes, Norrie."

"Good." He raised a hand to her cheek. "Christ, Vie. I'm just so glad you are all right."

And then his mouth seized her before she could think of anything to say. Her lips parted at the first insistent probing of his tongue. He tasted of brandy and man and something

Octavia had feared she'd never taste again—her dearest Nor-rie. She opened her mouth to him as she squirmed forward in her chair, eager to give as much as she wanted to take.

Her hands slid beneath his coat, feeling the heat and strength of him through the fabric of his shirt and waistcoat. Impatiently, she shoved, and he released her long enough to allow her to slide the jacket down his arms—their mouths still locked together.

He caressed her face, her neck and shoulders, sliding his fingers around to her back. As she fumbled with the but-tons on his waistcoat, he deftly unhooked the back of her dress.

Her tongue slid against his, stroking, tasting. She drank him in as though he were water and she were parched. And when she'd opened his waistcoat, she moved on to the simply tied knot of his cravat.

He broke their kiss long enough to toss his waistcoat and cravat aside, and when she tugged his shirt free of his trousers, he pulled the thin lawn over his head, baring his up-per body to her eager gaze.

He was golden perfection. From the jutting bones of his shoulders to the thick-muscled wall of his hairy chest, there was nothing finer or bonnier in all the world than North. And he was hers. All hers.

"You are so beautiful," she whispered, brandy and desire loosening her tongue.

He smiled, pulling the top of her gown off her shoulders. "I was just thinking the same about you."

She pulled her arms free of the tiny puffed sleeves, allow-ing him to peel the gown down to her waist, and when he tugged further she lifted her hips so he could pull the gown down farther, tossing it aside so it wouldn't tangle around her feet. Her shift followed, and soon she was sitting on the chair, the cool brocade against her bare flesh, in nothing but her garters and stockings. Those he left on. He seemed to like seeing her in them.

"So very beautiful," he murmured, sliding his hands up her thighs, up past her ribs to cup a breast in each palm. His thumbs teased her nipples, sending a hot wave of desire through her. The heat pooled between her thighs, and she gasped at the intensity of it. She watched, unable to tear her gaze away as he worked the pink crests into dark, hardened pebbles that begged for his mouth. She wanted him to suckle them, to tug on them until they were throbbing and distended, until they tingled with both pleasure and pain.

As though he sensed her need, he took a nipple into his mouth, laving it with his tongue, nipping it with his teeth until Octavia's head reeled. Her hands clutched at his head, holding her to him so he couldn't—wouldn't—stop this incredible torture. She itched deep inside, in a place only he could reach, an itch only he could satisfy.

North's hands went to the falls of his trousers. She could feel him yanking at the falls, peeling the fabric down his thighs to his knees as his mouth continued to bring moans of pleasure to her lips.

She still held his head with one hand. The other reached down between her splayed thighs, eagerly searching for what she craved. His hair brushed her temple; the velvety lobe of his ear was soft against her mouth. A sigh escaped her lips as her fingers closed around the head of his sex. He was hard and hot against her palm, slick with his own lubricant. He was ready for her, and wanted her so badly he pulsated in her hand.

Brazenly, she milked him. He thickened as her fingers moved, groaning against her breast. He nipped at her nipple with his teeth, one of his hands slipping between her thighs, to the heated, damp flesh that craved him.

Octavia gasped, her cheek abraded by the rough stubble of

his jaw, as he slipped a finger inside her. His intrusion was sweet and cool as her heated flesh opened to him, but instead of easing the wanton ache inside her, it only served to intensify it. Her hips moved as he stroked her, as his thumb parted her slick folds to rub the swollen hardness between. Gasping for breath, she pushed against his hand. It wasn't enough.

It would never be enough. She would never have her fill of this man. She loved him and wanted him with her, part of her and part of her life until the end of her days.

"Give yourself to me," she whispered against his ear. "Make me yours."

He withdrew his hand and released her breast, raising his hot, hooded gaze to hers.

"Come down here."

Even if she wanted to refuse him, the hypnotic timbre of his voice would have made it impossible. But she would never refuse him, not ever. Placing her hand in his as he scooted backward on his knees, she slithered to the floor as though her entire body were hot and melted enough to pour.

He didn't speak. He simply placed his hands on her shoulders and turned her around, gently pushing so that her head and upper chest rested on the seat of the chair.

"Grab the arms," he instructed, his voice rough and throaty.

Octavia did as he bid, her heart hammering wildly as she realized his intentions. This was how he was going to punish her for going to Harker. He was going to make her writhe and beg and squirm and deny her the pleasure of being able to watch him as he made love to her.

But it wasn't punishment. It was the only way he could do this and still keep himself apart from her. The emotion between them now was so heavy and thick it was terrifying. If they made love face-to-face it would be too much, too intense. As it was, she trembled with the need to have him, not just physically, but in every way possible. This was about release, about giving and taking, trusting and needing.

His fingers brushed the heated cheeks of her bottom, brushing the delicate flesh between, nerves jumping at his touch. Down to the heated opening of her body he caressed, spreading the wetness there back and forth. Heat flooded Octavia's face as she realized just how soaked she was, but despite her embarrassment, she spread her legs further when he pushed against her thigh.

God, it felt so good, so urgent. As she gripped the chair with all her strength, her body quivered like violin strings wound too tightly. She arched her hips, thrusting back against his hand, sweat beading her brow as she fought to ease the growing ache deep inside her. Still he teased her, his nimble fingers awakening nerves and sensations in places she never knew they existed, until she thought she might die from the pleasure.

The rounded, thick head of him pushed against her entrance as he stroked the tightened bloom of sensation ruthlessly revealed by his fingers. She arched again, trying to coax him inside. He didn't budge.

"Please." She didn't care if she had to beg. She'd beg if that was what he wanted.

Hot, moist breath brushed her ear. "Please what?"

Her eyes flew open. He was there, the hair on his chest tickling the sensitive flesh of her back.

"Do you want me inside you, Vie?" He slid the head of his erection just inside her wanting flesh.

"Yesss." Oh God, what was he trying to do to her?

"Do you want me to make you scream?"

"Please, yes!" Scream, sob, yodel, she didn't care as long as he gave her the release she needed.

"Tell me you love me."

So that was what he needed. She already knew he loved

her—how, she wasn't certain, but she was as sure of it as she was her own feelings. If he needed to hear it, she would tell him as much as he wanted, until he finally believed it.

"I love you," she murmured. "I love you."

He shoved himself inside her with one fierce thrust, and Octavia couldn't keep from crying out in gratitude. Frantically, he pumped, driving them both toward the edge of orgasm with deep, uncontrolled thrusts.

Faster he moved, their moans merging as her flesh clenched and constricted around his. Mouth open, brow furrowed in an attempt to keep from crying out, Octavia clung to the chair, incoherently begging him to take her further, thrust faster, harder.

And then the world exploded as spasm after spasm of mind-numbing release shook her. Burying her face in the chair cushion to muffle her cries, she allowed the vortex to carry her, the rapture of release wrenching through her body.

North stiffened behind her, a loud groan bursting free of his throat. He held her hips in his hands, his fingers digging into her flesh as he emptied himself inside her. Then he slumped against her, his torso resting on her back, their bodies still joined.

They stayed like that for some time, as their breathing returned to normal. Finally he slipped from her and then withdrew entirely so she could move.

Octavia sank into a sitting position on the carpet. She was hot and sticky and still a little unsteady, but she felt more relaxed than she had in a long time. North felt the same way—if the way he was sprawled against the side of the sofa was any indication.

She crawled over to him and curled against him, resting her head on his chest. He wrapped an arm around her shoulders, stroking her hair with his hand.

"I love you, Norrie," she told him softly.

His lips brushed his forehead. "Thank you."

What? Lifting her face, she frowned at him. "That is not what you are supposed to say."

His smile was sad. "I know."

Her heart frozen in her chest, Octavia stared at him, tears burning the backs of her eyes. Had she been wrong? Did she not know him as well as she thought? "You do not love me, do you?"

"You are my everything," he told her, his voice unnaturally hoarse. "You are my always, but I cannot give you what you want until I am certain being with me will not hurt you."

Grabbing her discarded gown, she staggered to her feet. Her legs trembled and an uncomfortable wetness smeared her thighs. "Being without you hurts me!"

He also stood, pulling his trousers back up his legs. Half naked and still too damned attractive, he tried to comfort her, but she pushed him away, struggling into her wrinkled gown.

"Octavia, please."

"No!" She jerked away from his beseeching hands. "It does not work that way, North! You cannot take my love and not give something in return."

His expression was wry. "I thought I did."

Shoving her arms into her sleeves, she shot him a dirty look. "Rutting does not count."

"Rutting?" His anger was evident. "You call what we just did rutting?"

Octavia scooped up her chemise, the open neck of her gown sagging around her shoulders. "It certainly was not lovemaking, was it? That generally requires both parties to be in love—hence the term."

He opened his arms, his palms up. "I told you—once I know you are safe, then I will be able to give you what you want."

What was he, deranged? "So, what? Until then you just

give me what is convenient? That is not enough. I broke promises for you, North Sheffield. I made changes and decisions that are new and sometimes a little frightening just on the hope that you might return my feelings, and now you have the gall to stand there and tell me that I need to wait even longer? I have waited twelve blasted years already!"

"Then why can you not wait a little longer? I'm not asking for a year, Vie. I just want you far out of Harker's reach."

She stared at him. There was something disturbing in the pale depths of his eyes. Something unfamiliar in his gaze. "You are scared."

He nodded. "Of Harker harming you, yes."

She shook her head, her crumpled chemise held tight against her chest. "No. You are more scared of me—of us— than you are of Harker. You are afraid that if you tell me you love me I will use it against you, or hurt you in some way. You think I will reject you like society did all those years ago."

North paled, but he did not deny it. If he had realized it himself before this, she would be surprised. "I am socially inferior to you, we both know that."

Scooping his shirt up off the carpet, she shoved it at him. "Obviously you are intellectually inferior as well, because that is the most stupid thing I have ever heard you say!"

His mouth thinned as he accepted the crumpled linen. "What if someday you regret your choice? You should marry a man who deserves you—a man that can give you the life you want."

"*You* are the only man who can give me what I want!"

He gaped at her, obviously as shocked by the force of her outburst as she was.

"I want you to leave," she told him, her voice shaking. "Come back when you have decided not to live your life based on what other people think."

"Vie—" But she didn't listen. She turned her back on him

and stomped toward the door. Only then did she turn to face him, her heart breaking in her chest.

"Come back then, Norrie. If you are lucky I might still be waiting."

What did she mean she *might* be waiting? She wasn't serious, surely. After all that had happened between them, after her ending her engagement for him, she wouldn't toss it all aside just because she didn't agree with him. Would she? No, he couldn't believe she would be that foolish.

But just because he thought it was foolish, didn't mean she would agree, North thought as the hack he was in swayed through the lighted streets of Mayfair. She hadn't been fooling when she told him to leave. She had meant it, and she had been genuinely hurt by his refusal to tell her he loved her.

It wasn't that he didn't *want* to say it, but those weren't words a man just tossed around whenever the mood struck— or at least they shouldn't be. Such a vow was one to be taken seriously, and such a commitment should only be given when he was certain he could hold to it. It was a vow he could not make while Harker roamed the streets. He was a threat to Octavia as it was, but if he learned just how much North thought of her—if she and North were to actually try for a future together, Harker would definitely not hesitate to use Octavia as a weapon when North closed in on him.

But that was only one of the reasons that he couldn't tell her he loved her. There were others—most of them stupid and silly. He wanted to give her time to reconsider. It wasn't going to be easy for him to step into society—they wouldn't readily accept him as her husband. He wanted to be certain he wasn't going to shame or taint her. He wanted to make certain he was accepted first.

He could spend all night rhyming off reasons why he and Octavia shouldn't be together, but it boiled down to one simple thing. She had been right. He was scared. Scared that he might lose her, scared that he might not lose her. Scared she might reject him, and utterly terrified that she might not reject him. Rejection and loss he expected. What the hell would he do if she didn't leave? There had been so little true happiness in his adult life, so few good memories since his mother's death, the idea of experiencing such things now was more than a little daunting.

Yes, his mother had loved him. Yes, his father had loved him. But his mother had loved his father more. And his father had loved wine and whiskey first, Nell Sheffield second, their son third. As good a man as his father could be, North could never depend on him to be there when he needed him, especially not if Viscount Creed found a drink first.

So yes, it was terrifying, the thought of putting his trust in Octavia. How could he be sure she would always be there? How could he be certain that he wouldn't end up hurt and disappointed again, with nothing to show for it but the vow to not be so stupid ever again.

He couldn't be sure. He couldn't be certain. What scared him the most was the thought of what might happen if he *didn't* at least try to trust that he deserved to be happy, that he deserved to be successful and content with the hand life dealt him. His brother Devlin had found such bliss. Why couldn't he?

Still, he had to do what he had to do. He couldn't go to Octavia as any less than what he wanted to be. And he could not be truly happy with her if he was worried every moment that Harker might try to hurt her.

And that led him full circle back to this badly sprung carriage, stinking of sex and feeling like shite.

Christ, he needed a drink.

*   *   *

"North, good morning." Brahm smiled as North entered the little area of the east parlor he liked to use as a breakfast nook. "Coffee?"

Bleary-eyed, with a tongue that felt like carpet and a head that felt like pounded granite, North nodded. "Please."

This was the room their father often used to entertain friends, its cherrywood paneling and dark green upholstery making for a very masculine atmosphere. The shelves were still lined with leather-bound volumes, the desk gleamed with a high polish—everything was exactly as their father had left it.

Except that where there had once been a liquor cabinet, there was now a breakfast table.

In fact, Brahm looked as though he had been eating a fair bit lately—making up for all those years of surviving on little but liquid, perhaps. He looked good, better than he had in years. Dressed in a dark wine coat and buff breeches, he looked hale and hearty—the way a wealthy viscount should look.

His brother eyed North with interest as he gingerly lowered himself into one of the chairs across the table from him. "You look like shite."

North tried to smile, but it turned out more like a grimace. "I feel like it."

"I thought you did not like to drink." Brahm's tone was hesitant, as though he feared that North might have changed his mind.

"I don't." That was true. He didn't like drinking at all, and despised the loss of control that came with being totally foxed. Last night, however, he had simply tried to shut himself down—stop feeling, stop thinking. He had succeeded. In fact, he couldn't remember much of anything—not about being drunk, at least. Unfortunately, everything else had come back to him this morning with painful clarity.

If he lived to be one hundred, he would never understand what appeal drunkeness held for his father or elder brother.

Brahm passed him a cup of coffee. "Drink this. It will help."

The coffee was strong and black as pitch, but so sugary sweet, North winced. "This stuff is awful."

His brother simply smiled. "I know, but it works."

It worked, no doubt, because it was so bloody awful people forgot about the pounding in their heads. "So, what is it you wanted to talk to me about?" North asked after ingesting half a cup of the awful brew.

"Your future."

His future was bleak. Without Octavia in it, the future was nothing more than the rest of his life. Nothing to look forward to. Nothing to hope for. "Christ, I should have stayed drunk."

Brahm chuckled. "I know you have as much interest in the topic as I do."

Draining the rest of his coffee, North set the empty cup aside with a shudder. Brahm was right; it did seem to be helping a bit.

His brother handed him a glass of water. "Now drink this. It will help, trust me."

It seemed bizarre to drink water for such an ailment, but if anyone knew a cure it would be Brahm.

"Is there sugar in it?" Any more sweetness and he was going to turn into a bonbon.

"Just water. It helps just as much if not more so than the coffee."

North didn't ask how he knew these things. It was obvious. Brahm knew because he had used them himself. North downed the water in one long gulp.

"I hope you have a chamber pot in here. I'm going to need it."

Brahm shot him a warning glance, so very much like that their father used to favor. "You know where the water closet is."

So he did. "All right, tell me what is so bloody important about my future that it couldn't wait until a decent hour."

"Why do we not start with you telling me why you look as though you have been to hell and back? You look even worse than you normally do."

It was on the tip of North's tongue to inform his brother that he had seen him looking far, far worse, but he didn't. He knew just how awful his appearance was. His hair was an unruly mess and in need of a good wash. He hadn't shaved for three days and his face itched, and he was wearing the same coat and trousers he had worn yesterday. This was disgusting, even for him.

"Octavia called off her engagement to Spinton," he admitted with a sigh, knowing full well Brahm would not stop badgering him until he confessed all.

Dark brows arched. "I thought that would be cause to celebrate—or is that what you were doing?"

"No, I was not celebrating." Would he look so wretched if he were truly happy? If he were celebrating, he and Octavia would still be in his bed, naked and sweaty. "She told me to stay away from her."

"Good God." Brahm refilled his coffee cup—no sugar this time. "What the hell did you do?"

North glared at him. Even his eyebrows hurt. "What makes you think *I* did something?"

His brother rolled his whiskey brown eyes. "You would not be so keen on self-flagellation if she were the guilty party. Besides a woman usually only tells a man to stay away if he has hurt her—badly."

Oh, this was just what he needed! First Octavia, now Brahm. Was there anyone else who wanted to tell him just what an awful person he was?

Another sigh. "I would not tell her I loved her."

Brows knitted in an expression of disbelief, Brahm stared at him. "Why the devil not?"

Did no one understand? He thought Brahm would. "Because those are not words a man should say when he is uncertain."

"But you are not uncertain, you great idiot." His brother graced him with a scowl that could have peeled paint from the walls. "You have loved her since you were old enough to know what love is."

He had? "I was infatuated with her as a boy, of course. And our friendship—"

"Oh stop." Clearly Brahm's patience had reached its end. "Do not insult my intelligence nor your own with insipid excuses. You love her, she loves you. Why could you not simply admit to it?"

North's mouth opened but no sounds came out at first. He tried again. "Because I am afraid that it will not last." There, he said it. He admitted it out loud, to someone other than the stray cat he fed in the back garden.

Buttering a piece of toast, Brahm shrugged. "Does anything?"

That was something of a cynical viewpoint, was it not? "Well, yes." But for the life of him, he couldn't think of what. "This house has lasted centuries."

Brahm glanced around him. "No more than two at the very most. And it may last for two or three more, but fire could just as easily destroy it tomorrow."

North raised his brows. And he thought *he* had a negative outlook.

Chewing his toast, Brahm swallowed and took a sip of coffee. "Look at this coat. It is a fine coat, is it not?"

North nodded. It looked expensive.

"It cost me a fair penny for this coat, but it was made by one of the best tailors in London, out of the finest wool. It will last me for years. In fact, I will probably be too fat to wear it in the near future. But as good as it is, eventually it will start to fray or moths will make a meal of it. However, does that mean I ought not to have commissioned it in the first place, if someday it will be gone?"

North saw his point—it was perfectly clear. "Octavia is not a coat."

Brahm smeared marmalade on another piece of toast. He was right. He would be too fat for the coat someday soon. "Of course she is not, nor is her regard for you. Love is not a tangible thing, North. One cannot predict its lifespan, but real love—true love—can last forever, I believe, or at least a lifetime, which is an amazing gift at that. Some people live their entire lives never experiencing what you have the chance to."

How effortlessly Brahm drove his point home and then twisted it.

"And I will experience it," he replied. "Once Harker is safely disposed of."

"Ah yes," Brahm's smile was twisted. "Harker. Whatever would you do without that villain to chase? You might actually have to stop running."

This was not helping North's temper. "Bugger off. Harker is my concern, not yours."

"You are quite right. My concern is for your future. You told me you were considering my offer to put you up for election in Hewbury."

North nodded, thankful that the subject of love was forgotten for the time being. "I am."

"I do not believe it will be any trouble to get you elected as member of Parliament. The people there know and like you and they are loyal to our family regardless. They will vote you in."

"But that is only half the battle," North reminded him, taking a drink of his proper-tasting coffee. "You are not totally without friends, but if I truly want to make a difference and have my ideas for more organized policing heard, I will need more peer support than merely yours."

His brother didn't seem the least bit offended by his words. "True, I am by no means a darling of the *ton*, but you have other connections that will help you achieve your goals. Spinton has indicated he will support you, has he not?"

North nodded. "Yes."

"And then there is Devlin's brother-in-law, the Marquess of Wynter. Miles will lend you whatever aid he can, I am certain of it."

Thank God for Blythe, Devlin's well-connected wife.

Brahm waved his toast at him. "And then there are all those poor unfortunate peers for whom you have worked."

Those numbers were great indeed. "But there is no guarantee all of them will want to publicly support me."

"Of course not. Some will not, but others will, and all you need is a few to plant a few suggestions in the right ears. Your views will find an audience in the House of Lords, mark my words." As if to punctuate his words, he tore another bite off his toast.

Could it possibly be this simple? North's heart sped up at the thought. The things he could do with the right people behind him. The changes he could implement, the laws he could help create. A whole new world was opening itself up to him.

All he had to do was let go of the old one first. Harker was his last bit of business. He would leave no loose ends. He couldn't afford to, not when the price could be so very high.

"But first," Brahm began, toast finished, his features twisted in distaste. "Before we try to convince anyone you are a man worthy of backing, I'm sending you upstairs to my valet."

Brahm's valet? Dear God. "He will not make me look like you, will he?" North asked in horror as he stood.

Collecting his cane, Brahm rose with him, and with a hand on his shoulder, led him toward the door. "He is good, but even he cannot work miracles."

Chapter 19

A week later Octavia, resigned to the fact that North was not going to come to her anytime soon, finally left her house for a bit of diverting amusement.

And without a doubt it would prove amusing. Tonight was the night Beatrice and Spinton were going to announce their betrothal. No doubt all of London would be flabbergasted by the news. It was a chuckle she sorely needed. People would speculate as to what happened between her and Spinton—and probably blame North. Never mind that Spinton had been falling in love with someone else at the same time.

No, not the same time. She had loved North for most of her life. Few people could say that.

In fact, her life had been fairly extraordinary in many ways, but she'd trade it all if she and North could simply live happily ever after. Alas, North would not have it. Or he would simply not have it *yet*. But when? How long was she expected to wait? How long would she have to endure the pitying looks of society matrons while her cousin married the man originally intended for her? How long would people whisper behind her back about North not coming up to scratch?

There was no point in thinking about it. It only made her grind her teeth in her sleep, and her left jaw ached enough as it was.

Still, she had taken extra care with her appearance, just so everyone would know she wasn't wasting away waiting for North to make up his mind. Her hair was artfully styled as a gleaming crown of curls atop her head. It had taken Janie hours to achieve, but it was worth it, for the look was very flattering to her face and revealed the long line of her neck—something she had been told was one of her best features.

The gown itself was beautiful—and new. Madame Villeneuve had outdone herself. It had an underskirt of rich burgundy with a shimmery gold crepe overskirt embroidered with hundreds of tiny burgundy crystals imported from Austria, which sparkled in the light. The crystals formed the pattern of a twining vine of roses along the bottom and up the right side of the skirt. The bodice was pale gold crepe ornamented with leaf-shaped pieces of burgundy velvet, and the sleeves were fashioned of similarly cut pieces of the burgundy crepe, sewn together to look like a bouquet of vines at her shoulders. Burgundy gloves and slippers completed the ensemble. For jewelry she wore a simple one-strand diamond necklace with matching dainty earrings. With a gown this strong, simple ornamentation was a must.

After dotting perfume behind her ears and at the base of her throat, she fetched her gold shawl and went downstairs. George, her coachman, had the carriage waiting, and the footman was lowering the steps when she stepped out into the warm night air.

The trip to Spinton's was blessedly short, giving North little time to plague her thoughts. She thought of him all the time now, instead of a mere hundred times a day. It was tiring, vexing, and more than a little heartbreaking.

When she arrived at Spinton's, the butler told her that Beatrice and Spinton were waiting for her in the white drawing room. Octavia thanked him and made her way down the corridor. She didn't need to be announced in this house, and probably never would.

It was odd, joining Beatrice here rather than the other way around or arriving together, but Beatrice had come early to oversee the final preparations. Spinton's staff had been planning his ball for months—it was supposed to have been *her* betrothal party. Of course, Spinton had never come right out and called it that, but he had made his hopes perfectly clear. How much happier he must be to be with someone who actually wanted to marry him.

She reached the drawing room in a matter of minutes. The door was ajar, so she did not bother to knock, assuming they had left it open for her arrival. She walked in to find her cousin and Spinton locked together in a heated embrace.

It only proved that they were a perfect match. Octavia had never inspired that kind of passion in Spinton. Good for Beatrice!

"Ahem."

They flew apart like frightened sparrows, both of them flushing a deep crimson.

"Not that it is any of my business," Octavia remarked with a teasing grin, "but the two of you may want to shut the door when you want a little time alone."

Beatrice blushed even further, but she smiled happily all the same. "Forgive us, Octavia. We were carried away."

She waved a dismissive hand. "Do not trouble yourself, Bea. I am not offended. Now, I see you have guests arriving; shall we go?"

She let them leave the room ahead of her, content to walk

behind and admire her cousin's happiness. Beatrice was clad in a gown of dark blue silk that almost perfectly matched the shade of Spinton's coat. They were both perfectly groomed and perfectly content.

And she was perfectly jealous, despite her pleasure at seeing such a perfect match.

They had no receiving line. Spinton, being a bachelor, greeted arrivals by himself as they entered the open rooms that served as a ballroom on the first floor. Both Octavia and Beatrice were nearby, saying hello as the house filled with chattering, glittering guests. No one seemed to think anything amiss, although Octavia heard a few whispered speculations on her relationship with Spinton. Apparently some people thought it was mighty generous of the earl to take her back after her "shameful chasing" of North Sheffield.

There was nothing shameful about her chasing of North. It was what she had done after she caught him that would burn their gossip-loving ears!

Oh well, they would never say anything to her face, and she truly didn't care what they said behind her back. She knew who her friends were. They would not turn their backs on her. And once something new to gossip about came along, society would forget all about her and North.

She milled about the crowded room, sipping champagne, chatting and dancing when it suited her. It wasn't until Brahm Ryland arrived that she felt as though she had a true friend in the room—other than Beatrice, of course.

The viscount's arrival caused a ripple of excitement through the crowd. Some guests were tickled by the scandalous peer's appearance. Others were dismayed. One very proper matron packed up her two daughters and departed in an indignant huff. Brahm watched her go with an expression of rueful amusement.

"You certainly know how to clear a room, Lord Creed,"

Octavia informed him with a smile. She wanted to ask him about Cassie, but even she wasn't that disrespectful of propriety.

Brahm made an expression of mocking regret. "I do. And to think that Lady Abernathy and her girls are going to miss the highlight of the evening."

Did he mean the wedding announcement? That was unlikely; no one had been told. But if he didn't mean Beatrice and Spinton's betrothal, what did he mean?

"To what do you refer, my lord?"

Brahm graced her with a smile that would have charmed a woman who wasn't in love with his brother right out of her dress. It was a smile so very much like North's own. "You will see, Lady Octavia."

That was it? He wasn't going to tell her?

Thankfully, he did not keep her waiting for very long. A short while later there was a commotion near the entrance that attracted everyone's attention, and then North Sheffield-Ryland was announced.

Octavia could scarce believe her ears. North hadn't used the name Ryland in years. He seemed to enjoy flaunting his illegitimacy. Why use it again now, when he had made it clear that he didn't care what society thought of him?

One glimpse of him answered her question. Ryland was his family name, and despite some negative associations, it was still a name belonging to a titled English family. Obviously, North had decided to join the family—and the society to which it belonged.

Her heart lurched at the sight of him. Gone were the unruly curls, replaced with neatly combed and tamed waves. His dark locks were still a little longer than fashionable, but had been recently trimmed, as had his sideburns. His jaw was smooth and freshly shaved, the skin there soft and as rosy gold as that on his cheeks.

He was dressed in austere black evening attire with a cream-colored waistcoat and snowy white cravat. The knot at his throat was simple yet elegant, his shirt points high, but not dandyish. The perfectly tailored coat showcased the un-padded width of his shoulders; the lean trousers accentuated the muscular curves of his legs.

He was breathtaking.

"You dressed him, didn't you?" she asked his brother in a low whisper.

Brahm grinned, tapping the floor with his cane. "I helped. And now that I have seen everyone's reaction to him, I will be on my way."

Octavia whirled to face him. "But you cannot leave now. He just got here!"

The handsome viscount nodded. "Exactly. Having me here—a virtual pariah—will not do him any good. Besides, our brother Wynthrope will be here soon, and he despises me even more than society does."

There was such a wealth of regret and sadness in his eyes when he mentioned his brother that Octavia's heart immediately went out to him. She knew the two of them had never been all that close, but she had no idea the dislike was mostly on Wynthrope's side.

"Thank you, Lord Creed." She wasn't totally certain what she was thanking him for, but it was a lot, whatever it was.

His body angled away from her, the oldest Ryland brother fixed her with a curious expression. "Why are you thanking me? I have little or no sway over any of my brothers. Anything North does is because of you, my lady. Not me." And with that he tipped his cane to her and limped through the crowd toward the exit.

Octavia watched him go in amazement. Her? North had done this for her? Surely not. He despised society. He wouldn't have entered this ballroom unless he wanted to. She had nothing to do with it.

Besides, it was obvious that he was up to something. This change in appearance wasn't solely for her benefit—not when he had yet to notice her attendance. Right now he was more interested in charming those around him than in whether she had noticed him.

Just as those cynical thoughts drifted through her mind, North's head lifted, and his pale gaze locked with hers. He had known exactly where to look, as though he had been aware of her standing there all along.

He smiled—not one of these false smiles he was giving everyone else. This was a real, honest-to-God Norrie smile—slightly self-deprecating, lopsided, and so uncertain that Octavia's heart clenched at the sight of it.

"He is a fine-looking man," a matron beside her murmured to her young daughter. "Aside from his own fortune, his father is rumored to have left him a portion equal to that of the three legitimate boys. If these political rumors are true, whoever marries him could very well be a very influential lady someday. He might make you a fine husband."

Might?

The daughter, turning her head toward her mother, made eye contact with Octavia and flushed a deep, embarrassed pink.

"Do not trouble yourself," Octavia said lightly as the aghast mother turned as well. "He would make a fine husband. You might want to snatch him up before someone else does."

There could be no doubt who that "someone else" was. No one—*no one*—was going to marry North Sheffield but herself. She'd die before she'd let another woman have him. He was hers.

Flashing both women a tight smile, Octavia left before

she could cause a scene and headed straight for a footman carrying a tray of champagne. Snatching one off the silver platter, she drained it in one gulp and returned the empty glass to the tray.

"Thank you," she said to the expressionless footman as she grabbed another.

"Be careful," a soft voice whispered near her ear. "You know how you get when you have had too much to drink."

The shiver had barely reached the base of her spine when Octavia whirled to face him. Had he followed her? He must have.

"What are you doing here?" she demanded.

Taking the untouched champagne from her fingers, he placed the glass on the tray of yet another passing footman. "The dancing is about to start, and I want to dance with you."

"You do not dance. Not well at any rate."

He chuckled. "I can waltz."

As the music started, Octavia smiled. "This is not a waltz."

"True enough. A turn about the terrace then?" He offered her his arm.

Leaving with him could be dangerous. People would talk and speculate. If they were carried away—and the chances were good they would be—it could mean her ruination. Of course, she was ruined already; people just didn't know it. As far as society was concerned, Beatrice had been there the entire time she was under his protection at his home. The fact that neither of them would say what she needed protection from drove the gossips mad, but the truth had a way of seeping out. Servants listened and then talked to other servants. No doubt some people knew about Merton's heir—his infatuation with her, the poor boy's awkward apology, and the banishment to the country his father had punished him with. And maybe a few had even heard that Octavia slept in North's bed while under his protection. How long would it be before others heard it as well? How long before that became the reason she and Spinton broke their engagement? How long before she became a source of innuendo and shame?

How long before she began caring what the gossips said about her?

She took his arm, and with it, her chances. If society was going to talk about her, she could not stop it. And she refused to allow the opinions of others to color her actions.

They made mindless small talk as they drifted toward the French doors, presenting the shared image of being totally unconcerned about what people would think of seeing them together. Only the absence of guilt would save them from the gossips.

Outside, the night air was warm, the slight humidity cut by a gentle breeze. They walked down the stone stairs to the gardens below, the scents of flowers and freshly cut grass rising to meet them.

Lanterns, held high on posts, burned and flickered as they walked the gravel path. Other couples and groups drifted past them, their conversations muffled, often punctuated with happy laughter.

Octavia and North were both silent. Anticipation churned in her stomach as they walked deeper and deeper into the garden. To all others they might have looked as though they had no destination in mind, but Octavia knew exactly where they were going. Veering off the main path that led to the maze, she guided him toward the northern edge of the garden, where an artfully designed wilderness waited in murky darkness.

The thickness of the trees made it next to impossible to light this area, which made it the perfect spot for trysting lovers. If the sounds Octavia heard as they entered the foliage were any indication, trysting lovers abounded.

But she and North would not join them as they groped and

moaned in the bushes. Even if there hadn't been the watery moonlight to guide her, she would know exactly where to go. A few turns and she found it—the little stone hut the gardeners used to store their tools. Even if another couple had stumbled upon it, they wouldn't have the key to open the lock. Octavia found it behind a loose stone in the outer wall. Opening the door, she let them both in, and then bolted it from the inside.

Two small windows gave enough light that she could see the outline of him and that was it, but that was all she—either of them—needed. They came together in a fierce embrace, their lips clinging as tightly as their arms. And when they finally broke apart, Octavia raised her gaze. Even though she couldn't see the whole of his face, she knew the exact moment their gazes locked.

"That was nice," she murmured. "Now tell me what the hell is going on."

North chuckled in the darkness. That was his Vie. Direct and to the point.

"What do you mean?"

He caught a movement of her hand in the dim light. She was waving it up and down in front of him. "This. Explain this."

Ahh, so she had noticed his change in appearance. She didn't seem as impressed as everyone else.

"I shaved and cut my hair." Actually, Brahm's valet shaved him and cut his hair, but that was a minor point.

"Why? You never cared about your appearance before."

Was that an insult or a compliment? "I have reason to care now."

He sensed rather than saw her nod. "These political aspirations I've heard rumor of."

Word traveled fast among the *ton*. "Yes."

"Why do you not simply marry some simpering idiot whose papa is in with Liverpool?"

Fortunately for him, she couldn't see him grin at her obvious jealousy. "I would rather take advantage of my brothers' connections—such as Dev's ties with Wynter and Wellington." Both men were well respected and very involved in politics.

"That will disappoint many of the mamas here tonight. I overheard one telling her daughter what a good catch you would make."

There was no disguising the caustic tone of her voice. "Me?" He laughed in disbelief. "A good catch? Since when?"

"Since you shaved and cut your hair, apparently." Her tone could have flayed to the bone.

"What do you think?" Wrapping his arms around her waist, he pulled her closer, until he could feel the soft, long length of her flush against him.

"About what?" There was hesitancy in her voice.

"Am I good catch?"

"You did not have to change the way you look to deserve some stupid girl's love, North. If all they care about is your appearance and connections, they do not deserve you."

How could she, of all people say these things? She was the one person other than his brothers—the one woman—who had seen him at his worst. She had seen him belch, heard him curse, had been around when he stunk as no gentleman should, and yet she talked as though he were a great prize without all the trimmings and wrappings. She didn't care if he tacked the Ryland on the end of his name or not. She didn't care about any of it. Only him.

His forehead lowered to hers. "Ah, Vie. I have missed you."

"I still reside at the same address, Norrie." Her breath was champagne-sweet against his face. "You could have come to call."

"No I could not. I shouldn't be here with you now. Being alone with you isn't wise." Just the scent of her, the feel of her was enough to make him want to lower her to the dirt floor and have his way with her.

"Why not?" Of course she wouldn't make it easy for him to resist temptation.

"It isn't safe for you to be associated with me."

"It has never been safe for me to be associated with you."

What the hell did that mean?

"My mother warned me away from you because she feared I would do exactly what I did and give myself to you. My grandfather feared people would discover the truth about my past if they discovered we knew each other. And I have always known that you were more dangerous to me than any other man. I have loved you since I was old enough to know what love was."

Christ, did she mean to make his heart feel as though it were about to burst?

Soft fingers brushed his cheek in the darkness. "My question to you, Norrie, is what do you plan to do about it?"

"What do you mean?" He meant to have her, that's what he planned.

"You have told me to stay away from you, that you are no good for me, and yet you keep coming to me, keep drawing me in. It cannot continue. If you want me, take me. If you do not, stop torturing me this way. Go back to your world and give me a little peace."

He'd had no idea that she was as haunted by him as he was by her. No idea that it was as difficult for her to let go as for him. How stupid of him not to realize that it hurt her to see him just as much it hurt him to see her—and just as much for them not to see each other at all.

His arms tightened around her. "I have no intention of leaving you, Vie. Or allowing you to leave me."

"You do not have any intention of being with me either." She was not going to let him off easily, was she?

"I do. I will. As soon as I can." It was a vow he intended to keep.

"As soon as you have caught Harker."

"Yes."

There was a beat of silence. A slight hesitation. "I do not know if I can wait that long."

His stomach clenched not only at the words, but at the pain in them. "Wait for me, Vie. Please. Just a little while longer."

"I have been waiting twelve years already. How do I know Harker is not just some excuse? That there will not be someone else there to take his place?"

"Because I am giving up hunting criminals. He is my last." Silence.

"Really?" The hope in her voice cut him like a knife.

"Really. Will you wait?" How glad he was that he couldn't see her face.

Her fingers clenched at his arms, digging into the nearly healed flesh where he had been shot. "I—"

He never heard her reply—if she said anything at all, because there suddenly was a loud pounding on the door.

"North, get the hell out here!"

"Who is it?" Octavia demanded, fear in her voice.

North gave her a reassuring squeeze before releasing her. "It is Wyn." Crossing to the door, his eyes having long since adjusted to the faint light, North slipped the bolt loose and swung the heavy oak open.

Wynthrope stood alone outside. "Are you dressed?"

North could have kicked him. "Yes."

"Good. Let's go."

North wasn't going anywhere. Not yet. "Where? And how the hell did you know where to find me?"

He could almost imagine the exasperation on his brother's

face. "After Spinton announced his engagement, I noticed the two of you were missing. One of your men was looking for you, so I asked Spinton where the most secluded spot on his estate was. I figured Octavia would know it as well. He told me here."

Good Lord, his brother should have been a spy—a legitimate one. Once, Wyn had thought he worked for the English government, but that was a long time ago.

"Why was my man looking for me?"

Wyn's face lifted in the moonlight. North could see the tightness in his jaw. "They think they have Harker."

North stopped breathing. Harker. Could it be? Could the end be this close?

"Take Octavia home," he instructed, stepping outside.

"I have already made arrangements for Francis to take her. I am coming with you."

"You are not!" The last thing he wanted to worry about, other than Octavia's safety, was his brother's as well.

Wynthrope would not be dissuaded. "You need someone to watch your back, and since Francis cannot be there, I will be."

There was no point in arguing. Not now. North held his hand into the darkness of the little shed. "Vie?" he asked softly.

She came to the door like a queen en route to her execution—all grace and dignity despite her fear.

"I will take you back to the house," he offered.

She said nothing. She merely took his hand and led both him and Wyn out of the trees and back to the garden.

"Go," she said, turning to him under the light of the torches. "I will find Mr. Francis."

But Francis was already striding toward them—North would know that burly silhouette anywhere.

"When this is over," North promised, "I will come for you."

Her fear was obvious in the tightness of her features and the quiver in her voice. "You had better."

Christ, leaving her was one of the hardest things he ever had to do. Careless of who might see, and ignoring Francis and his brother, North crushed Octavia to him and kissed her as though he might never have the chance to kiss her again.

"Be careful," she whispered as they broke apart.

Her eyes shimmered with tears. There was nothing he could do to take them away. "I will be."

"Take care of her," he said to Francis.

The bearded man nodded.

North had only made it a few steps before a thought occurred to him. He turned to face her once more.

"You look beautiful tonight, Vie. You always do."

She smiled in the flickering light. "So do you, Norrie. So do you."

Bow Street had Harker cornered in a pub, and although Duncan Reed had more than enough men to handle the situation, he knew how much bringing the crime lord down meant to North. He would have sent for him even if Harker hadn't grabbed one of the Runners, put a knife to his throat, and demanded that North be brought in to do the negotiations.

"Negotiations?" North shot Duncan a puzzled glance. "Harker does not negotiate."

His former employer nodded. "He does not. I think it's a trap for you, but I had to think of my man first."

Of course he did. North understood that. He would have done the same thing. "Harker!" he yelled. "I'm here. Let the man go."

"You come in here first!" came the slightly muffled reply.

Wyn grabbed his arm as he started toward the building. "You cannot mean to go in there!"

North nodded. "I do."

His brother scowled, disbelief in his gaze. "But Reed is right! It is a trap."

Another nod. "Probably. But I am not going to risk that Runner's life."

"But you will risk your own?" It was obvious what Wyn thought of that.

"Of course."

Understanding flickered in his brother's dark blue gaze. He released North's arm. "Go then."

He held Wyn's gaze just a few seconds longer before leaving his side. Cautiously, silently, he entered the tavern. How long his stealth would last before he hit a creaking floorboard was anyone's guess. Not that it mattered. Harker was watching the door.

The tavern interior was lit by wall sconces, lending a warm atmosphere to the otherwise dingy establishment. It was empty of patrons save for one man passed out at a table in the corner. Harker stood with his back against the far wall, his blind glinting as he held it to the Runner's throat.

"Here I am," North said softly as he stepped into the light. "Let him go now."

Harker eyed him like a wild animal. "Get away from the door."

Holding his hands slightly in front of him so Harker would trust him not to reach for a weapon, North did as he was ordered. Perhaps it had been stupid of him, but he didn't have a pistol on him. He had his own blade and that was it.

As soon as he was far enough away from the exit, Harker let the man go. The Runner ran from the tavern as fast as he could, tripping over a chair in the process.

"What is this all about?" North asked once they—and the man snoring in the corner—were alone.

"That." Harker pointed to a spot behind him.

Stepping closer, North narrowed his eyes. Harker moved aside to give him a better view.

It was a woman. North recognized her instantly as Cassie

Crocker, an actress he had known since his youth. She lay on the floor in a crumpled heap, her eyes wide and unseeing, her throat cut.

Christ.

She wasn't a common prostitute whose death could be swept aside. She was a public figure—a fairly well-known and popular actress. Her murder would be noticed, especially since Harker hadn't even bothered to dispose of the body.

"What did she do?" North asked, keeping his tone measured. "Refuse to take you back?"

"None of your business." Harker's eyes were wild, his expression that of a man who knew when he was cornered—and like a rat he was prepared to fight his way out.

"You have made it my business," North reminded him. "Although I have no idea why."

Sweat beaded above Harker's upper lip. "You are going to get me out of here."

That was laughable. "You think? If I do it will only be to take you straight to Newgate."

"You don't understand," Harker replied. "If I do not make it out of this tavern and continue on my merry way, your precious Lady Octavia is a dead woman."

Ice pooled in North's veins as fury and fear stoked a fire in his belly. "You cannot harm her from prison."

Harker grinned. "I have friends, Sheffield. All I have to do is say the word and she's dead. Maybe not right away. Maybe I'll keep you guessing. But she will die, make no mistake."

North's jaws ground together. "I will see you dead first."

His nemesis's grin widened. "We can do it that way, if you like. The idea of killing you and then going after your woman appeals to me. Although I'd much rather do her first."

Before North could respond, before he could even reach for the blade in his boot, Harker launched himself at him. North deflected the blow with his arm and caught Harker's wrist in his own as the bloody blade curved toward him once again.

This was why he was there—why Harker had asked for him. He had known Bow Street wouldn't let him out alive. Perhaps he had thought for a bit that he and North could work out some kind of arrangement, but he had to have known North wouldn't agree—although if letting Harker go kept Octavia alive, North would be tempted. It wouldn't work that way, though. North would always be waiting for Harker to make his move.

Harker knew that. Just as Harker had to know that North would always be after him. That was why he had demanded North come there. He wanted to end things between them. One of them was going to die that night. It was the only way.

Locked together, North and Harker struggled. Harker's desperation gave him inhuman strength. It was all North could do to keep the blade from plunging into his chest. North didn't know how long he could hold out, and even if he shouted for help, would they get there in time?

The muscles in his arms screamed in protest, as the tip of the blade pierced the fabric of his coat. It sliced through his waistcoat, his shirt and finally the flesh just below his left collarbone. He clenched his jaw, grinding his teeth to keep from crying out in pain. Still, he couldn't keep from hissing.

Harker laughed. And then there was a loud popping noise, and Harker's expression turned to one of surprise. The muscles once locked and tensed against North's own slackened, and after a few stunned seconds, blood began to trickle from Harker's lips.

"Sheffield—" And then he fell to the ground, almost taking North with him.

Shocked, North looked up and saw the man whom he thought had been passed out in the corner standing by the table, a smoking pistol in his hand.

"Brahm?" Was this a dream? Was he dead instead of Harker?

His brother smiled grimly. "I thought you might need some assistance."

Before North could say anything else, the tavern flooded with Bow Street Runners. Duncan and Wynthrope ran into the room, straight for North. But Wyn's attention was soon diverted, not only by Harker, but by the presence of their elder brother. He and Brahm stared at each other, one with an expression of mostly surprise and resentment, the other with no expression at all.

Limping forward, Brahm handed the pistol to Duncan. "I will be outside." Then, casting one last glance at Wyn, he turned his back and walked away.

Everyone stared after him.

"What the hell happened?" Duncan demanded.

North turned to him with a dumbfounded expression. "Damned if I know."

The Runner who knelt beside Harker's body rose. "He's dead."

It was over then. Harker was gone—for good. North was free.

Chapter 20

Hours later, after Harker's body had been taken away—after North made certain for himself that the bastard was dead—North and Brahm sat in North's office. North drank whiskey. Brahm drank coffee.

"Does this bother you?" North asked, holding up his glass.

Brahm shook his head, but he didn't look at the glass for long. "No. Thank you for asking."

Of course he asked. Brahm was his brother, and he loved him. As much as he wanted the whiskey to relax him, it wasn't worth Brahm's discomfort. Brahm didn't drink at all anymore. He couldn't. One sip would be all it took to sweep him over the precipice into the dark place where he had dwelled for too many years. Brahm became a different person when he was foxed—a person whose acquaintance North was in no hurry to make again.

Sinking into his chair, North put his feet up on the desk and leaned back, regarding his brother with a curious expression. Finally, after hours of questions with Bow Street and other officials, he was able to ask the question he'd been wanting to ask ever since he realized it was Brahm in the tavern.

Ever since he'd discovered that Brahm had been "visiting" Cassie Crocker. Had she been the one to tell him about Harker? Had she sacrificed herself to bring her former lover to his just reward?

"Why did you do it?"

Brahm smiled humorlessly. "Because he killed Cassie. Because he was going to kill you."

That was not a certainty. Not at all. "I might have killed him."

Brahm raised his cup. "That would have done wonders for your new career, would it not?"

His nonchalant attitude fanned North's temper. "To hell with my career! You could have been killed, you idiot!"

Brahm's gaze was level, even amused. "Better me than you. I am not afraid of death."

What did that mean, that he was? Hell yes, he was! Anyone with half a mind should be. "That seems to be a Ryland trait that thankfully decided to ignore me."

Shrugging, Brahm drained the last of his coffee. "Perhaps we get it from our mother. She never seemed to find much joy in living."

"No," North argued. "Not afraid of death. Afraid of life."

Now his brother's answering smile was sorrowful. "Yes. You have been afraid of it yourself for these past few years, have you not?"

North nodded, staring into his glass. "Not anymore."

"Good. Now, if we are done with this soul-baring discussion, I would like to go home."

Jerking his gaze upward, North stared at his brother in disbelief. "That's it?"

Brahm smiled kindly and nodded. "That is it. I am not certain what it is you are looking for, brother, but I do not believe I can give it to you. I have no remorse, no feelings of uncertainty or anything else that might make me restless. I did what I thought had to be done."

"How did you know where to go?"

"I spent a fair bit of time in London's dockside palaces. I asked a few people where Harker might be. They told me. Cassie confirmed it." Only at the mention of the actress did his face betray any emotion.

Christ, between Brahm and Octavia they could put Bow Street out of business. "You were going to kill him regardless, weren't you?"

If it was anyone else asking that question, Brahm would be a fool to answer.

"What do you think?"

North stared at him. "I think you might be one dangerous son of a bitch."

Laughter burst forth from Brahm's lips. Grinning, he grasped the head of his cane and pushed himself to his feet. "Not dangerous. Just protective."

No, dangerous as well, but North wasn't going to push that point. There was more to Brahm than he had ever realized, more than his brothers ever considered. He was the one who had found Devlin sick and feverish in a tavern; now he had come to North's rescue as well.

"I will have to tell Wynthrope to steer clear of taverns unless he wants you to come swooping in and save him."

The laughter was a bitter chuckle this time. "Wynthrope would rather shoot me than accept my help."

"But you would offer it anyway."

Brahm said nothing.

"Thank you," North spoke after a few seconds of silence. "Whatever your reasons, I want you to know how much I appreciate you being there."

Setting his hat on his head, Brahm flashed him a grin that looked more like the brother North knew. "I always will be. It is not as if I have anything else to do."

This time North laughed with him. He saw him to the door and watched from the step as his carriage bore him away. Then, shaking his head, he reentered the house.

Brahm didn't care that he had taken a man's life. Killing Harker hadn't bothered him at all because he knew Harker would never rest until North himself was dead. Brahm, who couldn't bear to see a dog suffer, had put a bullet into a man for *him* and wasn't the least bit remorseful.

Not that he would reveal to North, at any rate. There was undoubtedly some pain for poor Cassie. Brahm would never have intended for her to get hurt. One thing was for certain, however, his brother had done him a great service, ridding him of his greatest nemesis and allowing him to keep his hands blood-free. Someday he would pay Brahm back. That was a promise.

Well, truth be told, he was just mightily glad it was all over, although there was a sense of lack of completion hanging over his head. It was odd, knowing that Harker was gone, that he could go on with his life. Somehow, it did not feel real, as though there were still dangling threads left to be cut.

Such as Octavia and whether she would have him— whether he could find the courage to offer himself and trust in her love. Trust in his own.

He would go to her tomorrow, after he had bathed and sorted out the night's events in his own head. After he had thought of the right words to say.

There were so many things he wanted to say.

Before going upstairs to the bath he knew the servants were at this moment preparing for him, he made a detour by the parlor, the room Octavia had made her own during her brief stay with him. How amazed he had been that day when he saw it for the first time. All those memories of childhood had come rushing back. Happier days when both of his parents were alive. Days of knowing his father loved him, even though he could never trust that he would be there when North needed him. Days of security before he learned what the word "bastard" meant and all the whispers that came with it.

The delicate furniture that his mother had so prized, and his father had paid for. The upholstery that perfectly matched the drapes, the carpet that held the soft hues of the walls and furniture in its pattern. It was more tasteful than half the homes in Berkeley Square, and yet no self-respecting society matron ever had tea in it, or tasted the little cakes Mrs. Bunting made so well.

His mother had never cared about the *ton*. She had been happy with his father and her friends—and him.

His mother had never wanted more than his happiness. She hadn't laid any expectations or vows on him as Octavia's had, and yet Octavia had turned out the surer of them. Giving up old fears and insecurities had come much easier to her than to him. But the time had come to trust in her and himself. He had to if he ever wanted the joy his mother told him was waiting for him in the world.

A flash of color caught his attention. It was the pillow Octavia had made for his mother when she was but a girl. His mother had died not long after that, and she had kept that pillow with her, on the sofa in this room where she received callers, even though she hadn't the strength to hold her head up. Every morning her maid would wrap her graying hair in a turban and artfully paint her thinning features, giving color and life where it was steadily fading. She kept that little cushion there with her, a gift from the girl she always looked at as a daughter. Octavia spent more time at his house than she had at her own, but then her mother's circumstances had been far, far different.

Picking up the little patchwork pillow, he took it upstairs to his bedroom and set it on his bed. It was sorely out of place among his cream-colored sheets and wheat-hued counterpane, but he didn't care. He wanted the pillow here so it would feel as though he had Octavia with him that night.

The copper tub sat in the middle of his dressing room floor. Harriette, the maid, and Johnson stood with buckets in hand, having filled the tub themselves.

"Thank you," he told them. His mother had taught him to be polite to everyone. It was a nuance that seemed lost on the Upper Ten Thousand.

"Do not worry about coming back later. It will wait till morning."

The two nodded, wished him a good night, and left the room, leaving the buckets behind so the tub could be emptied later.

He rarely used this room except to bathe. He would probably have to use it more often now that he was trying to project an image suitable for a man with political aspirations.

That was, he would have to use it more if he and Octavia kept this house.

They would have to keep it. He wasn't about to let it go. Even if they didn't live there—and it was very likely that she would want to live in a more fashionable neighborhood—he could not let go of his home. Surely she wouldn't expect him to.

Stripping off his dirty clothes, he tossed them into a corner and stepped into the tub. The water was wonderfully warm without being too hot and smelled of sandalwood. The oil was soft on his skin.

With a sigh, he sank down, stretching his legs out to full length in front of him and resting his shoulders against the high copper back. Christ, it felt good.

He splashed water on his face, scrubbing with his hands.

Being on the docks always left him feeling dirty, and helping to lift Harker's dead body off the filthy tavern floor hadn't helped. His left arm ached.

The heat from the water seeped into his tired muscles, lulling him into a state of relaxation. The spicy scent of the soap and water soothed the tension in his neck and brow. His eyes drifted shut as he lay there, allowing the bath to work its magic.

Soft fingers stroked his brow and cheek. Had he fallen asleep already? If so, this was a wonderful dream.

No, not a dream. Those lips that brushed his were real. That perfume, sweet and gingery—that was real as well.

He opened his eyes, lashes fluttering in protest, and saw her—an angel smiling on him, her beautiful face just inches from his own.

"Vie."

"Hello, Norrie."

He hadn't the strength to sit up, and even if he did, he wouldn't want to risk splashing her. "What are you doing here?"

Rolling up the sleeves of her serviceable dark green gown—much less revealing than the one she had worn at Spinton's ball—she shrugged. "I was tired of waiting for you to come to me."

He smiled. She hadn't wanted to be away from him. "Patience never was a virtue of yours."

She arched a brow, her pert nose tilting as she lifted her chin. "Humility was never one of yours."

North chuckled. "No, I suppose not. What are you doing?"

Octavia gazed at him, washcloth and soap in her hands. "I am going to bathe you, what else?"

It was the "else" that got the wheels in his mind turning. Scarcely daring to breathe, he sat as still as death as she wet the cloth and rubbed the soap against it, creating a thick, rich lather. Then she applied the cloth to his neck and scrubbed with gentle, circular strokes.

"I will start here and work my way down." There was a teasing, seductive glint in her eyes. "What do you think of that?"

North sighed aloud as the cloth touched his heated flesh. "I think this night just got a helluva lot longer."

The cloth drifted over the large, firm muscles of his chest, over the fresh, small wound on his left breast, up to his shoulder and across to the other side, down to the scar on his bicep. She didn't ask how he had gotten this new hurt, or who had given it to him. She didn't want to know. All that mattered now was that he was safe. Mr. Francis had told her that he was all right, that Harker would never bother either of them again.

All she could think of was coming to him. She knew he would be tired, that she should wait till morning—that she should wait for him as she said she would, but that was stupid. Why sit there and wait with her foolish pride when she could be with North?

The bathwater was warm on her hands, the soap fragrant and silky. The cloth was soft, but a poor substitute for the flesh beneath it. Impatient, she dropped the cloth and took the soap in her bare hands. Sudsing her fingers, she put the soap back in the dish and began running her hands along his shoulders, up the strong, ropy column of his throat and down the warm, hairy expanse of his chest. He was all gentle hills and shallow valleys beneath her hands, solid and undeniably male. And he watched her with such an open and vulnerable expression that she couldn't bring herself to hold his gaze for long.

"Am I still bonny and fine, Vie?"

She smiled, even though tears stung her eyes at the lilting Scottish burr that deepened his accent. He wasn't asking her if he looked good, that she knew. He was asking if she still wanted him, because he was offering himself to her.

"Aye, Norrie Sheffield," she answered in kind—her attempt at Scots dialect nowhere near as lovely as his. "Bonny and fine indeed."

His hand came out of the water, suds running down the dark gold skin of his forearm. His fingers closed around hers, holding her palm against his chest. How did he get to be so brown? Even his chest, which should have been pale, was that same delicious rose gold color as his face.

And beneath that chest, right in the very spot he held her hand, beat the steady rhythm of his heart. Strong, steady—every beat made her own heart beat a little harder. A little faster.

"My brother killed a man tonight."

Of all the things she imagined he might say to her at that moment, that one was not on the list.

"What?"

Still holding her hand, North leaned back in the tub and closed his eyes with a sigh. He looked so very tired, tiny lines bracketing his eyes and mouth.

"Brahm. He killed Harker."

Octavia mentally shook her head. Harker was dead? And Brahm had killed him? Mr. Francis never told her *that*.

She didn't need to prod North to tell the rest of the story. He offered it willingly. "He was there at the tavern. I didn't even notice him. Harker and I got into a fight—"

"That is how you got the wound on your chest." Hadn't she thought just a few minutes ago that she didn't want to know how that happened?

He nodded, opening his eyes. "I might not be here if it hadn't been for Brahm. He shot Harker."

"He did it so you would not have to." She was certain of it. "He did it for you."

North squeezed her fingers as his gaze held hers. "He did it for us."

Us. What a wonderful sounding little word.

His fingers stroked hers, caressing the length of her hand from wrist to tip. "Marry me."

She might have fallen over were it not for the tub. Good God, did he mean it? Was she dreaming? God, she wanted so badly to believe he meant it. "What if you find another villain to chase?"

"I won't."

"How do I know that?"

A tiny smile tilted the right side of his mouth. "Because I have a new line of work now."

She stared at him, scarcely daring to breathe. "Politics."

"Yes. Brahm thinks I have a very good chance of becoming MP for Hewbury."

"What do you think?" Was this truly what he wanted, or what he thought she wanted to hear?

He leaned forward, water sloshing up the sides of the tub. "That none of it matters if I do not have you to share it with."

Tears burned her eyes as her throat tightened. "Oh."

Still clutching her hand to his chest, he reached out with his other hand and cupped the back of her head. Suds dripped onto her skirts. He held her head still, forcing her to look at him.

"I have spent most of my life either trying to be something I wasn't or trying to escape what I am. You are the only person who ever made me feel like none of it mattered. That I was fine just being me."

"Bonny and fine," she joked, her voice cracking with emotion.

He smiled in a manner that was almost sympathetic, as though he realized how close she was to losing control of her emotions. "*You* are all I have ever wanted or needed. I never knew it until you came here tonight. As soon as I saw you I knew everything was going to be all right."

A tear trickled down her cheek. "Whenever I come to this house it feels like coming home, because this is where you are. I have so many happy memories here."

His gaze bore into hers, all fire and ice. "Then live here with me."

"All right." God, was that shaky, whispery sound her voice?

He seemed surprised. "You will? You want to live here?"

She nodded as much as his hold on her head would allow, swiping at a tear with the back of her hand. "Of course I do. I love this house almost as much as I love you."

Obviously, that answer didn't tell him everything he wanted to know. "And you will marry me? You will be content to be a mere Mrs.?"

Reaching out, she brushed the smoothness of his cheekbone with her fingers. "There is no such thing as 'mere' where you are concerned. And yes, I will marry you. Gladly. Certainly. Without a doubt or a second thought. I will be Mrs. North Sheffield."

"Sheffield-Ryland," he corrected with a foolish grin.

She rolled her eyes. "I do not care if your name is Sheffield-Shitemonger. I will still take it."

Laughing, he pulled her closer, coming up on his knees in the water to pull her flush against his damp chest. "You have a dirty mouth, my love."

Glancing between them, Octavia smiled at his erection, which she could see growing beneath the surface of the water. She raised her gaze with a saucy smile. "Would you like to wash it?"

He groaned, a low, pained sound, just before crushing her lips with his. Wet fingers tore at the buttons down the back of her gown, managing to unfasten some and send others flying across the room. Clinging to his moist shoulder with one hand, Octavia tugged at the ribbon holding her hair with the other. After the elaborate hairstyle she had worn at the ball, she couldn't be bothered putting more pins in when she took it out—not when she knew she and North would probably— hopefully—end up in bed anyway.

She lowered her arms as her hair fell down her back. He pushed her sleeves down her arms until the offending gar- ment slid from her completely to pool around her knees. Then he pulled at the ribbons on her shift, discarding the fine lawn in one flick of his wrist.

Strong arms wrapped around her waist, and she clung to him as he lifted her over the side of the tub. Octavia kicked at the clothing tangling around her legs, sending her slippers hurtling into the air. They landed with soft thuds on the wooden floor.

"North, my stockings," she protested against his lips, but it was too late. He fell back in the tub and she landed on top of him with a loud splash that sent water sloshing over the sides—stockings and garters still secured above her knees.

Laughing, she gripped the sides of the tub and lifted her- self above him. "Look at the mess you've made!"

He didn't look at all. The only place his gaze went was her chest, where the cool air had tightened her nipples into pebbles—dusky and glistening in the lamplight.

Octavia's smile faded, her breath catching in her throat as his hands—long, broad hands—slid up her ribs to cup her breasts. His thumbs brushed the aching peaks, urging them into full distention. The hard, satiny length of his erection brushed the inside of her thigh beneath the water and she lowered herself to it, grazing the tip with the wanton cleft be- tween her legs.

His eyelashes fluttered, his lips parting at the contact. Gently squeezing her nipples, he arched his hips upward, shoving the blunt head against the opening to her body—not enough to gain entrance, but enough to make her want it.

She wanted him. In her life, in her body. This man was her best friend, her first and only lover, her perfect match, her other half. Only when she was with him did she feel complete. Only when he was with her did she feel like a beautiful and truly desirable woman. Her physical flaws didn't matter, her insecurities were of no concern. In North's arms she was a siren, a woman who wanted pleasure and knew how to give it.

She was everything she ever wanted to be when this man looked at her. The awareness of that, the full implication of what it meant and the joy it brought, sent a jolt of sensual need spiking through her body. If it was possible to have an emotional climax, she had one at that moment, every sense coming alive and opening to the pleasure her love for him wrought.

Slowly, she lowered herself onto him, positioning herself so that the thick length of him nudged, pushed, and finally slid inside. North's eyes widened as she took the sensitive head into herself, his brow knitting as she pushed down with excruciating slowness.

"Ah, Vie. Christ." He arched his hips, tried to thrust himself deeper, but she held back, squeezing him with her legs until he slowly relaxed and allowed her to take total control.

"Have you ever made love in a tub before, Norrie?"

Raising his gaze to hers, he shook his head. "No."

She lowered herself another inch, taking more of him inside, the warm water slipping into the crevices of her body, igniting already sparking nerve endings. She gasped. He groaned.

As her muscles tensed, it took all of Octavia's resolve not to shove herself down upon him and engulf his cock with her body. As much as she loved him, oh-so-dearly loved him, naughty words filled her head, danced upon her tongue. Things she had overheard in the theater and now knew what they meant. Love had nothing and everything to do with this urgency bubbling inside her. She wanted—needed—release, and he was the only one who could give it to her.

Further she slid, taking him deeper and deeper until her pubis came to rest on his. He filled her, stretched her in such a delicious manner that her reaction bordered on frenzy. Slowly, with all the control she possessed, she began to rotate her hips, undulating on top of him lazily, sending little waves of water lapping against the side of the tub.

North's hands tightened on her breasts, his fingers squeezing her nipples forcefully, drawing a gasp of pleasure-pain from her lips. Tugging gently, he guided her downward, so that her breasts were positioned in front of his face. Then, raising his gaze, his eyes held hers captive as he caught one nipple in his mouth.

Octavia shuddered. *"Ohh."* His tongue was rough and velvety, soft but ruthless as it drew back and forth across her puckered, tingling flesh. And she watched as he suckled, watched his as his mouth opened and the tip of his tongue flicked the dark bud.

Drawing her hips upward, Octavia thrust herself down hard upon him, drawing a loud gasp from them both. Body spasming in erotic shock, she arched her spine, sitting back on his thighs as she rode him, resuming her earlier languid pace.

North's hands came back to her breasts as his breathing became more and more shallow. He was like a selkie in the water—a mythical creature made for this kind of pleasure. For *her* pleasure. Her love. God, what a feeling to know he wanted this as desperately as she, that her body gave him the same pleasure that his was giving her.

Her hands crept down, one slipping between them to caress him whenever she lifted herself off him. The other hand eased between her own splayed thighs, the fingers parting her own flesh until she found the hardened spot that ached to be touched.

North's spine arched in response. "I love watching you touch yourself. I love you."

That drove her over the edge, snapping the fragile bonds of her control. He loved her. She had known it to be true, but never had she suspected that hearing him say the words would have such a potent, earth-shattering effect on her.

Down she plunged, then up again and down, until water sloshed over the side of the tub. Ruthlessly she stroked herself as she rode him, bringing them both to the crest of the waterfall and then sending them over in a crash and thunder of pounding water and dizzying, roaring rush of pleasure.

They collapsed together in the cooling, churning water, now at a significantly lower level than it had been when he'd first pulled her in.

"How are we going to explain this soaking mess?" she asked with a chuckle once she'd regained the ability to speak.

North stroked her hair. "We aren't. I do not think we have to."

True enough. "Did you mean it?"

Obviously she didn't have to tell him what "it" she referred to. "Yes. I love you. I always have. Always will."

Tears prickling the back of her eyes, Octavia lifted her head to look at him—at the beautiful rugged face that had haunted her dreams for most of her life. "Always?"

He smiled. "Even before I knew what love was. I think I have loved you since the day we first met."

"You hit me," she reminded him with wide eyes. "That does not sound very affectionate."

"Trust me, to a boy my age it was as good as a proposal of marriage."

Grinning, she kissed his jaw. It was starting to get stubbly.

"I am glad that this time you chose to ask me rather than punch me."

They laughed together and talked a bit, washing away the remnants of their lovemaking before climbing out of the tub together.

"Oh my Lord, I am stiff," Octavia moaned as she stepped onto the floor.

"I am not," North quipped as he handed her a towel. "But I could be if you give me a few moments."

Rolling her eyes, Octavia began to dry herself. One of her garters had slid down around her calf, taking the soaking stocking with it. She kicked it off and untied the other, peeling it off her foot and tossing it aside.

When they were mostly dry, North extinguished the lamps and took her to his bedroom, where they climbed into the large bed—the only bed they had ever shared. *Their* bed.

He brought her to climax again with his tongue, and when she was limp and sated next to him, she noticed the small pillow by his head. She smiled.

"What is that doing here?"

Smiling—he looked so boyish when he smiled!—North inched closer. "It reminded me of you."

That was all the explanation she needed. "I love you, Norrie Sheffield."

He opened his arms to her and she scooted into them. "I know. I do not know why, but I know."

"I just do." She stroked the hair on his chest. "Why do you love me?"

"Because you are my Vie. Nothing feels right unless you are with me."

His simple confession brought fresh tears threatening to burst forth. "I never have to pretend with you. I would never want to."

North gazed at the head resting on his good shoulder. Just

the sight of her hair filled him with a tenderness he couldn't describe. How had the world gone from being such a mess to being so utterly perfect in the space of a short time? How had he gone from thinking the world could only be one way, to allowing it to be whatever he wanted? It could not have happened overnight, and yet it felt as though it had. Everything that had seemed so impossible was suddenly within grasp. But the most important thing was already in his arms.

"Do you think you will be happy as a politician's wife?" he asked.

She raised her gaze to his, the golden candlelight highlighting the delicate bones of her cheeks, the dewy softness of her lips. "I will be happy to be your wife, no matter what you do."

"You will be safer this way," he reminded her.

The arm around his trunk tightened. "I am safe with you no matter what."

What had he done to deserve her? Thank Christ he had done it, whatever it was.

They lay together in silence for some time, until the soft gray light of dawn began to creep across the carpet and the candle sputtered out. And then she raised her face to his and he kissed her, thoroughly, passionately. They made love again as the sun lifted its sleepy head to the gleeful chirping of little songbirds.

And as they drifted to sleep, quieted by this perfect lullaby, North knew that everything was going to be fine. He and Octavia would not have a perfect life—there would be obstacles for both of them to face, concerning their pasts, their present, and their future—but it would be as close to perfect as anything could be, because both of them had discovered an important truth. Both had discovered where they truly belonged.

In each other's arms.